Genevieve is a writer from Melbourne. She writes character-led romantic comedies, pop culture columns for *The Age*, digital content, and not-great author biographies.

She loves croissants and her dog, Viktor. She hates being called Gen.

Her debut novel, *No Hard Feelings*, was published by HarperCollins in 2022. *Crushing* is her second novel.

Also by Genevieve Novak

No Hard Feelings

When do you stop starting over?

Crushing

Genevieve Novak

HarperCollins*Publishers*

This book was written on the Boonwurrung and Wurundjeri lands.
I acknowledge the Traditional Custodians of these lands and pay respect
to Elders past and present.

HarperCollins*Publishers*
Australia • Brazil • Canada • France • Germany • India • Italy • Japan
Mexico • Netherlands • New Zealand • Poland • Spain • Sweden
Switzerland • United Kingdom • United States of America

HarperCollins acknowledges the Traditional Custodians
of the lands upon which we live and work, and pays respect
to Elders past and present.

First published on Gadigal Country in Australia in 2023
This edition published in 2026
by HarperCollins*Publishers* Australia Pty Limited
ABN 36 009 913 517
harpercollins.com.au

Copyright © Genevieve Novak 2023

The right of Genevieve Novak to be identified as the author of this work has been
asserted by her in accordance with the *Copyright Act 1994*.

All rights reserved. Apart from any use as permitted under the *Copyright Act 1994*,
no part may be reproduced, copied, scanned, stored in a retrieval system, recorded,
or transmitted, in any form or by any means, without the prior written permission
of the publisher. Without limiting the exclusive rights of any author, contributor,
or the publisher of this publication, any unauthorised use of this publication to
train generative artificial intelligence (AI) technologies is expressly prohibited.
HarperCollins also exercises its rights under Article 4(3) of the Digital Single
Market Directive 2019/790 and expressly reserves this publication from the text
and data-mining exception.

HarperCollins*Publishers*
Macken House, 39/40 Mayor Street Upper
Dublin 1, D01 C9W8, Ireland.

A catalogue record for this book is available from the National Library of Australia

ISBN 978 1 4607 6932 4 (paperback)
ISBN 978 1 4607 1476 8 (ebook)
ISBN 978 1 4607 4782 7 (international audiobook)

Cover design by Mietta Yans, HarperCollins Design Studio
Cover image by Maria Jose Candela/stocksy.com/3688878
Author photograph by Miranda Stokkel
Typeset in Bembo Std by Kelli Lonergan

Printed and bound by CPI Group (UK) Ltd, Croydon, CR0 4YY

For Taylor, of course.

CHAPTER ONE

Dumped. Effectively homeless. Failing to black out on the only booze in Nicola's pantry (note to the wounded: when you think you've hit rock bottom, straight gin is the shovel that digs you deeper). Rapidly losing viable eggs. Enemy Number One in this sedate suburban cul de sac, owing to five straight hours of blasting Joni Mitchell's *Blue* album and disturbing the innate peace of the outer suburbs. And for fifteen more minutes, it was my twenty-eighth birthday: the age by which my mother had two kids, a husband, a master's degree and a manageable mortgage in an area where houses now cost north of seven figures. I had none of that. Eddie had even kept the dog.

Sweetie, our greyhound, had watched with pitying eyes as the elevator doors closed on me and my bags, while my boyfriend — ex-boyfriend — tried to nudge her back inside.

He had explained the problem in excruciating detail as he sobbed in my lap, so overcome with guilt about his decision that I had to be the one to comfort him through it. He had tried, he said, red-faced and sick with himself, he'd really, really tried, but he didn't love me anymore. Then he put on an Ed Sheeran song to try to better articulate his feelings, while I sat on the couch we'd picked out together and waited for the feeling to return to my extremities.

He'd been having doubts about the forever of it all, he said, squeezing my forearms while I tried to think of all the things I loved, but maybe wouldn't love forever. Really high waisted denim. A drizzle of chai syrup in my coffee. Binge-watching shows about amateur bakers. Three years together, and he loved me like a collapsed genoise sponge.

Now I was laying on Nicola's living room floor. The baby — Layla, my niece — had been lulled to sleep by the dulcet drone of 'A Case of You'. She had no choice. I wouldn't turn it off. This was my heartbreak party, which made me the boss of the music, entitled me to an entire bottle of gin, and demanded my sister's bottomless sympathy. Mitch, my brother-in-law, had been banished to his little man cave in solidarity.

I had nowhere else to go. I wasn't emotionally resilient enough for my mum's cloying pity. My only friends, really, were the girlfriends of Eddie's friends, and we weren't close enough that I could get away with crashing on their couches, monopolising their free time with long-winded rants about how much better I could do and how much he was about to regret losing me, until I almost believed it.

Were hotels up and running again now that restrictions had been loosened? I couldn't be bothered finding out. It was much easier to stay here and soak in my misery, annoying Nicola's neighbours, and doing all the things that Eddie hated, like lighting multiple scented candles at once and getting apocalyptically drunk.

'When Mum was my age,' I said, sniffing, 'she had two —'

'— two kids, a husband and a mortgage. You've already used that one. I have a kid and a husband and a mortgage, too.' Nicola grimaced. 'You're welcome to them. Layla bit me on the nip today. Where's the respect?'

'She's seven months old,' I argued. 'She doesn't know any better.'

'She can't use that as an excuse forever.'

Nicola and I had drifted in and out of closeness as the years passed, but she was all I had left. She was eight years older than me and got everything good in the gene pool: strong eyebrows, good lips, natural athleticism. I was left with half-decent hair and joints that clicked for an hour after I woke up. She got all the good adjectives, too: classic, striking, Grace Kelly-esque, while I got … tall. It wasn't fair.

And she had the perfect life: an okay husband with all his hair, a cute baby, and a back catalogue of thrilling anecdotes from her days on the international party circuit spanning 2010 to 2020, including one about a lingering hug from Mark Ronson at a BAFTAs afterparty. Before motherhood came calling, she had run glossy, star-studded events in London, living off catered leftovers and energy drinks as she ferried celebrities and their entourages between venues. Her life, new though it was — she'd taken a generous redundancy package when the pandemic had hit, moved home to Melbourne, married Mitch, bought a house, got pregnant and had a baby in the time it took me to grow out a fringe — was as idyllic as smug mummy influencers pretended theirs were, and she never missed an opportunity to grumble about it.

'Seriously Marnie, are you alright?'

'No,' I wailed. 'I'm going to die alone. My neighbours will complain about the smell coming from my apartment and eventually they'll break down the door and find a puddle of stomach acid and eyeballs where my beautiful body once lay.'

'Get over yourself. "Beautiful body". Don't you think I'll notice you're dead when you stop sending me fifty raccoon memes a day?'

I sniffed. 'You're ancient. You'll be dead years before me.'

'I'm thirty-six, you brat. I'm still young and hot.'

'You're geriatric.'

'Watch out, or I'll send Layla and her new front teeth to attack you.'

I crossed my arms over my chest to protect my vulnerable targets. 'I'm devastated. Give me a break.'

She clicked her tongue. 'Do you want the truth?'

'Of course I don't.'

She barrelled on anyway. 'Honestly, Eddie kind of sucks. We all think so.'

'Obviously Eddie sucks, Nicola,' I cried. 'He cuts his own hair. It's his dream to live off-grid in a commune. He calls espressos "expressos".'

'Then what's all this fuss about?'

'Because I loved him anyway,' I sobbed. 'And he's gone, and I don't know how I keep ending up here. I don't know what's wrong with me.'

'*Oh*,' said Nicola when she realised I wasn't kidding. She slid down onto the floor beside me and heaved my body, limp as a run-over ragdoll, into a comforting, maternal hug.

Breakup number five. That sounded like a lot and felt like even more. Here was another earnest attempt and jagged-edged failure to add to the ever-growing list.

In my mind's eye, I pushed back the plastic chair in the fluorescent-lit community centre meeting room and stood up to face my peers. '*I'm Marnie Fowler, and I'm a serial monogamist.*'

'*Hi Marnie,*' they droned back.

One or two big breakups in your twenties was normal. Three was bad luck. Five, though? Five failed long-term relationships in ten years was a pattern, and the only consistencies I could point to were:

- men
- myself.

Obviously men were the problem, always, in every scenario, but I wasn't blameless.

I'd been too opinionated for Ian, who wanted a pliant little ingenue who didn't question our age gap. Too needy for Guillaume, who only signed up to be my heartbreak holiday rebound fling but found himself trapped in an eight-month chokehold of unrelenting affection. Thomas grew bored of me after a year, and Martin couldn't carry all that baggage. I'd failed the girlfriend test all over the world: the wrong woman for every type of man I tried on.

And then Eddie. Kind and unselfconscious. He was supposed to be the nice guy, defined by patience. Not quite funny, but a willing and easily delighted audience. He loved the outdoors, so I loved the outdoors. He loved camping, so I learned how to drive a campervan and got used to falling asleep to the guttural sound of two possums arguing in a nearby tree. Even eighteen months of claustrophobic lockdowns in our prison of a flat hadn't been so bad.

Well, we hadn't killed each other. Good enough. We'd only just got our lives back on track. I'd finally begun to feel safe, even sure ... and here I was again. *Again*. I let out a yowl like a wounded animal.

'Oh, my love,' Nicola crooned, stroking my hair. I felt her inspect it for split ends and then decide to let it go. 'It's okay, I know, you're okay.'

These platitudes, mixed with how good it felt for someone to care enough to make them, brought on a new wave of tears. I moaned in agony and buried my face in my hands.

'He's the worst of them,' she said. 'Because he seems decent.

It's insidious. At least Ian was upfront about being disgusting. Eddie's worse than Tom — sorry, *Thomas*. What a prick. Worse than —'

'Can we not?' I whimpered. 'I don't need a tour of my failures.'

'I'm not! I'm just saying, if we thought Martin was bad —'

'Eddie isn't Martin!' I cried, wrenching myself out of her shoulder nook. There was a splatter painting of mascara on the neck of her T-shirt. 'I loved him — *love* him, I don't know what I d–did wrong. I don't know why this keeps — I —'

'Okay,' said Nicola in a maddeningly soothing voice, reaching out to pull me back to my crying spot as I choked on my words, coughing and gagging on renewed misery. 'It's okay, you're okay.'

I let her rock me gently in her arms as though I was a bereft infant and allowed myself to indulge in all the fantasies that had suddenly been wiped off the table.

The quaint house out by Altona Beach: a period home with an established lemon tree and a yard to raise dogs in. Taking a year off to drive around Europe in a caravan, him making friends with lifelong expats and me making myself sick on pierogies and Swiss chocolate. One very well behaved child, someday, who would never have meltdowns on the floor of a supermarket or be placated by an iPad. The dream life that I'd been working towards, waiting for, dropping hints about for three full years, now had been abruptly cancelled.

'I want to talk to him,' I said thickly. I reached around blindly, running my hands through Nicola's thick silvery shag carpeting to find the cool glass of my phone.

'Nope,' she said at once, grabbing my arm and pulling it away from the search. 'It won't help.'

'But he —'

'Not tonight,' she said. 'Not like this.'

My head throbbed with the pressure of an all-night meltdown. Snot streamed out of my nose and trickled down the line of my lip. I reached for the bottle.

'Maybe that's enough for n—'

'NO.' I snatched it away from her outreached hand and gave her leg a warning jab with my foot. 'Mine.'

'You're going to feel like shit tomorrow.'

'I'm going to feel like shit for the rest of my life!'

I knew, under the glug and burn of gin and the nineteenth replay of 'River', that I was being a tiny bit ridiculous. I was treating a kitchen fire like Chernobyl.

It was just embarrassing. To find out too late that it wasn't safe to let your guard down. To know that someone had made a list and found your cons column was infinitely longer than your pros. To have tried your hardest and come second place without any competition.

'Marnie,' said Nicola, pleading in mixed maternal concern and humiliating pity, 'I need you to take a breath —'

I was mid-swallow when I choked on a sob. My stomach convulsed, and I looked at her in panic. I coughed once. I coughed again, and it morphed into a gag.

'Oh no —' she said, springing into action as dread coursed through me. She hooked her arms under mine and dragged me, legs trailing, to the kitchen just in time for me to —

Splat. Splattysplattysplatsplat.

Gin and bile hit the clean steel of the kitchen sink. It swirled nauseatingly towards the drain, and I watched through streaming eyes as everything I had left in my stomach spilled out of my mouth to join it.

'That's real nice,' said Nicola soothingly as she held my hair back. 'You're okay. It's alright.'

I didn't know if the tears drying on my face were of heartache, shame or a body's natural reflex to mild alcohol poisoning, but it didn't matter. This, I decided as Nicola passed me a paper towel and rubbed my back, was the last time I would ever, ever let myself get this low.

CHAPTER TWO

Heartbreak hysteria looked pathetic in the predawn light of my sister's spare room. The hillock of unrolled toilet paper puckered and warped with tears and snot, mascara smeared on the crisp white pillowcase, the laundry bucket beside the bed painted glossy with dried bile and gin, and the same Julien Baker song playing on repeat through my phone for the last five hours of fitful, vomity sleep.

I laid there, numb and heavy, and indulged in the big grey fog as a treat. I prodded at my bloody fist of a heart and thought of the shape of Eddie's mouth when he told me it was over, and I braced for tears. But all I could think about was the sliver of plaque build-up on his slightly crooked incisor. When was the last time he flossed?

Maybe if I hugged my knees to my chest and pulled the sheet up over my head and stayed really, really quiet, Nicola might forget that she had a spare room or a sister at all, and my body would fuse with the mattress and I'd be found decades from now, preserved, and blissfully, mercifully dead.

Christ. That was bleak for a Friday morning.

I kicked the sheets off and began to stew.

Was I going to crawl into bed and wait for death over someone whose favourite book was *The Barefoot Investor*? Was I going to take long baths in the dark, blasting Phoebe Bridgers and lamenting my wasted time because a man who felt confident that three minutes of kissing and thigh groping was adequate foreplay decided he could do better? Would I obsess, pine, publish hammy poetry on public platforms, send him steamy texts and then pretend they were for my imaginary boyfriend instead, '*sorry haha*'? No.

Not again.

I caught my reflection in the mirrored wardrobe doors and saw a dishevelled gremlin, one tit having wandered out of the stretched armpit of my singlet, and thought: *This has got to stop.*

I would not become a caricature of the broken-hearted single woman slipping towards an existential crisis and relying evermore on pink wine and a horoscope app.

No, I thought, remembering that losing Eddie also meant never having to hear the anecdote about the first time he ate a jalapeño ever again, *that's quite enough.*

And that was that. Mourning complete.

This was what starting over looked like. Again. Five apocalyptic heartbreaks in less than a decade ought to entitle me to an honorary degree in humiliation and recovery.

Don't let Taylor Swift fool you. Getting over someone is not that difficult. All you have to do is focus on every negative thing about them for the rest of your life until you forget to stop actively hoping for their slow and painful death, then get a haircut.

It was thrilling to wake up into a brand-new life and find that the world outside looked exactly the same.

My face looked the same. My clothes fitted the same. The sleepy commute into the city followed a different train line, but the beep of my myki, the sway of the carriage, people's blank expressions — they paid no mind to the turmoil of an anonymous twenty-something's inner life.

I felt my phone vibrate in my pocket, and I fished it out.

Missed call (05:45): Nicola Fowler-Smythe
Nicola Fowler-Smythe (05:45): Don't hate me.
Marnie Fowler (05:46): What?

My phone lit up with an incoming call, which I immediately declined.

Missed call (05:46): Mum (Mobile)

She wasn't dissuaded.

Missed call (05:47): Mum (Mobile)
Missed call (05:48): Mum (Mobile)

Nicola's name popped up in another window.

Nicola Fowler-Smythe (05:49): SORRY!
Nicola Fowler-Smythe (05:49): IT JUST CAME UP
Marnie Fowler (05:49): You are dead to me.

The walk through the concrete labyrinth of Parliament Station and to the corner of Collins Street and Russell was no different than usual. It was too early for most commuters, leaving the streets empty and quiet. The towering office buildings stood as empty as they'd been for the last year and a half. The doorways of designer flagships and price-gouging convenience stores sheltered people sleeping there. A cyclist cried out at a delivery driver who had come dangerously close to knocking them off their bike. Par for the course, no life-altering drama here. I was so unbothered that I forgot to ignore the ding of my phone again.

Mum (Mobile) (05:55): My love ... So sorry to hear ... R U ok? ... ??? ...
Marnie Fowler (05:56): I'm fine and I don't want to talk about it.
Mum (Mobile) (05:56): Do U want to move in W me & Trent 4 a bit?
Marnie Fowler (05:56): No thank you

Marnie Fowler (05:57): Who the f is Trent?
Nicola Fowler-Smythe (05:58): Hell if I know. The newest squeeze.
Marnie Fowler (05:58): 🙄

Once upon a time, before the wire in a face mask wore a deep red groove into the bridge of my nose day after day, before my cuticles were permanently cracked from constant sanitising, before the world froze, collapsed, and feebly rebuilt itself on the tentative threat of a third, fourth, seventeenth variant, I had a career.

I'd been halfway up the ladder at a hospitality group — a wanky company that owned a dozen chic restaurants more concerned with being Instagrammable than making edible food in decent portions — having clawed my way up from nervy teenaged waitress to business development team leader.

But a year and a half ago, cases grew exponentially and restaurants everywhere closed their doors. Seventy-five percent of our staff were stood down while we waited for the worst to pass, and then it didn't, and then I was let go.

Eddie managed the bills on his own for as long as he could, smiling thinly as I apologised for every tin of chickpeas I dropped into the trolley, exhaling his resentment whenever I ran the dishwasher, murmuring his displeasure if I wasn't in the mood, as though it was the least I could do. My self-worth disintegrated with every polite rejection to a job application, every unreturned phone call to recruiters, every day wasted in front of the television.

Kit only offered me my job at Little George Gastronomia because I was the least annoying person he interviewed for it. He'd once said that his favourite things about me were, in order: I was born before 9/11, and I wasn't afraid of him. If those were the only qualities I needed to retain a job where I got to listen to music all day and offer biscuits to every passing dog, well, I could live with that.

Little George, named for its spot on George Parade, had been operating since the '50s. Kit's grandparents opened it after they emigrated from Italy during the war. It had grown from a poky espresso bar to a piece of Melbourne history. When Kit inherited it from his father two years ago, he had it gutted and renovated, keeping only the heritage-listed green neon sign, the imported tile and the original and highly temperamental espresso machine. I was the only one who could tame it when it was in the throes of a tantrum at peak hour.

Functionally, it was only a small place. Kit's family owned the building: a narrow three-storey space with bright, wide windows and a cafe on the ground floor, decades of storage and forgotten family junk on the second, and Kit's office (slash hiding space) on the third. We had ten tables inside and three out in the sunshine, and a row of bar stools along the long dark wood counter if you fancied a quick pastry and an espresso. In the renovation, he had had the place painted hunter green and white and replaced decades-old furniture with gleaming walnut tables and chairs.

Little George's side-street location, seasonal menu and rotation of chic black and white photographs by local artists in gleaming brass frames across all three walls contributed to the impression that the place was a local secret. A heavy swinging door separated the dining area from the kitchen, which was just as well, or else Sam — a full-time hornbag who moonlit as our day chef — would trap me in innuendos all day long. Monday through Saturday, we served breakfast, lunch and dinner to discerning Melburnians. I worked the daytime shifts, and what my awards wage lacked, I made up for in croissants.

The embroidery on my apron read *Marnie, Assistant Manager*, but my authority stretched only as far as my own set of keys, second dibs on the leftovers and handling needy customers on Kit's behalf. He oversaw the businessy bits, the kitchen had its own system, there were no other front of house staff to manage ever since Kit had fired Max, weekend barista and tortured Matt Healy desperado, for the sin of being '*fucking insufferable*'. Even though I could probably have done the job under anaesthesia, I had no complaints.

I knew I was supposed to want more. I was supposed to go all tingly when my LinkedIn profile got viewed. I was supposed to want a salary that curved upward, responsibility, five-figure bonuses. A career, not a job. According to, well, everyone, I should have used lockdown to retrain in a new field and viewed hospitality as a means to an end: a strictly temporary detour in my road to an acronym for a job title.

But when the morning rush petered out, the dishwasher was going and I was working on a particularly good daydream, I liked it here. The rushes and lulls were predictable, customers were mostly friendly and the biggest catastrophe I could face was running out of oat milk. I liked the early walk to open the cafe, and the sweet nonno who camped out at our window table with an espresso and three newspapers every Thursday. I liked that I didn't have to think about anything except accurate spelling on the specials board and the crema on my espresso pours. I liked that my body ached at the end of the day, the satisfying *pop* in my ankles when I rotated them on the couch each night. Everyone I spoke to brought me a problem I could solve: coffee, hunger — hell, a bathroom.

It wasn't like this before, when I would spend fifty hours per week panicking about deadlines and budgets and the passive-aggressive barb that Anna from marketing had made in the last team meeting. All of the exposure to the blue light glare from my laptop had given me premature forehead wrinkles. A salary, but at what cost?

I got to take home leftover cannelloni here. People greeted me with a smile. The staff got along, if you overlooked how often we told each other to fuck off. The worst I ever had to deal with was the odd sour-faced customer insistent on complaining. '*This coffee is too hot,*' they'd say, or '*This sandwich is too bready.*' But then they would leave, and I wouldn't have to deal with them again. They were a problem, and then they weren't. Here then gone, easy as that.

I unlocked Little George's doors, disabled the alarm, flipped on the lights and switched on the espresso machine. Soon the pastry delivery would arrive, customers would trickle in, and the day would look like any other.

I blanked another call from my mother. I wasn't in the mood to hear about the number of fish in the sea (rapidly dwindling) or how Trent was the love of her life (more likely, another puce-faced Liberal voter from OkCupid.com). '*Can't talk,*' I wrote. '*Call you later.*' (I wouldn't.)

I'd be in good company today. No one enjoyed the indulgence of a bad mood like Kit, and if my hands were busy and my mind was on hospitality service, I'd be fine.

I'd be fine.

I'd be fine.

I let out a determined huff, bumped the door open with my hip and heaved the first of the oversized striped canvas umbrellas onto the pavement for diners who liked it alfresco.

'There she is,' crooned Sam as he strode up the street. 'Light of my life. The most beautiful girl in the world.'

I responded without looking up from the umbrella ties, the way I always did: 'Get fucked, Sam.'

'And good morning to you too, my future wife. You're looking radiant.'

'You look like a cavoodle that's got caught in the dryer.'

He remained unperturbed. 'Our children will be beautiful.'

Uh oh — children. Future plans. Mine, eviscerated. I blinked hard, and when I focussed again, he was halfway inside the restaurant.

'Hey Sam?' I called.

He turned around hopefully. 'Hm?'

'Get fucked again.'

I didn't need empty flirtations from the horny puppy. I didn't need Julien Baker. I needed to tell more people about this, a receptive audience, a scrum of supportive women enveloping me in love and promises that I was better off. I reached into my pocket and pulled my phone out.

Girlfriend Chat was just that: a group chat comprising the five girlfriends of Eddie's friendship group. We weren't particularly close and didn't discuss much except the shows we were bingeing, discount codes we'd nabbed and elaborate viral salad recipes we wanted to try, but friends were friends.

You have been removed from Girlfriend Chat, my phone said.

'What the FUCK?'

A passer-by flinched, clutching her hessian bag to her chest.

'Can you believe this?' I asked her. Shouted it, actually. She looked too terrified to respond. 'What a bunch of treacherous little —'

I turned on my heel and stomped back inside, neck bent to the toxic glow of my phone as I tapped frantically at my screen, as though I could break past the block, grab them by the lapels and demand an explanation.

I slammed my phone onto the counter and stared at the history of the inaccessible group chat. Metres and metres of messages about nothing. Still, people to bounce the mundanities of my day off had been some comfort.

But I'd never really had a best friend. Ian, Guillaume, Thomas, Martin, Eddie: they'd all become my closest confidants by default, but that wasn't the same. Sometimes, when I needed a good cry, I would put on *Broad City* and lament my emotional loneliness, never sharper than when I realised I was an Abbi without an Ilana.

Was it sad that my closest confidants were either biologically coded to care about me or hinged the success of their family business on my ability to negotiate with an ancient espresso machine? What did I have in common with a retired party girl turned professional baby burper and a middle-aged man whose main passion was scoffing down all the mushroom arancini before we could sell any? How had I lost everyone overnight?

'Woah,' said Kit, freezing in the doorway, where he'd appeared with the plastic rack of the pastry delivery on his shoulder. 'Weird vibe in here.'

I jammed the portafilter into the machine to mask the sound of a sucked-back sniffle of tears.

'You have no idea.'

Kit delayed responding by putting the rack down. He seemed torn between curiosity and the unwillingness to care. Nosiness won out.

'Enlighten me.' He picked up a pain au chocolat and offered it to me. I waved him off, and he ripped into it instead.

'Oh, just my entire life falling apart,' I replied breezily. 'I'm crashing with my sister and my colicky niece because — *so* fun! — Eddie's left me.'

He choked on his next bite and sent a fleck of chocolate flying across the counter.

'That's the worst thing I've ever heard,' he said, and I revelled in the gratifying pang of pity. 'No one should have to live with a *baby*.'

I paused. 'You're a moron.'

Kit was fortyish, beardy and a bit of a shit. He had only ever been nice to Andrew, his partner of something like twelve years, and ever since they had split last month, he had been a shit times twelve.

His looks belied what a shit he was. Almost concerningly lean, with such long, delicate limbs that he seemed a full foot taller than me. He had soft, dark eyes hidden behind permanently smudged glasses, and you could tell how badly his day was going by the density of his scruff. Only once had I seen him clean shaven, and by afternoon — after he'd bitten into a doughnut and got splattered with jam, had an argument with the espresso machine, and got an earful from his mother for not answering his phone quickly enough — I swear he had a full beard again. He looked like a frightened deer most of the time, timid and docile, until he opened his mouth and gave away his saturnine nature. Just last week, a preschooler who often stopped by for a babyccino with her dad asked if he would hang up her drawing of the cafe. He took it from her, looked at it, looked at her, looked at it again, and said, *'Absolutely not.'*

Despite being the boss, he deferred all annoying customers to me to deal with, lest he permanently ban them for saying they preferred the place before the renovation. He never missed an opportunity to criticise the music I played (*'Drippy, whiny folk rubbish'* — say that to Leonard Cohen's face, why don't you? — *'Why can't we play Joy Division?'*), but he couldn't figure out how to work the Sonos. His insults were relentless and humbling. At last year's staff Christmas party — a couple of bottles of wine and a charcuterie board in the restaurant after closing — he leaned in close and whispered that I was his favourite employee. When I recalled this later, he insisted that he would never have said anything so stupid, and to shut my face and go find something to do. I adored him.

'Get a dog and move on,' he said indifferently. 'Actually, that might be cruel to the dog. Get a fish.'

'Hey Kit,' I said brightly, 'do you want to fuck off?'

'Oh, Marnie, you poor thing,' he said, changing tack. His brow creased in concern. He reached out to take both of my hands in his. For a moment, I thought he might be going soft. Maybe in light of his own recent heartache he'd developed the capacity for empathy and wanted to offer me a bony shoulder to weep on. 'I think I know what will make you feel better.'

'What?'

A raise would help. Or the offer to stay in the detached granny flat at his gorgeous Fitzroy North terrace house rent-free indefinitely.

He smiled and squeezed my hands. 'Making me a coffee and bringing it to me.'

I rolled my eyes, shoved him away, and reached for his favourite mug.

Some things, like your entire life, changed overnight. Some things, like Kit's commitment to being the most annoying person I'd ever met, never did.

CHAPTER THREE

'Can you say "misandrist", bunny? *Mis-an-drist*, come on.'

Layla wasn't listening. She was bouncing on my hip, kicking me in the ovary out of time with the music I'd put on to soundtrack Nicola's dinner routine, completely disinterested in learning her first word.

'Let's not turn my baby into a radfem just yet,' said Nicola from the sink. 'You aren't a misandrist.'

'I think I might be,' I told her. 'I don't like any men.'

'You like Mitch.'

I glanced down the hall to his home office — my bedroom, thank you very much — with its door firmly shut against the noise and chaos of his family. This had been his routine for the three weeks I'd been crashing here: he would get home from work, blow raspberries on Layla's tummy until she puked from laughing so hard, lock himself in the bathroom with an iPad for an hour, then retreat into his office to 'finish up a few things'. If it wasn't for the David Beckham fragrance in the bathroom and the souped-up Camaro in the driveway, you might never know a man lived here at all.

I shrugged. 'Eh.'

'You like Kit.'

'Kit's not a *man*. Kit's a … moody stray cat. He hates everyone until he's fed, and he has no genitals.'

'Why doesn't he have genitals? Why wouldn't a cat?'
'I don't know, have you ever seen them?'
'Kit's? Or a cat's?'
'Either.'
'No.'
'See?'
'You like Dad. Don't say anything about his genitals.'

I hid my grimace under the momentary discomfort of heaving a small person from one hip to the other.

'Next.'

Nicola paused with the tip of her knife in an heirloom tomato. 'David Bowie.'

'I'll give you that. I do like David Bowie.'

Mitch poked his head out from behind his door and called, 'Can you turn that shit down?'

I pulled into the hallway and frowned at him. 'Language. There are babies present.' (As though I didn't cry, '*Fuck*, she's so fucking *cute*!' every time I mashed my face against hers.)

'I'm trying to work.'

He spoke to me with impatience clipping the edges of every word. We'd never exactly warmed to each other. I saw through his weaponised incompetence and he saw through my thin-lipped tolerance.

He was the picture of the helpless manbaby archetype, uselessness amplified the day Layla was born, as though during Nicola's nineteen-hour labour he'd popped off for a lobotomy specifically targeting his ability to operate a vacuum or dump a bag of pasta into a pot of his own accord. He expected praise for taking the rubbish out before the bins overflowed. Nicola was called back early from every baby-free day out because Layla was crying and he didn't know what to do about it.

Nicola should have ended up with some British old money brat who had gone rogue and disappointed the family by becoming an acclaimed music journalist, with cheekbones that could cut glass and a mop you could lose a hand in. She had always been the adventurous one. She did things first, mapped the trail, cleared a path and made it safe for others to follow. When she was seventeen, she followed Big Day Out around the country trying to get Dave Grohl to spot her in the crowd and fall in love with her. She spent her gap year as a ski instructor in Crans-Montana. Family lore was that her first word had been the C-word, learned who-knows-where. She was supposed to have a life of thrills and adventure.

For all its sedate modesty, though, the life she had was the only one she ever really wanted. Her hedonistic twenties (and the first half of her thirties) had been a sparkly, boozy detour from her true goal. She had always wanted four kids, a Labrador, and a house near the beach.

Well, she had a baby, a husband who acted like a baby, a feud with the neighbour's cat, and a house on the very edge of town. Her adjustment to motherhood came in shudders and jolts. She would strap Layla into her baby sling, bounce up and down, and sing, *'I've never been so bored in my life! I can feel my brain cells rotting!'*

And Mitch ... tried, I guess. He'd flick the kettle on or swap the clothes from the washing machine to the dryer when she asked him to. He may have looked at her like she invented the sun and the stars, but he didn't make her life any easier. He enjoyed the perks of the hapless husband trope a bit too much. He was all thumbs when he changed nappies, pulling one tab too tight and the other not tight enough, so it was at constant risk of slipping down. He picked Layla up and tried to soothe her when her gums ached, but she would squawk and scream and reach her chubby little hands out for Nicola instead. I couldn't blame her.

He had been around for two years now, and I still knew hardly anything about him. His job was too boring for me to remember what it was. His interests spanned sport and complaining that no one could take a joke anymore. He never tired of commenting on the fact that I didn't eat meat, like it was a mental illness. The nicest thing I could say about him was that he adored Nicola, even if he did a lacklustre job of showing it.

But hey, he wasn't my husband. If he made Nicola laugh and put the toilet seat down, then it wasn't my job to point out his faults. (It was just an extracurricular I enjoyed immensely.)

'Dinner's almost ready,' called Nicola. 'Can you finish up?'

'What is this?' he asked, pointing at the speaker on the kitchen island.

'Um,' I said, using a smug note of incredulity, 'it's Alex Turner.'

'Who's Alex Turner when he's at home?'

'He's from the Arctic Monkeys,' I said, scoffing with more indignation than I felt. 'They're important. He's a genius.'

'You can tell Alex his music's crap.'

Mitch pulled plates out of the cupboard to set the table, but Nicola clicked her tongue. 'Not *those*,' she said. 'We need the pasta bowls.'

'But it's not pasta,' he said, frowning. 'Can't any bowl be a pasta bowl?'

'It's a wide, shallow bowl.'

'That's a *plate*.'

Nicola turned to me. 'Marnie, can you do it?'

'I can do it!' Mitch protested.

'Marnie will do it properly.'

He sighed his frustration and sat at the head of the table, abandoning the offer to help at all, and I could write a thesis on the patriarchal subtext of it.

'Thanks, Marn,' he muttered as I slapped a placemat down in front of him. 'How's the house hunt?'

'*Babe*,' said Nicola with a warning edge.

'What?'

'Marnie can stay as long as she needs to.'

'I never said she couldn't; I was just *asking*.'

'I've got four viewings on the weekend,' I said. 'Trust me, I'm not moving in for good.'

'Stay forever,' said Nicola. She arrived with a scalding baking dish between her oven-mitted hands and settled it on the silicone mat I'd placed in the centre of the table. 'Why do we have this massive house in the middle of nowhere if not to lend the spare room out when someone needs it?'

'Lilydale isn't the "*middle of nowhere*",' said Mitch as he loaded up Layla's fork, blew on the food and made plane noises as he guided it towards her open mouth. 'Nyoom! Isn't Mummy silly?'

'It's the very end of the train line,' Nicola argued. 'Ten minutes that way and it's regional Victoria.'

'Don't be such a drama queen,' he said. 'It's the suburbs, not the outback.'

Layla groped the air, mouth opening and closing like a fish as she waited for another bite. Mitch had dropped her fork to focus on the argument. I picked it up myself, aeroplaning a carrot at her and matching her delighted hum.

'If I can't get an Uber in less than six minutes, it's the middle of nowhere.'

'You don't even need an Uber! We have two cars!'

'We're moving to Parkdale next year.'

'Says who?'

'Says she who misses civilisation.'

Here was the silver lining: this wasn't my life. Sure, I was squatting at the House of Domestic Resentment, but my name wasn't on the mortgage. But for the momentary lapse of indifference when I shed an involuntary tear on the train yesterday — *'When can you pick up the rest of your stuff?'* Eddie had texted, knocking the wind out of me. *'Tuesday?'* — I could be grateful that the risk of falling into monotonous discontent was that much smaller.

'You and me, bunny,' I whispered to Layla under the ricocheting argument of what constituted a short commute. 'Swear we'll never settle for less than the best.'

She hummed around a mouthful of mashed carrot: a clear promise.

'Sorry,' sighed Nicola hours later. She peeled back the covers of the guest bed and flopped in next to me. 'Dinner was shit and Mitch is in a mood.'

'Dinner wasn't shit.'

'It was overcooked and bland.'

'Completely salvageable with enough parmesan though, so problem solved.'

She grumbled and hiked the tissue-soft sheets up to her chin. Even her spare linens were high quality. A real adult — with their life together enough to have a spare room — didn't subject guests to the plasticky sateen of Kmart sheets.

'You can stay as long as you want,' she said. 'Don't let him make you feel unwelcome.'

'I know better than to take Mitch seriously,' I replied.

She let out a grunt of appreciative laughter. 'I'll go to my own room in a minute. I just want ten minutes of peace in here.'

I went back to my phone. In the corner, a scent diffuser plumed sleepytime oil and water vapour into the air, dousing us both in drowsiness. Deeper in the house, the dishwasher sang to signal the end of its cycle.

I wondered how only children did it. Who held the strings of their safety net taut? Did they have no secret language with someone who had known them since before they'd mastered bladder control, share no knowing looks across the living room when their mum went on a tangent about another post middle-aged male disappointment? Who could you be your truest, most switched-off self with if not a sibling? I didn't even have to hide the fold of my double chin as I scrolled ever deeper in my blanket cocoon.

The algorithm was the usual jumble of nothing, somehow hyper specific and numbingly vague snippets of content targeting every other woman with wifi and a passing interest in pop culture. Recipes I'd never try. Makeup tutorials for hooded eyes. End-of-month wrap-ups from the girls from Girlfriend Chat: egg yolk oozing onto sourdough, Zara hauls, photos of them wrapped around their partners where she's made up like it's her rehearsal dinner and he looks like he's just come from the gym. Ads for oversized T-shirts with slogans like *TIRED FEMINIST* and *WINE AUNT*. Short videos of dogs dubbed with viral voice-overs. Aw, Sweetie with her chin on a girl's shoulder.

Wait.

Sweetie with her chin on a girl's shoulder?

'Get. Fucked.'

Without my brain's permission, my hand flung my phone across the room.

'What?' asked Nicola, looking up from her own screen. 'Is it a video where they slice into a roast dinner but it's actually a cake? I love those.'

'Get *fucked*,' I repeated, scrambling to fish my phone out from under the dresser. There on the floor of Nicola's pristine spare bedroom, I crouched, back hunched, neck craned, my phone mere inches from my face as I tapped for the profile I was looking for. When Eddie's popped up and confirmed I'd seen what I thought I had, I let out a shriek of disbelief.

A woman I'd never seen filled the screen. In the shade of an elm tree at a dog park I didn't recognise, she puckered her lips to kiss my dog — *my dog* — on the snout. 'These girls ♥' said the caption.

I pulled my phone closer. Did I recognise her underneath her heavy fringe and the primary colours of the mask around her chin? Was she Eddie's work wife, who he talked about constantly but never introduced me to? Was she someone brand new? Had he moved on already?

How had he moved on already?

I couldn't get enough air in. I heard myself dragging oxygen into my nose more than I felt it.

Nicola leapt out of bed and wrenched my arm towards her so she could see what I'd seen, any clue for what could have brought on such a reaction in a room so hazy with lavender, and let out a short, sharp, '*Oh*.'

'I'm done,' I told her. I was frozen, sitting so straight that I could only see her through my peripherals. I could feel that my mouth was a straight line.

'Oh, Marnie,' she said with nauseating sympathy. 'I'm so sorry. Eddie's such a —'

'I don't care about Eddie.'

'Of course, but it still has to hur—'

'I carried Sweetie twenty-five minutes to the vet when she sprained her paw,' I said. 'I cooked her steak on her birthday.'

'My love, she's a dog; she doesn't know. She's sweet to everyone; that's why her name's Sweetie.'

Against my better judgment, my mind pressed play on a supercut of happy memories. Throwing a tennis ball and not caring that it was drenched in drool. Drawing eyebrows on her in eyeliner and laughing every time she looked at me for days afterwards. Cheering her on as she zoomed around the oval near the old apartment. The happy thump of her tail when I turned off my alarm. My jaw gave a minute quiver, and I clamped it shut to put a stop to it.

I took a deep breath and braced myself for the sting of sadness.

My hand began to ache from the grip I had on my phone. When I looked closer, I was surprised to find it shaking. I felt my heartbeat, heavy and hot. My teeth sank hard into the soft flesh of my cheek. Aha! Finally, an emotion I could identify:

Anger.

Fuck this.

Fuck the whole fucking thing.

'I am done.'

'You'll get another dog someday.'

'Not dogs. Relationships. Men. Forever.'

'Eddie's a prick,' replied Nicola. 'But he's only one bad guy. There are lots of other guys.'

'Not interested,' I said. I sat rigid and tossed my phone back on the floor. 'No thanks. Not now, not ever.'

'You sometimes have a problem with over-commitment,' she said, giving my arm a supportive squeeze. 'Don't think in absolutes. Just have fun for a while. Being single was the best time of my life.'

She didn't understand. I didn't want to be *single*. I wanted to resign from having a relationship status at all. I refused to humiliate myself again. Absolutely not. Why play to lose? Why risk it?

This game was rigged and I was done tossing rings of hope and dignity onto slippery bottlenecks, and I was sick of partners with their own agendas. I was quitting. I was giving up. Thank you, universe, for the opportunity to learn what I didn't want.

'We all think we'll never love anyone again after we get our hearts broken.'

'Let's not give Eddie that much credit,' I scoffed. 'That's not what this is. I don't need to keep trying; I just know. Some things just aren't for you.'

Maybe it was the lingering scent of garlic in the air, or the fact that she had witnessed my breakdown and its epiphany because she was hiding from her partner, or just because I was right, but she nodded. 'Like anal sex.'

'*Exactly* like anal sex.'

CHAPTER FOUR

Here's the unlikeable truth: I had loved being a girlfriend girl.

Not in some regressive, stand-by-your-man way where I thought my place in life was as a supporting character in the hero's journey. I just liked being someone's someone.

A person to talk to. A steady supply of sex without caring about leg stubble. Claiming to not want dessert and still getting two bites of cheesecake. No second-tier relatives gave me a hard time about when I was going to settle down.

I rarely had a reason to get into Adele's catalogue. I thought the *Sex and the City* girls just had poor judgment and drinking problems. You'd have to lobotomise me before you'd catch me on *The Bachelor*.

I counted it up last night. In the last decade, I had been single for a collective hundred and twelve days. Every rebound was a rebirth. Every first date was an audition for the role of full-time girlfriend.

While everyone else my age was getting drunk at parties and making the mistakes that would fill their novels later, I was busy playing house with Ian, or with Thomas, pretending to be able to hear the difference between vinyl and streamed Lou Reed albums.

I didn't have to navigate sticky-floored nightclubs, freezing my mini-skirted tush off in the dead of winter in the hopes that someone cute would feel me up in the back of a taxi, because I was occupied with Guillaume's tongue in my mouth and hand up my top for eight steamy months.

I got to skip the utter humiliation of being ghosted by someone who owned multiple Tarocash suits because I was busy whooping and clapping through the second-hand embarrassment of Martin's attempts to crack into stand-up comedy.

I watched other girls go on bad dates, stress over the punctuation in texts and plot casual drive-bys to run into someone who wouldn't call them back. I thought I was the winner, spending my Saturday nights next to my boyfriend on the couch. A toothbrush in the cup on his bathroom sink was as good as an engagement ring.

I forced myself not to think about being relegated to the girlfriend corner alongside women I had nothing in common with while our boyfriends ignored us. I put a mental block on feeling unpedicured feet scratch against mine under the sheets. I ignored the fact that Nicola didn't like any of them. I ignored the fact that I didn't like them very much, either.

Single girls love to sneer at the women who disappear into their relationships, like they lack the courage to endure life without the armour of some guy named Dale or Johnno. They were right, and I'd worn it like a badge of honour.

I was a smug arsehole, now humbled by circumstance.

You only want what you can't have. Isn't that how it always goes?

It didn't take a therapist to draw a line between my relationships and my childhood.

I was raised on a steady diet of snipes and jabs, with an explosive argument for dessert. It was easier once resentment set in and the whole house froze over. I was the designated despatch rider by the age of eleven. '*Dad said to tell you ...*' I said a thousand times. '*Well, you can tell* your father *that I ...*' came Mum's reply, always.

Other families made it work, but ours seemed to be made of the wrong parts. Nicola and I were the only pieces that fit together, and I never knew if it was by design or by necessity. My parents finally split when I was eighteen, and all I felt was relief.

Dad married Susie within a year, and almost a decade on they were still nauseatingly enamoured with each other. They lived out on the peninsula with their three hairless cats, so I hardly ever saw them.

Mum threw herself into dating with more vigour and enthusiasm than I put into anything, so I hardly ever saw her either, too absorbed was she with the current love of her life. It was always some incredibly bland guy named Paul or Greg or Brian who was the answer to all of her problems for six months, until they committed the unforgivable sin of checking the football score on date night or failing to notice her new haircut. Then she would dump them, renew her premium dating app membership and start over.

So maybe this compulsion to attach myself to another was an effort to correct what went wrong. If I just gritted my teeth through the bad parts — projected a personality onto Eddie, tiptoed around Martin's fragile ego, taught myself to love Thomas' terrible band, pretended to love coke and breath play for Guillaume, and played the part of the wide-eyed ingenue who hardly noticed the fourteen-year age gap between me and Ian — then I'd prove that my parents just hadn't tried hard enough, and we'd melt into each other, and we'd be having breakfast in the garden on Sunday mornings, and everything would be wonderful forever.

But that wasn't happening. My Sunday morning wasn't spent

watching a greyhound wear a track into the grass around a lemon tree but dragging myself from share house to manky share house. I was ready to pack it in and become Nicola's full-time au pair by the third one. I pulled out my phone and messaged her:

Marnie Fowler (11:47): Another shithole.
Marnie Fowler (11:47): Mitch had better get used to me living in his office.

I sighed and my hot breath echoed back under my mask as the 6 tram lurched forward. Being single was expensive, and I couldn't afford to live on my own. I'd only ever lived with my parents and partners, and my expenses had just skyrocketed. All the mod cons I'd grown used to — interior laundry taps, outdoor space, bathroom walls that weren't bloated with water damage — were suddenly out of reach. It was discrimination. Punishment from the government for not having enough sex or anyone to talk to between *Queer Eye* episodes. Where were the tax incentives for people who shed the weight of another half? I wouldn't be having kids with anyone at this rate, so didn't I deserve a lifetime of offset carbon emissions? It was the pink tax without the negative press. A loneliness tax.

It wasn't just rent I couldn't manage on my wage, but the new couch, a fridge, the internet connection fee, the cleaning supplies and Pyrex you slowly accumulated. I couldn't ask Eddie to split the remaining dishwashing liquid with me. Most of the furniture in our flat was his, and what little belonged to me — a couple of lamps, a hanging shoe rack, a vast novelty mug collection — I didn't want.

Princes Hill, a pocket of the inner-north, with its village atmosphere and proximity to the city, was ever a mishmash of local lifers, cashed-up yuccies and students. It was half charming heritage cottages with box hedges, half soulless steel and glass apartments, so small you might as well move into a pod hotel. The top end of this suburb was devoid of mid-morning atmosphere: just a trickle of traffic and *For Lease* signs on every other fence. Melbourne had enjoyed the momentary respite of affordable rent during lockdowns, but now that personal freedoms had returned, so too had an eye-watering cost of living, and one by one people were squeezed out of their homes.

At least I wouldn't run into Eddie here. He was loyal to the west side. There were no haunted corners up this way, no forbidden brunch spots, no happy memories to stumble across. No chance that I'd run into him — *them*, ugh, the nerve — and descend into a violent rage when my own dog didn't recognise me, no police report and subsequent restraining order. The perks stacked up.

My phone buzzed with Nicola's reply.

Nicola Fowler-Smythe (11:50): How bad?
Marnie Fowler (11:50): Four cats. One litter box.
Nicola Fowler-Smythe (11:51): 😱
Marnie Fowler (11:51): Am I going to have to move in with Mum?
Nicola Fowler-Smythe (11:52): You could sublet while Trent takes her on a grey nomad trip to Vietnam. She's spamming me with travel brochures.
Marnie Fowler (11:54): Our mother?
Marnie Fowler (11:54): Who 'doesn't do' humidity? Who thinks pepper is too spicy? In Vietnam?

Fresh November sun bore down through the dark fibres of my T-shirt as I followed the pulsing blue barrow on my phone towards my last hope for independent living.

Share house four was the last in a row of single-storey terraces, each less maintained than the one before it. The one I was looking for looked like last year's gingerbread house: its red brick fading, white paint peeling from its accents. The squat fence had begun to bend at the hip; tufts of dandelion marked an early grave.

I held my breath as I pushed aside the painted iron gate, steeled for another mildewy disappointment or potential trap for human trafficking, and knocked on the rippled glass of the front door.

'Marnie?' asked Claudia. I recognised her by the wild dark curls seen in her profile picture, but she looked pretty small. If she was luring me into her kill room under the cover of needing a housemate, I could knock her down easily and get out of there.

I didn't say this. *'Good luck trying to kill me, bitch!'* wasn't the first impression I wanted to make. Instead, I said, 'That's me!'

She nodded without enthusiasm. 'You're the last one.'

Ominous.

Compulsive female politeness or just the pressing need to live without seeing Mitch's pubes on the toilet seat every morning pushed me along. I followed her over the threshold and made all the right sounds as she showed me through each room.

The place was dated but immaculate. You could forgive a lot for high ceilings and natural light. While my apartment with Eddie was stark — *'It's Scandi,'* he insisted, meaning everything was a shade of white, even Sweetie — Claudia's house could only be described as loud. It had all the hallmarks of a lifelong rental: milky white walls covered in old sticky hooks, scuff-proof laminate floors and an unstainable dark kitchen countertop, but every inch of it had been covered in aggressively feminine decor.

Palest pink tulle curtains hung over the living room windows, and the sofa was crammed full of so many purple and yellow throw pillows that there was barely space to sit. There on the bookcase stood a vase in the shape of someone's tits, a bloom of irises and daisies erupting out of her clavicle. Claudia had even framed her art: a Lichtenstein print in the hall, a French marketplace in the kitchen, and a charcoal nude smouldering down at us in the living room.

Sunlight poured through the windows. The dining table didn't even look like it had been pulled in from the street. The bedroom going was large enough for a bed and a side table. In the carport-turned-courtyard, weeds were optimistically curling through the concrete, as if to say, *'Everyone thrives here.'*

'I love it,' I said, clocking the ample pantry space and the distinct absence of testosterone. 'I'll take it.'

'Hold on,' she replied with the kind of bossy, take-no-shit energy afforded only to short women.

She had a mane that rivalled an eighties Nicole Kidman and ear cartilage strewn with gold studs and hoops. Her eyes, suspicious like a bouncer, said she could take me in a fight. The tattoo of a penguin in a bowtie on her left forearm said she was, secretly, a cupcake.

'Sorry,' I said. 'That was a bit keen.'

'Do you have a job?'

'Yes.' Why was I starting to sweat? 'I work at — I run Little George Gastronomia.'

It wasn't strictly untrue: in Kit's absence, I was in charge, but he practically lived at the cafe. My only contact with suppliers was high-fiving the guy who delivered the coffee beans. But I liked this quirky little house, I was desperate to impress the aloof woman in charge of letting me live in it.

'Are you messy? I can handle clutter, but I hate stuff left in the sink.'

'I hardly even use dishes,' I told her. 'Mostly I eat at work or bring leftovers home. In containers. That I recycle.'

'Do you invite people over a lot? I work long hours; I don't want a bunch of people around eating my snacks.'

'I mostly hang out with my niece, but she's seven months old. She doesn't really party.'

Claudia didn't laugh. I wondered if she'd even blink if I got up and left right now, mortified at my inability to land a joke, or if she'd keep asking questions to an empty kitchen.

'Are you going to be having a ton of loud sex?'

When I laughed, it tasted bitter. 'Um, no. No sex of any kind, loud or otherwise.'

'Good,' she said, nodding. 'The people in the place next door do. Constantly. That's why there's music on. I'm not trying to set the mood; I'm trying to block out the sound of my neighbour orgasming like a Tickle Me Elmo with a rip in the back all fucking day.'

I wasn't sure if she was kidding, so I strained my ears. Behind the twang of Dolly Parton was the repetitive thud of furniture against the shared wall. 'Here You Come Again' indeed.

'Yikes.'

She observed me for a moment, lips pursed and eyes narrowed in judgment, and I shifted from foot to foot.

'The rent doesn't include bills,' she said. 'Do you have a coffee table? My old housemate took hers. She's moving in with the most boring man I've ever met. They go camping. For *fun*.'

'Camping is the worst.'

'So!' Claudia stood up straighter and slapped her hands together. 'Do you want a wine?'

I paused. 'It's midday.'

'So ... white?'

'Does this mean you're offering me the room?'

'I can't be bothered doing any more of these walk-throughs,' she said with her freckled nose scrunching in a silent whine. 'Just say yes and spare me.'

Forty minutes later, we were pink and shiny from the spring sunshine in the courtyard. She'd dropped ice into my glass, turning our wine clear and the conversation easy. Claudia — Claud — was my age, a vegetarian too, and in her own words, had a soul-destroying, do-nothing, bullshit job in internal communications at a three-letter conglomerate (name withheld to protect the innocent) (and disinterested). What she lacked in career lust, she made up for with her obscene salary, which explained why she paid significantly more for the master bedroom with the ensuite and the walk-in wardrobe that was crammed floor to ceiling with luxury labels. By the end of my second glass, I'd decided that she was the best person I had ever met.

'Ew,' she said, scowling at her phone. 'This cretin on Tinder just asked, "*Are you submissive?*" Not even a hello. Just straight to, "*Can I disrespect you? By the way, I think the clitoris is an urban legend.*"'

'That's gross.'

'Dating apps are the worst place on the planet,' she said. 'They're punishment for the sins of my ancestors. Who were megalomaniacs, apparently.'

I tipped back to balance on the back legs of my chair. I teetered there, eyes closed to the pleasant breeze. 'Thank god I don't date.'

'Oh, are you ace?'

'No. I just have a rule about it.'

Claud frowned. 'So just casual sex, or ...?'

'Huh.' I snapped my eyes open and landed the chair back on the ground with a thunk. 'That's a good question.'

'What, you don't know?'

'It's quite a new rule.'

'How new?'

'About two days.'

Claud snorted. 'Right.'

'There was a whole thing,' I said, waving it off. 'The breakup and the breakdown. The panic attack when I looked at his Instagram and he's already moved on. The swearing off men forever. It's been a process. I haven't worked it all out yet.'

'Do we need another bottle about it?'

'Yes,' I replied immediately, and she went off to get one. 'I'm not even sad; I'm just ... finished. I've never really been single. Properly. Whenever I haven't had a boyfriend, I've spent the whole time looking for one.'

'You've *never* been single?'

I relieved her of the second bottle when she returned, twisting it open and refilling our glasses indecently full.

'I don't do it on purpose,' I said. 'I've just fallen for every guy I've ever gone out with.'

'That sounds like a chronic illness.'

I shrugged. 'We go out for a drink, and they like me, so I like them, and before I know it, I'm in his sister's wedding. It's like highway hypnosis.'

She smirked. 'Or dick paralysis?'

'It must be.'

'I think I envy you,' she said. She leaned back to observe me thoughtfully over the rim of her glass. 'All I ever do is go on crap dates that never turn into anything. I've been single for three years. It's fun, it's fine, but after a while I just want to get comfortable with someone.'

'Comfortable means not bothering to run the bathroom tap while you pee and not caring if they hear.'

'Ew,' she replied. 'Sometimes I think it's me, that I'm the problem, because no one pursues me that hard, or I spiral over rejection texts from people I'm not even into. But then I think, when was the last time I really liked someone? When was the last time I met someone who was interesting, or funny, or a good kisser? I'm interesting and funny and a great kisser. Why should I get down on myself when it's everyone else who needs to step up *their* game to be good enough for *me*?'

I raised my glass and cried, 'To being better off alone!'

'Amen!' Claud said as we clinked our glasses, and then we drank more than we should have, and another four glasses after that.

I had questions. Not about the gas bill, or if I had to sign a lease, but about how to live. All the people left in my life were heavily coupled. Nicola and Mitch. Mum and Trent/Paul/Brian. Dad and Susie and their uncooked-chicken-looking cats. Kit and Andrew, until recently. I had no single role models.

It felt childish and small, but I had to ask. 'What do you do with all your free time?'

'What do you mean?'

'What if you want to go out for dinner and no one's free?'

She frowned. 'I go alone …?'

'Don't you worry that everyone is staring at you? Thinking you just got stood up?'

'Who gives a shit?' she replied. 'If someone's reaction to seeing a woman alone is pity — pathetic.'

This laissez-faire attitude was fantastic and intimidating. I'd never met someone so self-assured, so in tune with themselves that they could deflect any nagging doubt without blinking. It was easy to let Claud take the reins. I had no desire to occupy a spotlight, happy to let confident extroverts do the talking. All I had to do was stay close and allow them to drag me along, accepting payment in the form of laughter and encouragement.

'You're amazing,' I said. 'How do you do that?'

'Self-esteem, babe.'

'Where do I get some?'

'You get a good dermatologist and a couple of friends who tell you how great you are until you believe it.'

'I need some of those.'

'You have one now,' she said with a wink.

I grinned, lazy and numb. By the bottom of the second bottle, I felt like I was a whole new person. The new house, new friend, and new life made the whole world look warmer and brighter. Wondrous, really, what a white wine buzz and thirty-some hours of enforced celibacy could do for your outlook.

I moved in a week later.

CHAPTER FIVE

'This is like a time capsule. What era was this from?'

I looked over to where Nicola was pressing an unconscionably short leopard-print number against herself and twisting in front of the mirror.

'Guillaume,' I replied. 'My party monster moment. You can have it. I'd get it dry-cleaned though.'

'Oh,' she said, and flung the dress into the growing donation pile in my new bedroom's doorway. 'Ew.'

We were sorting through the boxes that Eddie had dumped on the doorstep while I was at work that day. Ancient relics of a past life had been stacked up in our — his — storage cage for years, and I could no longer keep them in his house or my life.

Seven pm had come and gone, and the sun was still out. All of my unpacking had me hot and irritable, and the hair that had fallen from my topknot was slick to my neck.

Nicola had thrown herself at the offer to come over and sort through my stuff, whether for the chance to finally get her hands on the leather jacket we'd been squabbling over for half my life or for the excuse to get more than twenty feet away from a diaper genie.

A polyester bomb could have gone off in here for all the chaos reorganising had created, and my frown lines were growing permanent as I sorted vinyls into keep or sell stacks.

'This still has a price sticker on it,' I said, flipping over the sleeve of *Dookie* by Green Day and dropping it onto the sell pile. 'I paid fifty-five dollars for that and didn't listen to it once.'

'That's embarrassing,' said Claud from the floor, where she was digging through my jewellery box. 'Get a Spotify subscription, hun.'

'Why do I still have this? I don't even like these bands.'

The Doors, Journey, Don McLean: a rising stack of musicians I'd pretended to worship under Thomas' insistence, whose songs I could happily never revisit. So far, I was only set on keeping work from three artists: Joni, George Harrison and Jeff Buckley. It was cheaper and more effective than therapy.

'I don't know how anyone could like this,' said Claud, holding up a gingham romper by the tip of an uneasy finger. 'What look were you going for? "Sexy baby"?'

Nicola and I both spoke at once: 'Ian.'

Claud looked queasy and tossed it onto the donation pile. 'How do you go from party monster to grunge groupie to sexy baby?'

'It's what I was into at the time.' I shrugged. 'I wore it with knee socks.'

'It's *who* she was into at the time,' said Nicola, correcting me. 'She's a different dream girl for everyone she meets.'

'Am I?'

'In a good way!' she said, quickly. 'You're a chameleon.'

'Do I do that?' I asked. My frown returned. 'I don't think I like that.'

The longer I stood in the debris of my past, the truer it became.

I had a faded and blurred crescent permanently stained on my ribcage, the beginnings of the letter G before I panicked and called the tattoo artist off.

There were a dozen journals I couldn't throw away, bloated and dog-eared with glued-in ticket stubs and embarrassing poems. There were milk crates crammed full of vinyl sleeves of '70s nostalgia. A film camera pilfered from an op-shop that I used to obsessively catalogue our relationship: three months of bliss, and nine more trying desperately to reconnect with it, and the shoebox full of photos I'd never look at again.

The pearls and kitten heels I wore like badges of honour for my eighteen months with Martin, whose ill-disguised misogyny required me to play both doting mummy and vintage pin-up girl, owing to a complete misreading of and ill-advised fascination with Don Draper, a red flag I failed to notice at the time. All my equity was still tied up in Agent Provocateur.

And now I lived in outfits that prioritised practicality over style. Jeans and boots. Jackets with forty pockets sewn in. Clothes to survive the apocalypse, or a week spent in the Grampians away from modern plumbing, which was basically the same thing.

It occurred to me only now that my entire life was laid out in front of me, and it was filled with someone else's garbage.

I'd always had something to do and someone to do it with: flatpack furniture to put together, engagement parties to attend, department store aisles to wander looking for dinner sets to argue over. I'd spent so much time trying to fit into someone's life that I had forgotten to ask how they would fit into mine. An entire decade lost to people I didn't know anymore. In my righteous hurt and indignation, I'd failed to consider how much *time* there was.

I wasn't sure I'd thought all of this through, this foray into self-sufficiency. What was I supposed to do when the lonelies — a fluffy name I used to make them less threatening — struck?

I'd been a full-time girlfriend for nearly my entire adult life. I didn't know anything else. Who was I going to talk to when I couldn't sleep? What would I do with all the empty space on my mattress? What happened when everyone else paired off — as they always did, as I always had — and Nicola was too busy navigating Layla's preteen hysterics to answer the phone? Would I be the third wheel throwing my friends' and family's carefully calibrated machines off balance? Who would be my emergency contact? Who would remind me to buy more toothpaste?

'None of this is my stuff,' I said, frozen as my eyes swung from pile to pile. 'I don't even think I like any of this crap.'

'Well, now you can get rid of it and start fresh with stuff you do like,' said Claud bracingly. 'Blank slate!'

'But that's my point,' I said. 'What do I like? Who even am I without all of this?'

'Uh oh,' murmured Nicola. 'It's having an existential crisis.'

Heat bloomed in my cheeks. My throat seemed to swell shut. I could taste my teeth.

'I'm not a sexy baby.'

'No one is,' said Claud. Sensing the oncoming panic, she had risen to her knees to grab my wrist and pull me down to the floor beside her. I followed obediently.

'I'm not even a person,' I said, swallowing. 'I'm a mirror.'

'You *are* a person,' argued Nicola, joining us and taking my other hand. 'You've just taken on some of other people's stuff, too.'

'Which everyone does!' said Claud. 'We all plagiarise our personalities a little bit.'

'But I don't like any of these people!' I cried. I heard Claud wince from the grip I had on her hand, but I didn't let it go. 'I don't want to be like them!'

Beside me, Nicola clicked her fingers. 'Project!'

'What?'

'*Project*.'

'Say more words.'

'You can use this time to figure all of this out. Do everything you never got around to because you were too entrenched in boyfriend bullshit.'

Claud smacked her knee in enthusiasm. 'Yes! Project!'

'My life is not *Eat, Pray, Love*.'

'Why not?' asked Nicola. 'What's wrong with eating pizza and screwing Javier Bardem?'

'*Great* question,' said Claud. 'We love an ugly-hot guy.'

Nicola sighed. 'What I wouldn't do to sleep with an ugly-hot stranger.'

I shook her hand out of mine and clicked my tongue. 'Can you put your dick away and focus on my crisis, please?'

'Right. Sorry. Look — this is the first time in your life you've ever really had to yourself. Stop looking at it like a death sentence. You're *free*. You have three years, tops, before you need a prescription for tretinoin and a fibre supplement. You can do anything you want.'

'Like what, though?' I asked, exasperation leaking in. 'It's not like I've ever thought, "*I'd love to become a doula but Martin won't let me.*"'

'So try things on until you find your *thing*,' Nicola said. She cast around the room for ideas and said, 'Ceramics, maybe. Your calling in life could be to make cute bowls and vases.'

'You could learn a language,' offered Claud. 'So you can understand Javier's Spanish dirty talk.'

'Mmm. You could do a floristry course. Or creative writing. Take up taekwondo and become the vigilante Princes Hill has been waiting for.'

My lips pursed themselves as I considered this, mind reeling as I pictured myself in each scenario. The Marnie of my mind's eye looked focussed but serene as she glazed a bowl. She pulled off bright lipstick as she slotted a peony into a pastel arrangement. She was far removed from her existential crisis on the floor among everything she'd ever owned.

'I could be into this,' I said, relieved to find that my breathing had finally evened out. 'Hobby shopping. Until something sticks.'

'Exactly,' said Nicola. 'Get to know yourself.'

'I think quitting relationships is a great way for Marnie to *get to know herself*,' said Claud, elbowing me in the ribs. 'Get it? Wanking.'

'My god,' said Nicola. 'You're fantastic.'

'People can have sex without relationships, thank you very much,' I replied. 'I'm not a nun.'

'People can,' said Nicola. '*You* can't.'

'Says who?'

'Says the fact that you've moved in with everyone who's ever seen you naked.'

'That was old Marnie.' I bristled. 'New Marnie is probably great at casual sex. New Marnie could lead her own slut parade.'

'New Marnie fucks 'em and chucks 'em,' said Claud.

Nicola was on the verge of a perverted response when her phone dinged six times in short succession. She deflated as she went to check it, shoulders rolling in as she dug through her handbag for the message that summoned her home.

'Mitch doesn't know the bedtime song,' she sighed, her mouth thinning. 'New Marnie had better get an IUD, or the fun's all over before it even starts.'

CHAPTER SIX

There was never enough time with Claud. I'd lived with her for less than a month, and when we weren't on the couch watching B-grade movies over a shared container of leftover manicotti, we were drinking away our paycheques on Smith Street, laughing until our faces ached at the horrific dating profiles she encountered, or texting one another every detail of our days.

She wrote to me that afternoon:

Claudia King (13:50): The new EA just said she doesn't think Kacey Musgraves is very good. Why don't they screen these people in their interviews?

I replied instantly while almond milk burnt on the steam wand.

Marnie Fowler (13:51): Report her to HR for creating a hostile working environment.
Marnie Fowler (13:51): Also, should I shave my head or is that too tragic?
Claudia King (13:52): I shaved my head once! Half of it. When I was an emo teen. For a brief moment I was the coolest girl at my high school.
Marnie Fowler (13:52): I am obsessed with you.

So when she messaged me later that evening, half cut and barely coherent, to say her work Christmas party was kicking on to a rooftop bar with a tab open on her department head's credit card and to, '*comeocmeocmeome come!!!!ppp,*' I was rooting through her closet for something to wear within three seconds.

Another perk of living with a woman was that my wardrobe had effectively exploded overnight.

We had filled six garbage bags with old clothes and relics from my past lives, cutting my remaining wardrobe down to Soviet sparseness. All I had left were boxy tees from the Uniqlo men's department, half a dozen pairs of jeans, and shoes that prioritised comfort. It was the only way I could be sure I wasn't holding on to anyone else's ideas.

Claud saw me as both pet and project. Every day brought new spoils and sage advice.

'Dressing for women is more interesting than for men,' she announced last week, arriving home laden with shopping bags.

'What does that mean?'

'It means: this.' She pulled out a jumpsuit made entirely of fuchsia sequins, and I screamed.

I let her play Barbie, both because I loved every idea she had and because she had so much fun doing it.

Through another series of barely coherent texts, she had instructed me to pull a silky red wrap dress out of her closet, and it was easily the nicest thing I've ever worn. I held my arms away from my body in case the rising December heat created sweat stains and destroyed it.

It was as though the Thursday night crowd had consciously forgotten that only months ago we were prohibited from standing within six feet of one another. The entire space, with its view across a thousand other rooftops, was so packed that I had to squeeze myself between bodies, holding my handbag aloft as I shuttled and wove in the search for my friend. '*Bck cornR!!!!L*,' Claud had texted before I entered the veritable mosh pit.

The bar's retractable ceiling had been pulled back, and I could feel sweat running down my spine. The vines and fairy lights that wrapped around the support beams might have been pretty if the sun wasn't too bright to notice them. If there was music playing, it was drowned out by every corporate shill in the city shouting over each other as the day wore on and their HR representatives engaged in selective blindness.

It took an age to cross the rooftop, and just as I was beginning to wonder if I was heading towards the wrong back corner, I heard a familiar shriek.

'My love!' cried Claud, karate chopping people out of her way.

'Oh thank god,' I sighed, catching her as she launched herself at me. 'I was lost in a sea of navy. I nearly drowned in it.'

She was holding both of my arms and using me to dance. Only all the way over here, feet away from a speaker as tall as she was, could I hear any music, and still it was the tuneless thud of noise rather than any discernible sound.

'I think I need to get on your level,' I said, and when she made a face and pointed at her ears, I raised my voice to shout, 'I NEED TO GET ON YOUR LEVEL.'

'YEAH!'

Despite being the size of a pixie, Claud's capacity to drink outpaced my own. She was always two ahead of me and I was twice as sloppy.

'*This way!*' she mimed, dancing backwards through the thinning crowd, to where a second, less crowded bar had been set up.

There. That was better. It wasn't so loud I could feel my brain rattling around in my skull.

'We're going to find you a hot finance bro, and you'll be a whole new woman,' said Claud, loudly enough that the people lining up ahead of us turned around.

I pulled a queasy face. 'No thanks. I'm here to hang out with you!'

She whined and stomped her little foot. 'What is the point of your rumspringa if I don't get to vicariously relive my wanton youth through you?'

'It's almost like what goes on in my vagina is none of your business.'

Claud had been on this for weeks. When I'd let slip that I'd never slept with anyone I wasn't in love with, she'd spat sparkling down her front and began campaigning to change the fact.

I wouldn't have been bothered by it had it not been brought up so frequently, but the longer she nagged, the less sure I felt. Maybe I wasn't sex positive enough. Maybe I was repressed. Maybe I still had Eddie's fingerprints all over me, despite the fact that the closest I'd come to orgasming in the last year was when we went four-wheel driving and the car had shuddered over rocky terrain for an hour. Maybe Claud was right.

She was getting ready to protest but lost her train of thought when a pair of eyebrows made lingering eye contact as he passed us, making her practically pant.

'Fine,' she said. '*I'll* fuck a hot finance bro.'

'Thrilled we could negotiate.'

The people ahead of us cringed over their shoulders again. Claud poked her tongue out at their turned backs.

The fact was, I was twenty-eight whole years old and I didn't know how to make people see me sexually. I'd won my boyfriends over with polite laughter at their average jokes, and before I knew it, the lights were out and I was having a nice time underneath them. My body for their company.

I wondered how this would sound to a stranger. I didn't even have a bed frame yet. What if we had sex on the floor and the, uh, result got into my carpet? I imagined googling '*Semen removal polyester carpet*'. I imagined explaining a hard patch in the middle of my floor to a professional carpet cleaner and shuddered.

'Let's get you loose!' Claud cried as a space at the bar opened up in front of us, and she shoved her way into it. 'Two Long Islands, please!'

'Whoa —' I protested. 'I'd rather not end up in hospital.'

'Don't be BORING!' she said. 'Fine. Fine! Whisky gingers, then.'

'And a water for her,' I added.

'I'm going to go make out with straight Dan Levy,' she announced, jabbing her thumb at her newest crush, and I was seized with panic. I was still a nervous turtle in my shell. For all our weeks of gallivanting, the money I'd spent on nights I remembered like underexposed film, I hadn't navigated so much as a ladies' bathroom on my own.

As she moved to make her way over there, I threw out my hand and grabbed her arm. Suddenly, I wasn't sure this was such a good idea. 'What if no one talks to me?'

'They will!' she cried. 'You're amazing!'

'But what if they don't? What if I'm just playing mahjong on my phone all night?'

'Then come over and find me, and us and future Mister King will get outta here,' she said. '*Mahjong*? Are you eighty-five?'

'Okay but —' I squeezed her wrist as she turned to leave again. 'What if someone *does* talk to me? What do I say? What if they don't ask me any questions, and I can't think of anything to ask them, and they just stare at me like I'm an idiot and walk away? Can I play mahjong then?'

'I've never met anyone more high maintenance than me,' she said. 'Marnie. My love. Beautiful, stupid baby lady —'

'*Hey*,' I said, offended.

'This isn't complicated. We're at a bar. Your tits look great. Someone will talk to you, and when you have nothing to say, just look bored and do this.'

She took a sip of her drink, smirked and glanced around the room like she'd spotted someone wearing an outfit she liked.

'Okay?' she asked earnestly, breaking character.

'Yes,' I lied. 'I'll be fine.'

She shot finger guns at me and departed.

Immediately, I felt lonely. In my old life, I could text Eddie about the outrageous drinks prices, or ask how his night was going. But I had no one to text, and I wasn't allowed to play mahjong.

Okay. Fine. I'd have one drink, make some excuse to Claud, and go home.

One drink.

I could do that.

I took a sip and — 'Jesus fucking Christ,' I spluttered.

'Whisky on a school night,' said a man beside me. 'Aren't you brave?'

'Or a masochist,' I croaked.

'You could be both,' he said. 'You have to be pretty brave to get into a gimp suit.'

'Is that something you know from personal experience?'

'Yeah, definitely. I wear one under all of my clothes.' He pulled at his collar as though to show it off. His watch looked like it cost more than all my possessions combined.

'You know, Spanx will give you a smooth silhouette in a breathable fabric.'

'But do they have a little zip in the crotch?'

'A gusset.'

'Bless you!'

I didn't know if it was the whisky or the crass repartee with a perfect stranger, but I laughed. When I caught sight of my pink face in the mirror behind the bar, I remembered Claud's advice: I took another sip, ready for the burn this time, and glanced around the place. Claud was already perched on Eyebrows' knee, and I was satisfied I looked nonchalant enough to cover over my lack of anything new to say.

'Who are you, James Dean?' asked the guy as he hoisted himself onto the stool beside me. 'What a smooth move.'

'I don't know what you're talking about.'

'Oh, sure,' he said. He took my glass from my hands, sipped it and mimicked me, batting his eyelashes and giving the room a wide, indifferent glance.

'That's not what I look like!' I cried. I couldn't believe he took a sip of my drink. I hoped he was vaccinated. 'Is that what I look like?'

'But you're much prettier than I am.'

'It's just makeup,' I said with a dismissive wave. 'I have mascara in my bag if you want to borrow it.'

'I think I'm beyond mascara.'

I leaned back to consider him shrewdly. He had the kind of thick dark hair you could really get your fingers into, should the mood call for it. Good shoulders; broad and sharp. The perma-shadow on his jaw said, *'It's 5 o'clock somewhere.'* Yes, I decided. He was very easy to look at. 'I don't know. We could make you into a Kardashian with a bit of bronzer and tit tape.'

Grinning, he passed me back my glass, and I took care to trace my finger where his lips had been.

'I'm Marnie.'

'That's my favourite Hitchcock.'

'I've never seen it.'

He looked horrified. 'That's criminal. It's your namesake!'

'Well, I don't even know what your name is.'

'I'm Isaac,' he said, taking my hand and shaking it. Big hands. Long fingers. Interesting.

'And what does Isaac do when he's not squeezing in and out of leather gear?'

'Isaac works in finance.'

'That's vague. Are you a wolf of Wall Street or are you a teller at the Mordialloc Westpac?'

'Which one do I look like?'

'You'd be cute in a sensible heel and a French twist.'

'Where do you do your banking, the 1980s?'

'Gotta love that inflation rate.'

His laugh was wonderful, the kind that wrinkled his nose and forced his eyes shut. 'Do you have any idea what you're talking about?'

'Yes!' Pause. 'No. It's all about confidence, Isaac.'

'Thanks for the life advice.'

I didn't know what else to say, so I took another sip, and when he didn't come up with anything either, I took another.

As the cogs in my brain completed a single turn, I asked the only question I could think of. 'Are you from Melbourne?'

'Brighton, mostly,' he said, and then, to my disparaging face, 'Oh, come on. What's wrong with Brighton?'

Brighton was exclusively home to posh twats whose egregious generational wealth made you want to declare yourself a communist. That's what was wrong with Brighton. But I didn't think my proletariat soapbox rant was going to score me many points, so instead I said, 'So he's a *fancy man*. I didn't think they let you leave the house without a puffer vest on.'

He leaned in conspiratorially and whispered, 'I left it in the car.'

'I bet you did. In a dry-cleaning bag with your gimp suit.'

I couldn't believe how easy this was. No polite feigned interest here.

'Do you need another drink?' he asked. 'It looks like you're struggling with that one.'

'My friend ordered it.' I grimaced. 'I think whisky tastes like cigarettes and patriarchy.'

He flagged down the bartender, and moments later, my drink was replaced with a more palatable mojito.

Christ. He really was hot. Great bone structure. Eyes the colour of ... the perfectly ripe avocados I never seemed to find. Wait, that's stupid. Greener than, uh, Little George's branding? The mint in my drink? *Shut up Marnie.*

Whatever colour his eyes were, they barely left mine to blink. I learned he was an investment product expert, whatever that meant, and he thought my laugh was cute, which only made me do it more. He said he was impervious to the effects of gin; a claim I immediately contested by ordering another round.

There was a vague nerdiness to him, some almost-hidden, endlessly appealing subtext in his excitable character that suggested he hadn't always been good looking. Like he had only just come to terms with the idea that he was, maybe, sometimes, someone that women could find attractive. The way he lit up at every boundary-pushing joke, like he couldn't believe that anyone would be so forward with someone like him. As though he'd woken up one day and been shocked and impressed with who looked back at him in the mirror.

But of course that was all projection. No one who had mastered hair pomade or delicately matched their shoes and belt walked around thinking they were a gargoyle. His shirtsleeves were rolled to the elbow with a little too much perfect imperfection, like he'd studied it. His aftershave suited him too well to have been a gift.

This all said *effort*. This all said *curated*. This all said *confidence*. This all said *fucking delicious*.

Fine. Claud could win this round. I could sacrifice my pride for the sake of a string-free roll around on his memory foam mattress. This was the man I wanted to cleanse my palate with.

He was funny and quick and into me, evidenced by how often our conversation turned blue. He never let it enter into sleaze territory, only a wink here and there. '*I was bending over to —*' I was saying as the preamble to the time I popped my shoulder out at work. '*That's how all my favourite stories start*,' he said, and his grin got wider when I got flustered, and then we continued talking about perfectly innocent freak workplace accidents.

I liked being this girl, who could be crass and bold without worrying about the light it cast her in. Isaac didn't know anything about me. I could be whoever I wanted.

Now I was glad Claud insisted I borrow her dress. Réalisation Par knew how to make a uniform for the girl who was down for a good time, which helped, because I didn't know how to flirt except to keep the conversation light and mildly inappropriate. All I could do was hold my elbows in as close as I could to push my cleavage into his eye line. Don't you hate that saying, that the sexiest thing you can be is confident? How was I supposed to be confident if I didn't feel sexy? How was I supposed to feel sexy unless I was confident that I already *was*?

Calling on a mental catalogue of every romcom ever made and the confidence of two cocktails on an empty stomach, I took a handful of his shirt and pulled him towards me, angling my face to lean in for a timely and very sexy little kiss, then —

'Oh,' said Isaac. He stepped back, and I lost my grip on his shirt. 'I actually — sorry, I should say — I have a girlfriend.'

Did someone turn the music off? The only bass I could hear was the thumping in my ears as all my blood rushed to my face.

'Oh, I didn't —'

'I didn't either — sorry — I should have said before —'

'Well, why didn't you?'

'It didn't come up — we were just chatting — I just think you're cool.'

'It's fine!' I said with false cheeriness. 'It's totally fine! I'm just drunk, haha, whoops.'

'You're obviously very, uh, attractive,' he said, so apologetic it was humiliating. 'It's not that I'm *not* interested —'

'Totally! Yep!'

'I think you're *so* cool,' — oh, god, kill me — 'I've had so much fun hanging out.'

'Same!' My face was stretched into a manic grin to hide my humiliation. 'Really fun!'

'Maybe we could be friends?'

'Who doesn't love friends?' I replied, laughing to show how deeply, absolutely fine I was about this. 'Can't have enough friends!'

Miraculously, Claud reappeared right when I needed her to.

'Are you ready to go?'

'Yeah, I'm wrecked,' she sighed. 'I told that guy that Bruce Springsteen is the best musician to ever walk the earth —'

'An objective fact,' Isaac said at once.

Huh. I'd have assumed he was one of those men who could only express emotions when listening to Frank Ocean.

'— and he *laughed*.'

'He did not,' Isaac replied, affronted. 'I lost my virginity to "I'm On Fire".'

Claud froze, taken aback by this intimate fact. 'That's kind of a short song.'

'All the more reason to believe me.'

She turned to me. 'Do you want to stay and uh —?'

'Oh, no,' I said, feeling my face get lava-hot again, 'we're actually —'

'We're just pals,' he said smoothly.

'Yep! Just pals!' I drained my drink. 'I'll come home with you.'

'Oh, you should stay —'

'No, no, time to go!' I said. I didn't need to prolong this mortifying misunderstanding a second longer. I looped my arm through Claud's and dragged her away without more than a *'Thanks! Bye!'* to Isaac, who I hoped to never, ever see again so long as I lived.

CHAPTER SEVEN

'Nice of you to join us,' said Kit as we crossed paths; him with an armful of granola cups, me thirty-five minutes late. Thank god he wasn't the type of boss who cared about punctuality. Or performance. Or anything except having someone to talk shit with between tables.

'Sorry,' I groaned. 'Won't happen again.'

There was a queue three-deep at the counter, but they would have to wait. I reached for the portafilter and filled it before I'd even dumped my bag on the ground.

'Can I get an almond cap —'

'Just a minute,' I replied, with a hand up to silence them. They murmured among themselves as I pulled a double espresso and resisted the urge to press my forehead against the cool steel of the machine.

After last night's masterclass in humiliation, Claud had insisted on soothing my spirits with spirits, and I was powerless to her plea of '*just one more*'. I'd woken up on the couch, phone at eighteen percent, ten minutes after I was supposed to be at work. I hadn't even had time to look in the mirror; I'd just yanked on the first pair of jeans I found and ran out the door.

'Ex*cuse* me,' came the customer again. 'I'd like an almond milk cap.'

I turned to look at her, dead-eyed over the bridge of my sunglasses.

'I'll sort that for you,' Kit said to them, coming to the rescue. 'You owe me for this,' he muttered to me.

I took my coffee and a morning bun out of the case and plonked down on a milk crate.

It felt like my brain was leaking out of my ears. I took a bite of pastry and it turned to sand in my mouth.

'Did someone have a big night?' crooned Kit, letting the milk steamer wand gurgle obnoxiously loud.

'They should bring back prohibition,' I grumbled.

'God, I miss my twenties.'

'How do you take a look at this —' I gestured at myself, and in the reflection of the milk fridge I saw old eyeliner bleeding into my eye wrinkles '— and feel nostalgia?'

'This is the most fun you'll ever have,' he told me.

I tried to roll my eyes, but it hurt. 'I'm going to need a tactical vom. I'm sweating ouzo.'

'*Ouzo*. Now that's dangerous.' He slid the customers their coffees and bid them a good day. 'I'd love to be one of those chic men who could sip spirits neat. And a pinky ring, I always wanted to be a *rings* guy.'

'Like a mob boss?'

He flicked a tea towel at me and I yelped in protest.

'I used to be fun,' he continued, taking off his glasses and cleaning them with the edge of his T-shirt. 'I had four glasses of wine at a dinner party a while ago and tried to get everyone to do karaoke. Andrew had to fireman-carry me to the car.'

'That sounds like it was fun for you at least.'

'Getting tanked on pinot gris in the suburbs then getting the silent treatment for three days because I'd embarrassed him? Yeah, it was a riot.'

I never knew what to say when Kit made these comments. Until I'd queried Andrew's absence and Kit revealed that they'd split, and that he was sleeping in the granny flat, I had thought that they were the most well-adjusted couple I knew.

Not like Nicola and Mitch, who had mastered the art of passive-aggressive dinner conversation. Not like Mum and her flavour of the month. Not even like Dad and Susie, whose relationship had gone from 'honeymooning' to 'concerningly codependent' somewhere around their fifth anniversary. Certainly not like any relationship I'd ever been in.

It used to be that Kit couldn't say Andrew's name without smiling. If he knew he'd be dropping by the cafe, he used to zip to the bathroom to fluff up his hair and French tuck his shirt.

They alone seemed to have figured out the key to lasting love. After all the mundane details of a shared life and its many irritants had come and gone — delayed public transport, overbearing in-laws, the well-meaning kale bouquet rotting in the fridge — they just *liked* each other.

When Andrew pulled a shift at the same time as me, I'd stand in awe of the little things they did unconsciously. One would start telling a story, and the other would finish it. As they split a muffin, Kit would leave the blueberry globs for Andrew. Their hands would touch as they both reached for the card reader, and they'd share a flicker of an affectionate glance.

Invariably, these whispers of affection made me pick a fight when I got home. Why didn't Eddie put on the kettle and make me a cup of tea without being asked to? Why didn't his nephew ever call me Auntie Marnie — was it because his family didn't see me as part of theirs? Why wasn't it just *right*?

As I remembered how dismissed I used to feel, I kicked open the swinging kitchen door and dumped the half-finished remains of someone's breakfast in the kitchen mess.

Most couples I knew weren't happy. Even Kit and Andrew hadn't been an exception to the rule. You couldn't aspire to something as fickle as luck. When the reward was impossible, the risk wasn't worth it.

'You okay, lovely Marnie?' called Sam from the workbench as he spooned a poached egg onto a stack of zucchini fritters.

'I'm just taking a minute.' I hovered in the blissfully dark and quiet stock room.

'You'll take any excuse to be near me,' he said. 'Just admit it.'

'Right.'

Sam pressed on. 'You're *obsessed* with me. It's like, *give it a rest*.'

My temples throbbed. I wanted another pastry and to take a nap in the pile of clean tea towels in Kit's office.

'So,' Sam continued. 'It's been a few weeks since the big breakup. Is it okay for me to ask you out yet?'

'No.'

Once upon a time, Sam would have made perfect sense as a rebound fling. He was cute. Inoffensive, like a teddy bear, with the kind of soft, open features that suggested he wasn't capable of deviousness. He was a fraction of an inch shorter than me and in denial about it. His gingery hair flopped like a '90s heartthrob, tucked neatly behind his ears during service. He had the thick, dense eyelashes women were seldom allocated in the gene pool, and a pale mole right under his eye that caught the light whenever he smiled. He was sparky and extroverted, which I usually loved.

It wasn't that I didn't see his appeal. It was the relentlessness of his campaign. I'd made the mistake of smiling at him on my first day, and since then he had been like a dog with a tennis ball, dropping it at my feet and waiting, quivering with excitement, for me to throw it again.

Either because I was being rude or because he could see I was struggling and thought it would be funny, Sam punched down on the bell for service and called loudly, 'TABLE SIX, BEAUTIFUL.'

I murmured a few choice expletives as I collected the fritters and fruit medley and took them out to table six.

Which was worse: the slow recession of my blood alcohol levels or the vignettes that my sober brain was patching together from the night before?

Fighting my serotonin scarcity from last night's antics, I was trying to look on the bright side. That incident at the bar had been mortifying, but it was also an important reminder. I'd been too quick to get swept away with the first person to give me attention. I was an addict in recovery, and every interaction with a man was inherently risky. I'd wear off the embarrassment eventually, but I'd hold on to the lesson for as long as I could: I was not to be trusted unsupervised around good-looking men and alcohol. I'd text Claud to share this compelling insight as soon as I finished clearing this table.

'This is too cute.'

'Oh Jesus fuck!' I cried. I dropped the knife in my hand and it fell thunderously to the hardwood floors, and the dining room fell into a ringing silence. I grabbed it, straightened up, and froze in place.

What kind of sick joke was this? Was there no end to my suffering?

There was a toothpaste stain on my T-shirt, coffee under my nails and my mouth tasted like a sewer, and Isaac was here, in my cafe, polished and glowing in a pair of sexy little tortoiseshell glasses, looking down at me.

I wanted to say, '*Hi.*'

I wanted to say, '*You again.*'

I wanted to say, '*Who are you again?*'

Something small and indifferent, after which I'd breeze away, hide in the walk-in and refuse to come out until Kit promised me he was gone.

Instead, I felt my hand pop to my hip and heard myself say, 'Man, once wasn't enough? You're chasing me around town? Figure it out, Isaac, *I don't want to kiss you.*'

Where did that come from?

He grinned, big and delighted, but didn't say anything. I'd never had the confidence to *not* fill any moment of silence with inane chatter.

'I have a weapon, you know,' I said, holding up the butter knife. 'Stalking is a crime.'

'Not stalking,' he said, reaching out to take it from me, and I surprised myself by letting him. 'Just a lucky coincidence.'

I eyed him suspiciously, and he eyed me right back. I only broke it when I turned to slip behind the counter, the better to seem too busy to entertain him.

'I didn't know you worked here,' he said. 'I love this place.'

'She would remember if you had been here before,' said Kit, who looked like he was having the time of his life watching this all play out. The emphasis he'd put on *you*, there, like he was flirting with him *for* me.

Isaac glanced out the window when a passing car honked, giving me just enough time to turn to Kit and mouth '*Go. Away.*'

'So,' said Isaac as Kit turned his back and pretended to wipe down the menus I'd just cleaned yesterday. 'Can I apologise again for last night?'

'For what?' I asked, feigning innocence. 'I have the most amazing selective memory.'

'That's quite a talent.'

'I'm *so* talented.'

'I bet.'

'Uh huh.'

('God, get a room,' murmured Kit. I hid my blush by filling up the milk jug and Isaac cleared his throat.)

I didn't know what his coffee order was, but I could guess. You couldn't work in a cafe for more than a few weeks without beginning to draw patterns between the orders and the people who made them.

A long black for the man in a suit who gave his order without pausing his Bluetooth phone call. An extra dry cap with a sweetener for the woman in Zara who wished it was Celine. An almond milk flat white for the guy in his cutting phase. An iced coffee for the intimidatingly cool Gen Z kids, and a cold brew for the elder millennial having a crisis about it. You could become an expert in months.

'You've got to admit, though,' Isaac continued, 'twice in two days. What's that about?'

I pretended to think as I tucked a cup under the machine, poured a double ristretto and heaped half a sugar into it. 'The city needs a better variety of bars and cafes?'

'I think it means we're supposed to be mates.'

'Mates,' I repeated, my eyebrow quirking in disbelief. 'Right.'

'Yeah. You know, those people you like, hang out with, send stupid videos to?'

'Oh, I'm familiar with the concept. I just don't know if I believe you have any mates who are women.'

'Me?' he asked, pretending to be wounded. 'I have tons of them. They're my favourite people. I'll help them move their couch, offer perspective on their boy troubles ... I'm great value.'

I cast him a sideways look as I steamed the milk and wondered how much of that was the truth. He seemed earnest. He wasn't leering or unbuckling his belt, which helped. And we did get along well. I really did want more friends, and it would be good to have someone around to kill the silence when Claud and Nicola were busy.

I'd never had a straight male friend before. Being friends with Isaac could rewrite my internal narrative about the sinister intentions of their kind. It could be an exercise in self-restraint. And nothing could happen. Nothing *would* happen, because I'd tried, and he'd rebuffed me, and I didn't hate myself enough to try it ever again.

I poured the milk at an angle to avoid excess foam and shrugged. 'Okay.'

'Yeah?'

'It's your lucky day.'

I scribbled my number on a plastic lid and fitted it to his cup, letting my fours look like nines in the vague hope that he'd misdial, and he let out a whistle at such a slick move.

He got his card out to pay, but I waved him off.

Before he left, he sipped his coffee, paused, and frowned. 'How did you know my order?'

'She's *just that good*,' said Kit, interrupting. I closed my eyes in frustration.

'I'll message you,' said Isaac. 'Then you'll find out I'm incredibly boring and you can block me.'

'I look forward to it.'

And then he was gone.

I was still recovering from the speed of it all when Kit leaned over my shoulder. The door had just swung closed, and we watched Isaac run-hop through stalled traffic to cross the street, coffee in one hand and phone in the other.

'He's too good looking for you.'

Before I could tell him to fuck off, my phone dinged in my pocket.

CHAPTER EIGHT

Right. If I was going to carve relationships out of my life, then I had to backfill the space they left with something new. A career. Hobbies. A compulsive exercise habit. The only problem was, I had no idea where to start.

Every daydream I tried on felt wrong. I wasn't a serene florist in a messy bun, nor an aloof librarian in tweed. Definitely not a Pilates instructor with a high pony and an energy level only explainable by amphetamines. Not an academic, a dog trainer, or a data analyst, whatever that was. I flipped through ideas like fast fashion on cheap hangers; bad quality and unflattering fits. I'd never finished my degree, I'd been stuck at page twenty of *Anna Karenina* for years, and my core was too weak to plank for more than a few seconds, much less teach Pilates.

Even the core parts of my identity were stolen from stronger personalities.

I was running late to my own identity crisis. Usually reserved for people on the cusp of adulthood, I had only just realised on the edge of my thirties that I had no idea who I was, what I liked, or what I wanted.

To do something about it, I'd dragged Nicola along to an art exhibit on a rare Saturday morning off. I'd even raided Claud's wardrobe to dress the part, as though the NGV ticket sellers could spot an enthusiast from an amateur by the loudness of their outfit and the chunkiness of their jewellery.

I could be an arty person with the right exposure. I had no talent to speak of, but I could learn to form an opinion.

'What do we think of this?' she asked in a whisper as we paused in front of a towering ornate gold frame. A ship battled against a furious sea, grey waves crashing against its hull as it thrashed in protest.

'Big boat,' I replied, shrugging.

She sighed, considering it. 'But does it move us? Does it make us *feel* something?'

'I feel ... hunger.'

'For a naval adventure?'

'For brunch. I could murder an avocado toast.'

She kept exploring the details of the painting, frowning as she craned her neck to take all of it in. The textures in the waves as they broke; the splinters in the ship's wood; the admiral shouting directions at his crew, his hat miraculously still on despite the nightmare swelling around him. I looked at it and felt nothing.

'Imagine how long something like this takes,' she said in awe. 'Years. Not to mention the training. Imagine dedicating years and years of your life to a project, and having people stare at it a century later. Wouldn't that be so gratifying? Who do you keep texting?'

'No one!' I said at once. 'My friend.'

I shoved my phone back into my pocket. Even if she had got her hands on it, she wouldn't find anything incriminating. It was only my text chain with Isaac.

Isaac Abrams (10:17): Good morning, bestie
Isaac Abrams (10:17): Did you have sweet dreams?

Marnie Fowler (10:22): Yeah
Marnie Fowler (10:22): Of you ♥
Marnie Fowler (10:22): (Ew, can you imagine if I talked like that?)
Isaac Abrams (10:29): Maybe that's why you don't have friends
Marnie Fowler (10:29): Rude.
Isaac Abrams (10:30): You're just too cute for them to handle. They stay away for fear of getting cavities in your presence.
Marnie Fowler (10:31): I can't help that I just exist adorably

Fine, so I was on my third coffee of the day because we'd been up texting until two in the morning. He had insisted I watch *Her* with him and we were both feeling emotional and needy for human connection.

Don't look at me like that. We were friends now. Friends text each other. We were only taking the piss. It wasn't like he'd sent me anything pornographic, like a selfie in grey track pants.

Talking to Isaac — sometimes snippy wordplay, sometimes meandering paragraphs that spanned multiple subjects and moods within a single minute (***Isaac Abrams (01:38):** It's weird when you start to see your parents as people. People are idiots. There's every chance our parents are idiots. Sometimes I think, who gave these two emotionally vacant narcissists a baby?* followed shortly by, ***Isaac Abrams (01:39):** I LOVE* Bob's Burgers. *Linda is my celebrity crush*) — was a welcome distraction from the tedium of personal development.

I was spared Nicola's interrogation when her own phone rang. She clicked her tongue. We'd only been out an hour and Mitch had called four times.

'What now?' she hissed into the phone. 'No, she only likes the banana yoghurt. The strawberry one is mine. Yes, she — of course she knows the difference! Forget it, I'll just come home. Well then *give her the right yoghurt.*'

She paused and turned to me with a thin-lipped expression that I knew to mean, '*I'm going to kill myself. Or him.*' She took to a quiet corner to continue the spat about Layla's taste buds, and I pulled my phone out again.

> **Marnie Fowler (10:37):** Nothing like listening to a married couple argue over baby food to make you want to take a vow of celibacy.
> **Isaac Abrams (10:37):** I thought your personality was your choice of prophylactic?
> **Marnie Fowler (10:37):** WOW
> **Isaac Abrams (10:38):** Oh shut up, you know you're fantastic.
> **Marnie Fowler (10:38):** Do you swear you don't care about banana yoghurt?
> **Isaac Abrams (10:40):** I promise you, we'd never be that boring.

'I'm having a crisis!' I shouted into the house and launched down the hallway to throw myself onto the couch.

Nicola had just dropped me off, and I didn't even bother to unpack the shopping bags I'd acquired when we'd given up on art — containing a throw blanket, half of Sephora's stock, a coffee table book — before demanding attention.

Claud poked her head out of her room. 'A rosé crisis, or something harder?'

'I think I might be super into that guy. From the other night.'

'Oh. That's bad,' she said. 'A sweets crisis.' She went to the kitchen for a sleeve of biscuits.

The playlist I'd made to drown out the neighbours' relentless headboard banging was on, but ineffective. Try though she might, Florence Welch's echoing voice was no match for their guttural groaning.

When Claud returned, I had sunk further into the couch and draped an arm over my face dramatically. She'd had a coffee date this afternoon, but it mustn't have gone well if she was back already. Thank god. Doing this without an audience would have been pathetic.

'We've been texting non-stop.' Without bothering to sit up, I held my hand out for a biscuit, felt her put it in my hand, and crammed it into my mouth. 'Everything is a double entendre. He does boxing. I bet he has that one sexy vein up his bicep. *Ugh*. And he's super into movies, and he can probably reverse parallel park, and oh my god, it SUCKS.'

'But what about your rule?'

'I knew this would happen,' I told her. 'Didn't I tell you I'm never single for long? I wasn't bragging. It figures that I'd meet someone amazing right when it's inconvenient.'

'I'm sure he's not actually amazing. He's definitely just hot. Why don't you screw him out of your system?'

'Because I like him too much to not fall in love with him. I should only sleep with people I hate. And, yeah, tiny thing — he has a girlfriend.'

Claud looked unimpressed. 'And where was she when he was chatting girls up on a Thursday night?'

'Good point! No idea!'

'Poor thing. She has no idea her boyfriend sucks.'

'Maybe they aren't serious ...' I said, more to myself than to her. 'Maybe it'll fizzle out and I can get tired of him guilt-free.'

'How long have they been together?'

'A bit under a year. Not that long.'

'And how old is he?'

'Nearly thirty. Why?'

She shook her head. 'You might've missed your window. Once they hit thirty, relationships last two dates or five years.'

I let out a grunt of disbelief. 'Where do you come up with this stuff?'

'It's true! I've never been on a third date with a thirty-year-old man. What are you going to do?'

'I'm going to stop,' I said. She didn't look convinced. 'I should stop, right?'

'Probably,' she said, shrugging. She handed me another biscuit. 'You don't have to. Don't buy into that girl-code business. He's the only one responsible for his relationship. It's not your problem.'

I made a noncommittal noise. It was an appealing thought, that I didn't owe anyone anything, and that I could run around town doing whatever I wanted. But then, 'Isn't that letting me off too easy?'

'You don't know!' said Claud. 'They could have an open relationship. Monogamy might not be important to them. She could be texting some guy right now. You don't know, and it isn't your job to know. Their relationship is none of your business.'

'I'm just not sure,' I said. 'I think it's dangerous.'

'Not everything is kosher all the time. People meet all sorts of ways, Marnie. He could be the one.'

I choked on my biscuit. 'He's not the one.'

'That's all *you* know.'

'It'll go away,' I said, trying to convince myself. 'The more I get to know him, the less I'll want to jump his bones.'

'Or you'll ignore all his red flags and boring white male bullshit and only pay attention to the scraps of evidence that help you convince yourself that you belong together, start masturbating to his Instagram stories, rewrite your ethical code, and get completely obsessed with him to the point of imploding your own life, and require medical intervention to stop.'

I stared at her.

'What?'

'Are you speaking from experience, or …?'

'Of course not.' She grinned. 'I never had an ethical code to begin with.'

There was an annoying gnawing in the back of my mind, some echo of the answer to a riddle I hadn't heard yet.

'This is going to end badly, isn't it?'

'Yes,' said Claud. 'But that's what makes it *so much fun.*'

CHAPTER NINE

Two months of freedom — that's what I was calling it, not loneliness or voluntary celibacy — and I was a whole new person. I didn't even look the same anymore. Eddie loved my long hair, so I cut off five inches of it and lost another two to bleach. What was once dark and overlong was now bouncy and bright: a carefree take on Brigitte Bardot in her heyday. Shards of iridescent caramel and honey caught the afternoon sun as I leapt onto the tram, ferried plates to alfresco diners, or snorted at my own jokes in whichever beer garden Claud and I were using to recover from a big Saturday night.

Between playing dress-ups in Claud's closet, perfecting my winged eyeliner, constantly running on five hours of sleep, and every inane time-sucking hobby I could take up (a half-finished cross-stitch project stuffed into the junk drawer, a wardrobe overhaul mood board dumped into the recycling bin, the browning attempts to grow lettuce in a jar on the kitchen windowsill), I had learned an important lesson.

The single most underrated quality in a person was silliness. Of all the traits one could possess — empathy, patience, unnaturally high alcohol tolerance — silliness reigned supreme.

Whoever you spent your life with, if they didn't know how to take a joke and drag it out until it was clinging on with its fingernails then pull it back in and make you wonder how you ever saw the brighter side of things without them, then you weren't having enough fun.

Life was just *better* when it was filled with the kind of laughter that started as a shriek and dissolved into silent gasps for air and made your stomach hurt. I hadn't laughed like that in years.

I'd never gotten less sleep, been better at ignoring my existential dread, had such long conversations without burning out or had so much fun. Life with Claud was a Donna Summer song, loud and camp, and I was growing so used to the constant thump of a dehydration headache that I could keep a beat.

When we weren't harassing bartenders for refills, we were bingeing crap television shows or sunning ourselves in Princes Park as dogs zoomed around us. When Claud was around, the lonelies couldn't creep in and take hold.

Being my emotional support extrovert wasn't her full-time job, though, and she hadn't yet been convinced to swear off half the population with me. Usually when she had dates planned, I'd visit Nicola or take myself to see the films Isaac rated at the local arthouse cinema. It was harder to notice your loneliness in a dark room with two dozen strangers. But by now I'd seen everything playing, and Nicola's in-laws were in town, and I was faced with an intimidating, if novel, concept: my first night on my own in longer than I knew.

'But who's going to entertain me?' I whined. I was horizontal on the couch as I had been for an hour, too tired from work to close the three metres between the lounge and her room. 'What am I supposed to do? Be alone with my thoughts?'

'I've heard most of your thoughts,' Claud shouted from her ensuite, where she'd been holed up for an hour and a half. 'And they're all stupid. You *should* keep them to yourself.'

'My *Putin-is-Rasputin-reincarnated* theory is going to catch on. Tell it to this guy tonight! He'll love it.'

She made a noise like she was considering it. 'I *am* always looking for ways to weave crackpot conspiracy theories about the past lives of modern dictators into my first-date conversations.'

'Tell him Rasputin's penis is in a museum.'

'Why do you know that?'

'Why don't you?'

'Uh, anyway, what do we think?'

She had arrived in the living room, coiffed and spritzed and contoured to the hilt, wearing the same slinky wrap dress I'd borrowed that night at the rooftop bar.

'If that dress is *that* short on you and you're half my height, how was I wearing it?' I asked, frowning as I propped myself up. 'Was my entire business out?'

'Just about.'

'Hot.'

'Are the heels too much?'

I craned my neck to see the strappy wedges she had on and thought my ankles might break just looking at them.

'How tall is he?'

'His profile doesn't say.'

I snorted. 'That means he's short.'

'*I'm* short,' said Claud. 'He could be five-six and he'd tower over me.'

'Call me when you're five-ten in year nine and the kids at school call you a giraffe.' I paused. 'I can reel off a bunch of fun facts about giraffes if you stay home.'

'I have to go! He might be the love of my life.' She paused in her search through her bag for her phone and keys to pull a disbelieving face. 'Or it'll be another waste of perfume and car fare, and I'll be home in an hour eating ice cream with you. I'm still recovering from last week's horror show.'

'It's unlikely that you'll meet another guy with a soul patch.'

'Don't forget about the braided belt.'

'That was the worst part!'

'Why don't you go to one of your classes?'

She made a good point. In the last two months, I'd bookmarked dozens of classes and clubs to sign up for, and so far hadn't actually attended any. I'd been too busy having fun to care much for personal development, and too enamoured with my one new friend to remember that I should have been making lots of them.

'Okay,' I conceded. 'Good idea.'

'What'll you do? Rock climbing? Knitting circle?'

'I'm so much cooler than you take me for,' I scoffed. 'Do I look like someone who knows how to knit?'

'You tried to convince me to sign up for a macrame class two days ago,' she argued.

'They have a cool '70s vibe! If I made you a macrame plant hanger, you'd cry with joy.'

'I haven't cried since 1997.'

'That's concerning. You should cry more.'

'I can't,' she said simply. 'My emotional barometer only has two points: angry and horny, and it's usually right in the middle.'

That's how I found myself at the back of a black-lit room, deafening techno blasting from speakers in every corner while the seat of a stationary bike dug painfully into my crotch. I was fifteen minutes early to my first spin class, picked because the studio was offering an introductory week of unlimited rides at a steep discount.

I had to fill up my life with cool and interesting hobbies. Claud wouldn't always be there to keep me entertained, and my entire personality could not revolve around vodka and mummified penis anecdotes.

Maybe I'd hated running 10Ks with Martin because I was, in my heart, a spin enthusiast. (Spinthusiast?) Maybe this was the pastime I was looking for: a productive way to swap my rattling neuroses for the quiet thud of a raised heart rate. I'd collect a posse of likeminded gal pals and we'd stroll through life with a green juice in one hand and the ego we owed to our sculpted bums in the other, no broken hearts between us.

Look! There was one now. All glowy and toned with her life together in her matching activewear. I tried to find a natural way to make eye contact, but she was filling up her water bottle, then later tapping on her phone and mounting her bike at the front of the room. Well, that made sense. Accomplished spinners spun at the front, and novices, like me, who felt a bruise forming on their vulva, hid their inexperience in the back row.

Another version of the girl arrived, and another, and another. Sinewy men in tank tops joined their ranks. People older and younger than me strode into the room and filled the forward spots; even a seventy-something woman was confident enough to join the middle row. My passive fitness was not going to be enough here.

'Welcome Soul Spin! I'm Jen!' boomed a headset-wearing Lululemon model. She had teeth that shone white under the blacklights. 'Who's ready to WORK?'

Everyone except me shouted back, 'READY TO WORK, JEN!'

What kind of cult was this?

On the oversized monitor behind her, a scoreboard blinked to life. There were twenty names across it, sorted in order of the bike number. I blanched. Who said anything about competing?

'LET'S GO!'

The kick-off turned the volume up to deafening. I began to pedal in earnest.

'JUST A NICE, GENTLE WARM UP!' shouted Jen, 'TURN THOSE BIKES UP TO SEVEN!'

Okay, I thought, feeling the strain in my calves already. *I just have to come here every day until I fit in. No problem.*

'Every day' smacked of overcommitment. Claud wouldn't be out *every* night. It always went the same way: she would match with someone, get excited, make plans to meet them, then come home disappointed when he turned out to be allergic to asking questions, or shared custody of his cat with his ex, or was a secret smoker. Then we'd make fun of him, flick on an episode of something stupid, and have more fun doing nothing together than either of us did doing something apart.

But eventually one of these dates would stick, wouldn't they? She wouldn't be trapped on the bad-date circuit of doom forever. A firecracker like Claud, who had a sense of humour and a Burberry trench, was going to find someone wonderful. When that happened, I wouldn't have the right nor conscience to hoard her time and attention. So as the voice in my head panted, *I hate this, I hate this, I hate this,* I gripped the handles and persevered.

I would feather my own nest. I would form my own back-up plan.

'STANDING UP!' screamed Jen with an encouraging whoop. Every butt around me sprang up. Mine hovered mere millimetres above the seat, my torso was slumped over the handlebars as sweat beaded in my hairline and trickled down my forehead.

I hate this, I hate this, I hate this.

But that wouldn't happen right away, would it? The imminent arrival of Claud's perfect other half. It would be too cruel of the universe to give me a best friend for mere weeks before snatching her away again. I was here first, I had priority rights.

Plus, Claud wasn't like me. She wasn't going to disappear into her partner like I used to. She who juggled her job, six dating app conversations and a minimum of one date per week, near-constant hangovers, blithe indifference for her lactose intolerance, a needy housemate, the constant influx of deliveries from luxury consignment stores, a delicate hair washing schedule, and the management of our shared bills — was not going to drop the ball and get sucked into someone's world so easily. She had the right amount of contempt for people who did. She was a better friend than that.

I was dead last on the scoreboard. Even the senior citizen had surged ahead of me, rocking from side to side as we turned our dials up to fourteen. I felt sweat plunge across my chest and into my drenched sports bra. Someone had lit my lungs on fire. If I had a heart attack and keeled over, would anyone notice? Or would I die as I lived: surrounded by people who had their shit together?

'CLIMB THAT MOUNTAIN!' cried Jen. 'KEEP IT GOING BACK THERE, MARNIE!'

That was unnecessary.

Twenty-seven agonising minutes later, Jen led us through a cool-down that turned my legs to lead, and by the time I had gracelessly clambered off my bike and refilled my water bottle twice, the room had cleared out. My spin bunny gal pals had gone, the juice bar had closed, and I was faced with the same issue as before: an empty house.

It would be fine. Claud would be there when I got home, and all this panic would have been for nothing. I would face the idea of sharing her later — much later, when the world could conjure up someone who deserved her. That would take years. It would be future Marnie's problem, and present Marnie only had to worry about dragging herself twelve blocks home, collapsing on the floor of the shower, and then deciding how she was going to answer the door for the tiramisu delivery without using her legs.

It was fine.

It would be fine.

CHAPTER TEN

Wrong.

> **Marnie Fowler (19:30):** Two hours and you haven't got me to fake an emergency so you could leave ... unprecedented. How is it?
> **Claudia King (19:44):** Not the worst date I've ever been on!!
> **Claudia King (19:45):** Don't wait up xx

I used to crave alone time. Between a live-in boyfriend, public transport, and a customer-facing job, silence was so rare that I fantasised about it. I would send Eddie out on boys' nights or feign crippling period cramps as we were about to leave for parties so I could swing the door shut and revel in the peace of an empty flat.

I could watch my vapid shows. I could work on the ingrown hairs on my bikini line. I could over-order dessert and hide the evidence. I could blast my guilty pleasure music, prop Sweetie's legs on my shoulders and dance without an audience. But tonight, aloneness wasn't a treat.

There wasn't anything I could say about loneliness that hadn't already been said before. No clever phrase or floral poem could take the sting out of the feeling when it hit you.

The terrifying ache, like being choked. The arresting paralysis as the world moved on without you; how everything, everyone, everywhere was perfectly fine — thriving, even — without your presence. Existing half disconnected, half hyper-aware of every joke or meaningful look between two strangers passing you on the footpath, as though human connection was a club you were denied membership to.

They say that you don't know loneliness until you're in the wrong relationship, but even the wrong person could distract you, however briefly, from your nagging hunger for understanding.

The lonelies dogged me at every corner. They dragged me back to schoolyard slights, the awkward glances of people who decided against sitting next to me in lecture halls, and the huge, hollowing pain of feeling disposable after every breakup. I'd never let them grow wild before.

If Claud stayed out tonight, she'd only stop by in the morning for a costume change and a swish of mouthwash, and I didn't have a shift until Saturday, and Nicola's in-laws didn't leave until next week, and there might be nothing to do and no one to talk to for days, and who knew what the itch of isolation could do to me by then? Sitting in my empty little room in my empty little house, listening to my neighbours fuck themselves into comas. I could gnaw my hand clean off like a shelter dog. I could take a pair of kitchen scissors to my hair and make a mistake that would take two years to fully grow out. I could — horror of horrors — get hooked on all those superhero offshoots and allow them to become a defining part of my personality. There was no end to the number of toxic habits I could form, no ceiling on my capacity for unbridled psychosis, no chance I could ever actually survi—

He answered on the first ring.

'I need attention,' I announced. 'My housemate has abandoned me, and I don't know what to do with myself.'

'Sounds serious. What's at stake here?'

'Depression. Hysteria. Bad choices. I might cut a fringe or call some guy I met in a bar.'

'Heaven forbid,' said Isaac. I could feel his amusement through the phone. 'Would he be dangerously good looking? Have impossibly thick hair?'

'Spicy superlatives. Have you been reading the girl's trashy romance novels?'

'"*The girl*"?'

We texted about nothing and everything, but she rarely seemed to come up. All I knew was her name: Tash. He didn't have any social media (*hot*), so I couldn't narrow it down from his friends list. 'Tash' alone wasn't enough to dig up her profiles and learn everything about her, analyse it, and decide how I felt, so I stayed infuriatingly in the dark about it all.

I took a breath for courage and decided to go through with it.

'That less cool version of me you inexplicably prefer.'

Ooh. Risky.

He let out a laugh like a bark. 'No one is less cool than you.'

'Where is she tonight?'

'At her place, I expect.'

I heard him shift and wondered where he was. Home, going by the lack of background noise. One he didn't share with Tash. Interesting.

What did his place look like? We shared snapshots of our separate lives — a breakfast bagel here, a screenshot of eighty-seven open browser tabs there, a raccoon video for good measure — but building up his life in my imagination was slow work.

I pictured something distinctly bachelory with the adult touches of someone forcibly domesticated by their need to impress a frequent visitor. Dark fabrics and heavy, simple furniture. A framed poster of some well-regarded masculine film: *Taxi Driver*, probably, the way he went on about young De Niro. A naff bar cart packed with brown liquor and a cocktail recipe book gifted by an uninspired relative. I pictured lotion and a box of tissues on his bedside table and suppressed a laugh.

'Why has your housemate abandoned you?' he asked. 'Why do you put up with such abject cruelty?'

'Date. The audacity. Choosing the guy of her dreams, potentially, over a night eating a jar of Biscoff on the couch with me.'

'She is obviously insane,' he replied.

I grinned around the thumbnail I was chewing on, thrilled that he would humour me no matter what.

'Who would choose a *boy* over you?'

'When I was a teenager, I used to read these articles in *Dolly* — remember *Dolly* magazine? I used to steal my sister's, that's where I got all my sex ed — about what a faux pas it was for girls to ditch their friends once they got a boyfriend, and I thought I'd never do that. But then, I always ended up closer to all my boyfriends than my friends.'

'How many boyfriends? Could I take them?'

'Too many.' I rolled my eyes, although he couldn't see it. 'But I'm done with that now.'

'Why?'

'I don't believe in relationships anymore.'

'They're not the Easter Bunny. They're real, I promise.'

'The Easter Bunny is *so* real,' I replied, appalled. 'Or else how do you explain the egg he sends me every year?'

'C'mon. Why don't you believe in relationships?'

'Because they never last.'

'Did a tough breakup make you a fatalist?'

I made a noise of noncommitment.

'We all have bad breakups. You just do, until you stay in a relationship that never breaks up.'

'You only think that it won't, and then it does,' I argued. 'When you're too old and droopy for anyone to find you cute anymore, and then you die alone. Most marriages end in divorce anyway.'

'Actually,' he said, 'statistically, divorces are becoming less common.'

'Just the marriages I see then.'

'*That's* it.'

'What's it?'

'That's why you don't believe in relationships. It's not your broken heart.'

'I don't have a broken heart,' I scoffed. 'I'm just detoxing from a severe case of dick paralysis.'

Isaac choked on something. I heard him splutter and take a moment to regain his composure before he asked, '*What?*'

I'd tried to be mysterious. I'd been so good about mastering the urge to overshare and present myself as ever so slightly out of reach. But it was bound to come up eventually, and besides, we were friends. Friends talked about their lives. If Claud knew about it, if Nicola did, then why couldn't Isaac? Tales of rampant monogamy might have scared off a potential boyfriend, but a *friend* wouldn't care.

So I told him. I kept it light, skirting around my wounds and plastering over any real vulnerability with sarcasm and self-deprecation, as was our style. He howled with laughter at my most embarrassing anecdotes — the half a tattoo on my ribcage, the time I recorded myself singing 'Don't Speak' over an untuned guitar, dedicated it to Thomas, and uploaded it for all the world to see.

I told him how I wasn't sure I'd ever been exactly happy, but how I'd never learned how to leave before getting left. I said that being robbed of the last word stung as badly as any heartbreak, and that sometimes the only thing strong enough to blow the ennui out of your hair was Crosby, Stills, Nash & Young on a hot day, had he ever tried it?

His patterns weren't dissimilar, he said, that he'd floated from girl to girl since he shed his teenage uncertainties, never alone for long, and he liked it better that way. He'd never tried folk music and sunshine as a cure-all but found that two hours in a dark cinema was a good way to clear your head. We were all the hero in our own story, he said, but it was easier to be angry at people if we made monsters out of them.

'Don't humanise my exes,' I said, scowling. 'Leave me and my grudges alone.'

'You'll forgive them eventually,' he said. 'But it's easier to be angry than it is to be sad.'

'Did your therapist tell you that?'

'I've just seen *High Fidelity* too many times.'

'I don't wish them ill or anything,' I said. It was a lie. I had elaborate vengeance fantasies about them all, tailored to their exact idea of torture. I'd force Ian to spend three hours with a woman his own age. I'd make Martin read Clementine Ford's books. 'I just wish they'd all stop existing.'

'I love all my exes,' he said. 'Except Ella. She keyed my car.'

'I bet she had a great reason for it though.'

He paused, then laughed. 'Absolutely no comment.'

'You're a bit of a nightmare, aren't you?' I asked. 'You're the smug, handsome dickhead people write angry breakup albums about. You're Warren Beatty.'

'You're never going to let me get away with anything, are you?'

I bit into the pad of my thumb. 'I think you just like being in trouble.'

Don't think that this — whatever this was, since any labels I stuck to it peeled straight off — changed anything. Isaac was not some great contradiction.

If anything, he reinforced my resolve. That someone could have a girlfriend, be loyal to the point that they reject a kiss from a cute stranger, then go on to talk to them every day, lie in bed on the phone and reach new depths of intimacy when the moon came out — it only poured concrete into the belief that happily ever after was a falsity invented by romance novelists.

No, this made me strike harder. Every text confirmed that I was right. Every flirtation was another brick in the bunker I was building, protecting me from the nuclear fallout of another failure.

I could see all of his red flags. There were so many of them he was practically a Provencal poppy field. What was the harm in chitchat? My time and brain and body belonged to no one but me. He wasn't unavailable: *I* was. I got to enjoy him for what he was without ever having to entertain the prospect of disappointment. It wasn't real, so it couldn't matter.

I lay there on top of my sheets, listening to his voice like honey on a hot spoon, oblivious to the emptiness of the house. It was so easy, so fun to play the coy and unattainable girl he wanted me to be, making crass statements then backpedalling under false shyness. And when we'd run out of conversation and before I knew how many nights I'd spend replaying this one, he gave me a list of movies to see — wanky French new wave, golden age classics that took a whole day to watch, tiny indies with improvised scripts and moody palettes — and I gave him my favourite songs to listen to, and we fell asleep like that: Cat Stevens playing in his room and *Blue Velvet* downloading in mine, together and apart, tied together by an understanding that this would not be a one-time occurrence.

CHAPTER ELEVEN

'Maybe he died.'

'He didn't die.'

'That's the only reason I wouldn't text you back, and I don't want to get in your pants.'

Claud put her phone down for the first time all day. 'That's a good point. I'm extremely hot. You'd have to be at least in a heavy coma to pass this up.'

'Cold brew for Beth!'

Such was Claud's need for support in her trying time of a ghosting, she'd shown up at the cafe in the middle of Saturday brunch service and slumped onto the counter, loitering in the way of the outgoing orders.

That date the other day had lasted five hours. Jesse, a programmer from Richmond, had taken her out for an afternoon coffee, a walk, dumplings on Little Bourke Street, another coffee, gelato on the walk to her tram, and a chaste peck as it arrived. When she didn't hear from him by the next afternoon, she took charge: '*So lovely to meet you,*' she wrote to him. '*Let me know if we should do it again soon,*' and argued with me for forty minutes about whether or not an '*x*' at the end was overkill.

She had to keep a portable charger on hand from running down her battery by obsessively checking for a response. Eighteen hours later, she was spiralling.

What had she said? What had she done wrong? What was the exact moment — the exact phrase she used, the expression on her face, the lighting she was cast in — that earned this cold-hearted rejection? What deep inner wound, formed at the hand of a beautiful but cruel ex-girlfriend, was he carrying around that made him behave like such a prick? He hardly knew her; how could he do this to her?

'Okay,' she said bracingly. 'How did he die?'

'*Painfully*. He was in a hit and run, his guts got ripped open on the asphalt, and crows picked at his intestines as he lay dying in the street.'

'Is it possible for you two to have this appetising conversation on your own time?' asked Kit as he ferried eggs and lemon crepes to table four.

'No,' I replied, screwing up my face. 'This is important.'

Claud ignored him. 'What were his last words?'

I put on my croakiest voice. '"*I wish ... I'd seen ... Claud ... naked.*" And then he died. Dead! And one second later, your message came through. Matcha latte and an almond croissant for Jenny!'

'Oh my god,' said Claud, a hand to her chest. 'That's tragic. My tits were his dying wish.'

'It's my dying wish for you to get out of the way,' said Kit.

'We're talking about the love of my life here, Kit! He's DEAD,' she cried. 'Have a heart!'

'He doesn't,' I said. 'Where his heart is supposed to be there's just another arsehole.'

The bell dinged from the kitchen, and he left to answer it, muttering choice words under his breath as he went.

You would think that a centrally located cafe with deliciously cool air-conditioning would be thriving on a Saturday in February, that it would be packed with people who couldn't get a table at any of the overflowing hotspots on Degraves Street, but we had three occupied tables and an unsteady trickle of to-go orders.

I usually stayed away from the main drags, but for all the news articles crying about the slow death of the city, there never seemed to be a shortage of people anywhere. The Swanston Street thoroughfare and Bourke Street Mall were always a tsunami of bodies, all making up for lapsed social distancing rules by squeezing as close to one another as possible. Did these bodies not need fuel? Caffeine? Rest? Where had all the customers gone?

Little George had thrived since the day it opened. It had withstood the fickle economic tides over decades, luring people in and turning them into regulars. Along with the Flinders Street Station architecture, narrow laneways covered with every conceivable style of street art, and the fairy penguins at St Kilda Beach, Little George was a Melbourne icon. In a city defined by its coffee culture, it stood alone.

Nicola used to bring me here when I was a kid, when the tension at home got suffocating. We'd split a slice of cake, and I'd pour sugar into my cup until my nine-year-old palate could stomach espresso. I could only remember the place being busy. Even as years passed and the decor dated, tourists and locals spilled into the rickety chairs and squelched on the sticky linoleum, happy to pay modern prices in a place that hadn't had a lick of paint since the seventies.

Kit's makeover had had its big reveal the day before the city went into lockdown. All his hard work — the thoughtful design details he'd pored over with Andrew during months of planning, years of saving, and a lifetime of dreaming — went unseen. Now that we were free to drink and eat and roam as we pleased again, interest seemed to have moved on. The city had fallen out of love with Little George, and none of us quite knew how to win them back.

You might argue that Kit's gloomy disposition had driven people off to cafes with sunnier customer service, but I'd met his father, and Kit was comparatively chipper. Last time the old man visited, he actually drove customers out as he boomed criticisms about the way Sam organised the stock room. Still, we could have worked harder to swear less at one another, at least quite so loudly.

'What the fuck, though,' said Claud, ruining this idea in a second. 'If he's bird food, why is he posting about the cricket on his story?'

'You follow each other on social media? You went on one date.'

'We don't follow each other. I just found his account.'

'Claud! Don't be a psychopath!'

'His handle is just his first and last name; it's not like he's hiding it.'

'*Why* do you know his last name?'

'He told me about a website he just worked on, so I went on it, dug through the code, saw his agency's name in the metadata and looked them up,' she said, like this was normal. 'Then I went on LinkedIn and searched through all the Jesses that work there to find his surname.'

'*Claud.*'

'I didn't click on any profiles, I'm not stupid.'

'Aren't you, though?'

'Anyway, then I found his Instagram, and if you load someone's profile, turn on aeroplane mode and *then* watch their stories, you don't show up on their list of viewers.'

'You are unhinged.'

'What if he'd been a human trafficker? Do you want to run around interrogating every Jesse in the world to avenge me? You should be grateful I did this homework.'

'Tell me something.' I stopped rinsing the milk jug and put my hands on my hips to level with her. 'Why do we care about this person?'

'Because I really, really liked him!'

'Did you, though? Because you weren't sure when you told me about it yesterday.'

'I've had time to think about it and I decided I really liked him.'

'What happened to, "*He made this dumb noise when he got up or sat down*"?'

'Well I thought he was doing a bit,' she said. 'But maybe he just has early onset arthritis. Maybe he needs a chiropractor.'

'Didn't he say something weird about feminism going too far?'

'I think that was a joke.'

'Claud,' I said, leaning in. 'This guy sucks. You do not want him to text you back.'

She held eye contact for a moment, then broke it, pressing her hands to her face and giving an exaggerated sob.

'Why does this keep happening?' she groaned. 'I'm better than this. Obsessing about some guy I don't even know. What kind of fourth-wave feminist am I?'

'A horny one?'

'Sounds like I arrived at this conversation just in time,' said Sam, who had poked his head out from behind the kitchen door.

'Why, because we're talking about how all men are disgusting?'

'Not *all* men,' he argued.

I pulled a face. 'What do you want?'

If he was offended, it didn't show. One thing to like about Sam was that he was rarely precious. Although he couldn't dish it back, he took mine and Kit's cantankerisms in his stride and never sulked or fussed.

'I would love a special Marnie long black,' he said, palms pressed together in a plea. 'One made with love, not spit.'

'But the spit is what makes them so special.'

'Oh, go on then,' he said easily. 'Make it extra spitty.'

As he retreated back to the kitchen, Claud paused her misery to fix me with a look, lowering her eyebrows as she grinned devilishly. '*Cute*.'

'No.'

'Why not?'

'Because he would *Say Anything* me, we'd get noise complaints, I'd have to call the police and it would make work awkward.'

She sighed with longing. 'Young John Cusack.'

'I'm sure young Cusack ghosted plenty of girls in his day, too,' I said as I filled the portafilter for Sam, and she deflated again. 'No one is safe.'

'I don't know how much longer I can do this,' she said, now practically face-down on the counter. 'Matching, talking, making plans, buying a new dress, spending an hour on my makeup, going out, asking questions, getting my hopes up, getting let down, starting again. I try, try, try and it never goes anywhere.'

'Wow,' I replied flatly. 'It's almost like I'm right, and dating is pointless.'

Whether it was the scream of the espresso machine or selective hearing, Claud was too busy with her negativity loop to respond.

'I'm cute, right?' she continued. 'I'm interesting. I have a juicy caboose. What's so wrong with me?'

'Nothing!' I cried. 'The problem isn't your juicy caboose; it's your audience. Straight men. You know, there are studies that say single, childless women are the happiest demographic.'

'Do I look happy to you?'

I wanted to reach over and hug her until her brittle bones broke, and then squeeze her tighter still, until they mended stronger than before.

'Maybe you're right,' she said eventually, avoiding my sympathetic look. 'Maybe I'll just give up for a while.'

'It's hard to be disappointed when you don't have any expectations.'

She was on the verge of replying when the cafe door swung open and a group of four, six, seven trickled in, awkwardly bunching in the doorway and invading any space for personal conversation.

'Pass me that,' she said instead, nodding to Sam's coffee. 'I'll get out of the way and take it to Cute Chef.'

I slid it across the counter to her and said, 'Don't encourage him.'

Seconds later, before the group had finished settling into their seats, I heard a shout from the kitchen.

'You don't work here!' barked Kit. I heard a tea towel snap and Claud squawk. 'Get out, get out, get out!'

CHAPTER TWELVE

Nothing went better with a thudding margarita hangover than twenty squealing toddlers; the same eight Wiggles songs playing on repeat and worming themselves into your tired, dried-out brain; and your mother giving you hell for every life choice you've ever made as you sweated tequila in the fuchsia wonderland of Nicola's backyard.

Layla was turning one, and it was one of fewer than five times my parents had been in the same postcode as one another in a decade.

Claud and I had stayed up until dawn licking her wounds and failing to cover my lopsided birthday cake in enough icing and sprinkles to make up for my mediocre baking talent.

'But what are you going to do without a man in the house?' asked Mum as she coiled her bony arm around Trent's beefy one. She dropped her head onto his shoulder, and even under the olive tint of her sunglasses, I saw her eye wander off to where Dad and Susie were cooing at Layla.

'Just ... exist?' I replied. 'I don't know why it should be any different.'

'Don't you feel unsafe?' she pressed. 'What if there's a noise in the middle of the night; who's going to protect you?'

'Claud can be pretty intimidating,' I said, shrugging. 'The other day, a guy at the pub put his hand on her back when he passed her, and she made him cry.'

'When Trent was on his business trip to Brisbane last weekend, I went around with a knife checking inside every cupboard and behind every door, didn't I, darling?'

Trent grunted to confirm her claim and continued watching the golf on his phone.

'What about that family in Germany that was murdered after someone hid in their attic for days — or was it weeks? — and crept down and murdered them one by one?'

I frowned. 'When was this?'

'The 1920s.'

'Oh, Jesus Christ.' I rolled my eyes. 'Well, I don't have an attic, so I think I'm safe.'

'That you know of. Those old houses sometimes have a crawl space.'

'What's a boyfriend going to do if some psychopath is living in my ceiling? Do you think they have bulletproof webbing under their skin or something?'

'Fine,' she said, miffed. 'What about all the other things partners do?'

'Like what?'

'Changing light bulbs,' she said after a pause. 'Opening jars. Killing spiders.'

'Step ladder,' I answered. 'Run it under hot water until it pops. Bug spray.'

'Men can fix things around the house.'

'So can repairers.'

'Heavy lifting.'

'I'll get Claud to help. Or I'll start hitting the gym.'

I saw Mum's eyebrows raise and I knew what was coming. A symptom of overindulgence in female-driven dramedies was a complete lack of boundaries, and like other incurable ailments, this sickness weighed heavily not only on the sufferer, but their families as well.

'Stop,' I said, holding my hand up as her lip began to curl. 'Do not tell me what else men are good for.'

'We're all adults, Marnie,' she said scornfully. 'Don't be such a prude.'

'Trent doesn't want me hearing about this.'

'What?' he asked, blinking around at us.

'Just agree, Trent.'

'Oh. Yeah, sure.'

'Go and stand with the boys, love,' she said to him, squeezing his bicep and giving him a gentle shove in their direction.

Mum wasn't satisfied with the answers she was getting out of me, so she tried a different approach.

She was a tiny woman who favoured Nicola in every way. They had the same fuss-free shoulder-length haircuts, pinched nose, and critical stare that could wrench secrets out of you faster than US military-grade interrogation tactics. While I poured my time and money into the endless pursuit of new hobbies, Mum had hers worked out long ago: complaining. It could be a pristine summer's day, there could be a charcuterie board on the table and a pleasant breeze, and she would say the sun was too bright. Complaining gave her energy.

'She had to bring the biggest present, didn't she?' she hissed, scowling over at the neon plastic rocking horse Dad and Susie had brought over, wrapped in a bow bigger than my head. 'So obnoxious.'

'I'm sure she just wanted to get a nice present for the baby.'

'Whose side are you on?' she asked through an injured sniff. 'Why are you in such a mood?'

'I'm not!' I replied. 'I just think it's unhealthy to carry around that much anger after ten years.'

'I am perfectly entitled to my feelings, Marnie,' she said, giving me her patented scolding look. 'Until you've been through what I've been through, don't you dare —'

My head gave a painful throb and I sighed.

'You're right,' I said, holding my hands up in surrender. 'She bought Layla a lovely gift because you're her sworn nemesis. What a cunt.'

Defeated and offended, Mum huffed, muttered under her breath, and strode off to mingle.

I'd only seen Nicola in bursts all day. She was occupied ferrying platters and cups in and out of the kitchen, piling paper plates into rubbish bags, telling Mitch off for hanging the balloon arch wrong, wiping bits of food off little faces, telling Mitch off for getting the wrong ice, adjusting the music, fixing the streamers, telling Mitch off for putting Layla in the wrong party romper, refilling drinks, double kissing cheeks, telling Mitch off for being too slow to answer the door, and shouting down anyone who tried to help. She had been nervy about this day for weeks, slaving over details, desperately trying to revive the neural pathways once responsible for professional event planning. When I said no one would notice if anything went wrong and to please calm down, I received her inherited punishing look. Chided, I relieved her of the birthday girl and made myself scarce.

Except for my family, I didn't recognise anyone here. No one in her old life was all that interested in kids, she had told me as she pored over the RSVPs last week; they all preferred to rack up lines and frequent flyer miles than spend an entire Sunday in the nuclear idyll of suburbia. Everyone here was a new friend; relationships forged over teething and tummy time.

The genders divided: dads in a semicircle around the barbecue, beers held at their navels, a different shade of navy gingham on every shirt their wives picked for them; mums all playing babysitter; grandparents acting like this was all their achievement; and a sprinkle of infants hellbent on finding or creating chaos.

A pile of professionally wrapped plastic trinkets with a shelf life of two months in the house and two thousand years in landfill.

The immaculate guest list: inclusive and yet political. Nicola had had to invite Caitlyn from play group even though her daughter, Mindy, was a thirteen-month-old fascist, because Layla had been invited to Mindy's party, and it would go on like this every year until one of them moved away.

This birthday party, one that Layla would neither remember nor even particularly enjoy, was more elaborate than any I'd ever had. A bubble machine spewed iridescent blobs across the yard. Nicola had ordered a balloon arch and pink tulle backdrop for your most Instagrammable moments. There was a snack table piled so high with every iteration of sushi, crudité, hard and soft cheese, petit fours, fruit, and kids' party birthday classic you could name to tide you over until the barbecue fare was ready. There was a ball pit. A slushie mixer dripped icy watermelon and vodka onto the lawn. There was a rumour going around that later someone was going to show up in a fun-fur bunny suit to entertain the kids and drunker adults. Although designed with a baby in mind, this was a party for adults: a child-friendly pissing contest.

As I piled another plate high with fairy bread and chips, I pulled my phone out of my pocket. It was habit: every passing thought I had, I shared with him.

Marnie Fowler (13:03): I wish I was a one-year-old
Isaac Abrams (13:03): You wish you were bald and incontinent?

I coughed out a laugh and pocketed my phone again, seeking a shady spot in which to indulge my hungover binge, but I wasn't alone for long.

'Question,' I said as Nicola slumped down on the bench beside me. I accepted her offering of a third paper plate mounted high with pasta salad and a plastic cup of full-sugar Coke gratefully. She had her own cup of pink drink filled to the brim and drank heavily from it. 'Would you rather be a Mum or a Susie?'

Nicola's laugh came out of her nose. 'I'd rather be dead.'

'No, go on,' I said, nudging her knee with my own. 'Would you rather be a sixteen-year-old girl trapped in a sixty-year-old's body or would you rather have found the love of your life and be obsessed with him to the point of telling him about your every bowel movement, only he's ... Dad.'

'Our dad? Exactly as he is?'

'Yep.'

'Bald spot, old man gut?'

'That's right,' I said. 'No hair on his head because it's all migrated to his back.'

'And he's really into the weather channel.'

'And he thinks pull-my-finger jokes are the height of comedy.'

'And I really, really love him, and I see no problem with anything?'

'Correct. Or be ... Mum.'

Nicola squinted across the yard, hedging her bets. Susie had her hand in Dad's back pocket and was looking at him like he hung the moon while he told Mitch about a dust storm in Dubai this morning. Mum was clapping and pulling faces at a disengaged Layla, who was more interested in pawing at the bird shit on the lawn. Finally, Nicola nodded.

'I'd rather be a Marnie.'

I scoffed. 'That's bleak.'

'Cruising into parties stinking like booze, eating all the chips, then skipping out before clean-up to go find more trouble to get into? You're living my dream life.'

I leaned back on the bench, propped up by my elbows and ego. 'It sounds much more glamorous when you say it like that. I'm going home to eat pizza in bed and scroll through my phone until I pass out with mozzarella in my hair, but sure, dream away.'

'You're a disaster,' she said, pretending to wipe away a tear of pride.

I laughed through my mouthful of pasta.

Nicola had guests to entertain, but she didn't go.

'I don't know a thing about anyone here,' she said. I could tell by her pitch change that she had segued into the quiet honesty she only felt safe expressing with me. 'I've known them all for a year. We've been in this … tribe together. I know their kids' sleep schedules. I helped dip Rebecca's tit in warm water to clear a clogged milk duct one time. But I know nothing else about them, and they know nothing about me.'

'That's plenty,' I replied, frowning.

'I know that that one is a competitive rower; her arms are incredible,' she said, and I followed her eye line to tell which woman she was talking about. 'That one's in a spirulina pyramid scheme cult. That one won't stop talking about vaginal rejuvenation surgery.'

'Wow. Intimate.'

'This is where we all split off, they say,' she continued. 'Some of them will go back to work. Some of them will start trying for another baby. The baby bubble is bursting, and now they're toddlers, and it's every woman for herself.'

'Are you worried about it?' I asked. 'Won't you keep in touch with the ones you're close with?'

'That's what I'm saying. I'm not close with any of them. We're just bound by circumstance. I don't even think I like any of them.'

'They seem ... alright,' I said, unconvincingly. 'Well, not that one. She was complaining about no gluten-free options. They're a year old. It's not like they're paleo.'

'She's the scariest one,' she replied. 'She's the one who shamed me into making my own baby food. I spent the first half of Layla's life cleaning out the blender.'

'Only fancy mush for a fancy baby.'

'I'm sure there are cool, nice, normal mum friends out there. I just don't know where to find them.'

'Well, do you have to have mum friends?' I asked. 'Layla's a chill baby. Why can't you take her along to your plans with your old friends, the ones you do know you like?'

'Because then I'll have this weird, emotionally stunted child. Layla'll turn into a pyromaniac if I don't socialise her enough.'

'I think that kid is a sociopath,' I said, pointing my chin in the direction of a boy with his entire fist in his mouth. 'He pushed that ginger one over for no reason. Probably a gluten-induced rage.'

'It's lonely,' Nicola said into the rim of her cup. 'All my time is split up between being someone's mum and someone's wife. There's no time left to be myself.'

I didn't know how to tell her I understood, so I squeezed her arm. We were the same, even when we weren't. We both felt like we were looking into our lives through a pane of glass.

'Come on,' she said, slapping her knees and rallying as she sourced the gumption to join her own party. 'Time for cake, then you can sneak out before Mum offers to drive you home.'

'Um ...' I said, trailing behind her. 'You have a backup cake, right?'

'Why would I?'

'In case mine is disgusting. What if I send a bunch of babies to hospital with food poisoning?'

'What did you do?'

'It's just kind of ... ugly.'

Nicola waved me off as I followed her into the kitchen. 'I'm sure it's fine. She's one; she doesn't care what it looks like.'

'But don't you?'

By the time Claud and I were done, we were seeing double and ready to vomit from the mix of triple sec and buttercream, and our decorating skills had lost their combined edge. I braced myself for the horror within.

Nicola pulled the lid off the box and ... froze. I peeked in. The cake seemed to have grown uglier on the drive over here.

The middle had collapsed like a sinkhole, dragging my attempts at pink and yellow rosettes into the centre. The jam that was supposed to glue both layers together had cut through the rubbery vanilla sponge, and the colours marbled together sickeningly.

'This is the worst thing I've ever seen,' she said, altogether too calmly.

I nodded. 'Yep.'

'I can't serve this.'

'Nope.'

'It looks like a prolapsed anus.'

'We can fix it,' I said. 'It's fine! We just need more icing. Slather the whole thing in icing and no one will notice how it looks on the inside. Or — or! You can give me your car keys and I'll go buy four supermarket cakes and we'll just dump a bunch of strawberries on top and it'll look great. Or fine. Fine is fine!'

She blinked at the cake, trying to process how anyone could take flour, egg and sugar and turn it into this abomination.

'I'm sure it doesn't taste like an anus,' I said, reaching out to swipe some icing off its side and trying to hide the cringe when I licked my finger.

She copied me, tasted the metallicky sour frosting, and instead of bursting into tears or a rage, as I would have, she began to laugh. And then I started too. At first uncertainly, but soon Nicola's face was the same colour as the cake, and I gave into it, laughter coming out in hoots and huffs.

'What's going on?' asked Mitch from the doorway. Layla was wrapped around him, clinging to his collar as she leaned towards the noise we were making. When they made it to the kitchen island and looked inside the cake box, his face twisted in disgust. 'What is *that*?'

It only made us laugh harder. I snorted, so I slapped my hand to my face, and Nicola shrieked.

'What's taking so long?' came Mum's voice. She was dragging Trent across the threshold by his wrist. 'What's so funny?'

'Marnie's fucked the cake is what's happened,' said Mitch furiously. 'And these two are carrying on. Stop laughing!'

Nicola honked and fell to the floor.

'There are going to be photos of this forever!' Mitch continued. 'What the f—. Will you both cut it out?'

Mitch's indignation was kerosene on the fire, the splotchy red anger in his cheeks sending me to the floor too. Maybe because I enjoyed getting a rise out of him, or maybe because this was the worst moment he could have chosen to become an involved parent.

'Are you girls alright?' asked Dad, Susie a step behind him. 'What's gotten into —'

'Never you mind,' snapped Mum. 'Why don't you and your child bride mind your own business?'

'Oh, here we go,' he snarled.

They descended into bickering, as they always had done, and that was it. It was so predictable. Clutching each other, Nicola and I fell into silent gasps for air on the floor, holding each other for support, egging each other on, making everyone else in the room confused and irate.

'Stop laughing!' boomed Mitch over Dad's rising pitch, and Layla began to wail, and Mum had escalated to shrieking criticisms, and I was crying, tears turning my stale mascara liquid, and Nicola was on the floor, and the cake was still hideous, and I was still a mess, and she was still lonely, and there was nothing either of us could do about any of it, but we would always, always have each other.

Isaac Abrams (01:27): How have you never seen *Fear and Loathing*?

Marnie Fowler (01:27): Coming from someone who thought *Rumours* was a Lindsay Lohan song.

Isaac Abrams (01:27): Fowler, Fowler, Fowler

Isaac Abrams (01:27): I have so much to teach you.

Marnie Fowler (01:28): This is a weird way to bring up your teacher/student fantasy.

Isaac Abrams (01:29): Ha

Marnie Fowler (01:33): I'm going to make you a playlist. I can't live with your ignorance.

Isaac Abrams (01:33): You're going to make me a mixtape? How retro.

Marnie Fowler (01:33): Hope you like the sound of depressed women complaining.

Isaac Abrams (01:34): I like you, don't I?

CHAPTER THIRTEEN

'This is the dumbest thing we've ever done,' I said to Claud, prodding through a bowl of turquoise crystals in a dark shop crammed high with wishing candles, pentagram altars and ornate charms on silver necklaces: bait for anxious millennials and spinster aunts, of which I was both.

'Dumber than eating half a tray of edibles because you didn't think one was working fast enough?'

'I'm still stoned a week later.'

'Dumber than continuing to harass that stray cat even though it keeps giving you a rash?'

'Do not disrespect Bubula. She walks me to the tram every morning.'

'She *stinks*. I can smell her on you.'

'No, this place just smells like a litter box.'

She sniffed the air, grimaced, and shuffled sideways to poke at the bowl of black rocks that promised clarity of mind and pores.

'Why are you so against this? Don't you want to know your future?'

'I know my future,' I replied. 'It involves deep cleaning the milk fridge and punching Sam in the jugular if he tries to double-cheek kiss me hello again.'

'Well, I want to know mine. I don't want to go getting invested in Jesse if the universe isn't on our side.'

Oh, right. Jesse called eventually. Actually, he sent a croaky voice note that made Claud shriek and me queasy, to say he was free next weekend if she 'wanted to hang out, or whatever'.

$1,277.

That was how much money she had spent on new clothes for the second date that hadn't yet been planned. '*What if he wants to take a day trip out to the Heide museum?*' she asked. '*Outdoor art, I'll need a sundress. What do we think about, like, a fun, low-key Missoni something-something? Very '70s Palm Springs, very "High maintenance but I'm so hot it's worth it." Maybe not. Maybe just denim and a cute top. Do you think I can carry off a plum lip? Can we go to Mecca tomorrow?*' The boxes for every conceivable second-date outfit option stood precariously tall beside our recycling bin.

They would have a city-hall wedding, she decided. Followed by a luscious reception at Dessous, with signature cocktails and a thousand pink orchids. She had a birdcage veil and a white mini dress with a vegan feather trim in her Net-a-Porter wishlist, so it was great that she was consulting a psychic before she let her imagination run wild.

'You're right,' I said, insincerely. 'This is a totally normal thing to do. I hope the oracle has only wonderful and accurate things to say about your future.'

'Yeah, yeah,' she replied. 'You better be nice to her.'

Before I could protest that I was always nice, before Claud could talk herself into buying a clear quartz for courage and good phone reception, an ethereal voice called our names.

'Okay, now listen,' I hissed, grabbing her by the arm. 'Don't tell her anything about your life, or she'll use it to tell you what you want to hear. Stay quiet and let her out herself.'

'Stop being so boring,' she scoffed. 'It's just fun!'

The woman we followed up the narrow staircase was trailed by the hem of her violet kaftan and so petite she appeared to be drowning in her long, thick hair. She lifted an impeccably arched brow at us as we sidled into a dim room, cramped with old wooden furniture, antique lamps and rugs and throws in every moody colour.

'My name is Persephone,' she said as she sat behind a rickety table, gesturing for us to sit in the velveteen chairs opposite.

'I'm Claud, and this is my — ow!'

I had pinched Claud's thigh to shut her up.

'You girls have a strong bond,' said Persephone. 'Your energy is green; it comes from the heart.'

In my periphery, Claud beamed. 'She's alright, I guess.'

Persephone's long, maroon-tipped fingers shuffled her tarot deck. She laid them down in front of us in a stripe and asked us to pick three each. It took Claud a full minute to pick out the ones she wanted. I picked the closest three.

Persephone took her time turning over and examining each card, occasionally making an interested hum. Minutes passed in near silence, broken by Claud's restless fidgeting.

'You're a Scorpio,' said Persephone to me. 'You have several water placements.'

'Do I?'

'Do you?'

'I don't know.'

'No, no,' she said with a wave of her hand. 'You do.'

She turned over one of my cards and slid it towards me: The Fool. Claud snorted. I stomped on her foot.

'A new beginning,' she said, her tone brightening. 'A period of discovery. You're exploring a new identity.'

Claud sucked a breath in through her teeth.

'Have you started a new career path?' she asked. 'I'm sensing an opportunity coming your way.'

'Nope,' I said. 'Same job, and I'm not going anywhere.'

She made a tantalising and unconvinced sound. 'That's here in the reversed Six of Cups as well,' she said, tapping my second card. 'You're still holding on to some things in your past.'

I swallowed back a laugh. 'Who isn't?'

Her eyebrows rose and fell, but she didn't take the bait.

'This is an emotional reading,' she continued, sounding impressed. 'That's your water placements at work. This last one is the Knight of Cups. He's all about listening to your heart. There is an opportunity for great love here. It's your job to keep your expectations of it realistic.'

It took everything I had not to slump back and say, '*Oh, come on.*' It was all too perfect, too rehearsed, tailored for the app-swiping, horoscope-reading, burnt-out twenty-something caricature of her audience.

'You're going to be on this journey for some time,' she said, blinking serenely across her table. I blinked back, unfussed. 'All the way through next year. It may get tiring. Remember that you'll find joy in all the places you've yet to look.'

There was no hiding the disbelief on my face: a visual scoff. Beside me, Claud was rapt, with wide eyes and her chin on her hand.

But everything Persephone said boiled down to nothing: vague, smoky, something for someone who needed an excuse to believe. It wasn't prophecy, I thought. It was marketing.

'My turn!' squeaked Claud, wiggling in her seat with excitement.

Persephone smiled at her as she fanned out her cards, making a meal of choosing which to read first.

'This one,' said Claud, reaching out to tap the middle card. 'It has good vibes.'

'Temperance,' she said. Her voice dropped an octave, saving her performance for someone who would appreciate it. 'This is a very powerful card.'

'What does it mean?'

'Upright, it means harmony and balance. But you chose it upside down, which tells me that you're the kind of woman who believes in all or nothing. Intense relationships, working too hard, indulgence.'

'I definitely do that,' said Claud, turning to me. 'Don't I? Tell her. I don't know how to pace myself.'

'I sense a shift that will take you to an extreme. Soon; within the year.'

'Love that,' she said. 'Love, love, love that. What's next?'

'Five of Wands,' said Persephone, lips thinning. 'Conflict.'

'What kind of conflict? With who?'

'With loved ones, or maybe yourself. The things we leave unsaid always find a way to be heard.'

'Like, as in, "drunk words are sober thoughts"?'

Persephone seemed gratified that one of us was engaged with her work. She laced her fingers together and rested her chin on them, blinking dolefully at Claud as she considered her answer. 'It's more ... you don't resolve a problem by ignoring it. It repeats until you learn your lesson.'

This was the first believable thing she had said, and I fought to keep my expression neutral. I wouldn't give her the satisfaction.

'But what's the problem?' asked Claud. 'Can't I just deal with it now?'

'We all have truths we aren't ready to face,' she replied. 'Maybe your hedonism keeps getting you into trouble, and nothing will change until you change yourself. Your innate need to people-please will leave you in the cold until you stand up for yourself.'

Claud whipped around in her seat to look at me. 'Do I do those things? Am I a hedonist?'

I thought of the recycling bin sitting ajar on the kerb, crammed with sleek black boxes and empty sparkling bottles, and said, 'Um.'

'Am I a hedonist?'

'You enjoy being comfortable,' interjected Persephone.

'No one enjoys being uncomfortable,' I said. 'That's how you define uncomfortable.'

'Learn to live in discomfort,' she said, ignoring me, 'and you can overcome anything.'

'So I have to face my fears?' asked Claud.

'What are they? Your fears?'

'That I'm unlovable,' she said at once. I frowned. Claud usually saved her vulnerability for nine drinks in, and only once she was sure you were a safe mark. Where had this honesty come from? 'That everyone can see through me. That I'm the only one who isn't in on the joke.'

Persephone hummed her understanding. She held her long, bony finger on Claud's last card, like she could change the energy of something that had already been picked, then turned it over with a dramatic flourish.

'The Lovers.'

Claud's whole demeanour changed. Her fidgety shame disappeared and got replaced by bated excitement. She threw her arm out and squeezed my wrist.

'Tell. Me. Everything.'

'It's not necessarily what it looks like,' said Persephone. 'The Lovers represent choice and balance. They are two halves of a whole.'

'I'm going to be made whole?'

'You're going to be given a choice,' she explained. 'You'll need to understand what's important to you to move into the next phase of your life.'

'A life-changing choice.'

'That's right.'

'Okay, so I can remember, altogether ...' said Claud, reaching over to tap each of her cards in turn. 'Love taken to the extreme. Communication issues and over-indulgence. Two halves of a whole, taking my life to the next level. Marriage and kids and the whole lot of it.'

'Well, it could mean —'

'I love this,' she said, slapping her hands together. 'You're a genius. I'm going to fire my therapist and come here every month.'

We waited until we were out on narrow, rainswept Little Collins Street before we spoke at the same time.

'That was —'

'That was —'

'*Bullshit.*'

'AMAZING.'

Claud and I stared at each other in different shades of incredulity.

'How can you say that?' she cried. 'After the reading she gave you? It was spooky.'

'It was *crap*,' I said. I shuffled towards the nearest shop window to hide under its alcove as summer broke into autumn around us, a sprinkle threatening to give way to a downpour. 'You could squish what she said around to make it fit with anyone.'

'Like what? Name one.'

'Like, "*New beginnings, periods of discovery*" — that doesn't mean anything! That's just being a person!'

'But you *are* going through a period of discovery,' she argued. 'New *everything*. New house, new friends, new hair, new boy, new life. You can't tell me that isn't accurate. I thought mine was lovely.'

'Well of course you did,' I said, sucking my teeth as I dug through my bag for an umbrella. 'She just told you what you wanted to hear.'

'That's not true. I picked the cards and she told us what they meant.'

'Babe,' I said. 'She could tell you the eighteen of guinea pigs means your period is about to start.'

Claud looked torn between conviction and annoyance. Finally, I found my umbrella and opened it, holding it over the both of us as we idled in the worsening drizzle.

'I don't think it really matters if it's true or not,' she said after a pause. 'I think it just asks you to look at things through a different lens.'

'I bet that isn't even her real name. It's probably Louise.'

'Why are you being so negative about it?' she asked coldly. 'Who cares if you don't buy into it? You don't need to tear her apart. It's so easy for you when you have Isaac wrapped around your little finger.'

I paused, frowning. 'I do not have Isaac wrapped around my little finger.'

'Some of us need more guidance.'

I softened at the sight of her hugging her jacket closer around her collar. We usually agreed on everything.

'Okay,' I said. 'I'm sorry.'

'It's alright.'

We walked along Little Collins in silence for a minute or two, me taking long, slow strides, her trotting to keep up.

We hopped over shallow puddles and paused to peer through boutique windows until the tension dissolved.

Finally, Claud broke. She couldn't contain her excitement under my cynicism any longer. 'Okay but this definitely means that the universe is on my side re: Jesse, no?'

'Sure,' I laughed. 'If Persephone says so.'

'So I should double back to buy new underwear. Just in case it all goes beautifully on date two.'

'Well, yeah. What if the sight of all the underwear you already have makes his dick shrivel up inside his body permanently and you guys can't have kids?'

'I'm so glad you get it.'

'Here for you, babe.'

Once we could be silly again, everything was back to being okay, conflict forgotten under a premature March shower.

CHAPTER FOURTEEN

Isaac Abrams (10:12): Today's the day
Isaac Abrams (10:12): Moment of truth
Isaac Abrams (10:12): Do we really get along without the crutch of alcohol and the comforting anonymity of screens?
Isaac Abrams (10:13): Or will we have an absolutely terrible time, realise we're only good on the phone, make an excuse to leave and then politely never interact again?
Isaac Abrams (10:13): We're about to find out

'I have nothing to wear!' I called out to Claud. 'And neither do you. I need a 3D printer, so I can print myself an outfit from Pinterest. I know how you feel about Pinterest, but in a fashion crisis — whoa. Are you just getting home?'

Claud was rubbing her ankles on the couch, heels kicked off, still in last night's clothes, with a violet splotch down the side of her neck. She threw up a hand to silence me, beaming into the phone wedged between her cheek and shoulder.

'I know,' said Claud into her phone. A smile that big was usually reserved for a waiter handing us a second order of chips. 'I know. Ha! Haha! I *know*! I know. I miss you too. I know I know I know. Okay. Okay. I don't know. Any time. I'll make time. Okay. Okay, I can't wait. Stop it, me too. I know. Me too. Okay. I'll see you soon. Bye. Bye. *Stop.* Okay, bye.'

She hung up and looked at me, teeth sinking into her bottom lip as she tried to contain a giddy scream.

'What is that face for?'

'Persephone is a genius,' said Claud. 'And I've broken my drought.'

'You deviant,' I said, feeding off her joy. 'Depraved, perverted, shameless —'

'That's me.' She beamed, bouncing in place. 'I'm the deviant. I'm the hornbag.'

'So it was good?'

'Marnie, it was *great*. We had these really long debates all night, about everything. He asked me questions; he held my hand at the table. And then, well —' she gestured at her general disarray '— and on the way home I started thinking, *"Oh no, shouldn't've done that, should've played harder to get, now he's not going to call,"* but then he called! And we're going out *again*! *Tonight!*'

'Look at you,' I said. 'All those frogs, and finally a prince.'

She squeaked at her phone as it lit up with texts. I could see from the arm of the couch that Jesse had been added to her address book, half a dozen heart emojis trailing after his name.

'You were having a meltdown,' she said after a brief pause to respond to him. 'What's wrong?'

'Right!' I said, checking the time and remembering to panic. 'I'm finally catching up with Isaac and I have nothing to wear and I look disgusting.'

'Cut the shit,' said Claud. What a relief to know that even under the haze of new love, she was still her same, brash self. 'What do you need?'

'Everything I put on is too — *too —*'

Claud looked me up and down. My print dress clung to the sweat on my back, simultaneously too low-cut and too dowdy.

'You're overthinking it. You go to lunch with super-hot guys you have insane chemistry with all the time.'

'Uh, no I do not.'

'For all he knows, you do.'

I wrung my hands with nerves. '*But why* do I care what he thinks?'

'You want to control the narrative.'

'It's not a PR crisis. It's brunch.'

'What's the difference? You don't have to want to be with him to want him to want to be with you.'

'That's a good point actually.'

'I do make them occasionally. See, you're used to creating a persona in response to someone else, and you haven't figured him out yet.'

'Oh, yes I have. He wants me the effortless, indifferent, accidentally and obliviously extremely hot girl. Like I wake up every morning the picture of the male gaze.'

'Well that's easy,' said Claud, shrugging. 'Casual sexy. Jeans, flats and a slinky top. Hair down, unfussy jewellery, minimal makeup, and do your perfume right when you leave the house.'

I threw my arms around her and squeezed, even as she whined in protest. 'What would I do without you?'

Isaac Abrams (10:42): Just at the lights. Meet you outside.

I dashed down the hall and ripped my dress off before my door had even closed. There was no time to improvise. I would follow Claud's instructions to the letter. Jeans. A top that passed for silk. The same dainty silver *M* on a necklace

I wore every day and stud earrings. Flats. I'd just finished patting on a rosy lip balm when my phone buzzed again to say that he was here.

He was very tall, I realised as I pulled my front door shut and found him leaning against his car like a movie star. Much taller than he had seemed that night at the bar. Six-four was the tallest a man could be before he started to look odd. Their features got distorted that high above sea level. But Isaac was just right: long-limbed and lean, delicious in a grey T-shirt, with his ever-so-slightly overlong hair pushed back with the help of his sunglasses.

'There she is,' he said, grinning and unfolding his arms. 'She exists!'

'Here I am.'

There we were. I paused, uncertain of the appropriate greeting. Did you wave at someone you'd fallen asleep next to, digitally, for the last several weeks? Did you peck cheeks? My hesitation only lasted half a second, then he closed the space between us and pulled me into a hug.

God, he smelled good. I wanted to jam my face into the crook of his neck and breathe in his scent until it replaced all the oxygen in my lungs and I passed out and died from it.

As he let go, his hand lingered on my arm.

He nodded to suggest we head off, and we wandered towards Lygon Street in search of coffee, food and something to talk about. All these weeks of constant contact, the flow of conversation, once endless, seemed to dry up in an instant.

It was easier to be yourself, or whoever you were pretending to be, behind a screen. On the couch, hand wrapped around my phone as my cup of tea sank below optimum drinking temperature, my brain lit up like fireworks, blasting off quips and flirty comments, silly and coy in equal measure. Honesty, or a version of it, came effortlessly. Through the pixels I could sense the exact shape to become, finding meaning in his punctuation, gleaning his mood through the pace of his replies. The longer we talked, the clearer his picture of me became. It was so easy to like the idea of someone. It was so easy to make them like the idea of me.

But it was different face to face. My mind felt sluggish and simple. As we passed the pub on the corner, walked the outskirts of Princes Park, passed countless row houses and the cemetery and the towering red and yellow bricks of St Jude's Church, all I managed to say was '*Cat!*' when we saw one dart along a tall fence. Had I already asked how his day was going? We talked for three hours last night, me texting on the cool bathroom tiles after another gruelling spin class, so I couldn't even fill the air with empty chatter.

'So,' he said.

'So,' I replied, idling.

Say something, I told myself. *Say fucking anything.*

Anything!

ANYTHING.

I chanced a look up at him. His lovely face. His chic round sunglasses, thoughtfully chosen for his bone structure, colouring and taste. He hadn't simply grabbed the first pair of Ray-Bans on the shelf and been done with it. I could see him pinching the arms of different frames and delicately sliding them up his thin, straight nose, staring confidently into the mirror without a trace of self-consciousness. The payoff was subtle, but effective. Everything about him was delicately cultivated. I felt comparatively scrappy: a wrinkled Rouje knockoff against the clean lines of Comme des Garçons.

It was just new. A phone voice was only one part of a person. I didn't know how to hold myself, how to rest my face, what to do with my hair or hands, and in this pendulous silence, he wasn't giving me any clues.

Fine. I'd give in. I'd leave. I'd fake a stomach-ache and dash for the approaching 6 tram. Then we could resume our friendship from the safe margins of my messenger app, where it belonged.

As I inhaled to lay the groundwork for my lie, Isaac said, 'This is ... bad. We're bad at this.'

I tried to laugh, but it came out like a cough.

'Why is it so easy on the phone?' he continued.

'Because we're usually just talking shit.'

'Okay, so talk shit,' he replied, and I blanched. 'Don't think about it! Just say anything!'

'Everything I think of is stupid!' I argued. 'You're going to think I'm dumb.'

He leaned in, looking at me over his sunglasses, and said, 'We're way past that.'

Shoving his shoulder was like trying to shove a brick wall. It made him grin, and my hand ache. 'Fine,' I said. 'I think it's weird that I've watched so many shows about serial killers that I can fall asleep to them. I'm completely desensitised. They're like torture porn for women. It's like making a pig watch a documentary about factory farms.'

'Do you think pigs could follow the narrative form of a documentary?'

'I think pigs would love Ken Burns.'

'But their favourite movie would be *Babe*. Obviously.'

'That's the first good movie you've brought up,' I said. 'No more wanky, miserable indies, please. If there's not a talking pig, I don't want it.'

'Why, because you want to see yourself represented on screen?'

He only grinned wider as I cried out in offence, accepting each of my insults with pure delight. We had crossed the road by now, joining the flow of foot traffic along the brunch superhighway of Lygon Street. We continued like this, squabbling and hurling slights at one another. This was doable. This was fun. We'd save the substance and curated honesty for late nights.

As he put his arm around my shoulder to pull me out of the way of an oncoming pram, I found myself leaning against him, and lost track of how long it took him to let go again. Was it one second, or was it three?

Now that we'd found our rhythm, it felt like we were at the centre of everything. Carlton's village atmosphere existed just for us. The bustling crowd was background noise. We wandered into bookstores without explicitly suggesting it, strolling the aisles and making idle quips at bad covers and punny taglines.

We waited for our coffee orders and browsed through the titles being played at the cinema. He grilled me on the films I'd promised to watch, swelling with pride and nodding like a plastic dog on a dashboard as I waxed on about the yearning and pretty misery of *Doctor Zhivago*.

'Thank god you don't have a moustache,' I said, reaching up to press my index finger along his top lip, 'or else we'd really be in trouble.'

We dipped into junk stores, boutiques and toy shops. We bought him a new linen shirt. We stopped for refills on our coffees. The whole day was on low aperture, colours blurring as we clung to errands as excuses to drag out the time. It was a Haim song, bright and breezy. It was a hot exhale. As long as we filled every moment with conversation, we didn't have to acknowledge everything we weren't saying.

He walked me home and I invited him in, grateful I'd absently tidied up while we talked last night. I wanted him to think of me without clutter, unburdened and pristine.

I watched him from the kitchen doorway as the kettle boiled, feeling exposed as he thumbed through the library of albums I'd kept, like he could learn something true about me through their tracklists. He stroked the fibres of Claud's throw blanket, long fingers trailing over its frayed edge as he stood straight, taking in the details of the nude on the wall.

The gloopy quiet had returned as I set our cups on the coffee table, and we sat at the polar ends of the couch. He picked up his scalding tea, risked a sip and winced. We'd lost all our distractions now, and I couldn't figure him out again. Did he look odd in my space, all his long lines, smooth edges and carefully avoidant eyes, or was he the piece that tied the room together?

'Do we need to talk about it?' I asked, shattering the silence.

'About what?' I gave him a knowing look. He sighed. 'Do we have to?'

'Maybe talking about it will be so uncomfortable it'll cure us.'

'Of what? It's a crush, not chlamydia.'

'A crush can turn into chlamydia if you aren't careful.'

Isaac laughed and tried his tea again, and I wished I was the cup.

'I used to have a thing for John Mayer,' I continued. 'Do you think he has it?'

He thought for a moment, then said, 'I think it's impossible that he doesn't.'

'Ooh, talking about STIs is killing my boner. What do you think about herpes?'

'I think it'd be a shame to not be able to be mates just because one of us is spoken for.'

"'*Spoken for.*'" I snorted. 'You have a girlfriend, not an owner.'

He didn't rise to my bait. He set his cup down and asked, 'Why do you say girlfriend like it's a slur?'

It was important to play my cards right. There was a line, and I wanted to stay on the right side of it. It was a dangerous game I didn't want to play. I wanted to keep her invisible. Talking — even thinking — about her gave her depth and colour, when I preferred her as an abstract concept. '*Their relationship is none of your business*', Claud had said, and I kept to it like an oath.

'Because I was so boring when I was a girlfriend,' I said, a master of deflection. 'It's like I'd change my relationship status on Facebook and dump water over my fiery wit.'

'You change your relationship status on Facebook? Cheugy.'

I gave a shiver. 'I'm allergic to millennial buzzwords.'

'Hey Fowler, do you think I have —' he leaned over the couch cushion between us, a wicked look on his face, and breathed '— *big dick energy*?'

I dipped a finger in my tea and flicked it at him.

It wasn't even that I wanted him for myself. I was still learning the shape of my solitude. But I didn't want to be demoted. I didn't want to be any couple's single friend; a third wheel, tagging along as an afterthought, there as entertainment — the self-deprecating stories about bad sex and holidays by my lonesome — as though I existed to remind them how much easier life was together. If I treaded carefully, I could stay *his* friend and never become *their* friend.

'Does she know about me?'

He cleared his throat. 'Sure.'

'What does that mean?'

'She knows we're friends.'

'Do you think this is it?' I asked. 'The big one?'

'Do I think Tash is the one?'

'Yeah,' I replied. 'Is she?'

Maybe I asked because I *did* want to hear it. Maybe it was the reality check I needed to snap out of it. Hearing that he loved her, that they were agile enough to dodge a bullet like me — maybe that was the antidote to my toxic little crush.

He sighed, and I could hear in his breath that we'd switched from playful conversation to something deeper, the way we always eventually did.

'I don't know.'

I didn't say anything, and he avoided my gaze.

'I don't know if you ever really know,' he continued. 'I see pictures of my parents when they were my age, and they look so young, but they were further along in their lives than I am now. It's like they looked at the person they were with and thought, "*Why not?*" They weren't waiting for it to feel perfect; they just got on with it.'

He bought himself time with another sip, then said, 'I want to do that too, but I just ... can't. I'm still waiting for it to feel perfect. And sometimes it does, but then I wonder if I'm trying to make the pieces fit. I'm waiting for it to feel like a Linklater film, you know? I'm waiting for a sign.'

I heard him talk like this all the time, round vowels and meandering sentences, but watching him added another layer to it. The bob of his Adam's apple as he swallowed. His barely furrowed brow. Something I hadn't learned over the phone: Isaac didn't fidget. Even as he talked himself in circles of doubt, he didn't scratch at his arms or tousle his hair to indicate his cerebral discomfort. Was it his confidence, or that he was at ease here?

'That all sounds great and everything,' I said, crossing my arms and legs to complete my shrewd look, 'but you're full of shit.'

After a beat, he turned to look at me. 'Sorry?'

'"*Waiting for a sign*."' I snorted again. 'You don't want to be responsible for your own actions. You're waiting to be delivered an answer so you have someone to blame if it all goes wrong.'

He looked amused, not offended, as he turned to match my body language. 'Alright, Fowler — what do you suggest then?'

'Oh, hell if I know,' I admitted, and he laughed. 'I'm perfectly happy hiding behind my excuses.'

Isaac reached over, picked up his teacup and clinked it against mine, and as I watched the strain of his bicep, I bit into my cheek until I tasted blood.

CHAPTER FIFTEEN

My back pocket buzzed, and I ignored it.

Flipping delicious, I wrote, hunched over the counter, chalk turning my fingertips blue as I pressed it into the specials board. *Whipped ricotta pancakes w/ lemon curd and raspberry preserves. Yum!* I'd had four of them already, dipping them into a ramekin of jam and cramming them into my face over the kitchen sink while Sam took my enthusiasm as a declaration of lust.

My pocket buzzed again. It seemed more urgent this time. My butt cheek could just sense it.

It would be Claud firing screenshots of her never-ending conversation with Jesse at me, proof of his perfection, analysing the significance of orange heart emojis over plain red, a slate of exclamation marks following every humdrum interaction. I'd send heart reacts back, '*Aww*'s and '*Oh wow*'s, failing to meet her excitement but doing my best.

Or maybe it would be Mum, spamming me with texts about Trent. We could time her breakups down to the week by now. There were always signs. When she was in love, she would first inundate the family group chat with grinning couples' selfies taken from bad angles, showing off another in a long line of unremarkable boyfriends. She would drop off the map and forget to reply to us for weeks on end. We knew trouble was brewing when she began to call us again. Once or twice a week and then every day, we'd receive meandering voicemails peppered with negative comments. '*I'm sure it's nothing,*' she'd say, or, '*I know I'm being silly, but ...*' and then it would come out: he wore his socks to bed, or he watched the wrong newstainment programme, or he was too polite to his ex-wife, and by then it was done. She'd made up her mind: she was going to end it, and she needed our help to get through this trying time.

It could be Nicola, though, dropping hints to get me to babysit so she and Mitch could have a date night this weekend. These evenings usually ended with us on the couch no later than 8:30 pm, watching *Bake Off* with the zip of her cocktail dress undone, while down the hall Mitch sat on the toilet groaning about his decision to order scallops.

All I knew was that it would not be Isaac. Our text thread had dried up and wilted since last weekend. I'd dropped the act, acknowledged the truth, and sent him running. I'd begun to see my blank phone screen as a totem of embarrassment.

I blew at the board to scatter the chalk crumbs.

'Can you run the show for a while?' asked Kit as I propped it against the display case. 'I've got a meeting.'

'A meeting?' I replied. 'Are you looking for my replacement?'

'No one else could match your unique blend of useless and mouthy.'

I gave a gasp and pressed my palm to my heart, touched. 'Thank you! You really see me.'

Kit was looking increasingly harassed these days. His hair, always cropped and tidy, defied gravity in frazzled waves. The sleeves of his shirt were crushed from being repeatedly rolled and unrolled. He even looked paler than usual, with deep purple shadows barely hidden under his glasses. Usually I was the unkempt one, but lately, with my carefree-sexy bangs, permanent effortless cat eye and boat neck Breton tops, I was out-cuting him day after day.

'Is everything okay?'

'Fine,' he replied with a pursed-lipped twitch. 'It's just the accountant.'

Despite his flippant tone, it read ominous. I'd found Kit in his office muttering, *'Fuck, fuck, fuck,'* at his laptop more than once recently.

Were we going under? Had we survived the worst of the pandemic, only to crumble the minute we thought we were safe?

Odd and perhaps inappropriate that I thought of this place as *ours*, like I was as much a part of it as Kit was. I'd been here for a sliver of its history, yet I could sooner remember the alarm code than my own PIN.

Kit greeted the accountant — who was pointy and shrewd, like a dachshund here to drag a judgmental paw down a ledger of our incomings and outgoings — with frantic politeness. Kit exaggerated his vowels and kept his consonants sharp, a performance of put-togetherness. He gave me a passing, hopeful eyebrow raise as he ushered the man upstairs to the offices, and I managed a thin smile back.

What would I do without this place? I didn't want to think about it. This would have been a great time to have a real backup plan, or even a fantasy to fall into. A novel I wanted to write. A PhD to earn. A burgeoning love of pottery and a burning desire to sell it on Etsy. A secret singing talent and an extensive collection of floppy hats that I could take on the road.

Poor Kit, I thought. For all my inner panic, I didn't have a legacy on my shoulders. I imagined his guilt from their ill-disguised disappointment and felt my heart break on his behalf. Kit, who gave me a job when no one else would, who was cantankerous in one breath and funny in the next, who I loved like an annoying older brother — I couldn't bear the idea of not working together anymore.

I catastrophised the whole thing as I pushed through the mid-morning lull. Shortly, I would hear Kit exclaim through the ceiling. All of us, me, the nonno at the window table, the grumbling espresso machine, we'd fall silent and strain our ears for more details. Muffled shouting, and then thunderous footsteps down the stairs. We'd busy ourselves again, doing our best not to look suspicious as Kit stormed in, kicked the door open, and threw the accountant bodily onto the street.

'*Get out!*' he'd boom. '*We're finished! Closed!*' In distress, he would snatch a cup off the top of the espresso machine and smash it down in a ceramic firework. When the room was empty and we were alone again, he'd turn to me. I'd freeze in place while a panini burnt in the press. I'd feel my pulse in my throat as I waited to take the brunt of his rage, the nerve of his shame exposed, and then —

The bell above the door tinkled as the accountant pulled it open.

'Have a lovely day!' he said over his shoulder at me, and I flinched out of my nightmare.

'You —' he was gone '— too.'

Was that it? What had happened? What was *going* to happen? I needed Kit to come downstairs and offer answers to questions I wasn't within my rights to ask. I waited for the sound of footsteps, but the only sound I heard was Nick Drake through the speakers and the nonno's cup resting back on its saucer.

Habit sent my hand wandering, pulling my phone out of my pocket on muscle memory. Before I could tap it to life, I paused.

I promised myself I would not be disappointed if it wasn't Isaac. I would not.

I would not I would not I would not.

When it was only Claud messaging to moon over the double kisses trailing Jesse's description of his lunch, my heart dropped so low even two more pancakes and the machine-gun rapidity of Sam's compliments couldn't scrape it off the footpath.

CHAPTER SIXTEEN

'Hello stranger.'

'Who is this?' I asked. Sam frowned at me from across the workbench in confusion, and I pointed at the phone wedged between my ear and my shoulder. 'Have we met?'

'Once or twice, in my dreams.'

I snorted as I added cream cheese into the bowl of the stand mixer and turned it on, silky icing forming in seconds. I'd offered to babysit for Nicola tonight, and I was going to make up for the catastrophe cake from Layla's birthday by taking a fresh, edible cake with me so I could fill her with sugar and hand her back to her parents right as she turned into a monster. I'd watched a thousand hours of cake decorating YouTubes, falling asleep to them playing on my phone so that my brain could absorb the knowledge through osmosis, and and although I still wasn't confident in my abilities, I was at least sober this time.

The baking tin we had at home had been so heavily crusted with burnt cake that we threw it out, so I was taking advantage of the facilities at work for my second attempt.

I hadn't decided yet if this call was welcome or not. The knot that formed in my throat when I checked my phone and found a blank screen had just started to loosen as I began to accept the loss of him, and now, here he was again.

'Where'd you go?' I asked him. 'You triggered my abandonment issues.'

'Did you pine?'

'I was catatonic. Couldn't get out of bed. Had Morrissey on repeat.'

Behind me, Sam clattered through a stack of steel bowls. I clicked at him, shooing him away. *'It's my kitchen!'* he mouthed. I flipped him off and he returned it.

'You poor thing,' Isaac cooed. 'Sorry about that. Life consumed me for a minute.'

'Ah.'

'What've I missed?'

'Nothing,' I said, because *'I've been staring at my phone for a week and a half like a sap, arsehole,'* wasn't polite. 'I moved up a row in spin class. Now I'm second from the back.'

'Does the International Olympic Committee know about you?'

'If they don't, they will soon.'

He breathed a laugh through his nose, but he didn't speak, so I didn't either.

There was something in the room with us, and it wasn't Sam. It had all been so easy before, the constant stream of messages bookended with long calls, Isaac's midnight voice lulling me to sleep, the anticipation of his first message jolting me awake.

It had been nice, that's all, to have someone to talk to. Claud had a new toy to play with, and Nicola oscillated between calling with complaints about Mitch's dishwasher stacking technique and forgetting to call me back at all.

I listened to him breathe and continued what I was doing. I took the cakes out of the walk-in, undid their springform levers and peeled them from their tins.

'You okay?' I asked after a solid two minutes of silence. It came out squeakier than I meant it to, dripping with embarrassing sincerity.

Isaac sighed. 'In the doghouse for a bit.'

'What's wrong?'

'Nothing, just — nothing for you to worry about.'

'Oh,' I said. 'Right.'

'And what's my best pal getting up to tonight?' he asked, tone brightening.

'The usual Saturday night hijinks,' I replied as I cautiously sliced the peaks off the cakes to flatten them out, swearing internally as I left great divots in the sponge. 'Hopping onto my billionaire boyfriend's superyacht and getting sprayed with champagne.'

'Figures.' He clicked his tongue. 'I disappear for one second and Elon Musk snaps you up.'

'I would never fuck Elon Musk.'

'Not even once?'

'I do have standards, you know.'

'You *do*?'

'Occasionally.'

'That's bad news for me.' He paused. 'But then, everything about you is bad news for me.'

My voice dropped low in my throat. 'Which is exactly what you like about it.'

'So?'

'You're going to fuck that icing,' said Sam loudly behind me.

'Indulge my self-destructive streak, Fowler.'

I held my hand over my phone and mouthed, *'Fuck off.'*

'You're over-working it!' said Sam, elbowing his way to the mixer. 'You don't know what you're doing.'

'I know everything,' I snapped. 'I'm the smartest person on the planet.'

'What are you doing?' asked Isaac in my ear.

'I'm —'

'God doesn't give with both hands,' said Sam. 'You are objectively fucking your icing. Give it here.'

'I have to go,' I said into the phone. 'I'm about to commit homicide.'

'Call me from jail.'

I stuffed my phone into my apron pocket, pulled the spoon from my empty mixing bowl and wielded it like a weapon.

'Step away or I'll end your life.'

'With a wooden spoon,' he said with disbelief twisting his brow. 'I'm terrified.'

He reached out for the power button, and I screeched, 'Don't!'

'I'm doing it in the name of cake!' he cried. 'It's going to split!'

'Good! That's how I like it!'

The kitchen door swung open, and Kit, who hadn't shown his face all day, poked his head through and scowled at us, and we sobered right up.

CHAPTER SEVENTEEN

I did it. I had my first one-night stand. Finally!

And it was ... fine. The details were a bit fuzzy, owing to the white wine and rum headache throbbing behind my eyes the next morning.

I was getting better at coping with the empty house now that Claud was so frequently staying at Jesse's. I was halfway through a bottle of wine and a Michel Gondry film Isaac insisted I watch. I was chewing the cuticles off my nails and waiting for his name to light up my phone again, when someone else's did. Instagram notifications popped up, the bullet spray of a dozen likes on old photos from the cute, grammatically challenged firefighter I'd met at a house party with Claud a million drunken nights ago, and I thought, *why not*?

I asked if he felt like coming over, *winkwinkwink*, and he accepted. The validation felt the way I imagined heroin did.

Then the realisation hit. The house looked like a tornado had ripped through it, littered with laundry and empty teacups and junk mail and old post satchels courtesy of Claud's crippling shopping habit. A man was coming over, and he wasn't interested in my personality, or for professional advice about how many millimetres of foam constituted a flat white. It was all down to my sex appeal. I think I'd forgotten to develop any. I didn't even know the local customs around pubic design.

I had never acquired that smirking, feline quality of hot women who had discovered their power. I'd never exactly had complaints about my sexual performance, but now, as I tore through my drawer for something, anything, black and lacy, I couldn't remember any compliments, either.

Historically, I had won men over by being a flattering mirror for their own interests. No one had ever taught me how to flirt, or play coy, or how to smoothly reach out and stroke their thigh in a way that said, '*I am very good at giving head.*' I tried to picture myself doing it and cringed.

Why was I revisiting my latent sex appeal *now*?

I needed help. I couldn't ask Nicola: she'd be too excited about it, and she'd eat up valuable panicking time lamenting her envy. I really needed Claud, but where was she when you needed her?

Marnie Fowler (20:27): I've done something extremely stupid
Marnie Fowler (20:27): I have a man coming over
Marnie Fowler (20:27): For a booty call
Marnie Fowler (20:27): Do they still call it that?
Marnie Fowler (20:27): I'm too old for this
Marnie Fowler (20:27): What do I do?

And then, when he didn't immediately reply:

Marnie Fowler (20:29): Answer!!!

It felt oddly intimate, messaging Isaac about this: strategic honesty, almost weaponised. But I was entering new territory without a map. This was what friends were *for*.

I went about frantically stashing clutter in drawers while I waited for his answer. The loose tampons in the fruit bowl, cityscapes of wine bottles beside the recycling bin, stray socks that had fallen out of the dryer and been abandoned in the hall: our house, a museum of laziness.

I was throwing a clean top sheet over my bed when my phone buzzed. Finally.

Isaac Abrams (20:40): Who's the lucky boy?
Marnie Fowler (20:40): Some guy. It doesn't matter.
Isaac Abrams (20:40): What happened to 'I have standards'?
Marnie Fowler (20:41): Sometimes a girl has needs
Marnie Fowler (20:41): What do I DO?
Isaac Abrams (20:41): Well Fowler, when two people love each other very much …
Marnie Fowler (20:42): You are useless.
Isaac Abrams (20:42): Use a condom ♥

Right. That was a waste of time. I had candles to light and a casual-sexy playlist to source. I had barely finished dry shaving my legs over the bathroom sink when the doorbell rang.

Steven. I had to double check his name on his Instagram profile as I went looking for glasses and a mixer for the half a bottle of Malibu he'd brought. The coconutty smell of it made my stomach turn, recalling all too many mornings with my head in the toilet, but a good hostess didn't gag in the face of her guests. Only, uh, on their dicks?

I hoped he wasn't into dirty talk.

'You found the place alright, then?' I asked. Of course he had. He was in my living room.

'The Uber guy just followed the GPS.'

'Oh, good.'

He nodded.

I waited.

He sipped his drink.

On the speaker in the corner, The Black Keys' drumbeat thudded like my racing pulse.

Okay, so he wasn't a master conversationalist. I tried to come up with another question to ask, but the truth was that I didn't care. For once in my life, there was only one thing I wanted from a man, and it didn't go any deeper than that. I threw back the contents of my glass, poured another, drank it, thought *to hell with it*, and threw myself at him.

He choked on the sip he was swallowing, and rum from his mouth dribbled down my chin, and I ignored it. With all the confidence of half a bottle of wine and two Malibu and orange juices, I redoubled my efforts, getting my hands in his blondish, product-dense hair, and he heaved my body on top of his, and we were off.

Steven was shorter than my memory of him and built like a bulldog: all chin and chest. He made a point of blowing out the candle on my dresser before taking his shirt off, and it only made me more confident. I might have been the sexiest person he had ever slept with.

All I could think, as he pulled me back against him in the dark and jabbed me in the arse cheek with his boner, was, *I can't wait to tell Claud about this.*

He kissed dryly, without tongue, and he pinched my nipple so hard that I yelped. His jeans got caught around his ankles as he fumbled for the condom he had stashed in his back pocket. There was another pause as he realigned himself, and I tried to look down to see what he was doing at exactly the wrong time. Our foreheads knocked together, and we had to spend several seconds on opposite sides of the bed, nursing our aching skulls.

There was no passion here, only logistics. We were on a mission, damn it, and we weren't about to falter for something as fickle as desire. And so I did the things I was supposed to. I flopped and writhed under his tentatively bossy hands, panting and moaning, performing like a slutty seal.

He finished too fast — concerningly fast, actually; it seemed only reasonable to assume that I was just *too hot* for him to handle — and tried to make up for it with five minutes of well-intentioned but uncoordinated head, less satisfying than taking your ponytail out.

Knees apart, I lay there and watched as a set of passing headlights lit up the ceiling and plunged us back into darkness. Steven jabbed at my cervix with a lone determined finger. Down the hall, the playlist looped over and started again. I'd never be able to listen to Third Eye Blind without my crotch turning numb.

As I whimpered and wailed only half-convincingly, I realised that casual sex was not as exciting as the first season of every HBO show made it out to be. I didn't come like an opera singer hitting a high note. I faked it just to get it over with.

'That was so good,' he said into my neck, arm around me like a straitjacket as he forced me into a little spoon. 'You're so good.'

I wanted to snort and say, '*Uh, right.*'

I wanted to say, '*Was it your first time? Because nothing about that was* good.'

I wanted to say, '*You have no idea how much I wish you were someone else.*'

But instead, I asked, 'Are you staying?' and he heard, '*Will you stay?*', or maybe he didn't hear anything, because he was already snoring into my good pillow. I lay there trapped, unsatisfied, and just a tiny bit thrilled, because at last — at long, long last — I'd broken my own curse: I'd declined to fall in love with someone just because I'd touched their penis.

And in the morning, I woke up to an empty bed.

I searched myself for a feeling — disappointment, perhaps, that our deeply mediocre night was not enough to make him adore me instantly, or even stick around for toast and an uncomfortable peck goodbye — but I came up short.

Except for the sore nipple, I felt no difference in my body, either: no pang of loneliness in my stomach, or sharp barb in my chest longing for his approval. All that came was relief that I didn't have to keep pretending to enjoy his touch or company.

It took a while to even remember to check my phone to see if he had messaged me, and when he had (*@Stevo-0288: Thx for a fun night* 😊😊😊 *Txt me anytime*) it made no dent in my mood, because I didn't care if I ever saw him again.

I just got up and got on with it. For once, I didn't have a shift to go to, any obligations to fulfil, any meals to prep, a dog who needed a run, glitter to scrub out of my eye wrinkles, or even the looming threat of the lonelies to sour my mood.

I opened all the windows and let autumn flood the house. I lit the Diptyque candle I'd been saving for a special occasion. I had coffee in the French press and cold pad thai in the courtyard, *Song to a Seagull* on vinyl, and a phone full of messages I'd get to later. Sitting in the sunshine with Joni's guitar humming through my body, I appreciated for the first time that my weekend, and the rest of my life, belonged to me.

Isaac Abrams (00:07): Asleep?
Marnie Fowler (00:07): Not yet.

My phone lit up with his incoming call, and I answered it.

'Glad you're still awake,' he said.

'Yeah?' I sighed into my pillow. 'How come?'

It was late, so we were whispering.

'I like talking to you when I can't sleep,' he said. 'Sometimes I can't sleep without talking to you.'

'People tell me I'm exhausting all the time.'

He laughed and I heard the rustle of fabric as he shifted under his covers. 'Talk me to sleep. Tell me anything.'

I hummed and turned over, sandwiching the phone between my ear and the pillow and curling my knees up. 'Did I ever tell you about the time I got fired from my waitressing job for stealing bread?'

'What is this, *Les Mis*?'

'When I was nineteen, the restaurant I worked in made these incredible rolls, and London is so expensive …'

'Little teenage delinquent Marnie. I love her.'

I paused. It was nothing, a throwaway statement, but it left white marks on my skin like I'd been squeezed and then released. I took a breath and forced myself to move past it. 'Uh huh, so one day they pulled me aside …'

CHAPTER EIGHTEEN

The first heavy rain of May lashed against our kitchen windows as I dug through the bottom shelf in the pantry looking for the last bottle of white wine among a wall of vinegar and soy sauce. I'd always been told it was a bad idea to drink your emotions, but some days called for it. Claud had just texted to say she was about to make a run for it from the tram, so at least I wouldn't be drinking alone.

It had become my habit to keep Isaac in the loop of every micro activity and passing thought, so I pulled my phone out and filmed as I split an entire bottle between two fishbowl-sized glasses and sent it off with the caption, *This kind of day*.

'Home!' shouted Claud down the hallway a moment later, slamming the door behind her. 'Is it the end of times? Has some beardy guy in a kaftan been building an ark in Brunswick? I practically had to scale a fence to keep from drowning.'

She was drenched, water squelching in her pumps as she trudged down the hall, appearing in the kitchen with her hair slicked to her forehead. Her trench had turned grey in the downpour.

She sighed in relief. 'Oh *there's* my best friend.'

'Are you talking to me or the wine?'

She grimaced and held her hand out. 'Wine, obviously.'

I sniffed my offence. 'And to think, I put a towel on the radiator, ordered a vat of pho *and* spring rolls, *and* smuggled the sandwich cookies home from work for you.'

She made a touched expression around her glass, draining a third of it.

'Babe!' she said, jutting out her bottom lip. 'That's so nice, but I'm only here to pack a bag and hit the road.'

'You're going to his place *again*?' I asked. 'Give the poor man a break. He must have TMJ by now.'

If she heard my joke, she didn't acknowledge it. She took another heady gulp of wine, put her glass down and said, confidently, 'I'm in love with him.'

I choked. 'You are not. You're just in a fuck fog.'

'No.' She shook her head. 'I am. I'm in love with him.'

'It's been six weeks.'

'Sometimes you just know!' she protested. 'He's just … *perfect*. Haven't you ever heard those stories?'

'Yeah,' I replied, 'and they usually end with Ted Bundy skullfucking a severed head.'

Claud put on an exaggerated sneer and flipped me off.

'You heard what Persephone said. It's in the cards. The Lovers, two halves of a whole — *this is it*, I'm positive.'

I wanted nothing more than to convince her that the high-street psychic she'd fed her answers to was a fraud, but by the dreamy look on her face, the idea of contradicting her felt like kicking a puppy. I didn't have it in me to drag her down.

'Alright,' I said, surrendering. 'You're in love with him. Have you told him?'

'Oh god no!' she said at once. 'I'm not stupid. That's a great way to get ghosted. He thinks I'm seeing like five other people, and he's last on my roster.'

'But you've seen him four times this week.'

'I'm playing it cool,' she insisted. 'Trust me. Come and sit on my bed and talk to me while I'm in the shower.'

My wine and I followed her down the hall as she chattered away. She loved when he ordered for her, she said, because he knew how tired she got from making decisions at work all day, and he was trying to relieve her of another.

His ex was a nightmare, she continued through the ajar ensuite door with all the zest of someone revealing a piece of juicy gossip, a total narcissist. She didn't appreciate him at all, apparently, and made it difficult for him to trust women, but he found it *so easy* to trust her. Maybe he *just knew* too, she said. All she had to do now was stay relaxed and humble and supportive, and he'd see in no time that she, Claud, was the perfect opposite to his ex, and he'd love her for the relief she represented.

I bit my opinions back. There was an echo of familiarity, the rap sheets of old boyfriends' behaviour that coloured every flag maroon. I wanted to let Claud enjoy her lavender haze, so I chewed on the inside of my cheek and made all the right sounds of interest and appreciation.

Half my wine was gone by the time I felt my phone buzz in my pocket.

Isaac Abrams (18:04): What's got you so thirsty?
Isaac Abrams (18:07): I haven't sent you any shirtless selfies, so ??
Marnie Fowler (18:08): Where's the puking emoji?
Isaac Abrams (18:08): Right next to the eggplant one.
Marnie Fowler (18:08): Ha!
Marnie Fowler (18:09): Just a bad day at work.
Marnie Fowler (18:09): My boss is suspending dinner service indefinitely.

Isaac Abrams (18:10): I didn't think you worked the dinner shift

Marnie Fowler (18:10): I don't, but it's not great news. What if we close for good? Who else is going to let me eat croissants all day and swear as much as I want?

Isaac Abrams (18:12): You can be my horny assistant

Marnie Fowler (18:12): I'm calling HR right now.

Marnie Fowler (18:13): I'm not panicking, I'm just sad. I took this job as a means to an end, but I've fallen in love with it. It makes my heart hurt.

He didn't reply right away, so I closed the window and scrolled through my last conversation with Nicola.

Nicola Fowler-Smythe (16:44): That really sucks, hun

Nicola Fowler-Smythe (16:44): Why don't you guys start hosting weddings?

Nicola Fowler-Smythe (16:44): Talk about a cash cow

Marnie Fowler (16:45): Somehow I don't think Kit would be stoked at the idea of celebrating true love in the restaurant he lovingly redesigned with his soon-to-be ex-husband

Nicola Fowler-Smythe (16:47): All you'd have to do is put down a few tablecloths, order a shit-ton of flowers, and charge five figures for canapes and an open bar. He's not that bitter.

Marnie Fowler (16:47): Yes he is.

'He calls me sweet pea,' Claud said. I heard her shut off the water, and the squeak of her medicine cabinet opening as she began her skincare routine. 'Which is so cute, but I don't know if it's very *me*? I'm not sweet. I am objectively a sour little brat.'

Isaac saw my message but didn't write back. He usually responded so quickly I wondered how he'd even had time to read it at all.

'Maybe that's what I should ask him to call me,' she continued, appearing in the doorway in a towel turban and bathrobe. 'Sour brat.'

'Uh, no,' I said. 'Sour Brat is what we'd call our punk revival girl band.'

She gasped. 'I could shave my head again!'

'I've always wanted a nose ring.'

'You would look so good with one! Great, so that's our fallback careers sorted. Okay, help me choose an outfit that says, *"I've just come from work. I put no thought into this, now do me until you're shooting dust."*'

I laughed, threw back the rest of my wine, and while I waited for her to present her options, I checked my phone again.

Blank screen.

Had I overshared? I never knew how Isaac was going to react to reality. It wasn't a matter of honesty: sometimes our conversations would begin to orbit something true, our deep-rooted fears of inadequacy and indecisiveness, and he didn't mind that. I even found he kind of liked my insecurities; it gave him pleasure to be able to counter them, like I was fragile and he was my saviour.

It was the mundane things he didn't care about. Complaining about being skint. An unflattering but hilarious picture of me mid-squawk as Layla yanked on my hair. Details about my life that took the romanticism out of the idea of a wandering, wavy-haired dream girl and replaced it with constant effort and loneliness.

Usually I hid my brushstrokes better than this, and now I remembered why.

Marnie Fowler (18:27): Anyway. Boring. How's your day?
Isaac Abrams (18:27): Date night. Talk later x

Hot tip: don't whine about your life, or your imaginary crush will be so turned off that he'll run into the arms of his real-life girlfriend.

Great. No Claud, no Isaac, too much Vietnamese food and not enough self-control to keep from eating all of it in one sitting, and another night in a quiet house. The white wine sloshing around in my empty stomach turned this idea acidic, so while Claud compared two identical loungewear sets, I booked myself in for the last spin class of the night. If I was going to be left to the lonelies, I might as well tire myself out so sufficiently that I passed out in a sweaty heap no later than 8 pm.

CHAPTER NINETEEN

I lay in bed so still I could feel my heart thumping inside my ribcage. I strained my ears for the rustle of fabric, the murmur of a voice too close for comfort. There was someone in my house. I was sure of it.

When they'd snuck in, I had no idea. I hadn't left the house since my spin class the night before. They could have hidden in the hallway cupboard, where we kept spare towels and Claud's out-of-season clothes. Sometimes I didn't look inside it for weeks; how long had they been hiding in there? What about what happened to the German family Mum mentioned?

I strained my memory to think of anything that might have been out of place. I often found bobby pins and tester tubes of mascara in odd places, but did that mean I had an intruder, or was I just messy? We didn't have anything worth stealing, so whoever lurked in the shadows was here in cold blood. This was how I'd meet my end: alone and terrified, surrounded by junk.

Quietly, I reached for my phone on the bedside table. Claud was at Jesse's place. Again. Nicola would have been asleep for hours. For half a second, I thought of calling Sam and asking him to rush over to protect me, but I'd prefer to take my chances with the murderer.

Forget what I'd been saying all year; I wanted a man in the house. It was easy to make grand declarations of independence until you feared for your life.

> **Marnie Fowler (22:20):** Can you come over?
> **Isaac Abrams (22:21):** I think the phrase you're looking for is, "u up?"
> **Marnie Fowler (22:22):** I'm serious, I think there's someone in my house
> **Marnie Fowler (22:22):** I heard footsteps and this demony voice
> **Marnie Fowler (22:22):** Can I use a butter knife in self-defence?
> **Isaac Abrams (22:24):** How have you made it to 28?
> **Marnie Fowler (22:24):** Think about how bad you're going to feel tomorrow when you turn on the news and my mangled corpse is being carried out to an ambulance
> **Isaac Abrams (22:25):** Why would there be an ambulance? What's a paramedic going to do with a dead body?
> **Marnie Fowler (22:25):** ISAAC
> **Isaac Abrams (22:26):** Do you really need me to come over?
> **Marnie Fowler (22:26):** HURRY UP

Thirty terrifying minutes later, having received the message of his arrival, I was sitting up in bed digging my fingernails into my palm to brace myself for what I had to do.

Three.

Two.

One.

Faster than I'd maybe ever moved in my life, I flung off my blankets, ripped open my bedroom door and flew down the hallway. Shaking hands twisted the deadbolt and unchained the front door, and as I swung it open, I threw myself at him.

There. Safe.

'You cannot be serious.'

'Shh! They'll hear you!'

'Isn't that the point? Come on, stupid.'

'What's that?' I asked, pointing to his right hand.

Isaac looking embarrassed was a sight. The thin, shy smile and the pink blossom of a blush on his cheeks; the bashful shrug as he raised his right arm to show me a softball bat.

'Just in case.'

I didn't feel afraid anymore, but I still clung onto his arm as he let himself inside, flipping on every light switch as he went. He dutifully checked in every cupboard — even the improbable kitchen cabinets — behind the shower curtain, and in the dark corners of the courtyard. Only when he was satisfied that we were the only souls in the house did he accept the cup of tea I'd made him.

There seemed something improper about sitting in the living room in the middle of the night, so I didn't question it when he made his way into my room instead.

'Tell me something stupid,' he said, leaning back into my pillows.

I wanted to say, *'This is suddenly the best night of my entire life.'*

I wanted to say, *'The number of times I have thought about this exact moment defies human comprehension.'*

I wanted to say, *'Every single thing you do makes me like you more.'*

Instead, I said, 'I don't know if shih tzus have feelings.'

'What?' he asked incredulously, setting his cup down and turning onto his side to face me. A sliver of skin appeared below the hem of his white T-shirt, and I tried not to pant. 'You don't think they don't love their owners?'

'I think brains were bred out of them. Like jellyfish. Or rocks. I've never met one with any personality whatsoever.'

'What about chihuahuas?'

'Agents of hate. Sent to earth by the devil himself.'

'Those tiny fluffy ones? Pomeranians?'

'Adore! Sentient loofahs. Perfect animals. No notes.'

'Corgis?'

'Evolutionary mutants. So cute.'

'Cats ...'

'... are emotionally withholding, so I'm obsessed with them. I have so much love to give, Isaac; why won't they let me love them?'

'You're a psychopath.'

'I just want to be validated!'

'No shit,' he laughed.

'Validate me!'

'Never.'

'Do it! Validate me!'

'Don't pinch my nipple! Ow!'

It was the most sexually charged prodding and tickling event since the dawn of pastel-coloured male fantasies, and by the time we'd slapped each other away, my cheeks ached and I could tell I'd gone pink, but I didn't care.

'Who even are you?' asked Isaac, inches from my face, near enough that I felt the edges of his exhale on my skin, warm and cool at once.

'Your dream girl,' I told him dryly, breathing through my laugh and waiting for him to do the same. He didn't.

'Don't I know it.'

His hand hovered over me for a moment, and I wondered if he was going to touch my face and kiss me, or rest it low on my stomach and fuck me, and I didn't know which I'd prefer. Peripherally, I watched his palm hang there for the space of one heartbeat, then another, and just as I was sure he was going to make contact, he froze.

'What's that noise?' he asked, brow sinking into a frown. 'Is that what you heard? It sounds like someone's tunnelling through the wall.'

I strained my ears but heard nothing unusual.

'Did someone die in here?' he asked. 'Is your house haunted?'

'Oh.' I had to cover my mouth to laugh. 'That's my neighbours.'

'Are they …?'

'They're deeply in love.'

'Deeply in something,' he said, somewhere between impressed and concerned.

'It turns into white noise after a while.'

'How often is this happening?'

'It's constant.'

He raised himself on his elbows, listening intently. Muffled through brick and plaster, one of them yelped like a shih tzu locked in a hot car.

'Are they good looking?'

'Never seen them,' I replied. 'And I hope I never do.'

'Ugly people have the best sex,' he said matter-of-factly. 'It's why I'm terrible in bed.'

Maybe it was the comfort of being in my cosiest space, or his easy company, or the sheer unfathomability that he was anything less than a spectacular lay, but my ugly laugh came out, the one I reserved for Claud, and I forgot to be embarrassed. This, here, laughing as we lay side by side listening to two strangers have the time of their lives, was the most intimate thing I'd ever experienced, outpacing all the sex and pillow talk I'd ever had by miles. And when the tea had been drunk and he had gone home, I climbed onto the passenger side of my bed and buried my face in the pillow he'd been resting on.

Wood. Fire. Clove. I wanked until sunrise.

CHAPTER TWENTY

'It's just fucking inconsiderate,' said Claud as she kicked my bedroom door open and flopped onto my unmade bed.

One leg into my jeans, I nearly toppled over in shock. It had been a week since the phantom break-in, and Claud had been home two nights in seven. It took a moment to remember that I had a housemate at all.

'Isn't it just?'

'"*Let's hang out Sunday*," he says. Not Sunday brunch, Sunday afternoon, Sunday night. Just Sunday. So I ask, "*Cool, what time? What are we doing?*" — silence. So now I just have to sit around all day *waiting*. What the hell is that about?'

I hid my expression under the guise of following my hands up the buttons of my shirt.

'And I can't ask him again, or I'll be nagging. But I've already washed my hair and done my nails, and is that all for nothing? Where are you going?'

'I've got that dried-flower arranging class.'

'Dried flowers?' she replied, frowning. 'You mean dead flowers.'

'Well otherwise they're just plants, see.'

'Stay with me,' she whined. 'Entertain me.'

I turned and rifled through my wardrobe, then let out a confused, '*Huh*.'

'What?'

'It's so weird. I can't find my red velvet vest and hat.'

'Ew. What?'

'For my circus monkey outfit.'

'Oh *ha ha*.'

'I know you're too pretty to be smart, but you *do* know you don't have to sit around all day and wait for a boy to call, don't you? You're not under house arrest.'

'I cleared my day because we were supposed to be going out,' she said, with a contemptuous look at herself. 'I have officially regressed back to my teens. This is sad.'

I hesitated. I'd put a non-refundable deposit down on my spot in the class, and I'd be living on coffee and toast for the rest of the week as it was. But I couldn't stand the thought of her in the house by herself, ripping her nails off with her teeth to satiate the growing fear that the lonelies would take hold and never leave her again.

'I'll take you out,' I said. 'We'll do something fun together.'

In a defiant *fuck-you* to subpar romance, we staged a pantomime date for ourselves. Per her coordination, we changed into dreamy white dresses, straw hats and red lipstick for an afternoon spent drifting down the river in a rowboat, overtaking mushy couples and killing the vibe with dumb jokes and cackles of laughter.

The staff at Fairfield Park Boathouse didn't seem bothered by the absurdity of it, two idiots gracelessly collapsing into their blue boats for hire, overdressed and overexcited. It was pretty out here on the water, the banks lined with ancient trees growing at angles, their branches reaching towards each other and offering fleeting cover from the weakening sun as we floated beneath them.

This, I'd argue, was better, more romantic and more fun than whatever Jesse had in mind.

'I brought provisions!' I announced over Claud's prolonged grunt of effort as she rowed. I pulled a sweating bottle of rosé out of my bag with a flourish. Her face lit up for a moment, then fell again.

'I can't,' she said with an exaggerated pout. 'I'm trying to cut back.'

I booed. When had she ever declined the opportunity to drink pink wine on a sunny Sunday afternoon? She had maintained a two-glass buzz practically since the moment we met.

'But boat drunk is top-tier.'

'No, *pool* drunk is top-tier,' she argued, and let go of the oars. 'Then boat drunk. Then land drunk.'

'Wait,' I said, holding up a hand. 'You're forgetting about plane drunk.'

'Plane drunk! You're so right. Should we go on a holiday?'

'To wine country!'

'*Yes*! Or Singapore! No, wait — Capri.'

'Are you paying? Because that's the only way I'm getting to Capri.'

'Yeah babe,' she said, tapping her ankle against mine affectionately. 'For our honeymoon.'

I grinned at her, and she grinned back. A moment later, her arm was snaking into her bottomless tote bag and digging around in its contents. If she wasn't pulling out emergency snacks or aerosol sunscreen, it meant that her attention span had blipped again.

It was almost easy, out here in the good weather, away from the real world, to feel like nothing had changed in recent weeks. As though there hadn't been more nights alone in the house than nights with company. She was around so infrequently lately that I ruined the time we did have together by thinking about how much I'd missed it. When she was actually present, I could almost forget that Isaac was slowly ascending onto the best friend tier. Lately he was the one who kept the lonelies at bay. When he answered my calls, he kept me in his ear for as long as I wanted.

We talked while we cooked dinner — he weighed out portions for his macros, the vain little nerd, while I microwaved whatever Sam had set aside after service — and I propped my phone against the fruit bowl so we could video chat and eat together, too. I gathered minute details of his life this way: he ironed his tea towels. He poured salt into his hand before sprinkling it onto his food.

But it wasn't the same as having someone *there*. There was no one to listen to my dry commentary on whichever slow-moving dialogue-driven film he'd told me to watch; no one to chuck my clothes into the dryer so they wouldn't start to smell.

Company was only a phone call away, but sometimes, when the day was late and blue, that was still too far. I missed my friend. Claud's scattered, neon presence. And when she was around again, finally, she was only there in pieces.

'I don't think I'm getting any reception out here,' she said, frowning as she waved her phone around in search of a signal. 'How far from civilisation are we?'

'About thirty metres,' I said. 'Some guy is teaching his kid to ride a bike right over there.'

She squinted over to the riverbank and dropped her shoulders when she saw that I was right.

I tried to make it a joke, but all that came out was frustration when I said, 'I'm low-key impressed that he manages to be your main focus even when he's not here.'

'It's not Jesse,' she replied through an injured frown. 'I do care about more than just boys, you know. I'm not that vapid.'

Tension settled over us like a fog. 'I only meant — you were bothered by it before, him not answering. I assumed —'

'It's work,' she said with an edge. 'My shithead stakeholder is giving me a migraine.'

'Oh, fuck them. Fuck work. You hate it anyway,' I said, fighting to keep my voice light and airy. 'Don't let them spoil a lovely afternoon with your favourite person.'

'I don't mean to be a complete Miranda about it, but some of us don't have the luxury of switching off when it's convenient.'

'What does that mean?'

'It means I have responsibilities outside of whatever dumb thing we get up to on the weekend.'

'Whoa.'

'I'm just saying — if I have to check my phone, it doesn't mean it's some big attack on you.'

'This wasn't my idea,' I said. 'I had plans. I cancelled them to spend time with you.'

'And I appreciate that!' she insisted. 'But cancelling your life-drawing class isn't the same as missing an email and getting my department pulled into a disciplinary hearing.'

'Dried-flower arranging.'

'What?'

'I had a dried-flower arranging class, not life-drawing.'

She took a breath to steady herself. 'Honestly, Marnie?'

I folded my arms in my lap and watched her breathe through her frustration, feeling more hurt as the seconds ticked on. 'Why is your thing automatically more important than my thing?'

'Why are you so upset?'

'I'm upset that I made space in my day for you, and you can't even give me your full attention for a couple of hours.'

Looking baffled, she scoffed. 'It's not like we're doing anything. We're just hanging out. Why can't I check my emails?'

'I would have gone to my class if it wasn't going to make a difference to you.'

'You're being so neurotic about this,' she said. I wanted to disappear. 'It's not like I'm texting people for fun. It's work.'

This was humiliating, to have to beg for her time. I would have given anything to be able to stand up and storm off, but I was trapped out here. Because I didn't know how to say, '*I miss you and it's killing me,*' without crying, I decided to say nothing at all.

'Honestly I'm jealous that you don't get it,' she continued, trying to be diplomatic. 'I'd love for my job to stop the minute I left the office.'

'Can you cut it out?' I snapped. 'Stop acting like my life isn't important.'

'I didn't say it's not important!' she cried, offended at my offence. 'I would never say that — but it *is* different. If I screw up at work, there are consequences. If you screw up at work, what happens — someone's coffee sucks? It's just not comparable. I — what are you doing?'

I'd picked up the oars and with all the strength earned from inconsistent group fitness classes, begun to row us back to the dock.

'I'm going home.'

She grimaced with guilt when she saw where she had let the conversation get to. 'Marnie, no — I didn't mean it like that —'

'Yes, you did.'

'No, I really didn't — it's just, y'know — there are different stakes involved —'

'I'm not going to sit in a stupid fucking hat —' I paused my rowing to pluck the boater off my head and throw it like a frisbee into the nearby trees '— and watch you look down your nose at me. Sorry I'm not changing the world one internal news bulletin at a time.'

'That's not what I was doing!' she cried. 'I'm just saying, like, objectively, my career and your job are just different.'

I paused, and the boat floated on. 'Why is yours a career and mine is a job?'

'Don't read into that,' she replied, exasperated.

'Do you not buy coffee?' I asked. 'Is an almond croissant not the highlight of your weekend?'

I felt a pang of pride as I found that I was able to defend my point without deflecting my discomfort. Since the day I was hired, I'd struggled with the nagging idea that my job was a menial resting place while I searched for a greater purpose. But it was one thing to categorise it that way internally, and another to hear someone attack Little George for no reason other than to boost their self-importance. I was offended. I was indignant. I wasn't interested in hearing any more.

'I hear you,' she said, although I heard more placation than concession. 'I shouldn't have said that. I'm sorry if you —'

'My life might look trivial to you,' I said, stern and resolved, 'but everything about it is just as important as everything in yours.'

She nodded, and I rowed. My arms were heavy from the weight of the water, and the ride home on the tram was silent but for the tap-tapping of her thumbs on her phone as she hammered out messages to her shithead stakeholder and Jesse.

Claud was out the door with an overnight bag within ten minutes. No matter how many times I checked it, my phone screen remained blank, and the vase I'd set aside for my dried-flower arrangement sat empty on my bedside table, and my trivial little life felt emptier than ever.

Isaac Abrams (00:47): You have an opinion about everything

Isaac Abrams (00:47): Good god, you're mouthy.

Marnie Fowler (00:47): Would you want me any other way?

Isaac Abrams (00:49): I want a lot of things to do with your mouth

Marnie Fowler (00:49): Pervert.

Isaac Abrams (00:49): Would you want me any other way?

Marnie Fowler (00:49): I want lots of things.

Isaac Abrams (00:50): You're pretty good at this

Isaac Abrams (00:50): Whatever this is

Marnie Fowler (00:50): You wouldn't believe what else I'm good at

Isaac Abrams (00:50): I can only imagine

Marnie Fowler (00:50): I bet you do

Isaac Abrams (00:50): Yeah. I do.

Marnie Fowler (00:50): How often?

Isaac Abrams (00:52): All the time.

CHAPTER TWENTY-ONE

'Marnie, Marnie, Marnie,' said Claud as she bounced into the living room, bursting with the pride and excitement of a kid playing show-and-tell. 'This is Jesse.'

She tugged on the arm she was holding, and Jesse was pulled into frame.

I felt guilt before I'd even identified why: my first thought when I saw him was, *Oh*.

Nothing prepared you for the distinct blandness of someone else's boyfriend. After all their gushing and mooning, you began to expect a prince. Reality and more objective eyes eventually revealed that they were ... just some guy. Just skin stretched over a jumble of bones and nerve endings which made Claud prone to panic and hysteria if she ever lost sight of her phone.

Jesse was my height and just as lanky, heavy black glasses under his heavy black eyebrows. He had an unstyled dark mop that told the world that he had contempt for anyone who prided themselves on aesthetics, further confirmed by the rumpled khaki shirt he wore, curling at the collar. Claud had once lunged at me with a hair straightener when I tried to go out with a dimple in my T-shirt where a clothes peg had been.

I chided myself for being this judgmental. As though I was one to talk. As though I didn't require her sign-off on my outfits before I left the house; as though I hadn't spent a year in love with someone who dressed like a member of One Direction. When Claud saw a picture of Martin, she shrieked and made me promise to take myself directly to the psych ward if I ever went out with someone in maroon skinny jeans again.

Everything between us was fine. Not that we'd talked about it. She'd left a box of macarons on my bed two days later, and we called a truce. It had been our first ever tiff, and I couldn't put it behind us fast enough.

'At last we meet,' I said, leaning against the arm of the couch and rallying against my needlessly catty train of thought. 'The infamous Jesse.'

Claud beamed. 'The one and only.'

'What'll it be? Juggling, baton twirling — *ooh*, maybe Irish dancing?'

He blinked. 'Huh?'

'Your special talent to impress the judges. Me. I'm the judges. Some girls have their dad sitting in a recliner polishing his shotgun when the new boyfriend comes over. Claud has me.'

Jesse let out an awkward laugh and looked at Claud. 'If she doesn't approve, I'm dumped? Is that how this works?'

'Marnie gets her life lessons from Spice Girls songs,' she said through a mouthful of nervous laughter. 'She's being dumb.'

'I mean, they're modern philosophers, Jesse,' I said. '"2 Become 1" is about safe sex. You can't tell me they don't have important messages to share.'

'I think I'm good with Claudia's approval,' he replied, unbothered. 'She's the one I'm trying to impress.'

Uh, right. He was probably nervous. Claud on her own was a hurricane of noise and opinions and colour. Two of us piling on was nothing short of bullying. She had described Jesse as pretty quiet, with a dry, scalpel-sharp sense of humour. People like him often came off as aloof, she said; a bit hard to read.

It was what made it all the more exciting when they did finally let you in, like being granted access to an ultra-exclusive club.

I'd always played characters designed for someone else's preferences, so tonight I'd play the role of someone Jesse was comfortable around. It would be fine.

'And I am impressed,' she said, hopping up on tiptoe to peck him on the cheek.

'Sorry,' I said. 'I'm only joking. Claud's told me a lot about you, and you sound terrific.'

'Oh, thanks.'

'Are we ready for dinner?' Claud asked. 'Pizza? Pub?'

He'd made a reservation for us at the Egyptian place down the street, he said, and it was a nice night for a walk, so off we went.

Fighting through the Friday night dinner crowd was hard enough on your own. The footpaths were usually jammed tight with bodies marching agonisingly slowly from one of Lygon Street's innumerable Italian restaurants to the next, pausing to review their menus or else stand and engage with the jovial staff who performed cartoonishly to lure people inside. When you ventured out with a friend, you had to hold hands and snake through the crowd without losing one another, apologising for trodden toes and slamming into oblivious wanderers. In a trio, you could forget it. As we slipped into the dense herd, Claud reached for both our hands, but she was lost to the tide before my fingers could grip hers.

'I'll catch up!' I called, and she nodded, looking concerned as she got sucked into the scrum.

And so I walked alone, dodging and weaving and swearing under my breath. I missed the traffic light and watched as they crossed the road ahead of me, strolling hand-in-hand through the early evening. I did what I always did when left on my own: I reached for my safety blanket.

Marnie Fowler (18:48): Am officially third-wheeling Claud's date
Marnie Fowler (18:48): A fun look at the rest of my life

By the time I arrived at the restaurant, overheating under the trench coat I'd borrowed from Claud's wardrobe and exhausted from navigating the foot traffic, they were both already seated, and Jesse was pouring water into two glasses.

'You made it!' said Claud, rising to pull my chair out for me.

'And now I'm parched!' I said, slumping into it and fanning myself with the drinks menu. 'Let's replenish our electrolytes with pinot gris immediately.'

As I scanned the pages looking for a dry white in the ultra-budget range, it took a minute to clock their non-response. When I looked up, Claud was shifting uncomfortably in her seat and Jesse fought to hide a micro-frown.

I tried again. 'Or sauv blanc?'

'We don't really drink,' he said.

I almost snorted in response but caught Claud's warning eye before laughter rocketed out of my nose. I mined his tone for meaning: was it condescension? Was it judgment? Was I projecting my own shame around my social crutch onto his four innocuous words? What 'we' was he referring to?

'Get a wine if you want one, babe,' she said as his arm snaked around her back and gave her a supportive squeeze. 'We don't mind.'

'No,' I said, shrugging off my projections. 'Water's great.'

I wanted to like him. I *would* like him. I'd blink until the image of Claud's frustrated fragility at his earlier indifference disappeared, and all that was left were his redeeming qualities. He had to have a couple of them.

I coughed and waited for him to move the conversation along, but he didn't.

With her hair shielding her expression from his peripheral view, Claud made a pleading face that said, '*Say something!*'

'You're a programmer, right?' I asked. 'Tell me: are you an undercover anti-capitalist anarchist managing a dissociative identity disorder, or has Claud been lying?'

She laughed. 'You need to stop wanking to *Mr Robot*.'

'I will never.'

'Sorry,' she said with a flickering look at him. 'That was crass.'

'What? "Wanking"? I'm sure he's heard the term before.'

'I have nephews,' he said, smoothing out his brow. 'They'll pick up anything. We try not to swear.'

'Oh, I can't wait to teach my niece to swear!' I replied. 'She's only one and a bit, so her f's aren't great, but it's my duty as her aunt to make sure she stands up and shouts "*fuck!*" at an important family function while it's still cute.'

My phone pinged in my bag, and I twisted around in my seat to retrieve it.

> **Isaac Abrams (18:59):** Three wheels are better than two, Fowler
> **Isaac Abrams (18:59):** Can't fall over on a tricycle ♥
> **Marnie Fowler (19:00):** There's some remark about me being the town bike here that I can't quite put my finger on.
> **Isaac Abrams (19:00):** 🤐

'Who's that?' cooed Claud, pretending to reach out and snatch my phone away when I failed to hide my laugh. 'You-know-who?'

'He has a name.'

'And it's Loverboy.'

'And you're a moron.'

'Isaac is Marnie's grey-area friend,' said Claud, translating for Jesse. 'They're super hot for each other but nothing can happen.'

His eyebrows rocketed upward. 'Why can't anything happen?'

'Because we're friends,' I replied. If he didn't drink or even tolerate the word 'wank', Jesse probably wouldn't appreciate the moral relativism and deliberate ignorance I relied on to navigate that relationship.

He leaned forward on his elbows and asked, 'Do you really think men and women can be friends?'

I caught my laugh just as it escaped and glanced at my wrist like I had a watch to check.

'Is it 1995?' I asked. 'Of course they can. I'm friendly to men all the time without losing my clothes in a freak accident.'

'I'm not talking about passing interactions, though,' he said. 'I mean prolonged friendship. Emotional intimacy.'

'Don't you have any female friends?'

'Not when I'm in a relationship. I don't think it's appropriate.'

It was the most impassioned he had seemed all night, and I didn't know what to make of it. What had happened to friendly if banal conversations about each other's jobs, or siblings, or our guilty-pleasure binge watches? He'd latched on to the first opportunity to present me with a challenge, and I wondered if the sour taste in my mouth had anything to do with the tap water.

'I actually read something about this,' said Claud brightly, thrilled that the conversation finally had legs and doing anything to keep it moving. 'How our emotional support systems conflict with or reinforce our ideas of intimacy. So men — straight men — mostly get support from their partners, but women give it to and receive it from partners, friends, families, everyone. So when you're friends with a guy, he's thinking "*She must be into me*," but for you, there might not be any romantic or sexual element to it at all.'

'That's really intelligent,' said Jesse, squeezing her again. 'So you agree with me, men and women can't be just friends.'

'That's not what that means,' I said, interrupting before Claud could respond. 'It means that the kind of men who view women as porters for their emotional baggage can't have friendships with them.'

'Claudia called him your grey-area friend,' he replied. 'So you *are* porting his emotional baggage around, only without the perks of partnership.'

He had called her Claudia twice now, not Claud, and it grated for reasons I couldn't place. And what was that 'intelligent' comment about?

'A crush doesn't negate a friendship,' I said, hardly resisting the urge to roll my eyes. 'It only complicates it.'

Jesse observed me for a minute, conflicted like he was irritated to the point of amusement. 'You're a bit contrary, aren't you?'

'Only when I'm right.'

'Men don't like argumentative women.'

'I don't give a —' *We try not to swear.* Ugh. A 'fuck' would have felt so good, but I loved Claud too much to intentionally provoke him. 'I don't base my personality around what men like.'

'Okay!' Claud squeaked, sitting forward to interject. 'Let's relax.'

'I think that's wilfully naive,' he continued, ignoring her. 'Can you have an honest friendship when attraction is on the table? You can't. It's built on a lie.'

'I think we should change the subject before I have a rage stroke.'

'This isn't arguing,' he argued. 'This is discourse. You should be able to speak to your own point. Maybe you just don't want to admit I'm right.'

Claud's face, with her wide eyes and pursed lips, said *'Please.'* I'd never been so attuned to our silent connection nor confused as to how someone as outspoken, drink-happy, sweary or impatient as her had wound up on the arm of someone who opposed her — *our* — views at every turn. For her sake, I forced a taut smile. No teeth, dead eyes.

'You're so right,' I replied, sugar dripping from it. 'Men and women can't be friends. My platonic relationships with men mean nothing. I'm a liar *and* an idiot. Thank you for showing me that.'

'Ah, come on, don't be *offended* —'

'I'm not offended. I'm agreeing with you. That's all you want; what's the problem?'

I don't know when we turned the corner from surface-scratching disagreements to open hostility, but there we were. I hid my grimace in my water glass (what I wouldn't give for a bucket of vodka) and waited for a new topic to present itself.

'Let's order before we starve to death,' said Claud, waving her menu to waft the tension out of the air. 'Should we get everything to share? What are our thoughts on falafel?'

'Love.'

'Overrated, dry,' said Jesse over me. 'Let's get the lamb in pita.'

'I don't eat meat,' I said at once, 'and neither does Claud.'

Jesse frowned and looked at her. 'Don't you?'

'Oh, well — I have lately, a bit,' she said to me, looking guilty. 'I've always eaten sashimi because vegetarian sushi is so underwhelming. But Jesse made a whole roast chicken the other day; it would've been a waste not to eat it.'

'You love chickens,' I said. 'You think they're cute.'

She fidgeted in her seat. 'I know, but —'

'We'll get the calamari then,' he said, smiling at me through his victory. 'Is that a good enough compromise for you?'

I drained my water glass and waited for death to come.

'That did not go well,' said Claud as the front door slammed shut behind her. Jesse had just left, declining to spend the night at our place or have her stay at his.

Dinner had felt like it lasted half my life, each minute dragging out longer than could be counted on any clock. Once I went limp and stopped biting into his leading questions, he stopped asking them, and Claud had to keep the conversation afloat.

The poor thing walked us through the entire plot of the crime novel she'd borrowed from the library, what a difference pumpkin seeds made in her favourite salad, explained four different celebrity crises she was avidly following, and listed and ranked all the countries she had visited on holiday over two excruciating hours.

'Yeah, not great.' I sniffed out a laugh as I went about taking out my earrings and sliding off my rings, dropping them into the misshapen bowl I'd made myself at a ceramics class last month.

'I can't believe you.'

I whipped around. She had dropped onto the edge of my bed. 'Me? *He* picked the fight.'

'I know he did,' she said with all the cadence of someone being pointedly reasonable. 'But I wish you'd handled it a bit better.'

'You don't agree with him, do you?'

'Of course I don't, but it's like an atheist trying to argue someone out of their religion. There's just no point; you're only wasting your own sanity.'

'And, what, his religion is bad twentieth-century romcom tropes?'

'You have to admit he had a point.'

My eyebrows shot into my hairline. 'About what?'

'Well, you and Isaac aren't *just* friends. Sex actually *does* get in the way of your friendship, even when you're not *having* it. Just the fact that you both want it so bad.'

I pinched the bridge of my nose. 'That is so unfair.'

'Hey, it's not just you!' she said, holding her hands up in surrender. 'I don't have all that many straight guy friends. The ones I have, we've had to screw the sexual tension away before we can be just friends, and even then, it's always *there*.'

'People aren't helpless. We're not horny monkeys following our crotches wherever they lead. If *someone* —' I could hear myself getting shrill '— doesn't believe in self-control and emotional depth, maybe that's something they should be worried about.'

Not for the first time all night, Claud fixed me with a pleading look. 'I don't want to fight.'

I sighed. I fished my pyjamas out of their drawer and threw them over my shoulder, keeping my hands busy to contain the rant that threatened to explode out of me.

'I'm just really disappointed,' she said sadly. 'I wanted tonight to go well.'

I wanted to ask, '*What can you possibly see in him?*'

The man I'd sat across from all evening had, as far as I could see, no redeeming qualities. He was petty and argumentative and condescending and sexist in the infuriatingly circular way that made him tiring to fight and impossible to tolerate.

I wanted more for Claud. As with Nicola, her taste in men did not reflect how wonderful she was. It was crushing to watch my two favourite women, smart and funny and fantastic in every way, settle so far below their worth, and worse still, to hear them defend it.

'He was really nervous,' she continued. 'I've talked you up a ton and he wanted to seem smart in front of you.'

'Well now I think he's an idiot.'

'*Hey*,' she said, voice full of warning. 'Be nice.'

I grumbled my response.

'He asked me to apologise to you from him.'

'Why couldn't he do it himself?'

'He knows he pushed it too far. He's sorry. Can't you give him another chance? I think this could really be something.'

'Why?' I asked. 'Why do you think that? Not because of whatshername.'

'No,' she said. 'I had fun at the tarot place, but I'm not an idiot. I just … it's been a really long time since I felt like this about someone. I don't want to get it screwed up, because you're my two favourite people, and you're both stubborn and — sorry, but — a bit arrogant. Please.'

My stony resolve weakened at her pleading face, the ripple in her forehead.

'I'm sorry,' I said, dropping my shoulders. 'I'm premenstrual. I'll be nicer next time.'

'Yes, you will,' she said, smiling in an attempt to return to herself. 'And so will he. Promise.'

My jaw ached from clenching it.

I knew she was wrong. My own history told me so. How many times had I, in rose-tinted contact lenses, asked

Nicola for her glowing report on a new boyfriend and been disappointed, confused, even angry when she described him as '*fine*'? Years later I'd realised that '*fine*' was a generous assessment. I only hoped Claud was a quicker study than I'd ever been.

CHAPTER TWENTY-TWO

The sunshine that thawed my bones had to fight against a chill of dread as my phone lit up with a message from Claud, then two, then four, seven, thirteen. So many messages I'd dislocate my thumb scrolling through all of them. I watched them concertina in on themselves and rolled onto my back, prematurely tired of their content.

'That's a world-weary sigh,' said Isaac.

He was sitting on the rug beside me, throwing red grapes into the air and catching them in his mouth, his shoes off to reveal blessedly plain grey socks. (There was nothing more tiresome than a man who used his quirky sock collection to fill the space where a personality should have been.)

Picnics were a lingering relic of lockdown loopholes. Even now, on the last warm day of autumn, months after restrictions had been lifted, the great green planes of Edinburgh Gardens were chequered with people with wicker baskets and travel mugs of wine. We had joined them an hour ago.

It was such a wide stretch of nature that you could almost forget the rest of the world existed only a few minutes away. Elm trees clung to the last orange and yellow leaves, casting us all into warm relief. I didn't even care that once the sun disappeared it would be too cold to linger; I thought I'd stay even if it poured down with rain.

Isaac never complained when I dragged him over to my side of town. I liked an amenable man. More than that, I liked not having to slog through multiple methods of public transport for over an hour to see him and then feel scruffy and out of place on his bourgeois home turf. I called; he came.

I hadn't seen him in weeks, not since the night he came over, but he had been the one to suggest our plans this afternoon. I'd met him after my Saturday shift, having deflected raised eyebrows from Kit all morning when I turned up to work in an impractically flimsy dress, surviving the lulls and rushes of the day on bubbling anticipation. Seeing Isaac would be the highlight of my week. I brought him cake; he brought me relief.

'Claud stuff,' I said, with an arm over my face to shield my eyes from the weak sunlight. 'She's with the boyfriend. She's either melting down about him or making a list of baby names, and I don't want to deal with either.'

'You're not happy for her?'

'No. Yes. No, I am.' I groaned and heard him snicker. 'He's just a dick. She spends most nights at his place, which I guess is better than having him at mine, but it's like ... she's so different around him. I think he's bad news.'

'Are you concerned because she's your friend, or because she's *your* friend?'

I scrunched my nose to think. 'I just don't know what she sees in him,' I said delicately, because I didn't want Isaac to see me in the unflattering shade of a truthful answer.

'You can't control what other people do,' he replied. 'People are always going to do exactly what they want.'

'Even if it's bad for them?'

He held my eye for half a moment, then said, 'Especially if it's bad for them.'

'*People*,' I sighed. I dropped my arm and closed my eyes.

'Maybe in my next life I'll come back as a less complicated species. Wouldn't that be nice?'

'What would you want to be?'

'Anything else,' I said. 'Something with less autonomy. A bug or a tree or a star. Something where my only job is to live and do what biology says I should. Just exist.'

I heard the rustle of fabric on fabric and could feel the heat of his body as he lay beside me, but I didn't open my eyes.

'I hope I'm a tree in your forest.'

'You'd better be,' I said and felt around until I tapped his ankle with my foot. 'I'd get too lonely otherwise.'

I heard him sigh, so I sighed again too. It was easy to placate myself with silly conversations and imagined reincarnations, but then the topic would drop, and the weight on my ribs remained.

'I just feel like I'm losing her,' I continued. We usually saved our honest conversations for after dark, with the shield of a phone line between us. Maybe it was the cool change, or the assumed intimacy, or maybe I was just that lonely, but the words came out of their own accord. 'And I feel like such a terrible person because I love her, and I want her to have everything she wants. But I lay awake at night waiting to hear her key turn in the door, and every time I don't, I think, once she's gone, I'll have no one.'

I wasn't brave enough to open my eyes, but I heard him shift on the blanket as he turned to lay on his side. I waited for him to make a crack: a joke about adopting half a dozen cats or a suggestion to turn her relationship into a throuple, but his voice was earnest.

'That's not true,' he said. 'I'll be there.'

'This is temporary,' I replied. 'We both know it. You'll start your real life and you'll disappear.'

'No, I won't,' he argued gently. 'You'll be stuck with me forever.'

I could feel his eyes on my face, so I forced a smile and counted my breath.

'Come here,' he said a beat later. I cracked an eye open to see that he was handing me the bud of an earphone. I took it from him and popped it in.

'You sure?' I asked under an eyebrow raised in uncertainty. 'You might humiliate yourself.'

'Oh, probably.'

He lay back down, and I could have sworn he was a fraction closer than before. I caught a whiff of his laundry detergent and bit down on my tongue.

Surely this was some kind of move; a slick, well-practised tip that a secret society of men shared around like folklore, that all women were rendered weak over a private song in a public spot. I could have laughed, but I didn't. I chanced a glance at him, and he wasn't smirking, or making bedroom eyes, or even looking at me, but settling into his spot and scrolling through his phone for the track he wanted.

'What is it?'

'You'll see.'

I narrowed my eyes. 'Is this where I find out you're an Ariana Grande superfan?'

'I *do* love a good bop,' he said, grinning. He turned to look at me, and our noses almost touched. 'But this is better.'

He hit play, and as the twang of an acoustic guitar and the unpolished voice of Jackson C. Frank played out, I lost my breath. Maybe I'd mentioned him in passing in one of dozens of phone calls over these long weeks and months, or maybe — the thought made me want to cry — Isaac had simply heard 'Juliette' and thought of me.

Whatever it was that existed here between us, on this blanket, with our forearms pressed against one another's, it took a song about a girl we'd never met and turned it into something sticky and fraught. His pinky finger reached out and curled around mine, and I didn't pull it back.

We lay there together and watched the clouds drift and warp above us. There was nothing but time and breath and the thud of my heart beating in and out of time with the song. Everything else seemed so far away — responsibilities, distress waiting beyond my front door, unanswered text messages, nagging questions — there was no space for doubt here in a fresh cotton haze. I let myself exist between dream and reality, both soaking in the moment and watching it from outside myself, the red *record* light blinking in the top left corner of my brain.

Somewhere around the bridge, my head had dropped to the left, and the fleece of the blanket pressed against my cheek as cool air and hot want swirled around us.

Isaac was right there when I opened my eyes. The song faded out and started again. He was both too close and too far. I blinked and he didn't. I swallowed and he shifted.

This was it.

I could feel his exhale on my skin as I turned on my side, closing the space between us with mere millimetres to spare. He looked at me. I looked at his mouth. I was going to do it. I'd be brave. I'd tilt my chin and I'd just —

'I think it's going to rain,' he said, low and matter-of-fact.

'I — oh, right.'

It took a moment to collect myself, to pull the earphone out, to sit up and regain my place in reality. The sky had turned from blue to lilac to grey in the span of a song, and the abruptness of it all sent a shiver through me. I packed away the remains of our picnic to regain the feeling in my hands.

'This is always fun,' he said, rising to meet me. 'No matter how tough my week has been, seeing you always makes it better.'

'Why have you had a tough week?' I asked. 'You didn't say anything.'

He smiled and shook his head. 'No need. All better now.'

''Cause of me.'

''Cause of you.'

I reached over to smooth out the neck of his T-shirt where it had folded against his collarbone, and he beamed.

'C'mon,' he said. He launched himself up to stand and offered me his hand. 'Let's get you home before it buckets down and you're forced to listen to my bad jokes about being soaked.'

I cringed and shoved his hand away, laughing despite myself. 'Way to ruin a moment.'

'That's supposed to be your job.'

'Yeah, hey!' I said in mock outrage. '*I'm* supposed to be the walking mood killer.'

'You're okay, Fowler,' he said, and threw his arm over my shoulders as we began to walk. Despite the chill, my entire body felt like it was a scorching summer's day. 'I promise I'll never disappear.'

CHAPTER TWENTY-THREE

The lurching tram forced me to burp, and the dry, pink smell of pregamed rosé bounced back at me from my face mask.

'I heard that,' said Claud absently behind her phone.

'Is the tram driver on his L's?' I asked with a grimace, pinching the fabric back to let fresh oxygen in. 'I'm ready to vom.'

'Hm?'

She wasn't listening. I slumped back in my seat and sighed.

Getting south of the river was a pain, which was the excuse I used to never visit my mother, or go to the beach, or imbibe on seedy nights out on the decaying stretch of Chapel Street better known these days for bad coke than chic cocktail bars.

All cities divided by water did this, drew invisible lines and required its residents to declare a lifelong allegiance before rental agreements could be signed, but Melburnians acted like they invented it. Love couldn't cross the Yarra, but bar tabs and increasingly complex grey areas could.

We were skidding and sliding through the city, bodies flooding the streets as people refused to let the bitter chill of fresh winter keep them from a good time. It was my first night out in weeks — weeks and weeks and weeks — and I still felt disconnected and isolated from it all. With Claud so often occupied, I was filling my nights with spin classes, elaborate and flavourless attempts at baked treats, messy at-home pottery kits that stained the courtyard pavement, and more time on the phone to Isaac than ever before.

I kicked my leg out in front of us to get her attention. 'Do you think these boots were a mistake? I feel less like a gazelle and more like an undercover dominatrix. Which is a vibe, but ...'

I felt especially overdressed next to her. Claud usually dressed like an overzealous fashion editor, favouring the story her outfit told over its practicality or comfort. She owned a metallic purple leather jacket, for goodness' sake; what was she doing wearing a subdued black suit and a pair of almost-sensible yellow pumps? Where had all her zest gone?

'Mm.'

'How are you still texting him?' I asked. 'You've been glued to his face for a week. Honestly, what else is there to say?'

'You're in a bad mood for someone on their way to a party,' she said. When she glanced up and saw my sourpuss, she made an apologetic face and slid her phone into her jacket pocket. 'Sorry. There. I'm all yours. All night. Are you nervous?'

'Why would I be nervous?'

'Because it's a big deal! You two have been living in this weird vacuum. Inviting you to a party means he's bringing you into his *real life*. I — oh, is it his birthday?'

'It's his thirtieth.'

'Oh.'

'What?'

Claud paused. 'He's a male Gemini.'

'I guess. So?'

'Nothing.'

'*What?*'

'It just explains a lot.'

'Did Persephone tell you that?' I asked, barely managing to conceal my sneer. 'Is she who you're texting?'

Claud blew off the question and turned in her seat to face me, eyes alight with the thirst for drama. 'Are you prepared to meet the girlfriend?'

'I don't think there's going to be a quiz.'

'Well, what's her vibe?'

'How should I know?'

'You've never looked her up?' she asked incredulously. 'Not even for a drive-by?'

'You said their relationship was none of my business!'

'How are you supposed to defeat your nemesis if you don't know anything about her?'

'My "*nemesis*",' I scoffed. 'She's not Spider-Man.'

'But she could be, like, otherworldly hot. She could be so glamorous and condescending; she might cut you down to size with a single look. Really cruel, like this —' Claud leaned away, pulled her mouth into a line and looked me up and down '— and what will you do then?'

'Perish, I don't know,' I said, and hugged my bag to myself self-consciously. 'Stop it; she's not going to do that. That's a war crime.'

'*Or* she could look exactly like you. He could have a type. Which would be worse, do you think, if she was a high or low budget version of you?'

I fixed her with a look. 'Please stop. You're making me not want to go.'

The tram driver took a hard left, and we were thrown against the window.

Silence again. Claud hid half of her miffed expression under her mask and resumed typing on her phone while I sat there chewing at the tender flesh of my cheek. I'd worked tirelessly to block out precisely this type of thinking, both because I couldn't control the spiral it sent me on, and because at my core I knew it was unhelpful. The catfight trope, pitting two women against one another for entertainment: I wanted no part in it. No, I preferred to go on in my bubble, playing in the shadows of ignorance.

Off the tram, through the scrums of the bronzed and boozed teenagers off to their first forays into inebriation on Chapel Street's seedier corners, away from June's constant drizzle, we found the bar we were looking for. Through an unassuming warehouse door and up a narrow set of stairs, we followed where the noise led.

The place Isaac had picked to celebrate his birthday was a moody wine bar, so dim it was practically candlelit. Smooth floors were rendered cosy with several overlaid plush Persian rugs, and clusters of overstuffed leather armchairs around spindly tables dotted around the room. The twilit city sparkled beyond the iron-framed windows, and the terrace stood empty as the night's chill set in.

Inoffensive and uninspired jazz played overhead, some pre-made Spotify playlist with neither personality nor nuance, but hey — I was a dive bar girl in wine bar territory. I felt too broke to be here, ostensibly paycheque-to-paycheque, but Claud and her understated thousand-dollar outfit fitted right in. I was in their country now.

The back corner had been cordoned off with a wanky velvet rope and a printed sign that read, *'PRIVATE EVENT — ABRAMS 30th'*. Isaac was over there now, nursing a highball glass and talking to a trio of suits. I caught his eye and he winked without breaking the flow of his conversation.

'Here we go,' murmured Claud with a bracing smile as we headed towards the golden backlit bar furnished with more types of liquor than I even knew existed.

I knew her before I *knew* I knew her. Even with no prior awareness of her appearance — seriously, Isaac's lack of social media was both sexy and a real liability — even with her back to us as she chatted animatedly with the waistcoated bartender confidently pouring her French 75, I knew it was Tash. Maybe it was the curtain of creamy white-gold hair hanging down her back — another Hitchcock blonde notch on Isaac's bedpost — or the tinkling laugh that cut through the saxophone and sounded like the diametric opposite of my goose's honk of a guffaw. Claud knew it too and squeezed my hand for support.

'Hey,' said Claud to another bartender further down, knowing instinctively to put as much distance between Tash and me as possible. 'Can we get a couple of sparklings?'

As he turned to find a bottle and glasses, she grabbed my arm to make me face her, forcing my back to the room so she could play lookout for me.

'So!' she said. 'Hey!'

'Hey!' I cried, playing along. 'Night for it.'

'Oh wow,' she cooed. 'You're *so* interesting. Who's the prettiest girl in the world?'

I laughed and covered my face, but she didn't let up. I wished there was a way I could have expressed to her, without making a scene, how much I loved her.

'You've got hair like a caramel milkshake and legs like a racehorse,' she continued. 'The way you keep my plants alive is — god, frankly, I don't know how you do it. Are you a witch?'

'I am, *but* —' I said, gratefully accepting my coupe from the bartender and clinking it against hers '— do you want to know the magic? I *water* them.'

'Did you know we get a water bill?' she asked. 'We have to pay for water. I had no idea. We're like eight months overdue.'

'That's barbaric,' I said. 'Wasn't there a Tom Hardy movie about this?'

'Oh, I love Tom Hardy.'

'Of course you do. You have two eyes and a vagina, don't you?'

'Whoops,' said Tash, who appeared beside us in a cloud of Baccarat Rouge and the unmistakable air of honest-to-god niceness. 'Did I interrupt a private moment?'

'No,' said Claud lightly. 'We say vagina all the time.'

'I think one of you is Marnie,' she said, grinning as she eyed us both and finally pointing a playful finger at me. She had such shiny white teeth. I ran my tongue over my own from behind closed lips, comparing every slightly uneven edge. 'I think it's you.'

'Don't *I* look like a Marnie?' asked Claud, pretending to be offended. 'Brilliant and hilarious and a supermodel walking among mere mortals?'

'I'm Marnie,' I said. I tried to return her grin, but I felt thin-lipped and fake. 'This is Claud. She's my personal cheerleader.'

'There are pom-poms in my bag,' said Claud. 'Want to check?'

'You two are fun, aren't you?' said Tash with a splash of perky suspicion. 'I assumed that about you, Marnie, but it's good to know I was right.'

'Sometimes *too* much fun,' Claud replied. 'More fun than even we can handle.'

'We can't make it through a day without dancing on the furniture,' I added. 'Got a karaoke machine? We'll fuck shit up.'

Gosh. Up close she was really something else. Had she never had a pimple in her life? Was there some new treatment that allowed you to install warm lights *under* your skin? I'd always used my eyes as a fallback source of pride when I otherwise felt unattractive, but hers were bigger and bluer and brighter still.

I searched for a single flaw: an uneven eyebrow, a smudge

where her contour hadn't been fully blended out, even earlobes that drooped under the weight of her simple silver drop earrings, but nope, nothing. She was perfect. She didn't even have the decency to be unpleasant.

If I thought about it, it wasn't that surprising. She was exactly the kind of girl that someone like Isaac would be with: sparkly, blonde and pocket-sized. I would bet my life that she had never woken up still drunk with a half-eaten burger on her passenger-side pillow.

She didn't know what to make of us, like we were a joke she wanted to get in on. She looked like the embodiment of every insecurity I never knew I had.

'I'm Tash,' she said when we failed to enquire, and then a beat later, added, 'Ike's other half.'

'Oh wow, hi!' said Claud, doing a good impression of being delighted to meet her. 'You aren't at all what I pictured.'

God, she was good.

'Oh — I — thanks ...' replied Tash, her pristine smile holding strong through her confusion. 'Anyhoo, just wanted to say hi. Hi!'

'Hi!' I repeated.

'I've so looked forward to meeting you,' she said, reaching out to give my arm an overfamiliar squeeze. 'I'm going to be in a tizz all night keeping everyone's drinks topped up and keeping his dad away from the red wine —' she rolled her eyes good naturedly like I knew what she was talking about '— but you girls have so much fun, and Marnie, let's you and I grab lunch soon, okay? Ike's talked you up so much; I have to know everything about you.'

She left to greet the newest arrivals, and as soon as the coast was clear, my smile dropped and I turned to the bartender. 'Can we get those bubbles by the bottle?'

Claud was nodding before I'd even finished talking. 'Yeah, we're going to need a bottle.'

We mingled precisely as much as we had to. Isaac and Tash were friends with people like themselves: corporate southsiders, bloated bankers, people whose hair appointments cost as much as my rent. I felt like a child with Vegemite smeared on their face: grubby and tolerated.

Claud abandoned me for the bathroom, and I made it through ten whole minutes of conversation with one of Isaac's friends. Dev didn't mind that I knew nothing about NFTs, nor that I hadn't wanted to learn. He talked at me — not to me — about their place in the digital economy and the oncoming crypto-cultural revolution they represented, long after my eyes glazed over.

Isaac floated nearby, but never close enough to latch on to. Something about how Tash would breeze by — occasionally touching his arm in a way that was affectionate without seeming possessive — set my teeth on edge.

'Aren't they really bad for the environment, though?' I heard myself ask Dev. 'Aren't the carbon emissions from running the servers out of control, or something?'

'Well, everything has its cost,' he said indifferently. 'Who's to say that the economic benefit of cryptocurrency doesn't outweigh the environmental drawbacks?'

I didn't know anything about this. I couldn't explain the economy to you with a knife at my throat. I didn't know if this man — who could wank to the sound of his own voice, whose socks were woven with cartoon tacos, who was drinking his beer out of a glass — had any idea what he was talking about, either, but I knew I didn't care.

'I have to ...' I cast around the room again, and found the

back of Claud's head bobbing somewhere around the terrace doors '… go. Bye.'

Finally. I dragged her outside to be antisocial together. She was still nursing her first drink, but I'd left my glass somewhere inside and resorted to covert swigs straight from the bottle.

'She's *so* chic,' I whispered to Claud, tugging at my sleeve. I was fixated. I couldn't help it.

My outfit — a close-fitting knit dress from Reformation that I completely couldn't afford, long boots and a web of delicate necklaces I'd be untangling for weeks to come — was carefully planned so as to appear effortlessly sexy yet completely casual, but I now felt unimaginative and lazy.

In this labyrinth of glossy strangers, I felt scrappy.

In the shadow of someone I'd been unconsciously competing with for months, watching her chat animatedly with all the people she already knew, the tasteful drape of her backless black chiffon, I envied everything about her, and I hated myself for it.

'Is she chic, or is she just rich?'

'Ugh, I bet she's smart, too,' I continued, squinting through the glass at her. 'That's unfair. To be gorgeous and capable of forming a coherent thought. That's cosmically unjust.'

'I hear internalised misogyny,' said Claud as her phone buzzed. 'You're pretty and you're smart.'

'But I'm cute; I'm not *gorgeous*.'

I waited for Claud to argue, but she was frowning down at her screen. Her thumbs began to tap out a reply, her mouth forming the shape of the words as she wrote them. I waited a minute, and then another. She, apparently, was writing her manifesto in my moment of petty envy and self-flagellation.

'Excuse me, young lady,' I said, tapping the neck of the bottle against the edge of her phone. 'I just said *I'm not gorgeous*. This is where you rant about how wrong I am.'

'What?' She spared me a brief glance, barely a blink before her attention was lost again. 'Sorry, yeah. You're wrong.'

'Still Jesse?'

'Mm. What?' she sighed and put her phone away at last. 'There, sent. Sorry. Who's wrong?'

'What's the matter?'

'We're in a — a tiff,' she said, pursing her lips in a way that I knew meant she was biting back what she wanted to say.

'Why?'

'It's just something his mum said,' she sighed. I offered her the bottle in support, and she shook her head. 'We had lunch last week, and she —'

'You met his mum?' I asked. 'Why didn't you tell me?'

I heard myself doing it, pulling the conversation away from her and onto me, adding my needs onto her full plate, but I couldn't stop myself. It used to be that she talked me through every piece of punctuation in Jesse's texts. She'd waited until he'd gone to the gym one morning to video call me and walk me through his apartment, poking through his medicine cabinet, showing me how his Nespresso machine worked, naming his houseplants. If sending nudes was still in style, I'd know where his birthmark was. To think that she once came undone over an elongated pause between texts but hadn't needed to mention having met the milestone of meeting Jesse's family made it seem like the floor had moved underneath me.

Claud seemed to clock this, and her eyebrows tilted with an apology. 'It's just been such a hectic few weeks,' she said. I nodded because there was nothing else to do. 'Anyway ...'

'Anyway,' I replied, encouraging her.

'I thought it went great. I know I'm *a lot*, but I'm the kind of girl mums would like, right?'

'Absolutely!' I said fiercely. 'You're cute as a button and you look like you've never been in a bar fight in your life.'

She nodded. 'That's all she knows. Anyway, this morning he tells me she thought I was very sweet, but *did he think I was a bit old?*'

I paused. 'What?'

'Uh huh.'

'A bit old for what?' I asked, screwing my face up. 'To convincingly play a teenager on television?'

'He kept saying it like a joke, but I wouldn't let it go because — well, I'm into self-harm, apparently — but eventually he came out and said maybe I *am* getting a bit old to wait to have kids.'

'You're twenty-nine.'

'*I know.*'

'We are literal infants. We're practically still in utero.'

'She said if he's serious about me then he'd better *get serious* about me. Like I'm only an effing grandchild factory to her,' she sighed in apparent defeat. If ever a time called for the word *fuck*, it was being told that your boyfriend's mother thought you had a basket full of rotten eggs.

I paused and then asked, 'Why did he tell you this?'

She looked up. 'What?'

'She's obviously insane, and she can scheme to harvest your eggs all she wants, but why did you need to know about it?'

'I asked him for her review,' she said with a one-shouldered shrug. 'He answered.'

'But he could have just said the first bit, that she thought you were sweet, and left off the rest of it. Why would he tell you something like that? Were you supposed to find it funny? And why didn't he tell her to keep her mouth shut?'

Claud looked pained and exhausted, her face falling further the longer she looked at my hardened expression. 'It's not his fault.'

'It's not his fault his mother is nuts, but it's his fault you're out here feeling like you're past your expiration date.'

She flipped her palm up and down as if to say she could see both sides of the argument. 'If I think about the plan I used to have for myself, when I was nineteen and had the luxury of optimism, I *did* think I'd have a kid by now. Where did all that time go? I'm turning thirty soon.'

I put the bottle down heavily, no longer interested in drinking, too focussed on the growing rage I had to feel because she refused to. 'If you want to have a baby, Claud, have a baby. But she — *he* — shouldn't be making you feel like there's something wrong with you if you haven't gotten around to it yet.'

'I told him this!' she cried out in frustration. 'Of course I did! That's what we're arguing about! I do have a backbone. I had one before I met you.'

'Then why aren't you using it?' I asked, my pitch rising to meet hers. 'Why aren't you telling him to fuck off and find another incubator? Why do you put up with this?'

'I'm here, aren't I?' she snapped. 'You asked me to be here, so I'm here. I got dressed, I put on heels, I aged another twenty-nine years on a tram ride all the way out here because you asked me to. I'm here to support you, so why is it so hard for you to support me?'

'I *am* supporting you,' I insisted. 'One of us has to give a shit about you because you've obviously forgotten how to.'

Claud stepped backwards. 'Wow.'

'I just mean —'

'No, I got it.'

'No, you don't,' I argued. 'I'm so worried about you, you don't even know. It keeps me up at night. "*What is she doing? Is she taking care of herself? Is he being nice to her?*" You're not even yourself. You don't drink — since when don't you drink? You won't even swear. You don't have fun anymore. It's like you're disappearing and I'm the only person left to bring you back.'

'Well, no one asked you to!' she spat. 'That's not your job! I'm *not* an infant. I'm *not* in utero. I'm trying to make an adult decision and you're trying to drag me down into your second adolescence.'

I hugged my arms and didn't speak.

'You know what I think?' she continued, sensing my sore spot and going in for the kill. 'I think you feel out of control of your own life, and you're scrambling for the puppet strings of someone else's.'

'I don't want to control your life, Claud,' I said quietly. 'I just don't want you to get hurt.'

'Well it's my hurt! It's mine! Just back off!'

I shook my head in bitter disbelief. There was no talking her around from this. We looked at each other, fury and frustration, both too proud and too convinced of our own arguments to concede.

'Look, I'm going to go,' she said eventually. This wasn't defeat, but worse: resignation. 'You have a great night, ah —' she looked over her shoulder through the windows, back at the crowded room, full of all the many people who loved Isaac, giving it a wide and unimpressed glance '— coming second.'

CHAPTER TWENTY-FOUR

Back to the bar. A whisky ginger please, to take me back to better times. Hell, another, if the tab was still open. Dev asked if I wanted a shot of Fireball, and I thought — *why not?* I loathed the taste, but its burn would defrost my insides, and the peat and smoke and sugar was strong enough to wash the sour flavour of conflict out of my mouth.

The music had gone from New York jazz bar to throbbing warehouse party in the time it took for Claud's and my bond to crumble, and the deafening pulse of a late-night playlist was easier to listen to than the thoughts inside my head.

Here was the secret to navigating a party alone: obliterate yourself. I was *so* charming when I wasn't myself. Boundaries: never heard of 'em. I was talking to someone — I didn't know who, it didn't matter — about something — I didn't know what, it didn't matter — and I only realised at the end of my long, long tangent that I was giving a stranger an enthusiastic review of my vibrator.

'Uh huh,' she said, looking panicked as she backed away. 'I'm just going to —'

Well, that was silly. Whoops. Still. It was a public service. She would thank me tomorrow as her hangover ebbed and her curiosity piqued. Wasn't it funny how sometimes being horny felt like needing to — oh, no, I really did need to pee.

What kind of bar only had two individual toilets? Were we in communist Russia? Had I told anyone about my *Putin-is-Rasputin* theory yet? I hadn't thought about that in months. Not since Claud and I had joked about it all the way back before her first date with Jesse. *Jesse.*

I rested my forehead against the cool brick of the hallway, waiting ever so patiently for the people in the ladies' to finish doing their lines. Habit or desperation, I fished my phone out. Winking one eye shut to focus on the blurring letters, I found @Stevo-0288's profile and tapped out a surprisingly coherent message.

@marniemarniemarnie: Wanna come tto mine for some funny business tonight?
@marniemarniemarnie: Extra funny 😉😉😉😉😉

I hadn't seen that guy in weeks, or maybe it was months. He sent a fire emoji at every photo of myself I posted, and I left all his '*Heyyy*'s unanswered. Only when my validation stores were running critically low did I deign to respond. I'd half-heartedly sexted him once or twice. When he begged, I'd send him pouty, cleavagey selfies I'd taken years ago, knowing he couldn't tell the difference. I'd tell him I was touching myself when I was actually pumicing my heels. He loved it, and I loved having attention on tap again.

'There's trouble,' said a voice behind me; the only one I wanted to hear. I needed the support of the wall to turn myself over to look at him.

'That's my middle name, baby,' I said, shooting him with finger guns.

'Are you having fun?' he asked, reaching out to steady me as I stumbled on my heel. I looked down at my outfit, strategically chosen and bought on credit. The short dress and the long, long, long boots, the sliver of exposed skin on my thighs to make him imagine himself between them.

'A little too much fun,' I said, with a coy look like I'd been caught doing something bad.

The room was spinning, but he was remarkably still. I'd never met an open bar I didn't take as a personal challenge, but here he was, bright-eyed and self-contained. *Boring*, I thought. *Who ever got into trouble sober?*

'I'm glad,' he said.

What was going on? Where were the crass quips, the flirtatious insults, the private jokes? It was like he'd forgotten who I was; like he couldn't quite place me but couldn't say so for fear of looking impolite.

'So,' I said, sucking in a breath in an attempt to look and act more sober than I felt. 'That's Tash.'

'That's Tash.' He nodded, craning his neck past the doorway to see if he could spot her in the crowd. 'In the flesh.'

'She's ... really something.'

His knowing look cut through my bullshit like a knife. He tilted his head and a lone strand of hair fell from its place and into his eyes. The rebellious little thing. 'She's pretty wonderful,' he said, finally. 'She's been excited to meet you.'

'Oh, she adores me,' I replied sardonically. 'She wants to know everything about me.'

'C'mon,' he said. 'You had to know she'd be interested. She knows how much we talk.'

To avoid answering, I reached up to tuck his hair back into place.

'Where did your mascot go?' he asked, letting me. 'I thought you two came in a set.'

I shrugged and hoped I hid the resentment in it. 'Got a better offer.'

'Sorry to hear. I know you don't really know anyone here, so it's cool if you —'

'I know you,' I said easily, dropping a hand on his shoulder. Bony despite its breadth. I saw myself squeeze it against my better judgment. 'That's someone.'

Isaac smiled, patted my hand and removed it smoothly. Oh. Ouch. 'I'm pretty popular round here tonight. It's my birthday, see.'

'I know!' I cried. 'Happy *birth*day! You don't look a day over forty-five.'

He laughed as he rolled his eyes, and I felt the knot in my stomach loosen ever so slightly. There he was, and here I was: he recognised me, so I knew I'd found the right Marnie to step into. I took a step towards him under the guise of adjusting my balance, and I could feel the fabric of his pants against my leg.

He cleared his throat. 'Hey, I'd better get back.'

'Uh huh,' I said. 'Back to *Tash*.'

'She organised a lot of this,' he explained, rubbing the back of his neck in a bashfulness I knew he didn't feel. 'I can't leave her out there to fend for herself.'

'Oh, I'm sure she's the perfect host,' I replied. I ran my fingers through my hair and fluffed it for effect. *Look how unbothered I am*, it said. *Look how much of a fuck I give about hosting.* 'Perfect host, perfect girl.'

Isaac frowned. He stood straight and watched me like I was a riddle, and not for the first time all night, I wondered if I'd gone too far.

'She loves you, that's all I meant,' I said, using all my false indifference to paper over my mistake. 'She wants your night to be perfect.'

'I love her,' he said.

I smiled because there was nothing else I could do. He said he'd see me later, but I had to get out of there. I had to be anywhere else, be anyone else, be with anyone else. I pushed through clustered bodies and made for the stairs. Fuck my coat. It was polyester and pilling at the armpit and it wasn't worth the indignity stumbling around the room looking for the chair I'd left it hanging on while the party stared at the desperate, pathetic girl who'd thrown herself at someone who didn't want her.

There. Oxygen. I gasped for the cold night air, declining to care about the gaggle of foetuses in Shein dresses who made fun of me as they passed on the way to some neon-lit club.

I had caught myself getting into a bad place, somewhere more toxic than a mere grey area. This was somewhere I would live in wait, counting the minutes until Isaac would realise he didn't want to be with her, and he'd come screeching up to me on his motorcycle — he had a motorcycle in this fantasy, and a buttery-soft leather jacket and a good spritz of Tobacco Vanille by Tom Ford, *mmm* — profess his love for me, and we'd ride off into the sunset, in search of a good cocktail bar and a pair of Shiba Inu. I let out a screech of frustration at myself, and the drunk babies burst out laughing, and I was too angry at myself to bother being angry at them.

I'd travelled too far down the path of what-if and was reduced, now, to technicolour longing. Every time I picked up my phone and there wasn't a waiting message from him, I felt lost. I'd started wondering what he was doing with all the hours in his day. I'd stopped fantasising purely about the feeling of his hands on my skin and had let sugar-coated ideas of mundane routines slip in. Groceries. Sunday morning sleep-ins. The long, quiet drive home from an evening with my family. The sight of his rings on my bathroom sink. I was living in open defiance of my own rules. I was a hypocrite in every breath. *Relationships never work!* I shouted at myself, then turned to the side, cupped my hands around my mouth and whispered to no one, *but this one would.*

I'd given up the game. And worse still, he'd responded. He didn't need to say it for me to hear him loud and clear: the ringing subtext, the silent counterweight. '*I love her.*' I could read his voice well enough to know that *her* meant *not you*.

It all hit me at once, the pregame and the swaying tram and the bottle of sparkling and the fight and the whisky and the whisky and the whisky and the realisation that I'd asked for what I wanted and had finally, plainly, definitively heard a clear and clanging *no*, and it was all too much for my brain and body to take, and so I just didn't.

I floated somewhere apart from my consciousness, aware of my limbs but too detached to care where they went, as though reality was a television show I was only half-watching. I had to hold people's shoulders for balance as I navigated my way down the street in search of a tram to catch or throw myself in front of, and I felt nothing when they shrugged me off in annoyance or revulsion.

As I ventured back into the night, it had all deteriorated further. Every bar and club was full and spilling out onto the street, music blasting, competing with each other, the people waiting to get inside in less of a queue and more of a mosh pit of thirsty, blurry bodies.

And I still needed to pee.

Time warped and I lost track of it. I didn't know if I had joined a line or found a bar without one, or where I was, or if this was even the ladies' toilet, but I went, and it was glorious, and the lock on the door was broken so I had to hold it shut with my outstretched leg, requiring some purposeful angling, but it got the job done, and now I just needed to get home.

Home, home, home. Empty home.

Oh! Firefighter guy!

Despite the angry knocking on the toilet door, I kept my foot pressed against it and found my phone, and it only took four tries to get my password right.

No notifications. That was odd. Or was it? Sometimes my apps ate them. I pulled up Instagram, tapped open my conversations, but there was nothing there. The last message I had there was an endless thread with Claud, mostly the raccoon videos I sent her on a near-daily basis. (It was my love language, okay?) But where was firefighter guy? Where was @Stevo-0288?

I rerouted to my search history, but when I tapped his name, nothing came up. I couldn't even find him.

'Give me a MINUTE!' I shouted at the fist hammering on my door, kicking it shut again for catharsis as I reeled through all the possible explanations of how I could have sent the perfect cute-slash-crude sex invitation and not only receive nothing in response but get *blocked*.

Did he see my message and get so excited that he had a heart attack and died? And his housemates — if he had them — honoured his dying wish to have all his social media permanently deleted so no one could make those tragic memorial pages out of them? That had to be it. Because the only alternative was that I'd been ...

Ghosted. By the firefighter. How mortifying. Not even a polite refusal or a deflection to catch up another time. He had been presented with the option to come over and work through a value pack of condoms until daybreak, and thought '*Nah*' — actually, worse: '*NO THANKS cannot adequately convey my disinterest. I must make sure this woman can never contact me again.*'

I would have to go home, humiliated, rejected and sweaty, and I'd have to tap on every one of my molars to double check that I didn't have an emergency cyanide capsule soldered to one of them.

I'd have to pull the smoke detector off the ceiling and take it to bed with me so I would definitely hear it go off, so sure was I that the universe's vendetta against me could result in my hair straightener crawling out of the cupboard, plugging itself in, overheating and setting my towels on fire. My whole house would be engulfed in thick black smoke and my neighbours would call 000 while I lay unconscious, mouth slack to better amplify my snoring. Then the firefighter and his team of heroes would arrive in the fire truck — a red, huge metaphor for his penis, per the midnight message I received on Monday — and he would be sent into the embrace of the hot hungry flames to rescue me, and he would find me in my full-length flannelette Hello Kitty pyjamas, unflatteringly braless, clutching my phone with it open to our conversation that I'd been staring at for hours as I waited for his ellipsis to appear, and he would think, *bullet dodged.*

Wait a minute! I thought.

Who do you think you are, firefighter?

You are thirty-four years old!

Barrelling towards middle age with a velocity comparable only to the recession of your hairline!

Why!

Are you!

Ghosting!

Anyone!

As I sat there, my best underwear around my knees — honestly, Marnie, you tragic idiot, did you think he was going to fuck you at the birthday party his girlfriend threw him?

What is *wrong* with you? — roasting in shame and drowning in a supercut of a single night's humiliations, I thought fleetingly, longingly of Eddie, and how much simpler life and emotions and sex had been when I was with him. Before I knew better. Before I wanted anything else at all.

I pulled my knickers up, shoved past the bursting, waiting girls, dipped my hands in icy cold water in the grimy basin and tore out of there. I could see a sliver of the night sky beyond the throbbing dance floor and I flung myself in its direction.

A hand landed on my wrist and wrapped around it, and before I could jerk my arm away, the grabber's face appeared, and for the first time in what felt like hours, or years, or in my entire goddamn life, I felt relief.

'Sam!' I cried, but it came out silent against the pulse of the music. He pushed his hair out of his face with his free hand, beaming at me with the wide grin and slack eyes of someone who was at least as drunk as I was.

Sam mouthed something at me. I frowned and pointed at my ears to tell him I hadn't caught it, so he pulled me in, pressed his mouth to my ear, and shouted, 'FANCY SEEING YOU HERE.'

'I KNOW,' I replied. I stumbled on my heel, using a hand on his chest to steady myself. Huh. Surprisingly firm. Was his half-buttoned Hawaiian shirt an attempt at irony, or did he dress like a dad at a barbecue on his days off?

'DO YOU WANT A DRINK?'

My hair whipped around me as I shook my head violently. 'NO MORE DRINK.'

'THEN WE'LL DANCE.'

It wasn't a question. He took my hand from his chest and led me into the sea of writhing bodies. Density limits were a distant memory, even as we stepped over the blue and white fragments of forgotten disposable face masks stuck to the floor.

I didn't have to think about anything else, or maybe I simply couldn't. It was too loud, and too hot, and too blurry, and too much everything all at once to do anything but give in.

I didn't know what kind of dancer I thought Sam would be. The only time I ever saw him interact with music was when he bobbed his head along to the incomprehensible scream of whatever metal band he played in the kitchen, and the bone-rattling throb of late-night house music in here didn't exactly align with that scene. Would he navigate the dance floor with his crotch, I wondered, thrusting around and calling it rhythm? Or maybe his moves would be stuck in puberty, mortified by life and content to sway from foot to foot, always a beat out of time.

My brain was sluggish, utterly useless to come up with an excuse to leave and spare myself the second-hand embarrassment. I was having a hard time blinking, like my mascara had turned to glue and I had to wrench my eyelashes apart, and maybe it was time to go home.

But then he started to dance, and I was rooted in place. My eyebrows shot up in surprise, like I'd been woken up and doused with cold water. Sam was all shoulders and hips, cutting space around us with exaggerated steps and swishes straight out of a bad '70s montage.

Partway through a surprisingly smooth rendition of the running man move, his mouth moved in the shape of something like, '*COME ON!*' and I started to laugh in earnest. You couldn't make fun of someone who was making fun of themselves. So when he mimed throwing a lasso through the air, I was helpless but to let myself get caught in it and spin — haphazardly — in tight circles as he pulled me in.

It was so good to just be *silly* with someone and let go of any sense of dignity I might once have had. It was nice to not have to censor my ugly laugh, or care if I looked like a dickhead, because I knew Sam, and I didn't particularly care about his opinion. This wasn't a transaction. He liked me. He really, really liked me, he said so all the time, no matter how deep the bags under my eyes were at 6 am, or how rude I was to him any time of day. It was so easy, so freeing, such a *relief* to undo the knot in my stomach, that when he twirled me around and dropped me into a low, Hollywood dip, I looped my arm around his neck and kissed him right on the mouth.

CHAPTER TWENTY-FIVE

This was so much better than thinking. Thinking had only ever twisted me into knots and dragged me into unforgiving situations, severed my friendships, and ruined my life. Thinking wouldn't fix anything. You know what would? A body. And Sam's was warm and soft, and most importantly it was here.

Words came out of my mouth of their own accord, sloppy and jumbled and forgotten again in a blink, but whatever I'd said, it led us out of the hot, red, suffocating bar and into the backseat of a taxi. The driver scolded us as I lay flat against the seat and clung to Sam on top of me, but we wouldn't be the messiest fare he picked up all night, and anyway, this was too important.

Kissing was good. I'd missed kissing. The taste of someone's boilermaker mouth and my fingers in his hair, the delighted sound he made against me. Maybe the drive took hours or minutes, I didn't know, couldn't think, didn't want to.

There was a doorway, and Sam dropped his keys and picked them up again, unlocked the door successfully while I bit at his neck, and led me unsteadily up a flight of stairs, two, three, gosh, too many. The concrete hallway was cold and loud, and I felt the textured brick pull at the threads of my dress as he pressed me up against them to keep kissing, meaning I couldn't return it; the most expensive hookup in history.

But then there was a door, and we were going through it, and he flipped on the lights, and he pressed his mouth to the shell of my ear and asked if I wanted a drink, and I nodded as I idled in the entryway.

I'd never spared a thought for the way Sam might have lived when he wasn't in the Little George kitchen, but the living room of his flat seemed pretty accurate.

It was clean but cluttered: furniture made from wood pallets and handed down from share house to share house ad infinitum, curling edges of movie posters betraying a Blu Tack stain on the greying white walls, a shabby kitchen straight out of the '80s with exposed shelving crammed ceiling-high with every appliance, pan, spice and utensil known to man. Sam chose function over taste: there were no rugs, no lamps, no candles or trinkets to give the place warmth, no throw cushions or curtains, but there was — oh, why were my ankles warm?

'*Hi!*' I cried as I looked down and found a fat grey cat rubbing himself against my boots. 'Hi baby!'

I leaned down to scoop him up and pressed my face to his pillowy ginger fur, squeezing him as tight as he'd let me.

'I must've left my window open again,' Sam called over his shoulder as he glugged some unknown clear spirit and cloudy apple juice into a jam jar. 'He's not mine. I don't know whose he is, actually. I think he's just the building's cat. He's a vagabond.'

'I love him,' I whined into his cheek. 'I love love love love a handsome boy, so handsome so handsome so —'

'C'mon Kenzo, get outta here,' he said, giving the cat a gentle prod. He then looped both arms around me even as he held two jam jars full of emergency cocktails in his hands, nuzzling into my neck.

Kenzo shot off at the invasion, and I felt as empty as my arms were. Numb, I took a jar out of Sam's hands and drained it.

'Woah there, slow d—' I took the other one and drained that too, and with renewed courage and desperation, twisted around in his hold and pressed my mouth to his again.

I walked us backwards until his legs hit the couch, and then I was in his lap, and I was pulling off my dress. It was easier to dissociate with my eyes closed.

He wasn't the one I wanted, but he was the one I had, and that had to be good enough.

I was blindly working on the buttons of his stupid loud shirt when he paused for breath and asked, 'Why — are you crying?'

'Don't worry about it,' I replied, and pressed back into him.

His hands snaked up to my shoulders and created space between us, but I fought to close it again.

'What's the matter?' he asked. The low voice he'd been using was gone, replaced with a concern so genuine it made me queasy.

'I said it's fine, come back.'

This bubble wasn't allowed to burst. I wouldn't let it. I would not go back out there into cold reality. I refused. I redoubled my efforts, abandoning his shirt buttons for the waistband of his jeans, but he grabbed my wrist before I could do more than slip my hand down.

'Maybe we shouldn't.'

'This is what you want, so let's just do it,' I replied, throat sore in the grip of annoyance. 'What's the problem? Just come *on*, it's fine — *it's fine.*'

'You're upset,' he said. 'And you're really drunk, and I just don't think it's a great time? For us to hook up?'

'Are you serious right now?' I sat back, humiliated again, feeling ridiculous in my lingerie and boots, in his lap, in his crappy apartment, in the middle of the worst night of my life, and watched his face drift in and out of focus. I didn't want to cry anymore. I wanted to scream.

'Maybe we can do this another time,' he said. He reached out to put a gentle hand on my waist, but I slapped it away.

'Don't touch me.'

As I clambered off him, my foot slipped, and I kicked his coffee table and sent it skidding across the scuffed laminate floor. Our empty glasses slid off and smashed into a million pieces.

'You're pathetic, you know that?' I spat, scrambling for my dress and wrenching it over my head. 'You follow me around like a puppy for *years*, but the second you get me naked, you're not interested.'

I cast around for my bag. Where was it? Had I left it in the taxi? At the bar? At the party?

'God!' I cried. 'I'm so sick of it! Of you! Men! You! You're all bullshit!'

'Marnie, please — calm down.'

'Don't tell me to calm down!' I shrieked, and he looked panicked as he cast around the room, as though an onlooker would appear at his fourth-floor window. I didn't care if his neighbours heard. I hoped they would. 'Don't tell me what to do! You don't even know me! You're a —'

'Let's just talk about this.'

'— self-important prick — *using* me for your own amusement — slimy, arrogant fucking — treating me like a — a —'

Aha! My bag was hanging on the door handle. How had it got there?

'Don't go — please — just stay, I'll sleep on the couch — I don't think you should be on your own tonight.'

'Go FUCK yourself!' I shouted, slinging my bag over my shoulder and wrenching the door open. 'Jump off a bridge, do whatever the hell you want, just leave me alone forever.'

The door slammed behind me. I flew down the stairs, two or three at a time, risking a broken neck with every unsteady leap I made in the plight towards freedom and safety.

This wasn't happening. This *hadn't* happened. Not after everything else. When was enough *enough*? I'd already hit rock bottom tonight: I crashed into it when something I said — whatever it was, I couldn't remember — caused Isaac's eyes to drop, when they lost their sparkle and he saw who I really was. But this, now, losing Sam's good opinion ... that wasn't rock bottom. That was the nadir. That was the water table that flowed beneath rock bottom; it was the molten lava that surged and bubbled even lower still.

I hugged my arms as I made for the street. I had no idea where I was, how far away home could be, or how I was going to get there. Before I could find my way to a main road or steady my fingers long enough to unlock my phone and call for a taxi, I paused and gripped someone's fencepost, swayed on the spot for a moment, and puked up my black toxic insides all over their rosebush.

CHAPTER TWENTY-SIX

Claud wasn't home when I got back somewhere near dawn. She wasn't there when I woke briefly in the afternoon, dry-mouthed, fragile and still queasy, nor that evening as I was lulled back to sleep by the rhythmic yelp of my neighbour's three-hour orgasm. When I checked the following morning, Claud's toothbrush was dry.

> **Marnie Fowler (05:45):** I did the dumbest thing
> **Marnie Fowler (05:45):** Come home tonight and laugh at me ♥

I sat on the edge of my tram seat and waited for her read receipt. It was usually immediate. Claud was always glued to her phone, either for work or because Jesse expected a prompt response to a text any time of day or night. If she wasn't reading her messages, it could only be because she was with him and still angry with me.

Was that really only a day and a half ago? How many crises had been crammed into just a few hours? A spat with Claud that spiralled out of control. The entirely predictable but no less painful dismissal from Isaac; my irrefutable demotion. My complete breach of the boundaries between work life and sex life, just another thing to manage.

I tried again.

Marnie Fowler (06:01): Sorry everything got a bit out of control the other night
Marnie Fowler (06:01): Are you okay?
Marnie Fowler (06:02): Are WE okay?

She saw it immediately; I knew she'd be up this early, swishing mouthwash and dotting concealer under her eyes so she could tiptoe back to bed beside Jesse and wake up looking fresh and perfect.

An ellipsis appeared then disappeared. There it was again. I stared at it for two full minutes as the tram passed the museum and eased left onto Exhibition Street, watched as I pulled the cord to request my stop, as I hopped down the steps and made my way to work. Then it disappeared completely, and she went offline. No response, but a message received. A cold shoulder on a cold morning, ice in my stomach and aching fingertips around my phone.

Our disagreements usually resolved over a crass joke and the trust that our friendship was more important than any mindless tiff. I took the connection for granted. We weren't sisters.

I strained my memory to recall the argument. I'd lost most of it by now, retaining little more than the look on her face. I remembered that I had pushed her too far. I remembered the titbits I knew of the flimsiness of the human brain, and how often it showed you only what you were looking for, filtering out anything that didn't serve your argument.

I was never drinking again.

I'd never cared about my job less. I got five orders wrong before 7:30 am, forgot to charge someone for their pain au chocolat, spilled scrambled eggs in someone else's lap, and scalded my wrist under the hot water tap so badly that it glowed red a full hour later.

'Morning,' said Sam tentatively from the kitchen doorway in the lull between the corporate set's pre-work caffeine hits and their morning-meeting pick-me-ups. 'Any chance I could grab a long black?'

From my permanent position behind the coffee machine, which sensed my burning apathy and had behaved perfectly all morning, I replied without looking up. 'Nope.'

'C'mon Marnie,' he said pleadingly. 'We don't have to make it —'

'I just don't think it's a great time? For coffee?' I said, voice dripping in sickly sarcasm. When I looked around at him, every line on my face full of contempt, he was hangdogged and embarrassed. 'Maybe you could have coffee another time? When you're less ... of a dickhead?'

'Uh,' said Kit, pausing in the process of reorganising the muffin tower. 'What's going on?'

'Nothing,' said Sam at once.

'I can make you a coffee,' said Kit, nonplussed.

'No you can't,' I argued, throwing my arm out to block Kit's access to the coffee grinder as he made for it. 'He can drink 7-Eleven coffee for all I care.'

'Um, right, but —'

'I quite like 7-Eleven coffee, actually,' snapped Sam. It was the first time that he had ever bitten back.

We'd drawn customers' attention by now, all three of our occupied tables, their conversations paused to witness this interdepartmental breakdown. Breakfast and a show.

'7-Eleven coffee isn't a moody bitch all the time, but sure, *I'm* the one who needs to apologise for doing the right thing.

7-Eleven coffee wasn't four seconds away from being admitted to hospital with alcohol poisoning and didn't want me to solve all her problems with my penis.'

'Okay!' shouted Kit in a panic, holding up his hands between us to play umpire.

'Well I'm sorry if the natural response to being *harassed* for two years isn't to get on my knees and suck y—'

'ENOUGH!'

We both fell silent. It was only a small restaurant, and Kit's unpractised dad voice rang out sharp and rough.

'Sam — go back to work.'

Aware of his rank, Sam retreated through the kitchen door, and I heard steel slam on steel as he threw something in the sink in his tantrum.

I stood frozen on the spot, with hot dread rising through my body so rapidly I thought it might spill out of my ears. What had I just done?

'Listen,' I said meekly, although I knew there was no squeaky little girl voice that could manipulate Kit. 'I'm sorry — I'm so sorry — I'll pay for everyone's meals. I'm sorry,' I called to the traumatised customers, 'I'll pay for your breakfasts, order whatever you want, please, I'm —'

'Marnie.' Kit's voice, now, was unnervingly soft.

Oh god.

He was firing me. He was cutting me loose from the only job I'd ever liked. There would be no glowing reference. No one else would hire me. I wouldn't be able to pay rent — it wasn't like Claud was going to fight to keep me there now — and I was going to have to move in with Mum, and while listening to my faceless neighbours bang all day was painful, it was better than moving into the sparse guest bedroom of your mother's house where noise-cancelling headphones were required to drown out the sound of her and Trent's circular arguments as their love affair drew to a predictable close.

In the space of three days, I had destroyed almost every relationship that mattered to me.

My life was over.

I could hear my teeth chattering as I shook, hot tears spilling out and making it mercifully harder to clearly see the look on Kit's face.

'Marnie, I want you to go home —'

'Please Kit,' I said, and it came out as a sob. 'Please don't —'

'I want you to go home, and when you come back for your shift tomorrow, we're all going to pretend like this never happened.'

'I — what?'

'I don't know how to deal with this,' he said in that same eerily calm voice, 'so I'm just not going to.'

I could hardly breathe. Tears still came, thick and fast, and I had to suck back snot to keep it from dripping down my face.

'Are you serious?' I asked, barely daring to believe it. 'I can come back?'

'If I never have to hear about Sam's problem-solving penis again, you can come back.'

I wanted to throw my arms around him and squeeze until his eyeballs shot out of his skull, but something told me that would be a greater offence than screaming at another employee in the middle of service, so I clenched my fists to keep my arms by my side.

'Hurry up and get out,' he said, and finally he was his old brisk self. 'And you better bring me a treat tomorrow because I don't pay myself enough to put up with your shit.'

Marnie Fowler (10:31): That was some party
Marnie Fowler (10:31): I think I might be allergic to wine?
Isaac Abrams (12:59): Ha
Marnie Fowler (12:59): How was Ms Perfect's night?
Isaac Abrams (17:22): I don't know if that's cool
Marnie Fowler (17:22): I joke! I joke!

Marnie Fowler (06:07): Watched *Last Night* with Guillaume Canet. Thought of you.
Marnie Fowler (11:40): How's your day?
Marnie Fowler (14:19): I think I might be dying of scurvy. Are there enough vitamins in butter to survive on croissants alone?
Marnie Fowler (14:19): Quinoa is a superfood, but it's gross. Croissants should be a superfood.
Missed call (21:55): Marnie Fowler

Marnie Fowler (09:27): Look, I'm sorry. I know I made it all weird and awful and yuck and I crossed a line and made a fool of myself and I regret it. I hope you didn't have a bad night because of it.

Marnie Fowler (09:28): Can you just answer me?

Isaac Abrams (17:37): All good.

Marnie Fowler (17:37): Can we have a dinner call tonight?

Isaac Abrams (20:41): Another time.

Missed call (19:21): Marnie Fowler

Marnie Fowler (15:04): I miss you.

CHAPTER TWENTY-SEVEN

Isaac still wasn't answering, and it was making me desperate. My mind grew wild, fresh branches emerging with new imagined scenarios, each worse than the last. That he'd moved on to the next distraction. That he and Tash were scrolling through our messages and laughing at my naivety. That I'd pushed it all too far, exploded his life, and he now hated me so deeply that he was actively plotting my demise.

In a moment of simpering fragility, owing to the combination of five days of excruciating silence, a late period and the ill-advised choice to scroll through all of my ex-boyfriends' social media accounts to see how well they were doing without me, I'd sent him the most embarrassing message of my entire life. *I miss you*; what even was that?

It had been four hours, and every minute he wasn't replying was a minute he was purposefully digging the knife in deeper. As though every time he scratched his nose or changed the channel, he was making a deliberate choice to ignore me.

I'd been left alone with my thoughts for so long that I'd begun to draw patterns. I realised, as I dug obsessively through our text history searching for every instance of sincerity to convince myself I hadn't made the whole thing up, that every time I gave away too much of myself, he would withdraw.

We would text and talk endlessly, all day, most evenings,

and it was effortless. The constant commentary of our days. Meaningful discussions about the afterlife, and the validity of trashy pop songs up against the musical giants in my collection, and the mantras we used to make it through our twenties.

But sometimes I'd slip. I'd get sloppy and sleepy and forget to inject sharp quips into our conversation, or I'd reveal too much about the ugly truths of who I really was — flawed and slow and selfish and normal — and then he would disappear.

Like he needed a recovery period.

Like he remembered I was just a person, not a figment of his imagination, some sophisticated AI programmed to tell him what he wanted to hear.

Like he saw the real me and recoiled.

Part of me didn't blame him: she wasn't the girl I wanted to be, either. I liked the girl I was for him more than I liked who I was off the clock. I wanted to be her all the time.

I remembered, now, rehearsing her every time he was on his way to meet me. The exact position of my crooked smirk, the angle I held my eyebrow at, my slightly elevated pitch, the way I fiddled with the charm on my necklace in his presence as though I was nervous, but only just enough that it flattered him.

That was who he liked, and that's who I needed to be. For him. For me. For anyone.

This was *Eternal Sunshine*. This was *Melancholia*.

Why did I send that? Why was I so fucking stupid? There was no sentence less casual, less cool, less indifferent than *I miss you*. *I miss you* was the antithesis of everything I was supposed to represent.

He wasn't replying because he was repulsed. He was slumped over with his cheek against the toilet bowl, sweaty and groaning, because he was disgusted by three ugly, needy words.

'*Validate me!*' I'd cried, and he had responded, '*Ew, no.*'

It didn't matter that my next step was unlike myself because I didn't want to *be* myself. I wanted to be *her*, the character, the version of Marnie with eyelash extensions and hollow cheekbones and a rich history of hilarious anecdotes and an underwear drawer completely devoid of tatty Cottontails with bleach marks from her vaginal pH. I needed to be her again, to prove that I could outsmart this sticky, itchy feeling of self-loathing.

Tinder. Bumble. Hinge. All of them, the same three photos: a charming candid — actually quite heavily directed by Claud months ago, '*Chin down? Left shoulder back a bit? Now smiiile! No, not like that. Do it how you do it to get a dimple. There she is.*' — to show I was pretty, a full-length mirror selfie taken under the guise of showing off the pattern of my skirt but really to demonstrate the lines of my body, and an old photo of Eddie and me — a clown emoji covering his face — from his sister's wedding, to show I cleaned up nice and had, at one point in my life, been loved by someone.

Now wasn't the time to labour over a perfect profile. Did anyone read them anyway? I started swiping. Right to like them, left to reject them.

Anthony, a blond accountant with a tuxedo cat. *Right.*

James, 185 cm. *Right.*

Bryan, a big energy goofball with a hobby farm. *Right.*

Seb, an American who loved to cook and surf. *Right.*

Diego, who had one blurry picture and no bio. Whatever. *Right.*

Alistair, a dog dad who loved the gym and missed summer. *Right.*

Robbie, who was just hot. *Right.*

Right, right, right, right, right, right, right right right rightrightrightrightrightright.

No one was matching. I'd had a live profile for fifteen minutes — why wasn't anyone matching with me?

These people didn't even know about my shortcomings and irritating traits. They didn't know I got cruel and judgmental after five wines, or that I sometimes threw out perfectly good Tupperware because I didn't want to deal with the congealed lentil soup inside it, or that I was so desperate for attention that I would swipe right on Elan, who was *'Vaccinated and ready to fuck.'* I was only anonymous and interested, and even that was repellent.

I'd wasted it. My shelf life. I'd blinked and missed the window in which to find love and companionship or even casual sex, and this was it, this was how it was going to be forever. All that talk of independence and the road less travelled and a life full scintillating conversation without the burden of marriage and children and mortgage payments was bullshit. I'd never wanted that. I wasn't special. I wasn't different. I wanted to be loved, or even just wanted. I'd take tolerated if I had to, it didn't matter, I didn't care, I just couldn't stay like this, and why why why why why WHY had I sent Isaac that message? Why hadn't he responded? This weak display of open-hearted vulnerability, why didn't it guilt him into an answer? All these months, all the late-night phone calls, the secrets and jokes and connection, hadn't it meant anything? What happened to *'I promise I'll never disappear'*? What happened to *'Juliette'*?

My kingdom for a moment of his undivided attention.

Why wasn't it enough? Why had I never been good enough — for him, for Ian, for Guillaume, for Thomas, for Martin, for Eddie, for Claud? I'd tried. I'd held on. I'd twisted myself into the shape of all the things they liked, and it hadn't mattered. It was the *me* part that drove them away.

I choked on a sob, and realised I'd been crying. I held a hand to my throat and felt my pulse there, strong and frantic. With shaky fingers I found the number I needed and hit call. It only rang once before going to voicemail.

'I'm sorry. About everything,' I said into Claud's message bank. 'Please come home. I just really need you right now.'

Isaac Abrams (15:34): Fowler. I'm so sorry for the disappearing act.
Isaac Abrams (15:35): Can I see you?

CHAPTER TWENTY-EIGHT

This was by far the sexiest, most pretentious bar I'd ever been to. It was Isaac all over: sleek and a bit private, glamorous and inaccessible, towering above Melbourne with a sly wink. The dark fixtures and floor-to-ceiling windows, and the fact that it was mostly empty, gave the impression that we were in a world of our own, alone together.

I'd almost believed his message was a mirage, and that when I got here, I'd scan the bar, find it empty, then try to throw myself off the fifty-fifth floor. Still, I was desperate enough to risk my own delusion and raced home from work faster than a nuclear missile then tore through Claud's wardrobe in a feverish trance. When I found what I was looking for — a flimsy print dress, conservative and unassuming until I crossed my legs and exposed a stretch of thigh that bordered on obscene, and Claud's best trench coat — I hurtled into the shower, waved my razor around, smeared on just enough makeup to call it French girl chic, and threw myself into the back of an Uber. I'd barely had time to douse myself with the tester vial of Santal 33 in my handbag before the elevator doors dinged open.

But now that I was here, I wasn't giddy, excited, or even grateful. I saw him there with his neat suit and impassive face, and I was angry.

He'd let me soak in his rejection for days — *thirteen days* — without ever assuaging my shame, but all he had to do was ask and I'd come running. It made me want to pluck the drink out of his hand, throw it in his face, and storm out.

'I only have fifteen minutes,' I told him. 'It took me forever to find my way up here. Collins Street is a nightmare. And, sorry, what kind of wanker bar *escorts you* upstairs. What damage do they think I'm going to do to their elevator? Look at me. This coat is from Camilla and Marc. Have some respect. Anyway, what did you want to talk to me about?'

'Why don't you sit down and have a drink before you give yourself a stroke?'

He slid a glass of something lilacky and cloudy with a bobbing maraschino cherry across the table towards me. He'd taken the liberty of ordering on my behalf. Months ago, I might have found this charming, but now I just found it obnoxious.

'I'm going to spin class in a minute,' I lied. 'I'll have water.'

I hoped to convey through my posture that I wasn't in the mood for our usual hormone-charged banter and double entendres.

'Personally, I find a few drinks improve the technique of my hip thrusts.'

I ignored him.

'How long have you been here? All afternoon? Does everyone in banking drink like you? No wonder the economy is so shit.'

'I drink like this *because* the economy is shit, darling.' If he saw me roll my eyes, he didn't say anything about it. 'Cheers.'

He was determined not to cave to my cold shoulder. No matter how sharp my tone or stony my expression was, he remained relaxed. I had no right to be this upset with him. I'd given myself away: I was petty and jealous and obvious.

I pushed the limits of plausible deniability, and it had sent him running, and I had no one left to be angry at except myself.

I managed to sip my drink through a sourpuss, and found, to my great annoyance, that he'd chosen well.

'So?'

'How have you been?' he asked. 'I've missed you.'

I wanted to say, '*I'm very easy to miss.*'

I wanted to say, '*I forgot that you existed.*'

I wanted to say, '*Oh, didn't you know? They've invented these neat things called* phones, *Isaac, and you can pick them up and contact whoever you like, whenever you like! Here, I'll show you where to shove one.*'

When I didn't bite, he sighed.

'I'm sorry I haven't messaged you back. I wish I could say I've been busy at work, or that I've had some emergency, or, I dunno, that I'd dropped my phone in the urinal, but none of that's true.'

I scoffed into my drink but didn't reply.

'Things have been ... tough since the party,' he said wearily. He looked every minute of his thirty years all of a sudden, defeated and deflated, perhaps slightly paler and jowlier than I usually found him. 'I don't know. Tash isn't a shouter. But it isn't good. She wants us to see a therapist.'

'Oh,' I said dryly. 'Wow.'

'She thinks I was deliberately light on detail about this.' He motioned between us. 'It's rubbish. She knows we're friends. She knows we text and hang out. It's the same fight, hours of it, every day.'

'I'm sorry to hear that.'

'She wants to look through my phone. She thinks it's an admission of guilt that I won't let her,' he said, then added in a misdirected snap: 'She's got nothing to accuse me of.'

'Right.'

He took a swig of his drink, as though to give himself enough gumption to get through what he had to say next.

'She doesn't want me to see you anymore.'

There it was. The silver bullet to our friendship — relationship, grey area, whatever it was. The streetlights were flickering on and he was being called home.

He waited for me to respond. Out the window, Port Phillip Bay was a deep, cold grey.

How funny, I thought, that everyone had problems, and how none of them, none, felt anything as important as our own. The whole world was full of people trying to guess their partners' passwords; people lying awake at night trying to rewrite their memories; people making excuses for their unbalanced marriages; people brokenhearted or cautiously optimistic; people who had made a mess and hadn't a hope of cleaning it up. All of us just as clueless and clumsy as one another, hoping that our match was looking for us too; hoping that the people we met along the way would be gentle with us. So often they weren't, though, and you couldn't fathom their thoughtlessness until it was your turn.

It must have been delicious, I thought, to know someone was out there desperate for any word from you, to know how much the sound of your voice meant to them, and to not care. How natural it felt to inhale their adoration and exhale your indifference. If there was anything I truly knew, it was that there was always someone who cared less.

I wasn't sure how long I'd been silent for, but Isaac hadn't cleared his throat or waved his hand in front of my face. Either he was more patient than I'd ever given him credit for, or a thousand realities lived inside me in the space of a blink, the rush of a bad dream seconds before your alarm.

'How are we going over here?' asked a waitress, appearing from nowhere. 'Would you like to order another round?'

Isaac looked at me. 'Another?'

I raised an eyebrow at him. I couldn't help myself. The sickly sarcasm just poured out of my mouth of its own accord. 'I don't know, is it *allowed*?'

'A Negroni and an Aviation. Amazing, thanks.'

I waited for her to leave before I asked, 'Why are you here? If you're not allowed to see me anymore. You could've said that in a text. You could have ghosted. I already thought that's what you were doing.'

'You know why,' he said.

'I really don't.'

'*Fowler.*'

'I'm going to need to hear you say it.'

Somehow, suddenly I was winning. All these long months, the push and pull, the cat and mouse, the seduction dance, the constant battle for power, it all came to this point, and I was pirouetting on it. I had nothing to lose. I had already shown my hand and had accepted its humiliation. Now he was here, his whole fragile life in the balance, and what he got to do with it was up to me.

'I'm here because I had to see you,' he said, finally. 'Because I *can't not* see you. Because I can't help myself.'

And that's when it all went south.

I don't know how long we talked for, because the day blurred into sunsets and cocktails until I'd forgotten to be cold with him anymore, and we were laughing. Telling stupid stories of our weeks apart, competing for the most ridiculous take until our laughs came out as hoots and shudders, and the rest of the bar patrons — who had materialised instantly, I assumed, because I hadn't noticed them come in — were glaring at us in apparent distaste.

Through the blurry eyes of my gin-fuelled cloud, I saw us holding hands across the table. He turned mine over and traced the lines on my palm, and my next memory was of my lips on his, and the taste of Campari on his mouth, and the cool shiver of the elevator's glass wall as he pressed me up against it. I wondered absently where we'd go, but didn't care to ask, compelled to follow wherever he led.

In the movie version of my life, sponsored by Net-a-Porter and your preferred female-perspective-driven porn platform, Isaac would whisk me off to Rome for our drunken, sordid tryst, in one of those luxe first-class suites, and the airline would lose our baggage, figurative and actual, somewhere over the Indian Ocean, never to be seen or worried about again. We'd fast forward through immigration and customs and the chaotic Roman traffic, and find ourselves magically transported to the biggest, most luxurious hotel room you could imagine, and his chic off-white linen suit and my impossibly tailored Gucci sundress would — *poof!* — disappear, leaving us nothing to do but fuck endlessly, insatiably, for as long as it took for all of Italy to run out of Prosecco and condoms.

What happened next wasn't so far off, sans jet lag and Aperol. Soon, we were kissing again, though this time it was in the plush, gleaming InterContinental next door. My place was only a fifteen-minute drive away, but he couldn't wait that long, he said, slapping down his credit card at the desk and pressing himself against me in the elevator in what felt like a single blink. I could still feel his hands on me, firm and desperate, as though he couldn't let me dissolve out of them.

My heel snapped in the hallway, and dread and embarrassment mixed in my stomach, a fizzing panic that I'd spoiled the moment and he'd sober up and realise who I was: clumsy and imperfect, more reality than fantasy. I looked for him from under heavy eyelids, trying to make myself small and pleading, and then he laughed. His laugh that belonged to me, mine, a bright sharp bark of surprise and delight.

Soon, our bodies chased and met one another, reaching and pulling like the tide. Where he touched, I followed, and we turned into a gasping, compliant tangle of limbs and lips. Just like I'd pictured it. Just like he had, too.

Through the long, hot night, tangible reality and cloud-vapour fantasy blurred, I forgot everything I'd ever known or cared about. There was only the weight of his body, and the disbelieving and delighted laugh of it all before we were kissing again, touching again, coming again, and then it was dark, and every inch of me ached, and his arm was slung over my waist and pulling me against his body as we fell into a heavy, satisfied sleep.

CHAPTER TWENTY-NINE

And there he was. All of him. Good *god* he was hot. I'd never gone for that before: my boyfriends had been distinctly odd looking. They were cute at first glance, but you became less sure the longer you spent with the details of their faces. A character nose. A set of eyebrows that hadn't thinned out since the invention of fire. A snaggletooth. I liked that about them, that their personality had had to make up for what their genetics lacked.

But here, this, Isaac — it was unnatural. Like wanking off a renaissance painting. All his smooth lines and milky skin and the indecent curve of his top lip under a day's worth of stubble. I lay there on my side, on the heavy hotel sheets, and I ogled.

In all my logged hours of daydreaming, I'd never conjured up this particular image. The morning after.

Oh, I'd thought about the honeymoon period. I had thought about the weight of his arm over my shoulders, and how it would be to look up at him from that angle, and the scent and the heat of his body. I thought about the race up the garden path after our twelfth fantastic date. '*No time to waste, Fowler, get over here,*' he'd say, and he'd pick me up as though I weighed nothing, throw me over his shoulder, and charge into my bedroom, and for once my neighbours would know how irritating it was to hear a headboard slamming into brick for three consecutive hours. I thought about the pillow talk, practised the shy smile I'd wear, rehearsed a compliment or two. I'd memorised the details of his hands — long fingered like a pianist, ridged and veiny and positively erotic when he handled a gearstick — and thought of one or two things he could do to me with them.

And I thought of the relief I'd feel. The long-awaited proof that I had been wrong to doubt: that my silly rules were made of smoke and heartache, that I didn't believe any of it, that really, when the bottle was empty and the house lights came on and we were all too inebriated to lie to ourselves, this was what I had always wanted. That my mistakes weren't missteps, but gentle nudges in the right direction: here. Him.

It was all going to be easy now. Everything. Uncertainty erased. Career woes banished. Plans for the rest of my life sorted. I'd have someone to talk to and eat dinner with. Someone's T-shirts to sleep in. A travel companion. A buffer between me and my family's annoying questions. Someone to have a baby with if I ever decided I wanted one. A house and a dog, and a lemon tree in the garden with our initials carved into it. Framed photos on the walls and rumpled sheets on both sides of the bed. Company and security and the solid absolute hand-to-god certainty that life would never, ever be boring, because it was him, Isaac, who was always fun, who had a hot take on every topic, who didn't take anything too seriously, who was bright and dark in equal measure and here and perfect and mine.

I was sure now. I loved him. I did.

My contented exhale must have reached him because he stirred.

He blinked into the yellow half-light of the moon, eyes crinkling deliciously as he squinted to pull the room into focus. He found me and cracked into a smile, lazy and relieved.

'Hi.'

'Hi,' he replied. As he shifted, the sheet slid somewhere between a suggestion and an obscenity. His arm reached for me, and I wriggled towards it. 'You're still here.'

'Shouldn't I be?'

'Glad you are,' he said.

Something to add to the wank bank: his sleepy voice, low and gravelly.

'Me too.'

''Mere,' he said, and I obeyed.

And I forgot everything again, like I wanted to: every bad thing I'd ever done, every doubt or fear I'd ever had. Time warped in our bubble, stretching and shrinking and turning itself around as I existed as nerve endings and eyes and oxygen, giving and taking and touching and tasting while the moon rose outside the sliver of open curtain. I felt only safe and soft and seen, declining to feel self-conscious or to make a self-deprecating joke, because it was just easy, just right.

'I think I'm kind of terrified of you,' he whispered, like he hoped I might not hear him, somewhere in the coldest hour of the night as I hovered between heaven and sleep.

'Of me?'

'You're sure about everything you want.'

I hesitated for a moment, then said, 'That's funny.'

'Is it?'

'My sister called me a chameleon once, months ago,' I said. 'It's bothered me ever since.'

'Why?'

'Because it's true,' I replied. 'I just become who someone else needs me to be.'

Isaac shifted so we were both laying on our sides, nose to nose in the glow of late night light pollution, and I saw his brow crease ever so slightly.

'Are you doing it now?'

'I don't know. Yes.'

'What would you do if you were alone?'

'If I'd just had the wank of the century?'

His breath was a laugh, and it was wonderful to know he still thought I was funny after all of this; that he liked me even after he'd got what he wanted. He pushed a strand of hair off my shoulder and let his hand trail down my spine.

'How do you change for me?'

'The way I dress. The things I say. The things I don't. I carry myself differently.'

'Why do you do it?' he asked. 'What's wrong with how you are? I might like her better.'

I paused, holding my breath in my lungs while I decided how honest to be.

'I've let her down too many times,' I said. My eyes stung, so I closed them. 'She's not around anymore.'

I felt his hand on my face, and I pressed my cheek into his palm. There was a softness here I hadn't considered. For all the sharp edges of his flirting, the rough grip on my body and the teeth marks in my skin, the excitement and the rush, he was gentle now, earnest and affectionate, and for the first time in a long time, I let myself breathe out.

'Everyone I show her to runs away. It's safer to be the girl they want me to be.'

There was too much concern on his face when I opened my eyes again, and it ached. I wanted to turn over, to pull the sheet higher and hide myself, to drain the minibar and give in to a blackout, but I couldn't. He squeezed my hip, and I half hoped it would be enough pressure to crack my bones so I could crumble into dust and disappear.

'I love every bad thing about you,' he said. 'Everything you don't. All your bruises.'

I wanted him to mean it. More than that, I wanted it to be true.

There was nothing I could say that wasn't terrifying, so I kissed him instead, and that was enough to hit reset and wipe the look off his face, and I was her again, and again, and again, and again, everything he wanted for as long as he wanted her.

It was hours before my brain came back online, idled on the cusp of sleep. My mouth was dry and there was a ringing ache in every muscle of my body.

I eased onto my back to find him. There, miles away on the other side of this continent of a bed, propped against the headboard, neck bent to the glow of his phone.

'Hi,' I said again. He glanced over and smiled. Muted, even shy. 'Far. Why?'

'Just a sec,' he replied.

I scooted across the mattress until I could hook a leg around his. 'Have you been awake long?'

'Few minutes,' he said, dropping a hand to rest on my shoulder. 'It's still early.'

'I have a shift later, but I'm going to have to call and tell my boss some terrible pervert is holding me hostage.'

I waited for him to laugh, but he seemed not to have heard me. I thought of a stand-up comedian flicking a microphone cord as their jokes failed to elicit applause.

I drummed my fingers on his stomach to get his attention. 'You okay?'

'Yeah, sorry, just —' he made a frustrated groan at his phone, and it clicked.

He had an absence to account for. There was someone else who noticed when he didn't answer, who he wasn't allowed to ignore for days on end.

I untangled my leg from his and flopped onto my back, looking for patterns in the ceiling as my hot blood began to cool.

I swallowed. I tried to time my breaths to slow my thoughts, but no matter how many seconds I counted in and out, my mind raced ever faster.

'I need a glass of water,' I said. 'Can you turn around while I find my dress?'

He looked up, his frown lifting from concern to confusion. 'Well, I wouldn't want to miss the show.'

'I'm serious.'

'What's the matter?'

I spotted my underwear on the bedside table; as good a place for them as any. I wriggled into them gracelessly under the sheet, grateful for the excuse to continue avoiding his eye.

I didn't know what time it was, where I'd left my phone, or how I'd ended up here. Well, I knew *how* I ended up here, but I couldn't quite believe it. Somehow, I didn't want to.

That's the thing about fantasies. Reality ruins them.

I hadn't woken up into a gilded world of victory and possibility, but a cloud of regret, beside a man who wasn't mine to take, his borrowed body covered in my marks.

For all its plush interior and chic details, the hotel didn't feel glamorous, but seedy. I thought of all the people who'd checked into this room before us, what they did, what they were hiding, and who they were hiding it from. We were part of a long line of indiscretions, a secret society of selfish people.

I'd got what I wanted, learning too late that I didn't want it like this.

Only hours ago, a naked, bed-headed Isaac had been a privilege to behold, but it was indecent now.

I didn't need to force myself to feel guilty about it. Determined ignorance was long gone, and shame crashed over me like a tsunami, destructive and punishing, relentless and unforgiving. No one deserved this, least of all a woman whose biggest flaw was that she loved someone who didn't respect her. She had seen our friendship for what it was and had drawn a reasonable boundary around it, and Isaac and I — both of us, equally responsible and in full control of ourselves — had ignored her and then lit her life on fire.

For what? For who? Why?

If we had wanted to be together, then what stopped us from saying so? Why couldn't we have waited for him to break up with her to pursue this? What was so urgent that it warranted this slimy deceit?

And now there was no taking it back. She had to have known. There had to have been a sick feeling in her stomach all night long, the gnawing curiosity of his unanswered phone pulling her to the only logical conclusion.

What now? Would he go to her, show up on her doorstep, bite marks under his rumpled collar and tell the truth? Would he beg? If he did, would she stay? Would she ever trust him again?

And — I hated that I was thinking about myself right now — *what about me*? It was hard to imagine buttoning up my dress, hopping onto the tram and going home and continuing my life as though I'd had an ordinary night.

Would I ever hear from him again? Would we be together now? What would that look like? I tried to picture him in my house, soap bubbles sliding down his broad back in the shower he'd be too tall for, forced to crouch to wash his hair, a blue toothbrush on my sink for him. Sitting between me and Claud on the couch for movie night. His laundry in my hamper. His glasses folded beside a split, upturned book on his side of the bed.

'What are we doing?' I asked him, my back to him as I buttoned up my dress.

'When?'

'Right now, last night, tomorrow. What are we *doing*?'

When I turned to look at him, he was sitting on the edge of the bed, sheet pooled around his lap with his head in his hands.

'I don't know.'

'What do you mean, you don't know? Haven't you thought about this at all?'

'Of course I've thought about it,' he said. He sounded tired. Not sleepy, like he had been up all night, but exhausted down to his bones. 'It doesn't make this any easier.'

'This?'

'*This*. It's the same mess it's always been, isn't it?'

A knife to the chest might have hurt less.

I would not cry. I would not cry. I would not cry in front of him.

'Right.' I cast around for my shoes so I could make my escape. 'Well, that's that.'

'C'mon Fowler,' he said, exasperated. 'Don't be like that.'

'I'm not being like anything. I'm looking for my things.'

'What do you want me to say?'

Here was the moment to be honest. I was finally being given the space to shed my character and be myself. Not cripplingly amenable, not cool, not written by a hopeless romantic designing the girl of his dreams. *Here I am, take me or leave me.* I could tell him about that fleeting, desperate thought I had last night — that I loved him, and that I wanted to hear him say it too. It was halfway up my throat before something caught it, throttled it, and pushed it back down.

I heard myself ask, 'Do you want to be with me, or was this just a conquest for you?'

Isaac sighed heavily. 'I do, but ...'

It irked me that he was still sitting on the edge of the bed, tousle-haired and a strong breeze away from being naked, and yet I was the vulnerable one here.

What would I say if Claud were in this position? I'd tell her that everything before 'but' doesn't count. I'd tilt my head to the side, give her a know-it-all look and refuse to blink until she admitted I was right, that she was acting under the vain hope that her life was a romcom, and that she needed a sip of reality and a shot of self-respect.

'This is a disaster,' I said, near tears as I hugged my arms. 'This is the biggest mistake of my life.'

'You know how I feel about you.'

'No, I don't,' I said, faltering with a wobble in my voice and hating myself for it. I had to get out of there.

Isaac's face said, '*Come on.*'

'You know if I could, I would.'

'You could, though,' I said thickly, glad of the excuse to avoid his face under the pretence of stepping into my shoes. Fuck. My broken heel. 'You've always had that option. You aren't married. You don't have kids. You don't even live together. There was a choice you decided not to make. Or, well —' I gave a joyless laugh '— you did, and here we are.'

'It's just not that easy,' he said, pleadingly. He cast around the room for his clothes, aware of his shame, aware that arguments required underwear, aware that I was in the doorway, figurative and not. 'I want it to work out; I just don't know how. I'm trying.'

Pity was easy to grasp, but as I shrugged on my coat and flipped my hair out from under its collar, I wasn't sure which one of us it was for.

Him, for being torn in two directions. Me, for my naivety. Both of us, for the mess we'd willingly walked into.

'You have to choose, Isaac,' I said, my hand on the doorknob. 'I don't want to be second best anymore.'

'It's not that simple,' he argued. 'She's —'

'It can be so simple if you want it to be,' I told him. 'You just need to figure it out.'

Whether it was cowardice or the ick factor, he couldn't look at me. I swallowed hard and pinched the delicate flesh of my forearm to force myself not to cry.

'I want this,' I said, my voice cracking. 'And you need to work out if you do, too.'

'Fowler, don't —' He made a move to stand up, but I was gone.

The door slammed shut behind me, and I took my shoes off and bolted to the elevator. I didn't want to be caught out here in a whispered argument with a man in a sheet, begging for a place in his life and trying to cling to a scrap of dignity in the process. I hammered the call button until the chrome doors slid open, and then hammered the close button until they slid shut again.

Once I was alone, in my rumpled dress with last night's makeup, although nothing was very funny, I laughed. And once I started, I couldn't stop. It came out without my permission:

cold, sharp laughter. My cheeks ached and my teeth sank into my lip as I fought to steady myself.

As I walked my shame through the gleaming lobby in the unflattering light of the real world, I laughed until my head throbbed, until it wasn't laughter but gasps for air, and by the time I'd flung myself through the doors of the nearest tram, I was crying into my hands.

Ten years of this. My entire adult life, my twenties wasted, collagen stores squandered, trying to mould myself into someone small and easier to love, the male fantasy of an uncomplicated woman who lived to ask about his day and suck him off, asking for nothing in return but blithe tolerance. Ian, Guillaume, Thomas, Martin, Eddie, now Isaac — memories of them tore through me like bullets. Six men and six thousand mistakes, and there in the middle of it all, the one thing they all had in common.

I didn't care that the commuters around me looked edgy and panicked at the hysterical, barefoot woman causing a scene in the crowded carriage. I didn't care what anyone thought of me, because it couldn't be worse than what I thought about myself. I wished for something to snap in two. I wanted to kick something over, to rip it apart, to scream and shout and shatter something to offset this ballooning need to be someone, somewhere — anyone, anywhere — else.

CHAPTER THIRTY

'Oh, thank god,' sighed Nicola from her doorway. 'You're a lifesaver.'

'You look *fantastic*,' I said, cocking my head to the side and giving her a sympathetic look. 'Fresh off the runway, are we?'

She flipped me off. Her eyelids were as droopy as her oily topknot, her nose and lips chapped raw, the tails of her cardigan poked out of the bottom of her sweatshirt, and she had her trackpants tucked into a pair of Mitch's rugby socks. She was ready to make a rude retort, but her inhale got caught and she coughed — barked like a basset hound — into the pit of her elbow, and she decided to let it go. She stepped backwards to allow me entry, and I followed, laden with grocery bags and guilt.

I'd worked my Saturday shift on autopilot, unable to think, only do. Kit's barbs fell flat, customers' quips and chitchat went unnoticed as I pumped out coffees and distributed plates with numb fingers.

When it was time to go home, I came here instead, to Nicola's. Our childhood home didn't exist anymore. Mum and Dad sold it in their divorce, each splitting off into their beige empty nests. But even if I had a key to the old house, I wouldn't retreat into it. There was no comfort in the lilac walls of my bedroom. It was the same reason I couldn't stand to listen to The Killers: too many bad memories trapped between the notes.

Little George had always been a haven, but now every butter knife I picked up could have been the one I'd dropped at Isaac's feet; every creak of the door could have been him striding through it — or worse, Tash. Sam's cold shoulder was another reminder of the long, winding path that had led us here.

When Nicola messaged to say that the whole family had come down with a bug (*'We've done twelve RATs and they're all negative, promise!'*) and to ask that I drop some emergency supplies over, I agreed without a second thought. Anything was better than going back to my empty house.

She padded down the hallway, mouth-breathing, and said, 'Sorry about the mess.'

'Don't be stupid,' I said. 'It's fine.'

It was the worst I'd ever seen the place look. A puddle of dirty sheets lay in the doorway to the laundry, and the floor was sprinkled with baby debris: a dropped toy here, a fallen dummy there. The kitchen was worse: a sink full of swampy dishwater, cupboard doors cracked open, cardboard and plastic overflowing out of the recycling bin, bowls and mugs caked with old food littered across the countertop.

She opened the fridge to start loading in the milk and juice I'd brought with me, and I swatted her on the arm.

'Go and sit down.'

'I'm alright, I'll just put these away.'

'Sit down or I'll call Mum on you.'

She rolled her eyes but obliged, placing the bags down and dragging herself off to the couch, where she collapsed into the cushions.

'Death, please,' she moaned into a pillow. 'Sick bad.'

'You're so eloquent,' I cooed. 'Tea?'

The cupboard where she kept the mugs was bare, so I cracked open the dishwasher door. Clean. I began to unstack it for her, but before I could do more than put the forks away, a squawk echoed down the hall.

'I'll get her,' I said at once, but my sister was already up. 'Sit back down, Nicola, I'll go.'

It was too late. Before I'd even put the cutlery basket down, Layla was on Nicola's hip, her soft face flushed and miserable.

'There's my bestie,' I said. I reached out to take her, but she curled deeper into Nicola's clavicle. '*Hey.* No cuddle?'

She shook her head.

'Just needs her mum,' I said, shrugging to hide my disappointment. 'I get it.'

'She's probably forgotten what you look like. We haven't seen you in forever. Weeks and weeks and weeks.'

'*Weex*,' echoed Layla.

'It hasn't been that long,' I argued. 'It's only been, like, three weeks.'

'Try eight,' she replied, rubbing Layla's back and kissing her forehead. 'Your life is too fabulous for your boring old sister and her impossibly cute child.'

'Oh, yeah,' I said, snorting. 'Wild parties every night.'

'Knew it. Last-minute trips to Brazil. One-night stands with handsome strangers. Coke.'

'*So* much coke,' I said, rolling my eyes. 'It's the only way to make it through spin class.'

'That's life with Claud, I guess.'

I nodded them over to the couch and continued putting the dishes away, everything in its rightful home the way I knew she liked it.

'We haven't really been doing that lately. She's been busy.'

'Still with that guy?'

I made a disgruntled noise and called Layla's name. When she looked around, I gave her a meaningful look and said, 'I hope you'll listen to me someday, bunny. Some boys are *bad news*.'

I shook my head, and she shook hers back.

'Well, if she's happy,' Nicola sighed.

'She's not, though,' I said. 'She's fuc— she's effing miserable. She just thinks she loves him and keeps making excuses for him. It's infuriating.'

'She probably doesn't need a judge and jury about it, Marnie. Just support her. She'll figure it out for herself eventually.'

'"*Eventually*" is the problem,' I said. 'What if it takes years? What if I'm stuck with him?'

'*You*? What about *her*?'

'She adores him,' I said. 'Maybe she has a bland a-hole fetish.'

'Don't say "*fetish*" or it'll be her new word of the week.'

'Sorry,' I said, looking at Layla. 'I said "foetid". It means yucky.'

I filled up the kettle, flicked it on, and put a sleeve of biscuits down on the coffee table to tide them both over for a few minutes, but before Nicola could take one, we were interrupted again.

'*Baaabe*,' came Mitch's whine from the bedroom. 'Do you know where my heat pack is?'

Nicola heaved herself off the couch, sucking back phlegm and cradling Layla to her chest. She began to rummage in the credenza, junk drawer after junk drawer, freezing momentarily as the fever aches struck her.

'Sit back down,' I told her. 'I'll find it.'

'I'll get it, it's alright.'

Layla sneezed, lime-coloured snot coating her face and Nicola's T-shirt.

'Urgh – eff. That's okay, we're okay, let's get you a tissue.'

'Nicola, sit down,' I said, more forcefully this time, and still it went unheard.

'*Baaabe*,' called Mitch again, bleating like a sheep; brainless and directionless. 'My baaack.'

'I'm getting it!' she croaked.

This is what it is to be a woman: to give. To give life, to give support, to give herself, to give in. And in return she receives: contempt, indifference, more requests, his load. She gives until she breaks, a spiderweb of cracks in her porcelain skin, holding still until she shatters into a thousand tiny pieces.

And men take. Take the love, the support, the credit, our patience. They take and take and take what isn't theirs, what never was, what was designed to be shared, not stolen, until she is tired, angry, broken and useless, only then is she granted freedom from it all: the male gaze, the pedantry, the entitlement. They lose interest when she can no longer do anything for them; when they're no longer a doe-eyed plaything with pillowy cleavage and endless capacity.

'Daddy's a pain, isn't he?' she squeaked to Layla. 'Daddy's a big baby, just like you.'

She had located the heat pack and popped it into the microwave, wiping Layla's face with a tissue as they rocked on the spot waiting for the timer to beep.

Men — men like Mitch, men like Jesse — loathed an angry woman, so I got angry. Rage bubbled with the water in the kettle, what once was still and calm becoming rapidly hotter and more violent.

'You shouldn't be doing that,' I told her. 'He can get it himself.'

'I don't mind,' she said. 'He threw his back out sneezing yesterday. Nothing's worse than a bad back.'

I could think of a few things. Being used. Basing your value in your necessity. Balancing ever more precariously on the tightrope of wife and mother — which to whom? — your core spasming with effort.

What was Claud doing right now? I pictured her in an endless meeting, her teeth warping the cap of a pen in boredom, one eye on her phone, and I wanted to kick something.

I was saved by the beep of the microwave. Nicola retrieved the heat pack from inside it, adjusted Layla on her side, and narrated their walk down the hallway to give it to Mitch in bed.

The kettle popped. I made our tea and took it to the coffee table.

Nicola looked a little brighter when she returned, able to keep her eyes all the way open for minutes at a time. If the kitchen was messy, the living room was even worse. I collected the rubbish: the pizza box with splotches of oil breaking through the cardboard, the paper wrappers of cough drops littered on the rug. A glass with one remaining sip of flat lemonade in it. A cloth that had once been damp was now half dry on the arm of the couch, and crumpled socks strewn where they'd been kicked off in a fevery sweat.

She dropped onto the couch, slumping empty-handed against the cushions. Down the hall, I heard Layla babbling to Mitch. Good. Taking care of his own child for five seconds was the very least he could do.

'What's happening with whatshisname?' asked Nicola.

'Nothing,' I said at once. I pulled the collar of my jumper higher, like she might be able to see Isaac's fingerprints on my skin if she looked hard enough. 'Why do you ask?'

'Because I'm crippled by boredom.'

'Nothing's happening,' I said again. 'I don't know. I'm trying not to think about it.'

And I was. Trying. I'd zipped my phone into the pocket of my handbag and didn't let myself look at it more than once an hour, nerves too frayed to handle the crush of its perpetually blank screen.

But how could I not think about it? What else was there? Nuclear war could have broken out and I'd still think, *Is he okay? What's he thinking? The world is ending: whose arms is he running to? Thank god I had the best sex of my life before radiation poisoning melted my skin off.*

It had only been ten hours since I left the hotel room — ten hours and nine minutes, but who was counting? — and I knew it was too soon to expect him to have made his choice. Her or me. The girl he wanted or the girl he already had; the question he'd been squirming away from for months. At last — at such long last — a decision had to be made.

Part of me knew, as my insides turned to ice, that if you had to ask, then you already had your answer.

'That wasn't the salacious gossip I was looking for,' Nicola said, scrunching up her nose. 'How am I supposed to live vicariously through you if you refuse to get into any trouble?'

'I'm terribly sorry. Shall I go and ruin my life for your amusement?'

'Yes,' she said at once. 'If you wouldn't mind. God, that sounds like fun. Did you know, the highlight of my week, now, is when Mitch takes Layla to the park with his daddy walking group and he brings me home a hot doughnut.'

'That's sweet.'

'No, it's depressing,' she said. 'The *highlight of my week* is sitting alone in my house, waiting for a doughnut. I used to be so cool. Don't you remember?'

'You? Are you sure?'

'Now I'm just ... Imprisoned. Trapped! Marooned! Chained up in the kitchen! When did this become my life?'

I looked around their living room: stain-resistant charcoal fabrics, low furniture, Matisse prints on the walls. The corner Layla's play area was set up in, bursting with the primary colours of blocks and textured books and enrichment toys. Off the hallway, the washing machine and dryer took turns churning and beeping. The massive — truly unnecessarily oversized, like it was compensating for something — television blinking and flashing with muted cartoon characters on ABC Kids. An overgrown lawn just beyond the windows, and clean laundry twisting in the breeze. Chaotic though it was this week, this house and the family within it was all some people wanted, and she loathed it.

'If you hate your life, why don't you do something about it?' I asked. I picked at a biscuit for long enough to note the pause in conversation. When I looked up, Nicola's face had hardened. 'What?'

'Who said I hate my life?'

I let out a single *Ha*. 'Um, you? Constantly?'

She was chewing on the inside of her cheek, the way I did when I was fighting through all the wrong responses looking for the right one. A hereditary trait, perhaps, or one I'd picked up through years of imitating her.

'That's a terrible thing to say,' she said, crisp at all her edges. 'I've never said that.'

I wasn't sure what prickled me more: the fact that she was rewriting her history or that she was pushing back on me at all.

Nicola and I didn't fight. We never had. Our age gap had been great enough that there was never much to fight about. Her brattiest period had come and gone before I was old enough to clock it, and once it was my turn to be defiant and immature, she was old enough to handle it with indifference. We didn't argue about who got the front seat on the way to school or come to blows about whose turn it was to choose a Friday night movie. We had just coasted along, closeness ebbing and flowing as our life stages allowed. These days, we knew one another's pain points and rough edges and how to avoid them. But now, in the perfect house she so resented, in my corrosive state, as her husband whined that Layla might need a change and could she come help him out please, and my jaw ached from its ongoing clench, we'd found an unfamiliar plane on which to face one another.

'Okay, well, maybe think about that next time you call me to complain because you've been kicked out of the house for poker night.'

'Oh, okay, if you're going to nitpick —'

'Or tell me to get my tubes tied if I want to retain my will to live.'

'Layla cut four teeth in one night, okay; anyone would be pushed to the brink of sanity.'

'What I want to know is, where's Mitch in all this?' I asked, feeling myself sneer, feeling the sick, satisfying heat of years of swallowed comments finally coming out. 'When he gets home from work and locks himself in the office. When he's on a golf trip, or when it's time for the bedtime song, or for Layla to get her shots, or when the laundry needs to be hung out, or when you just need five minutes to yourself? Where is he? What is he doing? What is the point of relying on someone, and investing in them, and supporting them, building them up, putting them first, always, fucking *always*, when you're not even on their radar? Why do you always have to come last?'

My pulse was up by the time I was finished. I drained my cup and slammed it back onto the table with a satisfying *thunk.* 'I know such fucking wonderful women,' I continued furiously, too worked up to stop, to pause, to breathe. 'These smart, fantastic, funny, driven, generous, interesting, incredible women who let these *nothing* men, these mediocre, angry, no-effort, no-payoff men treat them like a chore. I watch them shed layers to fit in with this ridiculous male ideal, like it's anything worth aspiring to, like they're not all ready to throw you away and chase after the next most pliable option the minute you have a lick of self-respect. Why do any of you *care* what they want? Why do you make room for them? Why do you let them get away with it? What do you get out of it?'

'You need to calm down,' said Nicola coldly.

'I don't want to calm down,' I snapped. 'I'm tired. I'm so, so tired of watching the women I love settle for scraps. You all deserve so much more, and you need to start acting like it.'

'You —' she cut across me, razor-sharp and at the edge of her patience '— need to stop talking about *women* when you mean *you*.'

'I'm the only woman I know who isn't tied up in this bullshit.'

Nicola's sneer was imperceptible to anyone who hadn't known her face for nearly three decades, but I saw it. The pulled lip, the micro lift of an eyebrow, the joyless amusement.

She lifted her cup to her mouth took a tiny sip, swallowed, and asked, 'Aren't you?'

CHAPTER THIRTY-ONE

I never seemed to get sensation back into my extremities. I raced home, gripping the edges of my seat on the train to will it faster, desperate for peace and safety. The whole world felt like an ice bath, turning my insides blue, agony at first then quickly becoming too numb to feel anything.

I tried. I thought endlessly, digging through my memories, trying to turn scratches into wounds, but nothing had any effect. It was as though I'd simply run out of emotions, shielded by the bulletproof glass case I'd boxed myself into, able to see but not feel.

It was a waiting game. Waiting for Jesse to send Claud running home, waiting for Nicola to call and say we'd only misunderstood each other, waiting for time to pass, waiting for a word from Isaac, waiting for anything to happen and shake the big grey melancholy out of my mood.

It was almost funny how long I had convinced myself that I wanted a different life. All year long, I'd grimaced at the memory of sexless weeknights and the death marches down supermarket aisles, how boring it was to know someone so well you could recite their jalapeño anecdote, and how the key to avoiding it was to reject intimacy and companionship altogether.

It was embarrassing, now, to be wrong. Eddie and I had been in a rut, and I was in one with myself, and it was a hundred times more claustrophobic when you could only blame your suffocating boredom on yourself.

Everything just seemed like too much effort. Chasing the high of a dopamine hit my whole life, never satisfied by good wine or a $20 note found in my pocket, itching for the next good thing to come along and distract me from my own oppressive ennui.

All that sadness and fear had curdled, and when I could summon a whisper of a feeling, I could only identify brittle anger. The way my baggage coloured the way I saw men, blaming all of them for the shortcomings of a few, every clumsy mistake further evidence of their collective depravity. I reached for anger over acceptance, because if Mitch and Jesse and all my mother's forcefully ordinary boyfriends were fundamentally decent people, then it wasn't men that were the problem, it was me, and that was too much grief and guilt to process.

Anger was easier. I could externalise it. I could feel the hot flames of it flicker whenever I glanced at my phone screen, as if another log was thrown onto the fire every time it came up blank.

'*Sorry I missed your call, babe,*' Claud had said in a returned voice message. It felt like I'd called her weeks ago, not two days. '*Everything's okay. I'm not ignoring you. Jesse and I – well. I don't know. It's all a bit ... anyway, I'll be home tonight.*'

What did that mean? It's all a bit what? Hope felt dangerous, so I sunk back into my melancholy to avoid the inevitable disappointment.

I counted every minute until she usually got home — usually, back when she still pretended to live here. I was desperate for someone to talk to, the high highs and lowest of the lows. I chewed my nails down to tender pink stubs.

I didn't know what to do with myself, but Claud would know. She always had the answers. She hadn't meant what she said that night at Isaac's party; she had been riding the low tide of Jesse's unending inadequacy.

The real Claud would walk through that door any minute. She'd tell me it was about time I screwed Isaac out of my system, and that now I was ready to enter the next phase of my life.

She'd pull a bottle of vodka out of the freezer and we'd sit on the couch and laugh and talk like we always had, before all our missteps had led us miles from one another.

And when the buzz hit our systems just right and we slid to the floor, we'd make a pact. We'd both be done with bad guys and fuckboys for a while — for good — and we'd sit slumped against each other, content that we were all we needed. In the morning, dry-mouthed and delicate, all our bad choices would be out of sight and mind forever.

It had been so long since we had properly connected, and in this moment of crisis, I'd never missed her more.

At 6 pm, after what felt like a lifetime of waiting, I heard her key turn in the door.

'Finally!' I cried. 'You're not going to believe this.'

'Hey, babe,' she said, flatter than I expected. 'You good?'

'Far from,' I replied, following her down the hallway. 'It's a Russian novel, honestly, the longing and the drama and the depravity, but the gist of it — wait, are you okay?'

Claud had climbed into bed, shoes and all, and turned away from the door. Muffled through a mouthful of covers, she said, 'I'm sad.'

'What's happened?'

I waited for her reply, but instead, I saw her shoulders shake. My problems, once all-consuming, seemed suddenly small.

Claud, who hadn't 'cried since 1997', was crying.

Without another word, I crawled in beside her, wrapped an arm around her middle and held her. I stayed close as tears turned into sobs turned into a dry choke. It was impossible to know if she cried for minutes or hours, because the toughest person I knew was in pieces, and it could only be one thing.

I hated him. Jesse. The toxic little fuck. She didn't have to give me context: I knew instinctively who and what this was about. Had she not needed to be hugged like she needed oxygen, I would have pulled her phone out of her bag, worked out his address, gone over, hammered on his door until his ugly weasel face appeared behind it, and headbutted him, knocking him to the ground and proceeding to unleash a fury on him so violent it would give Tarantino pause.

But I didn't. I stayed with her while she cried herself out and didn't say a word until she sighed, exhausted, and pushed herself up to sit against the headboard.

'It's not that I'm not enough,' she said with a sniff. 'I love myself. I am enough. I am all I need.'

'Of course you are.'

I rubbed her arm, and her composure wavered.

'But what about what I *want*?' she asked, crumbling through a fresh wave of tears. 'I want *more* than enough. I want all of it, from everyone, all the time.'

She choked on her own breath, her face pink and twisted behind her hands. My lip wobbled in sympathy, and I pulled her in and let her weep into my shoulder again.

'I don't want to be on my own because there's no other option,' she squeaked. 'I don't want to be my own fallback plan.'

'You deserve everything you want,' I told her. 'Everything you want and more than you need.'

She cried and cried, and there was nothing I could say to fix her aching heart, so I didn't try.

It was unsettling to see her come undone like this, over a man like that. All this time, I'd been sure that I could outrun pain, that all it took was a sharp tongue and steely resolve, but here was the truth: even the strongest armour couldn't protect us if we let someone in.

We lay like that for an eternity, alternating between tired silences and bouts of tears. The deepening darkness was the only hint that time continued to pass.

Eventually, when she seemed to have run out of energy, Claud rubbed her eyes. 'What did you want to talk about?' she croaked. 'Isaac did something?'

'Nothing,' I said. 'Don't worry about it.'

'I can't do it again, Marnie,' she said, like she hadn't heard my answer, like she'd forgotten she had asked. Her eyelids were heavy, and she seemed ready to surrender to her misery. 'I think you had it right. No relationships. I just end up feeling like this.'

Now wasn't the time to tell her that I was complicit in putting this ache in someone else. If Tash ever found out. If Isaac ever owned up to it. Claud was right, and I had been all along, too. You couldn't count on anyone. If your head and heart were misaligned, as mine were — torn, constantly, between the need for respite and unquenchable greed — you could even betray yourself.

To spare her this in her moment of agony, I nodded. She nodded too, between long blinks, and finally gave in to sleep; the only safe place left.

I lay still as my mind raced, cutting seamlessly between memories of the night before (his hands, his body, the pressure and the release, how good it all felt, the sound of his gasp and the shape of his mouth when he made it) and snippets of what I imagined Tash's reaction would be (the shattering of ceramic as she threw everything in her reach and let it smash on the floor in a hot rage, or a single glistening tear cutting through her immaculate makeup as she cried, glamorous even in her grief) in a montage of mixed emotions. I felt weary, like I'd made it through a battle, and then guilt came crashing in.

Shame had reawoken with fresh hunger. It had waited patiently for seven long months, earning interest while I ran all over town, ducking and weaving away from the consequences of my bad behaviour, and finally, time was up. A woman's life was about to be turned out because of me, and there was no clever phrase that could untangle me from the blame. No semantics, no claim that Isaac alone was responsible, no convenient belief that their split was inevitable and so this indiscretion hardly counted.

I thought of the explanation tour she'd have to give. Telling people that her world had changed and why. Her miserable search for a new life without his fingerprints on it. The questions she would never have answered: *What else could she have done? What made him change his mind? What inner deficiency did she harbour to push him between someone else's legs? How could she have let it happen?*, and the baggage she would carry for the rest of her life. The people she would punish for our mistakes, and the pain that would ripple from one night and a thousand moments of weakness. It all looked too familiar.

I lay in my guilt for all the women I'd betrayed lately, and waited for the answer to come. For the buzz of my phone or knuckles on my front door or a way back to December, to the rooftop bar, so I could nod out of that very first conversation and save us all from all this mess. I slept there on the edge of Claud's bed, cold and curled like a dog, and waited for the absolution I didn't deserve.

CHAPTER THIRTY-TWO

A shrill alarm and no notifications. I expected it, but it stung all the same. Even after the most innocent encounters, Isaac always disappeared. He wasn't going to call. Still, I kept an eye on it in the shower, held it in my hand while I brushed my teeth, compulsively checked it on my ride to work and between every coffee I poured, but nothing. My battery was drained by midday with nothing to show for it.

Had I been too quick to go? Did I regret it? Would I? Which part?

It was easier to box it up and put it on a shelf where I could forget it until I had enough resilience to handle it. So I worked, and I relished in the sublime relief of routine.

Greet the customer, take their order, charge their card.

Grind the beans, steam the milk, pour it, call their name.

Toast the croissant, bag the croissant, pass the croissant.

Don't think; just serve.

It was fine. It would be fine. Claud was home again. She'd remember herself. We would talk it out and she would make it better. She would listen, pausing to pull the conversation aside for a joke or to ask if he was better at giving head than his height and general handsomeness suggested, and she would take a deep breath and say something healing and brilliant.

Something like, '*Sometimes self-care means making choices that hurt right now, but protect us from something much worse.*'

Something like, '*Never underestimate a man's ability to make you feel guilty for his mistakes.*'

Something like, '*Well, you're excellent and he sucks, so who cares? Let's make margaritas and get matching tattoos.*'

It was the only thing that kept me going all morning through the rushes and the lulls of a shift: the promise of old times.

The cafe was actually busy for once. The sporadic downpour had lured people inside under the promise of warmth and cake, and Kit had had to refill the coffee grinder twice. I'd snuck off to the upstairs toilets for a moment to lock in tonight's plans.

Marnie Fowler (11:15): Let's bust out the big guns tonight
Marnie Fowler (11:15): Emotional Armageddon
Marnie Fowler (11:15): Pizza, ice cream, and every Dev Patel movie we can find
Claudia King (11:18): Are you suggesting a suicide pact? Because that sounds like heaven
Marnie Fowler (11:19): You jump, I jump, Jack.
Claudia King (11:19): Would love love love to, but I'm out with Jesse tonight
Claudia King (11:19): Soon?

I blinked at my phone. I even closed the window and opened it again to make sure that there hadn't been a glitch, that the software hadn't become sentient and started sending text messages posing as an intelligent woman who inexplicably makes stupid decisions. My jaw gave a throb, and I realised I was clenching it.

Put the phone down, I told myself. *Do not respond now.*

That was what a sensible person would do. They would come back to the problem with a cool head, capable of seeing reason and helping their friend through a difficult time with sensitivity and generosity. They would pause before judging and choose empathy. They understood that we could not fight other people's battles, that we could only control our own reactions.

I took slow breaths, inhaling cool and exhaling warm, relishing in the control of it all, and the self-awareness, the frankly impressive maturity. My god, who was this fabulously level-headed person I was becoming? I could almost —

My phone buzzed again before I could put it away.

Claudia King (11:21): Don't start, ok?
Marnie Fowler (11:21): I didn't say anything?
Claudia King (11:22): I'm a big girl, it's my life
Claudia King (11:23): You know what, Marnie? I don't need this from you
Marnie Fowler (11:23): ???
Claudia King (11:23): I know you hate him but I never asked for your opinion
Claudia King (11:24): You're supposed to be on my side. I'm happy. Leave it alone.
Claudia King (11:24): Not everyone wants what you want.
Claudia King (11:24): God, can I live?

What had just happened? And so quickly. I expected myself to panic. I expected, as in all our pointless tiffs, that I'd feel my heart thundering at five hundred beats per minute.

I expected the urge to fire examples of Jesse's shortcomings at her, to want to quash any arguments in his favour with a thousand reasons why she was better than the treatment she was accepting, to whip out anecdata from my own history to show her what craters they had left in my burnt and frayed nervous system. I would have strapped myself to her like a baby sloth if it would help, repeating it in her ear until it sunk in. That she loved herself, that she was enough.

But it wouldn't matter. No number of desperate manifestations prescribed by a fraud in a kaftan would ever sway someone from who they were and what they wanted. I knew all of this, and it still made me want to cry.

Because I remembered how I used to be. The relationships I couldn't be talked out of. No matter how many times Nicola told me that it was weird for a thirty-three-year-old man to have a nineteen-year-old girlfriend, that Guillaume was only good for a fling, that Martin spoke in condescending circles that made me feel bad about myself, or that Eddie was a black hole that sucked all the joy out of the room — it never mattered. Any slight strengthened my resolve; every insult made me hold them tighter.

I couldn't tell her to leave him, because it would do nothing but push her further into his grip. I felt my throat squeeze tight as I realised that after all of that, Nicola was right. Claud didn't need a judge and jury about it. My job was to be supportive. Because we only ever see what we want to see, and this is both a gift and a curse.

Marnie Fowler (11:27): I'm sorry. I want you to be happy. I'll be here whenever you need me.

It was the best I could do. I couldn't get the passive-aggressive flavour out of it, and she was so fired up that she would read even the most earnest of messages through a sarcastic lens.

She saw it but went offline. I heard footsteps on the stairs and knew I'd be getting called back down to service, but I lingered, waiting for her green light to reappear.

'Can you get out here, please?' called Kit from the hall. 'Someone's asking for a caramel latte, and I don't know where you've hidden the flavour syrup. Stop taking toilet selfies and come downstairs.'

I swung the door open and pulled a face. 'Taking what?'

'When you take a selfie on the toilet.'

'Why?'

'I don't know why millennials do what they do. What's wrong with your people? You're all fundamentally broken, needy, difficult ...'

We bickered the whole way downstairs, and the place was full to bursting. It looked like I always remembered it: crammed full of people shoulder to shoulder with other tables, conversations loud enough to drown out the sound of Depeche Mode and Tears for Fears — Kit's choice, and the very height of my indifference.

I got back to work, returning to my other character: the helpful barista who hadn't, in just a few days, expertly sabotaged her life and seven months' worth of productive emotional repression.

The rush lasted all day, and I lingered after close to avoid going home. I tidied more thoroughly than usual. I deep-cleaned the espresso machine, disinfected the sandwich press, vacuumed and mopped, pulled outdated flyers off the noticeboard, refilled the stack of paper cups, wiped a day's worth of dust off the windowsills. I considered offering to make sense out of Kit's filing system upstairs, but I could hear him up there now, pacing across the floorboards over one half of a conversation.

Finally, there was nothing left to do; no one left to cushion the impact of my empty house; no one left to call. Finally, I was truly — in every sense of the word now, no hyperbolic flourish for the love of drama — alone.

Isaac Abrams (08:47): Hey

Isaac Abrams (14:15): I keep seeing raccoons all over my feed. Your influence?

Isaac Abrams (10:07): 'Waiting Room' by Phoebe Bridgers. Thought of you.

Missed call (22:18) Isaac Abrams

Isaac Abrams (18:50): You okay?
Marnie Fowler (19:22): I don't know what to say.
Isaac Abrams (19:30): Anything.
Isaac Abrams (19:58): Come on, Fowler.
Marnie Fowler (21:41): What? Do you want me to ask how your day was? Want to hear about mine? Want me to ask about your girlfriend? Should I act like nothing happened? What should I say? Which girl am I supposed to be for you today?
Isaac Abrams (21:48): I just miss you. I miss how it was.
Marnie Fowler (21:57): Do you still have a girlfriend?
Isaac Abrams (22:00): Yes.
Marnie Fowler (22:00): Then what's the point?

CHAPTER THIRTY-THREE

Spin class. Vegan Iranian cooking class. Hot yoga. Painting classes with wine. Book clubs in suburban book franchises. A free lecture on ethics at Melbourne Uni. Sensory clay hand building workshop. The Scandinavian film festival. Kintsugi for beginners. Group boxing.

I filled every moment of exile. The results included a mountain of sweaty laundry, inedible leftovers, hangovers, canvases thrown out before they even made it through the door, a stack of books on my bedside table left unread, a lumpy vase I'd never remember to pick up from the kiln, a bunch of films I didn't understand and sore arms.

I was drowning. Every time I turned over my blank phone — it was always blank — a knife went through my heart. I fell asleep with the television on. I listened to podcasts to trick my brain into thinking it was part of a conversation. I stopped people on the street to talk about their dogs.

Every day felt like 'These Days' had got stuck on repeat: resigned and hollow and quiet and raw and so big and empty and echoing and just ... sad. All the time.

And when I wasn't sad, I was angry. At them, at myself, my exes, my parents, everyone who had ever declined to save me from myself. I spat at my reflection, the pathetic and detestable shape of her.

The lonelies were out in full force for four agonising weeks, bigger than ever with no relief on the horizon.

I'd given up on waiting for Claud to come home for longer than it took to stuff some clean clothes into a bag.

I didn't know if Nicola would ever speak to me again, or if I'd only see her graveside as our family members died off. I wondered if she would talk to me then, or if she would sweep away with the family she'd chosen for herself, and I'd be left talking in circles with our aunt's rapidly advancing dementia.

Even Mum was too busy, too invested in the honeymoon phase with her new beau, Doug, to do more than make vague plans for lunch next week, which she'd cancel at the last minute to wander the aisles of hardware stores with him.

I'd tried to feel wounded by the concrete order of her priorities, but this was just how she was. This was where I got it from: in Mum's personal hierarchy of needs, *love and belonging* came first, not third. She needed Doug, or Trent, or Brian, or Paul or who-the-hell-ever like oxygen, and no number of pleading phone calls or passive-aggressive remarks about her youngest child being replaced by some man from the internet would change her mind.

She had been raised to believe that her place was at the side of another, and whether she knew it or not, she'd raised her daughters that way too. The three of us, we were incapable of change; our sweat and tears to prove otherwise rendered irrelevant. That was just the kind of women we were. Desperate to love someone; our entire validity hinged on someone loving us. This went deeper than self-esteem; it was genetic.

I'd lay awake with my messenger app open waiting for an ellipsis to show that Isaac was trying to find the right thing to say, too.

Part of me — a tiny, ridiculous sliver, driven by my repressed biological clock, I was sure — wondered every day as I reached for the front door handle, if I'd find him on the other side of it.

Some days, in the fantasy, he'd be slumped against the frame, out of breath and rubbing the stitch in his side. He had run from Brighton to Princes Hill because he couldn't wait one second longer to tell me that he was sure now, finally, that I was who he'd been waiting for.

Other days I dreamed I'd open the door to find him waiting there on bended knee, presenting me with a diamond and a question. And I would say yes, because in the moment, in the daydream, it would solve everything. I would never have to be alone again.

Every morning when I opened my door to nothing was both a let-down and a relief, and always started my day off on an unsettled note.

I was running out of ways to keep my hands busy and to pay for these distractions. Strangers and small talk: every time I got a hit, it was never enough. I could see people's eyes glaze over, the way I dug my nails in and dragged every interaction out. I asked too many questions about their day. I gave too many details about my own. I was repellent. I could hear it. I couldn't stop.

And when there was no one left, when the cafe had cleared out and its surfaces were clean and Sam had again gone home without a word, I would stay behind and read, or scroll, or dissociate, just to be anywhere other than home. Anything from anyone, I'd take it: let me give you my problems. Please show me how to fix them.

It was early on a Friday evening when Kit stomped down from his office and gave a yelp when he found me still in the building.

'What time do you call this?' he asked, rubbing his chest like my presence had given him angina. 'You only get paid until close.'

'The number of croissants I eat, I still come out ahead.'

'Can I start paying you in pastry? That would actually work out great.'

'Take it up with my landlord.'

He pointed at the espresso machine with a lifted brow, and I nodded, so he went to make us coffee. For all my professional expertise, I had never become a snob about it. I didn't care about crema integrity, flavour notes on the beans, or why plant-based milks were better for the planet but a middle finger to the way coffee was meant to be enjoyed. I drank whatever was put in front of me. A scalding mug of Blend 43 had the same effect on me as a perfect ristretto. He'd never say it, but Kit was the same.

'You okay?' he asked, so tentatively I wasn't sure he actually wanted to ask. 'You look ... sick.'

The drought had robbed me of my motivation. Gone was the styled hair, the paper-thin T-shirts so oversized the neckline hung off my shoulder, the casual red lips, the confidence and silkiness I'd employed since December. It was back to scruffy ponytails and chin acne, the only colour in my face the dark purple bags under my eyes day after day.

'Just my life falling apart,' I said with a breezy false indifference. 'Nothing to worry about.'

'Oh, phew. I thought you were phoning it in because you were getting ready to quit, but if it's just your life falling apart ...'

'I'm not going to quit. No one else would have me.'

'That's true.' He slid my cup and saucer across the table to me and sat down. 'I'd tank your reference checks. Not 'cause I want you to stay, just because I'm a prick.'

'You love having me around.' I rolled my eyes. 'It gives you someone to blame everything on.'

'Yeah!' he said heartily. 'That's what I'll tell my dad. *I'm* not a failure. *Marnie's* tanking the business.'

I clicked my tongue. 'He does not think you're a failure.'

Kit laughed. 'Yeah, what seventy-year-old man doesn't want to watch his son haemorrhage money from the family business two and a half years after he took it over?'

'It's not your fault,' I argued gently. 'All city cafes are struggling.'

Kit brushed the idea off. 'It's easy to tell yourself that's an excuse. It's easy to think you're the only one who can't get it right. My friends are having their second and third kids, and I'm further behind in my forties than I was in my twenties.'

He looked a little appalled with himself for being so open. Kit found no pride or comfort in vulnerability. His life was made of mirrors too, all his parts reflecting each other endlessly into the ether.

Funny how the thing that troubles you most also troubles the people around you. Frustrating, too, to know that relief and solidarity was only a question and answer away, and that suffering within the confines of your own head was unnecessary punishment for someone doing their best to survive.

'Anyway,' he said, shuddering to shrug off the honesty. 'Don't quit; I need you as my scapegoat.'

'I love working here,' I said, 'but I wish I didn't so much. I wish I knew what I was really passionate about so I could chase it. I wish I had a clue. Maybe if I did, it wouldn't feel like I'm working backwards.'

'How old are you now?'

'Thirty is getting pretty close.' I winced. 'I know I'm running late. I should know by now.'

'Why? I'm nearly forty-five and I don't. Last week I looked into running a daffodil farm in Ireland. Why do you have to have it all figured out by now?'

I shrugged. 'Because everyone else does.'

He gave a bark of laughter. 'No, stupid. They don't. Maybe if you're really lucky, but most of us ... you just pick something you don't hate and do it until you don't want to anymore. Life isn't a storybook. There's no arc. You just live and try to have a good time doing it.'

'That's pretty wise for a failure.'

'Eh,' Kit grunted. 'Broken clocks.'

He smiled at me, and it was too genuine for us both, so we screwed up our faces and flipped each other off.

For the first time in weeks, I walked home without a podcast on.

The last spin class of the day had been and gone, and I couldn't watch anything without thinking of someone I missed. No story could hold my attention for more than a few minutes.

Time was up.

I went home and sat with who I was now. No distractions to lean on. Not even Joni for company. The neighbours must have sensed the need for peace and reflection, because for once, no one was yowling into their pillow on the other side of the wall.

I was a woman who liked wine a bit too much. I was a woman who gave up too easily, who found it safer to blame others' failures for every minor inconvenience than to stay and learn and fight for anything. I liked storms and hail and the sound of someone's voice breaking over an acoustic guitar.

When I went shopping, I would have to touch the sleeve of every shirt in every store before doubling back to the first thing I had set eyes on. I had to know all of my options before making a choice, no matter its significance. I was paralysed by indecision, idling for years. I let myself be led by stronger personalities to absolve myself if — when — things went wrong.

I was a bad feminist. I was one more bad experience with men away from committing to hand-on-heart misandry. A socialist, in theory. A cynic masquerading as a realist.

I cared about the environment and how many pandas were left in the wild, but I could have cared more. I could have composted my food scraps, convinced Kit to ban disposable coffee cups, separated my soft plastics instead of feigning ignorance.

I believed I was the only person on earth without a clue what they were doing, and that when other people said this, it was only to placate me. Everyone else was a whole person, complex but complete, a finished puzzle, and only I was still a thousand cardboard squares in a box. I had questions; they had answers.

I used music to understand the world around me, windows into people's heads, characters to become and lives to live for three and a half minutes at a time.

I was a woman capable of terrible spite and brutal jealousy. Once formed, my opinions set like concrete begging for a sledgehammer. A woman who loved reluctantly, and then deeply.

I wanted to be known, but accidentally, by someone listening for a thousand tiny details and piecing them together in a notebook, arriving at the finished story without me ever having to be brave and reveal myself.

I was a woman who was tired of herself and the places she had been.

I had never really known what I wanted, not in any significant way. But inaction was action; opting out was a choice. I'd floated along and called it fate. But the riverbed was rising now, and I had to choose to swim against the tide or climb up on the bank. Who I was, or who I wanted to be.

I'd tried to stand on fragile sands of anger and resentment, working on the belief that I could outsmart myself. As though I was a binary being, as though I wasn't made of shadows and fog. As if any of us were.

And I supposed that I was a woman without much left to lose. Already I'd isolated myself, hurt people I loved and people I thought didn't matter, shed my comforts and kept breathing. I looked in the mirror and, for better or worse, understood who looked back.

I was a coward and a wallflower, and I wanted to be better. And after months of lying — to myself and the people in my life and to the whole world — I was ready, finally, to do the work.

CHAPTER THIRTY-FOUR

How clearheaded we become when we come to terms with ourselves; our ugly and our redeemable. The weight hadn't eased but it was easier to carry now. I was a person in progress, and there was so much work left to do.

I woke up. I commuted. I worked. I went to spin class and pedalled harder than I ever had despite my tired muscles' protest, hair slicked to my forehead, drenched T-shirt clinging to my clavicle. I went home exhausted. I took a sleeping pill to avoid bad dreams. I woke up and started again.

I had no soundtrack for this.

It felt good to slam the portafilter against the bar of the knock bin under the guise of dumping out old coffee. It felt good to take control: of my breathing, of my thoughts, of the temperature of the milk.

'To-go order up,' I said to Sam, clipping a docket from a delivery app up on his workbench.

It was the tail-end of a sluggish breakfast rush, and every minute of the day had seemed to take twice as long as it usually did. Kit was off sick, so I was on my own again.

'You look terrible lately,' Sam said in response.

I was already halfway out the door by the time I heard him. I paused and turned on the spot. 'I thought we'd agreed on passive hostility.'

'Kit thinks you're depressed.'

'I'm not depressed,' I told him. Wait, was I? 'Why do you care if I am?'

Sam didn't say anything. He just squinted at the docket I'd pinned up and went to pull the ingredients from the walk-in. I stayed where I was, warmed by the heat of the oven and how good it felt to talk to someone who wasn't ordering from me, even if it was just to tell me I looked terrible.

'I'm sorry,' I said, half of me hoping he wouldn't hear it. 'For being so —'

'It's cool,' he replied without looking up. 'I get it.'

'No, it isn't,' I said, looking at the floor instead of directly at him. 'I never should have spoken to you like that. That night, or that day here, or — or the last couple of years. That wasn't okay.'

I could feel him looking at me, so I dug my thumb into the sensitive flesh of my palm.

'I thought we were playing around all this time,' he said quietly. 'I didn't know you meant it. I didn't know you thought that way about me.'

'I don't really,' I replied at once. But then came the instant guilt at this easy lie. 'Or maybe I did. But I don't now, and I never should have. And I was so upset that night, and it wasn't about you at all. That's not — it's not an excuse. And I'm sorry.'

'Well, maybe I shouldn't've been so … relentless. I just thought I was being cute, but Kit's told me I was a bit of a pest. And I'm sorry for that.'

I nodded, and so did he.

'I also wanted to say thank you,' I said, and it took hearing my voice come out flat and nasal to clock that I'd become teary. 'I was in a bad state and you were trying to do the right thing. You're a good guy, and I'm – well, kind of an arsehole.'

'Let's call a truce,' he said. When I looked up, he was leaning on the workbench, balancing on the elbow of his outstretched arm. He had his hand extended for me to take.

'A truce,' I said, reaching out to shake it.

'Friends.'

'Friends.'

Proper friends, not the charade I talked myself into with someone else. On reflex, I reached for my back pocket to check my phone, but I must have left it out under the counter. I thought of going out to the empty dining room, leaning against the counter and scrolling endlessly while I waited for someone to show up and need me, and I paused.

'Do you need any help?'

'With what?' he asked.

'Anything, I don't know. Lunch prep.'

'You don't need to be out there?'

I shrugged. 'I can prop the door open and keep an ear out.'

Sam considered the offer, presumably battling between the reflex to make a comment about spending time together and the lingering pity he must have felt.

'Do you know your way around a paring knife?'

'I know how to use a knife, yes.'

'Can you resist the urge to slip into a falling-in-love-while-baking montage?'

'Sam.'

He grinned. 'That's the last one, I promise.'

'Give me the knife, moron.' I paused. 'Last one, I promise.'

I wedged a milk crate in front of the kitchen door to keep an eye out for customers, and we got to work. He needed to get rid of a surplus of sour cherries and apples, so we made a pie with them. It wasn't anything particularly complicated, but there was peace in the process.

'Do you want to talk about it?' Sam asked, folding up the cuffs on his sleeves as he prepared to rub butter into flour to make pastry. I was focussed on cutting apples into identical slices and didn't look up.

'About what?'

'Whatever had you so upset that night.'

I swallowed and moved on to the next apple. I supposed I could have told him everything. He wasn't judgmental; he had proven that over and over. He was safe because we really didn't know that much about each other. I knew how he took his coffee, and he knew I could be abominably rude. That was where our intimacy ended, and who better to unload on than a stranger?

But I didn't know how to articulate it in a way that a stranger could follow. I didn't know how to give words to describe the enveloping, pulsing loneliness and the counterproductive way it made me push people away. I didn't know how to explain how angry I was at everyone I loved, or indeed why, and I feared that if I tried to talk my way through it, it would mean twisting off a jar lid I'd never be able to get back on.

'No,' I said. 'Is that okay?'

'That's okay.'

'Okay.'

He didn't press any further. We worked quietly, then, him rolling out pastry and me working on the filling, breaking the silence only when I had to hand off the to-go order or make the occasional customer a coffee. I cut petals out of pastry to decorate the lid. He coached me patiently through the latticework.

'That wasn't so hard,' I said as he brushed an egg wash over the whole thing.

'You can do one on your own next time.'

'Let's not get ahead of ourselves,' I said. 'It might taste like vomit.'

'Is that what Marnie magic is? Puke in my coffee?'

'Hey, if you deserve it …'

He laughed through a queasy expression and opened the oven door to slide the dish in.

'You and Kit talk about me when I'm not here?' I asked.

Sam frowned across the room to query what I meant.

'When he said I was depressed and you'd been inappropriate.'

'We chat,' he said with a micro shrug. 'Just sometimes. Not every day.'

'What do you talk about?'

'Anything,' he said. 'Stand in silence for long enough and eventually people come out with what they want to say.'

'What does he tell you?' I asked. 'I'm not being nosy. I worry about him. I worry about what he does with all that anger.'

'I don't think he's angry,' he replied. He had turned his back to begin stacking the dishwasher, the functional autopilot of someone with a meticulous process. 'He's just got a broken heart. Their house sold a while ago, and I don't think it hit him until now that this is really it. He's got to move out, and it's like he's bottled up all his grief, and suddenly there's nowhere left to put it.'

This wasn't gossip. There was nothing juicy or salacious about it; no thrill for knowing something I shouldn't. All it did was make my heart ache harder. I wanted to tell him this, to ask him to pass on my love to Kit in some quiet and tolerable way in their next meaningful talk, but I didn't know how to phrase it.

'That'll be the lunch crowd trickling in,' I said reluctantly as the front door creaked open. 'Let me know when the pie's done?'

'You got it, boss,' he said, saluting me.

That was nice, I thought as I left to seat the customers and take their orders. *It was okay. It wasn't nothing.*

CHAPTER THIRTY-FIVE

The *honk-honk* of my alarm was as unwelcome to me at 7 am on a bitingly cold Sunday morning as my blank screen when I blinked it into focus. My toes ached inside my socks, and I could feel an unsqueezable pimple swelling to life on my hairline. When the packing boxes I'd so awkwardly heaved onto and off the tram slipped from under my arm and fanned out across the road, I was ready to throw myself under the wheels of the Range Rover beeping at me to hurry up.

'Do you think I'm doing this on purpose?!' I shouted at its driver; dignity lost in the wind. The catharsis of screaming at someone was as close as I'd come to an orgasm in weeks. 'I'm doing my fucking best! Toorak wanker!'

So when I'd finally dragged myself down the right street, looped around and traipsed back because I'd been going in the wrong direction for three hundred metres, found the right house, wrestled the boxes up the lavender-lined path and punched the doorbell, any interest in altruism I'd once had had long waned.

'What are you doing here?' asked Kit, gruff as ever.

Huh. I would have guessed his loungewear would consist of consciously coordinated cashmere sets. The cartoon otters on his pyjama bottoms betrayed a secret silliness he seldom revealed on the clock.

'Helping,' I said. 'Let me in.'

I didn't wait for him to step aside to nudge the heavy white door wider and let myself in.

I'd been here once before to drop off a care package when he and Andrew had caught Covid last year, but since I'd had to treat the house like a biohazard, I'd never been any further than the front gate.

A double-fronted two-storey terrace house in the inner suburbs was middle-class pornography. I'd even pulled up old real estate listings of the place now and then and scrolled through slide after slide of high-ceilinged rooms, soft golden lighting, and tasteful staging furniture, longing for a spare three million dollars of my own. I once almost asked if he would leave the place to me in his will, since he hated children and was so near to dying of old age.

I'd expected to see gigantic canvases smeared with the kind of loud modern art I'd only pretend to understand. I'd expected the floor-to-ceiling bookshelves crammed full of *very serious literature* and trinkets from their sixth, seventh, eighth honeymoons to Morocco and Greece and Costa Rica. Where was the delicate pink orchid I imagined bobbing on a narrow table in the long hallway?

A single oversized print sat off its hook. The bookshelves had been ransacked, with the remaining books and empty picture frames at awkward angles. A candle sat in the middle of the coffee table, its creamy wax blackened and lumpy from misuse. The shadow of old tape on the hardwood floors in the hall betrayed where a rug had been rolled up and taken somewhere else. What had once been a dream home was now Kit's personal museum of loss.

I dragged my boxes and bones from room to room, ignoring Kit. He shuffled behind me, grunting and sighing with the heavy-handed hints that he didn't want me there.

'This kitchen is making me horny.' I blinked in the white downlights of the expansive kitchen, giving in to the urge to rub my hands along the smooth white benchtop, leaving my fingerprints along the stormy blue cabinetry.

'I'm not interested in helping you with that,' said Kit from the doorway. He tugged his pants higher and folded his arms over his grey T-shirt. Underfloor heating negated the need to dress for the weather.

'Yeah, cool, I'd rather die.'

'What are you doing here?' he asked again, his emphasis squashing out any patience he might have had before.

'I'm helping you pack up,' I said.

'*Ugh. Sam,*' he muttered after a pause. 'Look, I'm not really in the mood to do this, so you should just go.'

'Do you think *I* want to spend my day off going through your stuff?'

'Yes.'

'Well. Yeah. A bit. But I'm doing you a favour, so just shut up and appreciate it. Where are we starting?'

'*We're* not starting anywhere. I don't need your help.'

'You have a whole house to pack.'

'Hardly,' he grumbled.

I grunted my agreement as I looked around the room. The dining table stood alone, chairs nowhere to be seen, and the glass kitchen cabinets were conspicuously bare of glasses and plates.

'He cleaned you out. You must have a terrible lawyer.'

'I don't want to talk about it.'

'Fine,' I said. I pulled a tape gun out of my bag and dug my nails into its plastic wrapping to rip it open. 'Then pack.'

'No!' he said, so loudly that I took a step back. I'd grown so used to Kit's broad-sweeping surliness over the last couple of years that it rarely made me flinch anymore, but this was new. Anger was a different colour on him: a black cherry of contempt and gritted teeth. 'I don't want your help. I don't want to talk to you about my divorce, or let you look through my shit, or pretend like you don't see how pathetic all of this looks just so you can feel good about yourself for helping someone. We have one sincere conversation and you think we're friends, but we aren't. Go home.'

Once upon a time, a statement like that would have seared into me like a cattle prod. It would have decimated me. I'd have crumbled, instantly, falling apart the moment my bottom lip began to quiver, and I'd need a month in the bath with a box of wine and Elliot Smith on repeat before I could regain any semblance of composure. But today, I searched myself for wounds and found the smooth steel of boredom instead.

'Bullshit.'

Kit balked, his frown disappearing as his eyebrows shot up. 'Excuse me?'

'Bullshit we're not friends,' I said.

'We're not,' he insisted. 'We just work togeth—'

'First of all, you do not pay me enough to come to your house on a Sunday as an employee. Second, we see each other almost every day. I know that you take your coffee differently in the afternoon unless it's Friday and you're going out later. You handle that Margot lady when she comes in so I don't get arrested when she snaps her fingers at me. You like my playlists. You think I'm funny. You like having me around, and I love being around you. We. Are. Friends.'

'Well, that doesn't mean I apprec—'

'I don't think this house looks pathetic, but if you're too busy feeling sorry for yourself to let me help you, I'll think you are.'

We glowered at each other. A vein in his forehead throbbed. A beat passed.

'Fine,' he said at last, rigid and arrogant. 'Stay out of my bedroom.'

'That's the first place I'm going,' I countered. 'I'm going to go through your bedside drawer and find all your gross dirty secrets.'

'What? Ew.' Kit's face puckered in disgust. 'Why would you want to?'

'Because you don't want me to and that's good enough for me.'

'I'm going to put some real clothes on,' he said. 'Make me a coffee.'

'It's your house!' I cried. 'You're supposed to offer *me* coffee!'

'Make the sad divorcé a coffee!'

'You make it!'

'You!'

'*You!*'

'Fucking, YOU!'

'Hey Kit,' I said through a grin I knew he'd hate. 'Love you.'

'Okay, enough, that's disgusting. Go and pack up my office.'

Eventually he did bring me coffee, grumbling as he placed a mug on his desk, scowling down at me on the floor covering his picture frames in bubble wrap.

We worked wordlessly, painstakingly sorting through years of accumulated clutter and memories. Linens were folded into neat squares, summer shirts packed into storage containers, stray cords wrapped and tossed into boxes never to be used again. I cleared out his fridge and pantry and felt an ache in my stomach when I saw that he, too, lived on cafe leftovers, biscuits, and the odd piece of fruit: perfunctory meals eaten in front of a screen.

We didn't put on any music, even though if I was ever going to suffer through hours of The Cure without complaint, it would be today. For hours, we communicated through grunting and pointing and waving our empty cups at each other when it was time for a refill.

It wasn't until I was stripping the sheets off the bed in the granny flat — still more than a hundred grand outside of my own housing budget — that I heard him speak again.

'Lunch!' he called from the courtyard.

I paused in disbelief when I saw what he was holding. 'That's not what you're eating.'

He rolled his eyes as he settled onto the back step and rested the pizza box on his knees.

'You are the heir to an important Italian dining legacy. You do not eat Domino's.'

'I do so.' He tilted his head and looked over his glasses at me conspiratorially. 'And I absolutely love it.'

'You should be more embarrassed of this than anything in your bedside drawer.'

'Don't be such a snob,' he said, shuffling aside to make space for me. 'Yeah, sure, Nonna would turn in her crypt if she knew about it, and yeah, alright, my parents spent a fortune on this authentic Napoli wood-burning whatever-the-fuck pizza oven for my wedding present, but this —' he flipped open the lid of the box and made an obscene noise as his glasses clouded with steam '— is comfort.'

He handed me a slice on a shred of paper towel, and despite my ridicule, I took it.

Our silence was different from the silence I had with other people. I didn't spend it panicking about the next interesting thing to say, like when I was with Isaac. It wasn't broken frequently by bursts of laughter at some video or disgusting message from a dating app like it was with Claud. It wasn't even the well-earned quiet of a long drive with Nicola, when quiet usually meant we'd run out of things to talk about and were content to drift off into our own internal worlds side by side. What Kit thought about when he was next to me was none of my business, and after all this time, I knew better than to ask.

It was only once the molten cheese had scalded a layer of skin out of my mouth and we were left with an oily circle in the empty box that conversation felt inevitable again.

'Where are you moving to?'

'I've got a soulless one-bedroom over on the west side lined up,' he said. 'What's that look for?'

'Nothing!' My eyebrows had shot upward against my will, and I had to consciously lower them again. 'I just can't picture you anywhere else. You're *so* ... here. This place. Big Edwardian terrace, massive trees, independent grocery shops, two Frenchies on a split lead.'

'They have Frenchies and IGAs in Yarraville, you know. They have trees, too.'

'I know that. I do leave my inner-north pocket occasionally. I used to live there. But I haven't been back since that guy dumped me.'

'He who must not be named.'

'He *wishes*,' I said with a phantom spit, although I noted absently that the anger I'd so long carried with Eddie's name had mostly evaporated. Except for the nights I scratched at my scar tissue, I hardly thought about him at all.

'You're missing out,' said Kit, shrugging. As ever, he was too void of empathy or curiosity to ask more. 'It's a nice area.'

'I miss Sun Theatre. And my dog. And the best injera you'll ever have. But I have this uncomfortable sense that the minute

I step off the train there I'll revert back to the needy, weepy, simpering mess I was back then.'

'When have you ever *simpered*?'

'God, you have no idea. I had no sense of self. The only thing I wanted to be was someone he loved, and still, it wasn't enough.'

'You can't love someone into loving you back,' said Kit. He wasn't looking at me, but out at the bare and brittle wisteria. 'They just do until they don't, and then it's gone.'

Heartbreak aged most of us, made our eyelids heavier and our lips drop in a permanent frown, the stress of grief wearing us thin, but not Kit. He looked younger than ever, smaller, his eyes wider and less certain of the new, half-empty world he found himself in. If it wasn't for the scruff on his chin, he might have been a lost little boy.

'Oh, fine, here we go,' he said under his breath, and pulled his knees up into his arms. 'How do you forgive someone for letting go of something that died years ago? And how do you stop blaming yourself for not being the first to leave?'

It was better that I didn't speak. Not because I didn't understand, didn't empathise, didn't have my own thoughts and tips on repressing the same questions until you forgot to keep asking them. But Kit expressed himself through grunts and insults. He panicked in the presence of emotions, preferred to put them in a lockable drawer and toss the key into a storm drain. But there was nothing to put away anymore. We sat on the step of his big, lonely house, and the emptiness grew around everything that was gone. He might have suffocated on the loss if he kept it inside.

'It was good when it was good, and it wasn't when it wasn't,' he said. 'It used to be that the good outweighed the bad so much that it didn't even matter. Then it started to get a bit more even. Then it got bad a lot. Then it all just stopped, and that was worse. And by then we'd been together so long, the idea of leaving seemed so much harder than just hanging on. For the last couple of years, he and I — it was just easier to lie. To ourselves, to each other.

'It would almost be easier, I think, if something awful had happened. If someone had cheated. If it had all got toxic. I remember coming home that day and knowing. Something was different. He was waiting at the table, and I looked at him, and I didn't recognise him; this person I'd orbited around. I'd loved him, but I didn't know anything about him anymore. I had all the pieces; I just couldn't make them fit. And I said, *"This is over, isn't it?"* and he nodded, and that was it.

'I keep losing everything. Him, our house, and any day now, the restaurant too. It feels like my organs are made of granite. I keep forgetting where I left my keys, or what day of the week it is. But I haven't cried, and every day I don't is a day closer to the day I will, and I think I'm afraid that if I start, I'll never be able to stop.'

I watched him breathe for a while. I watched the fine lines on his forehead smooth out, relieved of his perpetual frown.

'I'm sorry,' I said. 'I'm really sorry.'

'I'm sorry too,' he replied. 'It's fine. Or it will be. I've been alone before; I can be alone again.'

It was instinct, then, or irrepressible empathy, but I looped my arm through his and pressed my cheek against his shoulder.

'You're not alone,' I told him. I felt him tense for a moment, but then he relaxed, and I felt the weight of his head resting against mine. 'And when you feel like you are, you'll call me. I'll come over, and then we'll be alone together.'

There we were, two people with no one left to lose, friends by circumstance, and finally, by choice.

CHAPTER THIRTY-SIX

The Fowlers weren't great communicators.

Oh, we could talk. We could fill an empty room with boundless conversation about the news, fun facts we'd picked up online, or idle gossip, but substance stumped us.

In the throes of teenage mood swings and perceived injustices, my mum and I would get into screaming arguments about anything. Instead of ever apologising or talking it out, we simply moved on. There was nothing so big we couldn't ignore it for the sake of our pride.

If we never acknowledged it, we would never have to address the root of the problem, and we'd never have to admit we were wrong. Was it any wonder we kept our conversations at surface level?

But Nicola wasn't my mother, and she wasn't my friend. We were sisters, and sisterhood was like friendship in as many ways as it wasn't. There were things we could hide from the whole world, but there was nothing sacred between sisters.

The truly unconditional love repeatedly tested. The unshakeable intimacy of having grown up under the same roof, the secret language of pointed looks and private references. Defence strategies we'd developed to survive the whims of domestic disharmony. Whenever we reunited, we would pick up from the last page. It went beyond love and into biology:

two bundles of atoms, made up of the same stuff. Knowing — not just believing, but really *knowing* — that we would be connected throughout this life and into the next.

You could walk away from friendship, injured but fulfilled, disappointed but stronger, shivering from the loss and warmed by the memories. You could never stop being someone's sister.

It was wonderful, and terrible too, to be born with the right weaponry to wound one another in a way that few others ever could. We knew everything about each other. Too much. Too close.

For a moment when she found me waiting on her front step, I wondered if Nicola was going to slam her door shut. I saw her hand grip the edge of it, the tips of her fingers turning white, then pink as she relaxed.

'Hi,' I said. She frowned down at me from her high ground. I held up the cake box in my hands. 'Cannoli. I thought we could talk.'

It had been six weeks since our fight, and the longest we had ever gone without speaking. We had been in near constant contact since the day I was born, and even as our closeness waxed and waned, there had always been an open line of communication. But all of my texts had gone unanswered, from the unproblematic '*Hi*' to an offer to forget my horrible outburst had ever happened, to the photo I took of a pair of tiny glittery rain boots for Layla. I got the hint: she didn't want to talk. But if I waited for her resolve to soften, we'd be ignoring each other into retirement.

The thing was, in between these hobby classes and heart-to-hearts with Kit, I'd picked up a bit of wisdom. The only way to beat the loneliness out of your bones was to connect with people and make peace with your alone time. You couldn't feel at ease in an empty room if you were too clouded with anger and shame to notice your breath.

Perhaps she sensed I was desperate. Perhaps she'd been lonely too. Or maybe I looked pathetic enough there on her stoop, jittering on the spot in the brisk chill and the noncommittal drizzle of late winter, because she held the door open for me and stepped aside.

The house was quiet, without a whisper of ABC Kids or sports commentary to be heard, and tidier than I'd seen it since Layla was born. Through the open doors I saw crisply made beds, folded laundry and vases of white chrysanthemums.

Nicola led the way, keeping her posture perfect and her gaze forward. The tension in her shoulders, visible through her oatmeal-coloured cardigan, signalled a tension that suggested this wasn't going to be a smooth ride into forgiveness.

'Where are Mitch and the baby?' I asked while she flicked on the kettle.

'Oh, I got rid of them,' she replied brightly.

'What?'

'I thought, you know what? Marnie's right. If something in my life isn't working, I should just cut it off and start fresh. No responsibilities. I should just do whatever I want. If my marriage is struggling, the way all grown-up relationships sometimes do, I should just leave my husband, right? If I'm grumpy from four hours of sleep a night, if I can feel my brain smoothing out because I spend my life talking to a seventeen-month-old, while I'm also doing a dozen loads of laundry a day, trying to keep any semblance of my old personality or sense of identity, *and* keeping my phone on loud in case my little sister wants someone to complain about her fundamentally easy life to — well, I should just kick my family out and go back to how things used to be. So that's what I've done. Are you proud of me now?'

I couldn't bring myself to look up from the floor, but I knew she was looking at me with her mouth pulled in a tight, unpleasant smile and her eyes cold and judgmental. She was right, and I was a coward.

My heart thumped in my ears and all I could do to keep from crying was count the beats. *Fourfivesixseven. Twelvethirteenfourteenfifteen.*

The kettle popped. Nicola poured hot water into two porcelain cups, and I watched it turn mahogany as the tea steeped. She tipped milk into mine and strained the bag. She stirred sugar into it, the way she knew I liked it. She took care of everyone, and the thanks she got was an unsolicited lecture from someone who used anger like armour against honesty.

'I'm sorry,' I said to the buttons on her cardigan. She pushed the cup and saucer towards me. 'I shouldn't have said any of that. It wasn't my place. I'm so, so sorry.'

Finally, I was brave enough to meet her eyes. Her glare remained, but it might have softened somewhat. Her eyebrows were less straight than they had been.

'Okay,' she said. 'You're sorry.'

'It was ignorant and cruel.'

'Yes,' she said. 'It was.'

'I should have been more supportive and less judgmental. I should have thought about it from your perspective. I was a massive dick.'

It took a minute for her to form an expression, as though she was mentally running through a spinning catalogue of responses and struggling to find the one that both fitted the situation and maintained her right to indignation.

I saw her mouth twitch into a smirk, then drop again. 'It's really unfair for you to set me up with a massive dick joke when I'm so angry at you.'

A snort bubbled out of my nose before I could stop it. Gingerly, I asked, 'Would cannoli help?'

I flipped the box open and pushed it across the kitchen island to her, and she eyed them suspiciously.

'I made them.'

She paused, frown deepening. 'But they don't even look disgusting.'

'Sam helped. Well, he did most of it, but he let me do a couple.'

'The hornbag chef?'

'He's not so bad.'

She looked surprised but didn't say anything. She nodded us over to the table, so I took the box and my tea and followed her there.

'Are you, like, into baking now?' she asked. 'Is this your romcom route? Are you opening a cupcake shop?'

'No,' I said. 'It's just nice to make something for the people I love.'

My earnestness made her joke fall flat, so she picked at the pastry shell. She lifted it up, inspected it, sniffed it, and bit tentatively into it.

'Is it that bad?'

'It's kind of …' She paused to chew. 'It's kind of good, actually?'

The tension was thinner now, just a mist, and I finally felt it was safe to ask, 'You didn't really kick them out, did you?'

'No!' she cried, indignant. 'They're out at baby bocce.'

'Baby bocce?'

'I know.' She shook her head. '*Baby bocce*. But apparently she loves it. They go every week now.'

'That's actually so sweet.'

The idea of my tiny niece strapped to Mitch's chest in one of those front-facing baby harnesses as he leaned down to throw silver balls across a pitch, the only father in a field of mothers, was too cute to bear thinking about. I bit into my cannolo to keep from grinning too widely.

'He's a good dad,' she said softly, and shook her head as I rushed to respond in the affirmative. 'You only ever hear me talk about the negative stuff and none of the good. That's my fault. I can't blame you for thinking I'm miserable when that's all you ever hear.'

She had air to clear, so I rolled a shard of broken pastry shell between my fingers to keep from interrupting.

'You really hurt me when you said all that stuff about Mitch, that he was useless,' she said. I hung my head. 'But mostly I was upset that that's what I'd let you believe. I didn't know I was painting such a bleak picture. I didn't know I was that unhappy. It's just so hard to ask for help, and then it's hard when you get it, because you realise what a heavy burden you've been carrying when it could have been shared all along.'

She spoke easily, without pauses, because this was how her brain worked: she struggled over a problem endlessly, laboured over it and taught herself to see it from every angle before arriving at an understanding. Then, when she was ready, she could talk about it with perfect clarity.

Nicola wasn't like me, who needed every thought to be verbalised the moment it arrived in my head or else it might get lost in the wind.

The problem was, then, that when she was drowning, she didn't know how to ask for a life raft. Certainly, she'd never asked me to keep her afloat, always putting my safety first.

'That's where it all came from,' I said. 'Seeing you so upset. Being angry for you. Wanting better for you. But I didn't say it like that, and I shouldn't have said it at all. It wasn't my place.'

'Maybe not,' she replied. 'But it might be more accurate to say that it isn't your responsibility.'

'That's letting me off too easy. I'm always going to have an opinion.'

'God, I know. You never shut up.'

I kicked her under the table. She kicked me back.

'I think I've been using it as a cautionary tale,' I told her. 'You and everyone else. Like if I can just learn from someone else's experience, I can avoid screwing up in my own life.'

'First of all, there's nothing wrong with my life,' she said, but held up a hand when I tried to explain myself. 'But ... I don't blame you for thinking there is, because I've complained about it a lot. But the thing is, you acclimatise.'

'Meaning what?'

'Meaning you think you know what you want. Maybe you've wanted it your whole life, and every decision you've ever made, you made in pursuit of that. And getting there takes so long, you believe – you *have* to believe – that it's going to be worth it. And then, finally, you get it! And it's wonderful! It's everything! And you look out at everything you've achieved, except now it's just your life. The thing you always wanted is just something you already have. Pursuing something feels great. Getting it is something else completely.'

'And there's no getting around that?'

Nicola gave a short, kind laugh. 'I don't know if wanting more ever goes away.'

I made an exaggerated sulky face and collapsed, comically, onto my hands folded in front of me.

She reached out and messed up my hair. I didn't bother swatting her away, just turned my head to rest my chin on my wrist and looked at her.

'But are you *happy*?''

She paused to consider the question. 'I'm happy in the big picture. And I'm happy in this minute, here with you. In between … I wish I got more sleep. I wish there were more hours in the day, and more time to do the things I want to do. I wish I had more friends. I wish you were happy.'

I knew I was supposed to push back here and say, '*But I am happy.*'

'I'm … so angry at so many people,' I said instead, because it was time to be honest. 'And I don't know how to stop because they don't deserve forgiveness.'

'But don't you?'

I frowned. 'What else do I need forgiving for?'

'Maybe you need to forgive yourself for getting hurt.'

I exhaled the leaden weight on my shoulders. This would stick to me for weeks. It might take years to unpack; revisiting old memories, watching a shadow of myself make mistakes, forgive too much and accept too little, and feel not shame, but empathy. A heavy sadness for the girl who would contort herself into someone she thought deserved love at the expense of her happiness. I thought of her — the gamine, the groupie, every character she took on — and for once, I didn't think she was pathetic. I didn't think she was stupid, or desperate, or weak. I just thought it was sad. If only I could have reached back through time to hug her. I wouldn't tell her it would all be okay, just that it would be different, and that was going to be enough.

'*Heavy.*'

'Well, I'm pretty smart.'

'Because you've been on the planet for so long.'

She rolled her eyes. 'Because I'm ancient.'

'Old enough to be your own great-grandmother.'

'You're an idiot,' she laughed, and I could breathe again, because the best part of my life was settling back into itself. 'But I like you, and I love you.'

CHAPTER THIRTY-SEVEN

The wood squeaked underfoot as I headed to Kit's office on the third floor, the building's age showing with every step up the concaving stairs. It forced me to take my time, focussing so I wouldn't drop the coffees in my hands.

I hardly ever came all the way up to the top floor. I usually only called up the stairs when I needed help with something, and Kit would come. There wasn't much to it: a narrow hallway with three doors leading off it. There was the office, a bathroom and another storeroom full of dented and scratched pots and pans, aprons with retired branding, and box upon box upon box of old records and files.

I knocked on the office door and waited for Kit's grunt of response before I pushed it open.

His chin rested on his fist as he scowled at his laptop. Was there more grey in his hair, or was it just the way the weak September sunlight streamed in through the window?

Two more lonely weeks had passed since the day we packed up his house, and we'd agreed not to speak about it. He arrived at work the following morning, stood in the doorway, and gave me a hard look — a quarter stern, a quarter vulnerable, half asleep — to which I nodded, and it was simply understood.

'Close up okay?' he asked.

'All good. Made you this.'

'You're a star,' he murmured as I passed him his cup.

'Do you have time for a chat?' I asked. 'Can I sit?'

He paused, piccolo halfway to his lips and a concerned wrinkle in his brow, then nodded.

The visitor's chair was much nicer than the one behind his desk, I noticed, its buttery leather moulding around me as I sank into it. The faded wheely chair he sat slumped in must have worn out any ergonomic cushioning a decade ago and was now probably filled with crumbly sponge and dead skin cells.

I was nervous. Our friendship was still adjusting to the light of day. I had to be careful not to push too hard in case it sent him back into his shell.

I was finding the right way to phrase what I had to say, because I didn't know how he was going to take it. We worked best when the conversation was about annoying customers, what Sam had set aside for lunch, or whether the Lycra-clad sixty-somethings who piled their expensive racing bikes against the windows and took up all the tables to linger over a single macchiato all morning deserved the death penalty. (They did.) Whenever I'd made passing suggestions — that we could start offering puppuccinos for the city's burgeoning office dog population, or even just the offer to correct the typos on the menus and get them reprinted — he would blow me off. But this was bigger than that, and I had to ask. If he wasn't interested, that was fine — I could go back to slinging coffees and quality testing pancakes, knowing that I'd tried. I squared my shoulders, fixed my posture, and took a deep breath.

'I have some ideas,' I told him. 'For the business.'

Kit raised his eyebrows. 'This business?'

'No, for my fantasy girlboss league. Yes, for this business.'

'I didn't know you were interested,' he said. 'In business or ... girlbossing.'

'I feel like I need to sort my career out, but I keep running into the same problem: I like it here too much.'

'That's flattering. I think.'

'I want to try to make things better here,' I continued. 'Not that it's not great. But I know — or I get the sense that things could be better. Business style.'

'*Business style.*'

'It used to be busy all the time, and I know that's flattened out a lot since everything shut down.'

He didn't say anything. It wasn't like he needed reminding. I downed half my coffee to keep my mouth from drying out.

'Don't close the restaurant,' I said. I'd tried to keep the note of pleading out of my voice, but it slipped in. Kit looked slightly surprised, and I pressed on. 'I know everything is tough right now. You can't justify a whole kitchen for ten tables a day. But we need to find a way to bring people in again.'

'Wow,' he replied flatly. 'Why hadn't I thought of that?'

'We have to create our own demand,' I said, ignoring his sarcastic barb. 'We host events.'

He grimaced and waved me off. 'I wouldn't know how.'

His dismissal only made me more determined. As Kit leaned back in his seat, I leaned forward in mine. It had been Nicola's idea months ago, and I'd shrugged it off, but it was such an obvious solution. To need help and to ask for it. To invent a situation that demanded assistance.

'I know how.'

'How?' he asked. 'Like what?'

'Okay, so, lately, I haven't got anything to fill my nights,' I told him. 'I've watched everything on Netflix twice. There are only so many times a week I can go to spin. I don't go on dates; my housemate has turned into a pod person; I can't drink a bottle of wine in the bath every night —'

'If you're trying to make me feel sorry for you, it's working.'

'Fuck off. My point is: I need something to *do*, and I'm not the only one.'

This wasn't born of my loneliness, but of its collective power. The longer my exile dragged on, the more I resigned myself to it. Nicola had too. She had gone into lockdown as one person and emerged another, and in her metamorphosis she had lost her bearings. The empty cafe didn't appeal to a hungry passer-by. Breaking your patterns took gumption.

'I can't keep the restaurant open to keep you entertained,' he argued.

'I started signing up for all these classes to keep myself busy,' I pressed on. 'It cost a fortune. Language classes, pottery, jewellery making ... I made the worst terrarium you've ever seen.'

'What's a terrarium?'

'You know what else I tried?'

He paused, pretending to think. 'Did you join a fight club?'

'Cooking. I paid $70 for a pasta-making class.'

Kit choked on the sip he was taking, spraying his laptop and paperwork with coffee in a satisfying and genuine spit take.

'You work in an Italian restaurant!' he cried, outraged as he wiped his face with his hand. 'Do you know how much flour and egg you can get for $70?'

'But that's my point! That class was full of girls like me, who just want something different to do on a Thursday night.'

'Okay, but this is a restaurant, not a cooking school.'

'It doesn't have to be a class. It's not really about the skill you're learning; it's just about getting out of the house and doing something.'

Kit screwed up his face.

'It could be a singles event,' I continued, 'but for friends. A dinner club. Single tickets, randomised seating, a cocktail hour so everyone can mingle and chat. People want to make friends, they just don't know how.'

'You're monetising your loneliness?'

I ignored him. 'And if that went okay, we could start dinner service again, and do prix fixe menus one or two nights a week, maybe just Friday and Saturday when we know people are out looking for dinner. And I bet if we cleared all the crap out of the second floor and gave it a coat of paint, we could rent it out for private events.' As he opened his mouth to protest, I added, 'Private events that you wouldn't have to run, I promise.'

Despite his permanent frown, I could see a hint of excitement. 'That wouldn't be terrible. Necessarily.'

'See, I'm not completely useless.'

'News to me.'

'And me!'

'But how do we do all of this?' he asked. 'I can run a restaurant, but I don't know the first thing about event planning.'

'My sister used to do it professionally,' I told him. 'She'll help, and I'll use my other brain cell to figure it out. I'll create an event, post it on a ticketing platform, then we'll advertise it. It'll work. Come on. Come *on*. Can we try it?'

It used to be that my life was spent waiting around to hear three words. '*I love you*' came first. No matter how rocky the relationship became thereafter, we could always retreat back there. *I love you, I love you, I love you*, I'd chant, I'd cry, I'd beg, both safe harbour and weapon.

And immediately, the wait began for the next three. It didn't matter if we'd been dating for two months or two years. As soon as we established that we were serious about one another, I was preparing to hear them say, '*Let's get married.*'

I rarely wondered if I wanted to marry them. The point was only to be asked. I was glad, now, that I never was. I might never have been here, in front of this man — my favourite one by default — waiting for him to say the best three words I'd heard in a while:

'Let's do it.'

CHAPTER THIRTY-EIGHT

Missed call (11:33): Isaac Abrams
Isaac Abrams (11:33): Call me back? X

I locked my phone and put it back in my pocket, then lifted the milk jug to the steamer wand to finish a flat white.

When had we rounded the corner on October? Winter had come and gone in a sheet of rain and Radiohead, and I'd learned to treat chronic codependence like an addiction from which to get clean. Every day that I didn't type out a long message to Claud and delete it, didn't cruise by the Instagram of everyone from my past life, didn't linger at the front of spin class waiting to see if anyone would suggest grabbing a green juice — I'd count it as a win. Eight weeks sober and a lifetime to go.

It was a relief to have something new to focus on. I wasn't spending my nights giving myself a migraine in perfume-mixing classes, or painting with acrylics, or attending handywomaning workshops where it was a defiantly feminist act to nail stuff together. I was instead, finally, doing something productive. Afternoons slipped into evenings as I hunched over my laptop designing promo tiles on open-source photo editing software, writing and rewriting ads, working with Sam to design a cohesive menu and bumbling through social media data analytics until I found just enough information to get confused and overwhelmed. And now, today, it was time to see if it would all pay off.

The Little George Pasta Social had sold eighteen of its twenty tickets, and only one of them had been a pity purchase from Nicola. It turned out there was no shortage of people who had a blank calendar on a Friday night. If only the clock would work faster.

Kit crossed the restaurant with his head down, like he hoped I wouldn't see him and ask him to run another errand.

'Are you going to get my menus printed?' I called out to him.

'What?' He paused in the doorway and pointed to the stack of menus tucked between the register and the pastry case. 'We have menus.'

'For tonight.'

'It's a set menu tonight,' he argued. 'There's nothing to choose between.'

'Soy cap for Marco! — You have to have menus!' I cried. 'People want to know what they're eating.'

'Then we'll tell them when they get here.'

'People are dumb, Kit. They're going to need it in front of them.'

'People are not that dumb.'

'They are. They're so, so stupid.' I turned to the next waiting customer. 'Not you, obviously.'

'She *does* mean you,' he murmured to them. 'Her customer service is terrible.'

'Can you just go and get them printed, please? I spent a whole night working on them —' I nodded at the next customer to let them know it was their turn. 'Almond milk macchiato and a morning bun, no probs. Tap when you're ready — you'll like them; they're super cute.'

'That's what I'm going for in maintaining my family's legacy,' said Kit. '*Super cute.*'

'And call the linens guy again; he was supposed to drop them off by ten and it's nearly twelve.'

Kit nudged the customer. 'Which of us do you think is the boss here?'

They swallowed. 'Her?'

He huffed, threw his hands up in defeat, and made for the exit.

'Menus!' I called as he reached for the door handle. 'And bring me back a bag of oranges!'

I saw him flip me off through the window, but I was too busy attending to the buzz in my back pocket to retaliate.

Missed call (11:50): Isaac Abrams
Isaac Abrams (11:55): I wouldn't ask if it wasn't important

Nope. Not today. I couldn't think about anything except tonight.

As long as everything went exactly according to plan, it would be fine. We would close the cafe as usual at 2:30 pm, wipe down the surfaces, vacuum, mop, set the tables and dress them. If the linens guy ever arrived, we'd have white tablecloths and serviettes to elevate the space and make the room feel special.

I'd get home by 4 pm, shower, put a wave in my hair, and get dressed. Tonight I was playing both host and help, and finding an outfit to fit the character had been a challenge, but I'd done it. In all of my abundant free time, I had found a dress that balanced perfectly on the tightrope between *competent* and *hot*: black, long sleeved and low backed, with enough give that I wouldn't bust a seam or pop a tit free if I reached for someone's dropped fork. It was hanging on my bedroom door, pressed and waiting to transform me into the poised, confident showrunner I would pretend to be. No pressure.

Lunch came and went, pasta and salad served and cleared by the time Kit got back carrying a stack of menus. I'd found a font that came close enough to the Little George branding that only we could tell the difference, and spent an entire night getting the formatting just right. For someone who could hardly match two black items of clothing without her housemate's intervention, they weren't terrible.

The menu itself was straightforward: house classics done perfectly. *'When you get the classics right, there's no need to deviate,'* Sam said more than once, his overlong catchphrase. *'Overcomplicated dishes denote insecurity.'*

We were offering Aperol spritzes and antipasti over cocktail hour before moving on to the pasta course (spaghetti with prawns, rocket, sundried tomato and white wine, and wild mushroom gnocchi with sage and butter), the main (eggplant parmigiana with fresh basil and a spring side salad of radish, kohlrabi and fennel), and either classic tiramisu or vanilla panna cotta for dessert, before resuming cocktail service until last man standing.

I would be living off the leftovers for a week. I was leaning through the kitchen door to ask Sam if he could make me an extra portion of the gnocchi to eat over the sink later, when my pocket buzzed again, and in an instant, two words undid weeks of progress.

Isaac Abrams (14:18): Please, Marnie.

Maybe it was because he never used my first name. It was always *Fowler*.

When he'd used it that night — 'Fuck, Fowler, that's so —', both f's dragged out in a shuddering breath — it had been delicious. But in all my navel gazing I'd begun to resent it. Every time I revisited a memory — and I so often did, not against my will but always against my better judgment — and I heard his voice say it — 'Fowler. You gorgeous idiot. It's pronounced Zelenskyy. Don't you ever watch the news?' — I felt like one of the boys. I'd come to find that it wasn't a pet name, but a rank.

'What's up?' asked Sam as I lingered in the doorway.

'What?' I looked up. What had I come in here for?

'Is there a late order? If it's that guy who asks me for lasagne without bechamel, I'll go out there with my cleaver. I'm not joking. It would be worth the prison sentence.'

I tried to pull one single memory of the sound of my name in Isaac's mouth, but I couldn't find anything. Having it here in black and white gave it gravity: his earnestness on my screen where I could stare at it forever and wonder.

It would feel good to maintain the upper hand, to leave him on read, delete the text thread and move forward. The winner, at last, because I was finally, finally the one who cared the least.

It was the not knowing that would kill me.

What if I always wondered? How would I ever put the question to rest? I'd had nearly a year of dreaming. Could I take anymore?

A sound like a gong pulled me back to the present. Sam had thumped his hand on his workbench to get my attention.

'What? Sorry. What?'

'I said *what do you want?*'

I spent every second of the tram ride home doubting myself. I stowed my phone in the zip pocket of my bag and sat on my hands, convinced that they would move without my permission and tap out a response I wasn't ready to give.

It had been a horrible few weeks. I'd laid awake so often and dreamed about him making everything better. Kissing my fingers and proving me wrong about everything: that my strike had been silly, that this had been real, that there was a chance for us. Here was the door: all I had to do was open it and let all that hope back into my life.

But I had been looking forward to this night for weeks. I'd planned every detail of it. It had been the only thing that had kept me from collapsing under the weight of all this isolation and self-doubt, and now it was here, and it felt like the floor was falling out from under me.

Maybe he knew how to fix it. Maybe he had left her and was finally ready for this thing between us to really start. I could wish, even if it was bad for me. There was nothing wrong with a sliver of optimism.

I had to, just this once, resist his pull and see this through. If it was meant to be then it would keep. I'd waited months for him; he could wait one night for me.

I repeated this to my reflection in the tram door as I waited for it to open. *I waited. He can wait for me. I waited. He can wait for me.* There was a time to be emotional, and a time to be practical, and I had to choose the latter.

I rehearsed tonight's speech in my head as I strode up my street. '*Hi everyone and welcome to the —*' no, wait. '*Hi everyone and thanks so much for coming —*'

It was one thing to be a waitress: to serve and be polite, to deliver and clear plates and hand people a bill without making them feel hurried along. I'd been to enough of these cobbled-together social events to watch them go wrong. You could tell when someone didn't know what they were doing. The goofy look on their face as they searched for a sympathetic eye. The jokes that didn't land, and the sickly pity you felt watching them. It took a masochist or a moron to put themselves up for it.

The lump under Claud's sheets as I passed her room made me jump.

'*Christ!*' I cried, hand to my chest as she rolled over to look for the source of my shriek. 'I thought we had a squatter situation.'

'No,' she said. 'Just me.'

'You're home,' I said, when what I meant was, '*You're home?*' 'Are you sick?'

Her eyelids were heavy as she blinked, slumped against her bedhead. She was still in her work clothes, the remnants of the day's makeup lingering on her pillowcase. She took a long time to answer, and then shook her head slowly as her face crumpled.

Not again.

I dropped my bag on the floor and sunk in beside her, arm open for her to lean into.

'What happened?'

'He kicked me out,' she wailed. 'He said he was just sick of me.'

I had to sink my teeth into my tongue to keep from reacting with violence. I squeezed her tighter instead, and said, 'I'm sorry.'

'I just don't understand,' she continued. 'He wanted me and now he doesn't and I don't know what I did.'

I made a noise of commiseration as I rubbed her arm, and she didn't slow down.

'I just can't seem to do or say or be what he wants and I don't know how to figure it out,' she said into my shoulder. 'I get it wrong and he screams at me — screams — and then it's like the real him comes back and he's sweet again and he begs me to forgive him, and then it happens again, and I just don't know what to do. I want to make it work. I just — just —'

I frowned and said, gently, 'I don't think you should be with someone who makes you feel like this all the time.'

'It's not *all* the time,' she argued, sitting up and fixing me with an irritated look. 'I just have to learn how t—'

As she leapt to Jesse's defence, as she always did, as she always would, something in me broke. I'd been stretched between my love for her and hatred of him, and finally, I couldn't hear another word of it.

'I don't have time for this,' I cut her off, withdrawing my arm.
'What?'

'I'm sorry you're hurt. I just can't sit and comfort you when you're going to go running back for more tomorrow.'

Claud's face was frozen halfway between anger and indignation, and mine felt determinedly blank.

Maybe it was the nervous adrenaline coursing through me ahead of tonight. Maybe I was angry at Isaac's timing. Or maybe I was just hurt by the order of her priorities, and her eternal expectation of my available shoulder. It burned to think that as I sat at home gripped by fear and loneliness, she was opting to exist as Jesse's emotional punching bag, content to be berated so long as it meant feeling wanted.

I wanted to think I would be on Claud's side no matter what, that some friendships were untarnishable. I wanted to believe that the love of a best friend endured long journeys on different roads, but for the first time, I felt like giving up on her.

Emotion I'd been holding back all afternoon had made its quick ascent up my throat. It was too much hurt to process; I'd maybe even been holding it in all year.

Certainty, then uncertainty.

Respite and racket.

Attempt after failed attempt to work out who I was and what I wanted and which people I could rely on, only for the answer to change every other minute.

I was tired. I was burnt out. I was done.

'I get it, you meet someone and your whole life becomes about them,' I said. 'We've all done that. But you lean on me when you need me, and I drop everything for you, and then you disappear, or you take the things he does to you out on me.'

'I know,' she said, her voice watery. 'I know that's how it must feel bu—'

'But what?' I asked. I grit my teeth against the tears. I would not cry. *I would not cry.* 'Where have you been when I needed you?'

'You don't understand —'

'And I don't want to. I don't care what you do. I just can't keep watching you degrade yourself.'

Claud began to splutter a response, but I wasn't interested. I pulled my dress off the hanger on my door, picked up my bag and left without looking back.

CHAPTER THIRTY-NINE

When I made it back to town, Little George was a warzone. I froze mid-step, paralysed by the chaos of it all.

Chairs were stacked on the footpath outside, a tower of wooden legs and hope. Tables were in a huddle in the middle of the room. The back wall, usually stocked high with the bottles of top-shelf booze we no longer served, was blank, its contents in milk crates across the counter, with one propping open the door to the kitchen. The espresso machine, poor old girl, was at an angle, hissing furiously from the steam wand as Kit flapped at it with a tea towel.

'What the hell happened?'

'I don't know!' he cried, looking panicked at my arrival. 'I was trying to help!'

A cloud of steam billowed out of the kitchen, and the dining room's smoke detector began to scream in protest, and I had to shout to be heard over it.

'By blowing up the place?'

'What?!'

'WHAT?'

'SORRY —' called Sam from the doorway, flapping his arms at the vapour cloud '— DISHWASHER.'

'Can someone get me a broom?'

'WHAT?'

'A BROOM.'

I hoisted myself onto the nearest table, took the broom handle Sam passed me, and jabbed it at the smoke detector until it stopped shrieking.

There. Silence.

I looked at the scene below, to a sweaty, sheepish Kit huddled in the corner. It was even worse from up here: everything from behind the counter had been pulled out of its place. A puddle of espresso leakage was dripping down the fridge doors. The noticeboard on the far wall, where we kept posters for upcoming theatre shows and ads for garage sales, had been taken down, leaving a stretch of deep green paint darker than the rest of the wall.

I checked my phone for the time. 4:40. People would be arriving in less than two hours, and I'd never seen the place in such disarray. It made my house, which I'd been neglecting in my enduring bad mood, look sterile.

With as much authority as I could muster against a man more than fifteen years my senior and in charge of my livelihood, I asked, 'What did you do?'

Kit had the decency to look embarrassed. From under his eyebrows and beneath his smudgy glasses, he mumbled something about *'Trying to help.'*

My impulse was to shout again. I felt my stomach jolt with the effort of swallowing it down. I took a steadying breath. 'How?'

'I was going to mop.'

'I mop the floors every afternoon,' I told him. 'I do it after I lock the door.'

'You do?'

'Yes.'

'I didn't know that.'

'You don't need to move the tables. You stack the chairs *on top* of the tables, and you mop *around* them.'

'Oh.'

I was enjoying my high ground, actually, so I waited for him to continue.

'I thought the noticeboard looked messy, so I took it down, but I didn't think about the paint fading around it. I tried to put it back up, but it won't hang straight, so I was waiting for you to help me with it. I was tidying up back there while I waited, and it got ... out of hand.'

I sighed. It was hard to sidestep pity. 'Why did you need to go through the old dockets?'

He rubbed the back of his neck. 'They were in the way.'

'On the spindle? Behind the counter?'

Kit didn't say anything; a child caught doing something bad. I felt a pang of sympathy for Nicola and her days spent trying to maintain order in her house.

I tried another question. 'And what happened to the espresso machine?'

He jumped, throwing his arm out to point at it and snap to his defence. '*That* is not my fault!' he cried. 'That thing hates me. It always has. It's sentient. It's evil. It can smell fear. Like a horse!'

This time, I had to bite back a laugh. I squeezed my eyes shut and breathed in and out. It felt good, so I did it again, and then I nodded. 'Okay.'

'What?'

I crouched down on the table and lowered myself off it. 'Okay. It's all going to be okay.'

'No, it isn't! Look at this place! We're going to have to cancel. We're going to have to give people refunds. We're going to *lose* money on this!'

Kit flinched when he felt my hands on his shoulders. He'd been ranting at his shoes and hadn't noticed me approach.

'Here's what we're going to do,' I told him. Even I was impressed by the tranquillity in my voice. 'I'm going to chat to the espresso machine. You're going to put the tables back and bring the chairs in.'

'I am?'

'You are.'

'Okay.'

'Then I'm going to put the bottles back on the shelves, and you're going to go down to that flower stall on Swanston Street and buy out the rest of their stock.'

'But they're always so ugly — gerberas —'

'You're also going to go to Uniqlo and get a new shirt because that one is disgusting.'

He looked down at his white shirt and the splotch where stale espresso had exploded on his stomach and he made a grunt of agreement.

'And you're going to get yourself together, because this is not that hard, and you're being a massive twat.'

Remembering himself, Kit screwed up his face and shoved me away. 'Okay, that's enough.'

Just like that, I blocked everything else out and switched into work mode, even forgetting to nervously check my phone for another missed call or text that I wasn't sure I didn't want, whoever it was from.

Once I'd lulled the espresso machine back into submission — a gentle combination of hushed compliments, creative insults and switching it off and on again — I wiped the cornices, glued a ten-cent coin to the foot of that one wonky chair, hand-dried the wine glasses to make sure there were no water spots and narrowly avoided slicing off the tips of my fingers as I sliced oranges for the aperitivi.

I unpacked the tablecloths and serviettes from the laundry service and set the tables. In the depths of the junk room upstairs I'd found a store of white candles and set them in spare water glasses and saucers around the room.

It was a masterclass in compartmentalisation. If I had space for one more emotion in my ribcage, I could have added awe for how successfully I swallowed it all down, the whole day, its lows and its lower lows, and just got on with it.

As peak hour passed and the traffic had slowed, the dining room looked perfect, Kit had lost the crazed look in his eyes, and I was salivating over the smell of fresh focaccia. Everything was perfect, but the crowning jewel of tonight was the soundtrack.

I had been poring over it for weeks. It was timed to move with the night's schedule: warm and welcoming for cocktail hour (Al Green, Etta James, The Teskey Brothers), mellowing into something quieter yet temperate for dinner (Leon Bridges, early Winehouse, Chets Baker and Faker), then we'd lift the energy up again once dessert was out and the wine pours got increasingly generous (Blondie, Flight Facilities, Robyn and the Spice Girls, just for fun). Finally, the after-hours set would kick in (Tame Impala, Mark Ronson, Honne), sending everyone out into the night happy and hyped. This wasn't a playlist. It was a love letter to Little George itself.

I slipped upstairs to get dressed, resisting the impulse to grumble about the inconvenience of storming out of the house without getting primped for the night. I only had to hold on a little while longer: just a few hours and I could fold.

The dress fitted just right. The flowers Kit had brought back had come wrapped in a black ribbon, so I wound it into my hair. There was a tube of pinkish lipstick in the bottom of my handbag, and a can of deodorant they used as air freshener in the men's bathroom. (Gross.) The loafers I'd worn all day didn't quite work with the dress, but I could get away with them if we dimmed the lights enough.

Back downstairs ten minutes later, the dining room had filled. It was mostly women, with only a couple of nervous-looking men among them. People hung in detached clumps, making uncomfortable small talk as Kit worked furiously to pour as many drinks as we had glasses.

'Ready?' I asked him.

He mimed swigging from the bottle of gin in his hand, which I took to mean, '*No, but let's go.*'

I cleared my throat. 'Hi …'

No one heard me. A woman in polka dots saw me, watched my mouth move, then turned around to face the other way. The conversation seemed to balloon in earnest.

What if this was a total waste of time? What if they all went home and made fun of us — *me* — for even trying? But as panic set in, a voice in the back of my head argued back. No, it was time to back myself. I had more in common with the people milling around here than I gave myself credit for.

I'd been every one of them, showing up to an unfamiliar place with expectations simultaneously high and low, uncomfortably alone and desperately sober. I'd wanted empathy and direction then, and that's what I'd give these people now.

I grabbed the milk crate we kept behind the counter and stepped onto it.

Deep breath.

'Hi everyone!'

It worked. Kit dimmed the volume on the speaker, the chatter died down, and people turned towards the sound of my false confidence.

'Hi — hello, thanks so much for coming. Welcome to the inaugural Little George Pasta Social!' I heard Nicola's voice give a *whoop!* in the back, and people tittered. 'I'm Marnie, and this is Kit, and if you strain your necks over that way, you'll see our excellent chef, Sam.'

He winked at me. I grinned at him.

'To get all earnest about it, it can be really hard to make new friends. You can get a date, no problem, but a friend? I've spent so much money on so many weird classes trying to meet people I wanted to hang out with, but sometimes it's easier to just have a wine and a chat. And cheese and pasta only make everything better.

'So have a drink — have a few — and talk to each other. In a bit, you'll sit down, you'll eat, you'll love it, you can drink all the wine in the building, and hopefully we'll all go home with a few new friends.

'If you need anything at all, just flag down Kit. He'd love to answer all of your questions, big or small. Okay. Cool. Have fun!'

I hopped off my crate and bounced on the spot. As though someone had hit play, the room's noise swelled. I bit into my cheek as I listened to it, and my eyes widened with excitement as I met Kit's faux-irked frown, and I thought: *Yep. It's going to be okay.*

CHAPTER FORTY

The Pasta Social was a success. No, scratch that: it was a *huge giant raging knock-it-out-of-the-park, forget your delusions of mediocrity, career choice affirming* success.

The last of the guests didn't filter out until well past 11 pm, all a little sloppier and more shrill than they had been on arrival. To my surprise and utter joy, Nicola was one of them.

'Best night EVER!' screeched a woman in tall black boots. She threw her arms into the air, and the contents of her clutch exploded onto the street. 'Oh no!' she cried, and as she reached for the stray lipstick rolling down George Parade, she overbalanced and toppled over.

Nicola and one of her new friends collapsed on themselves, heaving with laughter as they watched her fall, absurdly slowly, onto the footpath.

'You — *fucking* — *dickhead!*' Nicola wheezed, and then, when she saw her friend convulsing on the ground. 'Shit. Shit! Erin, are you okay?'

But when Erin turned over, she was shaking from laughter, her face screwed up ludicrously as she hugged her stomach. That, right there, made the late night and the blister forming on my heel worth it. If any of them caught up for brunch or walked their cavoodles around Albert Park Lake some Sunday morning, it was my doing, and I'd never been so proud of anything.

Nicola had gone the whole night without being summoned home to her responsibilities, and now she was drunk as a skunk, ready to totter off to the next bar, looking and sounding more like herself than she had in years.

Once I'd checked that they were fine and didn't need an ambulance, I kissed Nicola on both cheeks, waved them goodnight, and flipped on the house lights.

Claud had shown up somewhere around the gnocchi and sat tucked away on the staircase with a drink and her phone while the night raged on below. I'd been too busy to engage, a blur of a woman ferrying plates and glasses all night, and I'd hoped she would have given up and slipped out by now, but she was still here, helping bundle the stained tablecloths into Kit's arms.

'You don't need to do that,' I told her coldly. 'We can clean up.'

'I want to help,' she said. 'Wait, someone's dropped a serviette on the floor.'

'Just stop,' I snapped, but she reached for it anyway. 'Stop it! Stop helping! It's my job; it's my event; it's my mess; you don't need to be here; stop!'

The room stilled. Claud froze, scolded. I stared, scolding.

Kit, sensing a battle he wanted no part of, cleared his throat, 'I'll just, uh ...' and dipped through the kitchen door.

I exhaled stiffly. Now that it was just us and I had the privacy to let loose, I had nothing to say.

It was my own naivety, believing we'd formed a sisterly pact when we'd agreed to nothing. This was just what happened: eventually, most people found their other halves, and they didn't need their friends the way they used to. Someone else would fill that space more completely than I ever could. I knew, deep down, that my anger was with myself. But it burned all the same to see it play out this way: the first domino of the rest of my life. I would continue like this, making friends and losing them when their real life arrived, and it was better that I got used to it early.

I bit back something unforgivable and started loading dirty wine glasses onto the nearest tray.

'I hate fighting with you,' she said. I set my jaw. 'But it made me realise something, and I didn't want to wait for you to get home to tell you.'

I scoffed. I couldn't bring myself to pretend. If they were engaged, I would combust.

'It's over,' she said. 'Bridge burnt. Rock bottom reached and filled back in. Done.'

Relief didn't come because I didn't believe her. 'Right.'

'I know,' she pressed. 'I know you don't trust me not to backslide, and I don't blame you. I didn't really trust myself, either. So I had to make sure I couldn't. I took screenshots of all of the horrible texts he sent, calling me stupid, telling me I'm worthless, saved the voicemails of him screaming at me —'

'What the fuck?'

All the sound had gone from the room. It felt as if my eardrums had been blown out, like there had been an explosion inside my skull. Brain matter would start leaking out of my tear ducts. The tinkling of the tray of wine glasses being set down was the only sign I hadn't gone spontaneously deaf in response to Claud revealing how bad her relationship had become.

'And I sent them to his bitch mum.'

'What the *fuck*?'

'"*Thought you'd like to know what kind of person you raised*," I told her. "*Never contact me again*."'

'Why didn't you tell me any of this?'

'I don't think you'd do well in prison. You're kind of ... soft.'

'That's true.' I nodded. 'I'm glad one of us thought ahead.'

'There's only room for one dumb bitch in our house.'

I held a finger up to correct her. 'One dumb bitch *at a time.*'

She smiled, and that was all it took for me to start to cry. In two steps, I closed the gap between us and threw my arms around her. The dam was broken. The smog was clear.

We stayed like that for a long time, hugging in the empty restaurant. The late-night playlist looped over and started again, bass and horns, and we were well into it before she gave me a parting squeeze.

We dropped into the nearest empty seats and unloaded it all. Tears burnt hot and dried cold on my cheeks as I listened to her talk about where she had been and what she had done to herself. How she knew it wasn't good for her to keep returning to someone who kept her on a leash, but how, if someone wears you down and tells you enough lies about yourself, you start to believe them. How he would push her off a ledge, watch her plummet, then pull her back to safety at the very last second, and the way she learned to be grateful for it. The way that self-love isn't guaranteed, but has to be practised, or else it can chip away to nothing. How you'll do desperate, stupid, reckless things when you're no longer on your own side. How long she knew it would take her to work through all of it, that she'd need a professional and perhaps a prescription, but now, finally, she pointed the blame at Jesse instead of herself, and that was a start.

I was only now grasping at how much time we had spent apart. I'd grown so used to having her in my ear all the time, and then felt so hollow in her absence that I'd forgotten what the sun felt like.

She didn't even know about the night with Isaac. I had rehearsed the story for her that morning, and I never got to share it, to listen to her gasp and cackle or feel my face go red when she demanded exact details and dimensions. But she was here now, and so much had happened since, and I could finally tell her everything.

Claud was the perfect audience. She listened intently, interjecting only to ask tiny questions at the right moments. She sniggered through the good parts and bit her tongue through the bad, slamming her hand down on the table in righteous satisfaction when I told her about his increasingly desperate texts. I found it harder then, no longer gossiping but confessing. Although I had thought about it endlessly, lying awake and trying on different ideas and outcomes until I could dream about it no longer, I was further from an answer than ever.

'That's tragic,' she groaned, slumping back against her chair in sympathetic agony. 'The melodrama. All the *longing*. The *burning loins*.'

'I never said anything about burning loins.'

'It was implied.'

'*Was it?*'

'What do you want to do about it?'

'I don't know.'

'Yes, you do,' she said. 'You know exactly.'

I sighed and covered my face with my hands. 'I know.'

'If he's left h—'

'Don't!' I cried. 'Don't say it, it'll jinx it, and then you'll have broken the laws of manifestation. We never, ever say that.'

'I don't think you've been to a psychic enough times to be an expert on the laws of manifestation.'

'Well, you haven't either,' I argued. I got up and took a saltshaker from behind the counter. 'Throw this over your shoulder just in case. Karmic reset.'

Claud frowned. 'I think those are different belief systems.'

'Do it anyway.'

'Stop dodging the subject,' she said, obliging. 'What are you going to do about this? If the thing we can't say might have happened has happened?'

'It's too much.' I wilted. 'I don't know if what I want is what I want, and I don't know how to know. And I hate hearing myself say it, even thinking it, because I've been trying to force myself to believe that I don't need it, but maybe I do. Or maybe I just want to believe I could, theoretically, be open to it, but someday, in the right circumstances, with the right person.'

'Use more definite words, please.'

I frowned at my hands, watching them as I splayed my fingers on the table. I waited for them to shake with uncertainty, but they didn't. I expected my voice to quiver, but it came out crisp and quiet, so it must have been true.

'What if I do it: say yes, jump in, and it doesn't work? And what if, after all that, I undo all this hard work, all the stuff I've been trying to teach myself, that I'm fine on my own and I don't need anybody — what if I'm right back to being a fragile baby bird again?'

'You'll survive,' said Claud, maddeningly logical. 'You have before, and you would again.'

'But then I think, what if I'm just scared and —'

'You are, for the record.'

'— and I don't answer and I don't go and see him and I make that choice, what if after all that, I —' I faltered, and my face felt hot, and I felt queasy with betrayal and ugly neediness as I gave language to the quiet fear I'd been repressing since my last birthday. 'What if I never find someone to fall in love with again?'

This was when Claud was supposed to stand up, lean across the table and wrap me in a rib-cracking hug. She was supposed to tell me in no uncertain terms that it was a preposterous fear, that I would get everything I ever wanted and more than I dared to hope for.

Instead, she sneered. 'That's bullshit.'

'I know that's pathetic, but —'

'It's not pathetic,' she said. 'It's just bullshit. How many times have you fallen in love *this year*?'

'Just this once.'

'What about me?' she asked, and this time her voice came out kind. 'What about yourself?'

'That's not the same.'

'Why not?' she asked. 'Why is romantic love the benchmark? Why do you think it's more meaningful than any other?'

'I'm not trying to downplay our friendship,' I rushed to tell her. 'This, you and me, we're magic. But a real partner, that's what we all really want, isn't it? A life together.'

'What do you call this if not a life together?' she asked, gesturing between us. 'I know we've had our rough patch, but haven't we all had enough meaningless sex to know the difference between love and lust? We're a family, you and me.'

I held my hand out to Claud and she took it. It was the safest I'd ever felt.

The next song started, and I felt fresh tears brim. Of all the thousands of songs in my phone and of all the moments in my life, well, 'Moon River', right now, was about as perfect as anything ever got.

CHAPTER FORTY-ONE

It was unfair how good he looked, even when he looked awful. I could see from across the room that he had lost weight, hollowing his cheeks and making the details of his face sharper. Even his shirt collar seemed to droop miserably away from his neck. He had on his glasses, and it occurred to me that he was tailoring his character for me, too.

It had been two more weeks since he last reached out and asked to meet, and I'd run through my options a million times. I'd explored all their challenges and potential roadblocks, every variable, the romcom trope fantasies, the worst-case scenarios, and 2 am nightmares, and still decided to come. Poor Claud had sat through hours of talk and kilometres worth of text messages with the patience of a saint. Perhaps she felt guilty about her absence and wanted to make up for it with a sympathetic ear and creative licence. Maybe she was just a better friend than I was. Today, though, she hit her limit.

'*Oh my god,*' she groaned, barely conscious. I'd burst into her room at 7 am, thrown myself onto her bed and told her about the scenario I'd imagined where Tash had stolen Isaac's phone, texted me as him to lure me into a public place to shame me with a megaphone and an audience. '*ENOUGH! Just GO and we'll get revenge later! Go AWAY!*'

I told him I'd meet him at midday, and it was four minutes past.

The laneway cafe he'd picked was dark and narrow, lit by heavy Edison lights and a sliver of early summer sun. I felt his glance as I ordered my coffee, and he stood up and held his arms out as I approached. The hug was made brief by the heady smell of his aftershave and the way I wrenched myself away at the first whiff of it.

'I can't stay long,' I told him as I dropped into the seat opposite his. 'I've only got a couple of minutes.'

'Ah.' He grinned. 'Now, where have I heard that one before?'

'No, really. I'm looking at a flat in a bit.'

'Are you moving?'

I nodded. 'I figured it's about time I got my own place. Be a little less codependent with Claud.'

'Exciting,' he said. 'You'll have to invite me to the housewarming.'

I gave him a warning look. 'I don't know if Tash would like that.'

I'd tried to make it a joke, but all that came out was a mouthful of razors.

'We broke up,' said Isaac.

Three sharp syllables that I'd been waiting to hear for nearly a year: one, two, three. I was surprised to find I was surprised. I had started to believe that he would never tell her, and that one day morbid curiosity would get the better of me, and I'd look him up and find evidence of their happy family — maybe with a dog, a baby and another on the way — built on a lie simultaneously too big and too small to reveal.

'I'm sorry to hear that,' I said, although I wasn't sure it was true. 'Did you …?'

'I think she put it together,' he told me, scratching at his bicep in apparent unease. In spite of everything, my eyes still followed the curve of its flex, and I fought the impulse to lean over and lick it. 'She asked, and I didn't deny it.'

'Oh,' I replied. 'I see.'

'Anyway,' he said, shaking it off, 'I don't want to talk about her.'

'Okay.'

'I want to talk about this.'

'This.'

The waiter deposited my coffee at the table, and I muttered, 'Thanks.'

'Us.' He swallowed. It was flattering to find I could make him nervous. 'What do you think?'

There it was at last.

Not a defence strategy or a coping mechanism, not a steamy, hazy daydream to make it through the day, but a choice. Will or want.

It would be so easy to say yes. To watch as my nod melted his pinched hope into a smile. It would solve so many problems.

The enveloping panic that still lingered in the shadows when I was left alone too long. Another body in the house to help get through a loaf of bread before it turned green with mould. The inherent danger of wanting to have sex and being forced to call in someone from an app. The great big question of who I'd spend my life with and what we'd do with all the years ahead. Trips overseas and trips to Kmart, equally fun with the right person. A pair of waiting arms to collapse into after a bad day. Someone to call with good news.

It would be lovely, too, to be with someone who got me, who pushed me and challenged me, made me laugh and blush.

Not someone like Ian, who loved what he could turn me into. Guillaume, a beautiful little fling with an expiration date. Not like Thomas, who wanted a cheerleader. Martin, who never really saw me. Nor an Eddie, who needed me until he didn't.

When you're young you believe you'll connect with people at every turn. In the great big roadmap of your life, adventure and understanding seem so easy to find. You just had to follow the signs: a shared look in a crowded room, a mutual affection for James Taylor, compatible energies and pet peeves. You would spark with them. They would see who you were and fall for everything about you, and the blank spaces inside you would be filled by their laughter.

But a few years in, you find out how few and far between these experiences are.

You get older and lose track of all the parties you've been to. Soon — much sooner than you think — the pours get more conservative; the music gets quieter and your capacity to connect recedes. No matter how well your jokes land or how soft the lighting is, people just find you less compelling, and you're forcing conversation with them, too. Your references fall flat. Their anecdotes are too rehearsed. You're bored and you're boring. You go home half sober wondering where all of your people went. You could have sworn they existed en masse, once, for a while. Suddenly it feels as though you're floating through life on a lazy river or terrible mid-Atlantic storm, untethered and adrift, and so aimless you've begun to forget what the shore looks like.

And Isaac was the shore. Soft and sun-drenched and tangible, waiting for the tide to bring me in. No one chooses to stay lost at sea.

I thought of the storms I'd endured so often at my own hands. The overwhelming loneliness, the confusion, the starvation for affection. The ache of rejection and inadequacy, and how I never, ever wanted to feel that way again.

And here was the way out.

Isaac would love me. He would keep me safe. He would hold me after a bad dream and make me feel like a whole, finished puzzle. He would be — could be — the love of my life, casting such a long shadow that all the earlier candidates were left to wither in darkness.

And I would love him. I had missed loving someone. All this tenderness inside me with nowhere to put it. The feminine urge to nurture. Palms to trace, films to quote. I would rub his sore muscles and remember his nephew's birthday and glue his broken pieces back together. Kintsugi for beginners. My name in his mouth would turn all the others sour. None of it would matter anymore, our histories would be erased to leave two brand-new people with nothing but time to talk.

I watched his hands cradling his cup. Maybe one day I'd wrap a platinum band around one of those fingers, or maybe we would stay together for years, decades, so secure in our connection that the government and organza never need get involved. The house, the dog, the lemon tree. White sheets drying on the line. Hair ties on his gearstick. Two half-finished mugs of coffee in the sink.

All the things I used to see as bars on a cage, now flipped to become markers of security. My Isaac, mine, from the moment we met and inside every minute since, even when it wasn't allowed, even when I couldn't admit it. It would be so nice to give us our happy ending. There was the sunset, and here was the chance to ride off into it.

'No,' I said. I heard it before I thought it. 'I don't think I can.'

'Marnie,' he said, and I wavered at the sound of my name on his lips. He closed his eyes, midway between disbelief and prayer. 'Come on.'

'I don't want to be anyone's second choice.'

'You *aren't*. I know, before — but that's just logistics.'

I took him in in pieces: his chin, his ear, his bottom lip, his eyebrow. I was afraid that if I got the whole picture, I'd cave.

'I would have left her for you at any point,' he said fiercely. 'If you'd ever asked, if I thought this could be a real thing, I would have left her in a second.'

'But that's not good enough,' I said gently. 'You didn't want me enough to leave on your own.'

'What's that supposed to mean? Was I supposed to blow everything up on the off chance you wanted this?'

'I don't know,' I replied. 'But I don't want to be anyone's backup option.'

I'd never been here before. I was always the one getting left, the one making wild and desperate promises I could never keep, so long as it was what I thought they wanted to hear. It had always been someone else's choice to stay or go, and I'd been just a passenger on their journey, kicked out halfway to the destination.

They had made it look so easy. Their faces set with benign acceptance. A decision had been made and they were sticking to it: '*Marnie, I don't think we should see each other anymore.*' Rehearsed and resigned. Don't shoot the messenger.

For years I would scratch at my scars with their aggressive indifference, spinning blue-tinted narratives of their cruelty, harbouring disbelief that they could do this to someone they loved, convincing myself that their desertion meant they could never have cared at all.

But I didn't feel good about this. I didn't feel victorious. I wanted to cry, to crumble, to climb outside myself and grip my own shoulders and shake and scream, *'Stop! Take it back! Don't do it!'*

In the end, which was harder on your heart: to love the wrong person or to be loved by them?

Did he want me, or was he just out of options? Did he know the difference?

Perhaps my ambivalence showed, because he reached out his hand and rested it palm-up on the table. I hugged the elbows of my jacket.

'I know that it isn't the cleanest way to start things,' he said, pleading now. 'But that doesn't mean it can't go somewhere. Some of the best relationships start as friendships.'

'But we weren't ever really friends,' I said. 'It was never for free.'

'We *are* friends,' he said, pressing down on each word. 'We used to talk about everything, every day. We get each other. We're great together. You know everything about me.'

I shrugged my doubt.

'I don't trust you,' I said, and the hypocrisy tasted bitter. 'You made a promise to someone you cared about, and you broke it every day, talking to me.'

'That isn't fair,' he said, his brow creasing in pain. 'You can't blame me for something you took part in.'

'I know. It isn't fair.' I pressed my nails into my cuticles to keep from apologising. 'But it doesn't change how I feel. I'm never going to be sure you're not talking to someone else when I'm asleep beside you. I'm never going to believe that I'll be enough to keep your attention.'

'You have to have faith in me. That I mean it.'

'That's naive,' I told him. 'I'll tell you I do to keep you happy, but I won't. And every time you're late coming home, every time you get a text, I'll wonder. I'll never be sure.'

'But I'm not like that,' he argued. 'You're assuming this is habitual, that I'm some slimy guy who's not content with what he has. I'm not that person. I wouldn't be.'

'I don't think that's true.' It came out quiet, because it was an awful thing to say, and I was sorry as I formed the words. 'I think we're the same. We both see other people as solutions to our problem.'

'Our problem?'

There was a prickle of frustration in his voice now, his pleading was bleeding into agitation.

'We don't like to be alone,' I said, 'and that's not a good enough reason to be with someone.'

As I watched him grapple for the magic words that would change my mind, as I lingered on the threshold of a new kind of ending, I finally understood that no amount of tears or shame would bring back the love I spent on other people. The logistics of heartbreak became irrelevant the moment the spark died. The resentment I carried only punished myself and the people I met thereafter. I could never make right what was always going to be wrong.

At last, I located my courage. The space he took up with his shoulders, usually broad and confident, had shrunk inwards. It hurt to hurt someone. It took every ounce of self-control to resist the urge to people-please, to not take it all back, to not give in and follow his lead all the way to the edge of my sanity. He looked so small now. Gone was the godlike quality I'd seen for so long, the uncanny handsomeness, the appeal of his permanent smirk, the playful sparkle I sought behind every lingering glance. He was neither my soulmate nor a prize, just a person with whom I had too much history to have any kind of future.

'So that's it?' he asked, his voice acidic. 'You've got what you wanted and now you're not interested?'

'That's not how I see it,' I replied. 'But I can see why you do.'

'How do you see it? Let's hear how you're the good guy here.'

I smiled at him sadly, finally able to look at him without blinking or slipping into a daydream. 'I see two people who might have worked in another life, but not this one.'

'That's crap,' he said. 'You can't just destroy my life and walk away like nothing happened. You're punishing me for *our* mistakes. That's not fair.'

'But that's how it is.'

This was not how he had expected the afternoon to go. The way he had his jaw set, his determined stare out the far window and the watery shine in his eyes threatened to shatter my resolve.

'I wish we'd met at another time.'

He gave a dismissive scoff at the consolation prize. 'Right.'

'I do. I think we could have really been something.'

'No one's stopping that but you,' he said moodily. 'You don't need to bullshit me.'

I reached out and put a hand on his wrist. 'I'll regret this my whole life.'

He pulled his arm away. He was rightfully hurt, and I wasn't going to make a scene. I turned to hook my bag over my shoulder so I could leave.

'*Don't*,' he said at once. 'Stay.'

'I can't,' I said, my voice twisting. 'That would be the worst thing for both of us.'

'But I'm in love with you!'

He was panicking now, sullen one minute and desperate the next. I was surprised at the distance from which I watched him, more audience member than participant, as though this public breakup — if that was what it was — was the crescendo of one of his cult films watched from the back row of an empty cinema.

I hoped my smile was gentle and understanding, not cruel and condescending in a moment where Isaac needed a kind of safety I couldn't offer him. I smiled through the sadness, too, the bittersweetness, because acknowledging what he'd said meant accepting my role in his life as a fantasy, never a real option, but maybe it was better this way.

All the nights I lay awake dreaming of passing flirtations, and all the wonderful lives I'd lived inside them, wonderful only in their impossibilities. All the happy endings, happy only in their unending nature, constantly rewritten and refilled with a rosier tint than could ever really exist. I thought of how perfect and terrible it was that this was all we could ever be.

In a jumpcut to decades ahead, I imagined myself remembering this, savouring the fantasy of the what-if. How fulfilling it was to believe in, and how brittle it would become once acted upon.

I thought, then, how much more appealing it was for us to stay here in an endless memory, holding each other close and still so far apart.

'No,' I said at last. 'I promise you. You aren't.'

It wasn't a tactic to win the argument or get out of here. I wasn't gaslighting him into believing I knew his feelings better than he did. It was just the truth. Because somewhere along the way I'd learned that being in love with the idea of someone wasn't a feeling with any merit. Because I'd perfected a character for him, yet another girl in the shape of all the things someone else wanted, carefully airbrushing out that which he wasn't interested in. I would show him a scratch and tell him it was a wound. We'd spent all these long months competing for airtime, for who could make the crassest comment, who could balance on the razor-thin line between our grey area and the black and white objectivity of honesty, and in between we had forgotten to be ourselves.

Most of all, I knew that this was the right decision for both of us. I knew how ugly the reality of it would be, and the immediacy with which our spark would extinguish when the lust and adrenaline wore off.

How quickly we grew bored of the thing we'd always sworn to want. Some gifts were better left in the wrapping.

As I left the cafe, the skin of my palm rang hot where I'd rested it on his shoulder as I passed. I blinked away the last sight of him, with his head bowed to avoid meeting my eye, and the shell of his ear burning pink. I felt every muscle and nerve in my leg work as I took the first step out of the doorway, knowing I had one foot in the right direction, and one in a dream I'd never be able to return to again.

It had always been so much more beautiful inside my head.

CHAPTER FORTY-TWO

'This place is revolting,' announced Claud from the doorway, grimacing as she found she was able to take in the entire flat in a single glance. 'What is wrong with you?'

'It isn't that bad!' I cried, smacking her on the arm with the bottle she'd just handed me.

I had only moved in the day before and I was already unpacked. It wasn't difficult to move house when all you owned was a bed frame; a new armchair; a second-hand fridge with a chipped handle; a bookcase full of lightly scuffed vinyls, and a vase in the shape of a pair of tits, stolen from your former housemate.

'Where is she?' she demanded. 'My replacement. The other woman.'

When she found her, she pointed an accusatory finger at Minnie, whose warm smile of greeting faded when she heard Claud's tone.

'Why did you let her do this? You promised me you were going to take care of her.'

You know that infuriating adage that people always drip onto single girls as they teeter on the edge of hopelessness, '*You'll find someone when you stop looking*'?

This trite advice was always loaded onto you apropos of nothing. It suggested that you were doing both too much and not enough. You couldn't win. It was your own fault. It made me want to spit fire every time I heard it, not least because it turned out to be entirely true.

Because I stopped looking for romance — for real this time, pinky promise — and I met the love of my life.

She had the best smile I'd ever seen. It took over her whole face and never seemed to fade, as though she knew the world to be a kind and wonderful place and she was just happy to be part of it, as long as she was by my side. Her dark eyes were all kindness and adoration. Her golden hair hung in effortless waves around — oh, fuck it, she was a dog.

I went to the shelter, intent on signing up as a volunteer dog walker, and like a sucker, I fell for the first one I saw.

Minnie was some kind of golden retriever mix. She'd been surrendered in middle age when her elderly owner had grown too frail to take care of her. She had two goals in life: to rip apart every soft toy I bought her, and to do it lying across my feet. She took up eighty percent of my bed and I often woke up clinging to the edge of my mattress or else contorted around her. She loved funk, especially James Brown, and put her whole body into her howl whenever he played. And I loved her.

Such was her joyful energy that she had even won Kit over. She spent her mornings greeting people at Little George's door and afternoons sleeping in his office. Once I'd caught her and Kit spooning on the floor, which he vehemently denied.

Dogs had it figured out. They knew that the only way to love someone was to throw yourself into it, to dive in and have faith that the love you gave would come back to you.

'It *is* that bad,' said Claud. She groaned as she swung open my fridge and found it empty but for two bottles of rosé, a jar of pickles, a wedge of brie with an indisputable bite taken out of it, and a carrot cake big enough for a party of twelve. 'Why would you leave our lovely house for this *hole*?'

'But it's miiine,' I sang, throwing my arms out wide and spinning around on the spot. A small spin because if I went too wide, I'd be able to touch both sides of the kitchen in a single turn.

She didn't indulge me but went about looking for something to pour the champagne she'd brought into, opening and closing cupboards until she found one with glasses.

'Things can belong to you and still be shit. My first car was a piece of shit. That breast cancer gene, I probably have it, that's shit.'

'My apartment is not cancer.'

'But it is shit.'

Claud wasn't wrong. My new place was nothing special. It was the antithesis of special. It was where special went to die.

The kitchen was dated, with black and white checkerboard laminate floors and blue cabinets with naff gold seashells for handles. I was pretty sure only two burners on the gas stove actually worked. There was an empty space under the bench where a washing machine or dishwasher could go, but since I had neither, it had become Minnie's preferred nap nook. A manky lilac blanket and decapitated stuffed hedgehog lay there now.

You had to press yourself against the wall and suck your stomach in if you wanted to stand in the bathroom and close the door. The showerhead wasn't much better than a knotted garden hose, drizzling at you as you rotated and tried not to catch your death. All my makeup had been piled into a mop bucket; there was nowhere to put it away.

The bedroom, too, left plenty to be desired. It fitted a queen-sized bed, a narrow side table and nothing else. I had to keep my clothes in the linen press, but it didn't matter, because I had neither spare linen nor access to Claud's depthless closet anymore. My jeans, work T-shirts and single nice dress fitted just fine.

A few optimistic plants hung off a balcony with cracked and flaking grey paint, just wide enough for Minnie to wedge herself onto for an afternoon spent sunbathing.

It wasn't all doom and bacteria. There was the light. Sash windows in every room welcomed golden hour in a wide embrace, bathing every inch of the place in a gradually deepening orange that had me believing everything was going to work out.

'Listen, listen, listen,' I said, shushing her with flapping hands.

Claud tucked her hair behind her ears to improve her hearing. She waited a minute, then looked at me with a question mark on her face.

'Silence,' I said. 'No one is having sex in this whole building.'

'Not even you.'

'Definitely not me.'

'Ever.'

'Well, I don't know about *nev*—'

'If someone brought me back to this apartment — I don't care if they're Chris Evans in a chunky sweater — I'd leave. I'd walk out and I'd call the police.'

'To report what?'

'Indecent exposure to ugliness.'

'Do you hear this?' I asked Minnie. Her tail thudded against the floor in response. 'The way she talks to us. I don't know why we put up with her. I agree with you; we should cut her out.'

'Um, fuck off,' said Claud. 'She would never suggest that. She loves me.'

'We bitch about you all the time. It's all she ever wants to do.'

'She wouldn't say that if she knew what I have in my bag.'

'What do you have in your bag?'

She reached into the depths of the bag hanging from her shoulder, and from within it came a sharp squeak.

Minnie shot up to sit perfectly straight and still except for the golden blur of her wagging tail. Claud withdrew a stuffed purple octopus, squeezed its squeaker and threw it, and Minnie shot after it. Claud yelped with delight and chased after her, calling out encouragements, taking back the disgusting sodden toy without a word of complaint and throwing it for her again.

It was shrill and loud and wonderful, the squeaking and shouting that carried on as I popped the cork on the Perrier-Jouët and filled up the glasses I'd indefinitely borrowed from Little George.

'I brought you something too,' said Claud as she accepted the glass I was handing her. Elsewhere, Minnie worked to rip open the octopus' seams.

'For moi?'

'It was too big to put in my bag, so I left it in the hall. But from the looks of this area, someone might have stolen it.'

'We're three blocks away from your place,' I said, rolling my eyes on the way to the door. 'It's the same area.'

A potted miniature lemon tree stood in the foyer with a ribbon looped around its branches. I spun around to beam at her with a hand to my heart.

'Stop it,' I said through the wobbly line of my mouth. I was too close to tears to grin and too happy to cry. 'You love me.'

'Ew.' She cringed. 'I do not.'

'You do!' I insisted. 'You listen when I talk because you love me.'

'I only love two people: Minnie and my reflection.'

'*And me.*'

I cradled the pink ceramic pot in my arms and brought it inside, careful not to let its branches scrape the ceiling, and nuzzled my face against the leaves purely for the look of disgust it got from Claud.

'Happy birthday, dickhead,' she said. 'I'm glad you were born.'

'I'm glad we met.'

'I'm glad we got rid of those terrible boys.'

'I'm glad we're cute enough to get by on our looks, but ugly enough that we had to learn how to be funny too. If to no one but each other.'

She paused to think. 'I'm glad we ... have a superhuman tolerance for wine.'

I settled onto the floor in front of her and drank heavily from my glass to support her statement. Minnie sandwiched herself between us, offering her tummy for rubs, and we obliged.

'I'm glad we live within walking distance of the best croissants in the world.'

Claud sighed with longing. 'Can we go to Lune in the morning? I'll buy you one for your birthday.'

'Good,' I said. 'Because I spent all my money on this horrible apartment's bond.'

'Babe, it's so shit.'

'It's really shit,' I agreed, laughing into my glass as I scanned the room. The greige vertical blinds with a panel missing, the ancient and non-functional gas heater painted into the wall, and the mushroom-coloured carpet I suspected had once been white were all remnants of an indifferent landlord and a competitive market. 'But I like it. It'll grow on you.'

'As will the mould.'

'To mould poisoning!' I cried, holding up my glass to toast. 'May it kill me before I have to worry about how I'm going to pay for retirement!'

'To realistic life plans!' she called, matching my energy. 'Happy birthday, you!'

'Happy birthday, me!'

We drained our glasses, refilled them and drained them again, and again, and again. There was pizza delivery and music and pictures and chat and laughter and more fizz until we were red in the face and numb in our extremities.

'Look what else I got,' she said, somewhere around midnight as double vision set in. She pulled a small pink box from her bag, gold embossed letters spelling out *Tarot of Light*.

'Stop it,' I said, snorting. 'You're not serious.'

'I figure, everything she said was right, so tarot can't be the problem,' she said, her eyes slits as the fizz hit her bloodstream. '*Plerstephanie* just sent us off in the wrong direction. We gotta take charge of ourselves.'

'*Plerstephanie*. Really.'

'Shut it,' she said and handed the box over. 'Tell me my future.'

I took it from her, withdrew the cards and began to shuffle them. She watched me with her glass against her cheek, cooling her flushed face and scrutinising me. She was a lit fuse again, just like she used to be.

Despite this year and all of its challenges, Claud was someone who wanted to believe in good things. It was her flaw and her strength, and she wasn't going to let something as inconsequential as a bad boyfriend get to her. It was enough to make you cry. If souls were split in two and it was our life's work to seek out our other halves, then I'd found mine, and was only grateful we had so much time left together: as long as we wanted.

I fanned the cards out and told her to pick one, and she did. I turned it over to examine it.

'Hmm,' I said, thumbing through the accompanying guidebook to find the meaning of the Five of Cups. '*Very* interesting.'

'What does it mean? *Don't* say it's that I'm going to have five more cups of champagne.'

I found the page at last, and the longer I read through it, the deeper my frown became. I bit my tongue and made a warning noise.

'What is it?' she asked. 'Is it awful? What didn't Plerstephanie tell us?'

'It means you're ...' I reached out to take her hand, and she let me. I gripped her fingers and took a shaky breath, swallowed hard and whispered, '... a fucking moron.'

More champagne and laughter. More cake and indie pop and polaroids. Against all that angst all year, there was more joy in my life than I knew what to do with.

Claud fell asleep on the armchair after too long, covered in a towel (*Reminder: buy a spare blanket*), snoring grotesquely through her open mouth thanks to a bottle and a half of bubbles and an entire half a birthday cake. There had been twenty-nine candles, and by the way the room swam as I drank right from the tap, it felt like I'd had as many drinks.

The checkerboard design of my kitchen floor blurred when I blinked at it. On the fridge, Claud had stuck a series of Polaroids from the night just gone: a selfie she had taken in my bathroom mirror, tongue out as she flipped off her reflection. Minnie beaming at the camera from her bed, the guts of a destroyed stuffed octopus between her paws. And one of both of us, out of focus: her arm around my neck as I used my champagne bottle as a microphone. If photos could project sound, the kitchen would be cursed with my pitchy attempt at 'Jolene' forever.

On the bench sat a grocery bag of cleaning supplies, toilet paper, teabags and microwaveable popcorn that Nicola had dropped off on her way to her Spanish class that afternoon after she rightfully assumed I'd forgotten to buy essentials.

This, more than anything, made the place feel like a home. It didn't matter that my fridge was old and slightly yellow, or that I could only watch TV on my laptop, or that everything in here echoed without the rugs or curtains I'd yet to buy. I didn't have all the things I needed yet, but I had stuff. A dozen candles, a record player, a basket full of dog toys, a few homewares and a deck of tarot cards for party tricks. Everything that mattered.

Minnie had taken herself to bed hours ago, and I found her curled up against my pillow. I kissed her on the head and went to brush my teeth.

I was a year older, and everything was different, and everything was the same.

Thirty was right around the corner now, practically tapping on the window with its sensible manicure to coax me into developing a complex about it. Birthdays always seemed like the right time for an existential crisis, so I stared at my reflection with a mouth full of toothpaste foam and gave it permission to arrive. I could cry it out and get it over with: a third of my life wasted on men I no longer knew, my potential squandered for the easy route, the line between my eyebrows I couldn't afford to get Botoxed out. The emptiness of my nest, and how unlikely it seemed that it would ever get full.

I stood braced. I scrubbed and spat. I strained, tensing my stomach like it might force the tears out. I screwed up my face and tried to remember every sad Julien Baker song in my catalogue, just like I had a year ago, but still, nothing came.

It wasn't as though there was nothing to cry about. No matter how the sun bathed my apartment, life was not a glorious haze of a golden fog. My thoughts were still consumed with dissatisfaction and doubt.

I thought about him most days. Healthy, sensible, rational or not; sometimes I missed him so much it made me want to vomit.

Sometimes, when someone goonishly tall passed the cafe window, my heart would jump into my throat and I'd be seized with panic. *Was it him? Was he coming in here? What was he going to say? What did I want to hear?* But then I would see that it was no one, just some stranger, and the feeling would pass.

Other days it would consume me completely, and I would have to shut my phone in a drawer and take Minnie for a long walk just to stop myself from googling *How to restore deleted messages* so I could scroll endlessly through them and make myself sick with longing.

How strange it was to grieve something you never really had in the first place. It wasn't the friendship I missed, because there wasn't one there to begin with. It was the daydream.

How nice it had been to want something without ever having to risk getting it. How lovely it had been to fall in love a thousand times and live a thousand lives inside my own head, excited and enthralled and safe, always, from the real pain of real life. That was what I missed: delirious, irrational hope. How funny, too, to have broken your own heart. There was no recourse. I'd just have to live through it.

Nicola was right: you couldn't outsmart getting hurt. Life and people and circumstances and self-destructive patterns would always find a way to hold your expectations up to the light and then smash them into pieces. But for now, I was okay with that. I was okay with getting it wrong. I welcomed my attempt and accepted my failure.

It was all about perspective, wasn't it? I was as alone as I'd ever been, and I was getting better at it. I was learning to fill up my days with things that felt good — time with my friends, pasta and wine, teaching Layla how to swear, new and old music, fighting with Kit and planning events for Little George, dog parks and their politics, coffee and fresh flowers, Sunday evening trips to the coin laundry with a book — and spending less time thinking about what I thought was missing.

Maybe my birthday drink with Sam tomorrow would lead somewhere, or maybe it wouldn't. Maybe I'd get a rash from my shower, and I'd move back in with Claud before the year was out. Maybe I'd find a new job, or a new haircut, or a new way to kill all the time I had ahead of me. Maybe everything would change in a blink, the way Nicola's life had. The rest of my life felt like such a long time.

As I climbed into bed beside Minnie and pulled her in to cuddle, I noted, in my fuzzy champagne haze, that I had everything I ever wanted, even if it looked nothing like I expected it to: a home, a dog and a lemon tree.

ACKNOWLEDGEMENTS

No one deserves more gratitude than Taylor Whitington, who read incoherent first drafts, listened to frantic voice notes, suffered my circular panicking and plotting and ranting, and did it all with more support and enthusiasm that no amount of therapy will ever convince me I deserve. We've known each other a long time. Let's know each other for a lot longer.

A big happy warm thank you to Daniel Barnett, Erin Hunter, Sam Smith, Rachel Coop, Raquel Gazzola, Nick Tattam, Emma Webster, Ainsley Thompson, Keera, Ava and Otto Hoogendorp, Hugh Hundertmark, Patrick O'Loughlin, David Adams, Anna Burke and Luke Beck. This book has made me a frazzled, grumpy recluse, and you're all blissful relief.

Thank you to Victoria Brookman for your unwavering patience and support while I whined endlessly about Marnie finding her way. Clare Fletcher, Carlie Slattery, and all my other wonderful writer friends too; the combined trauma of this agonising hobby bonds us all.

Thank you forever to Jane Novak and Anna Valdinger for always making this tired author feel safe and heard. Lucy Inglis, Mietta Yans, Jacqui Furlong, Rachel Cramp, Samantha Sainsbury, and the HarperCollins family: talented and hardworking people who take the mush in my drafts and help turn it into something I'm so proud of.

My unending gratitude for MA, today and the rest of my life.

VK again and always.

And to the people I've loved the wrong way.

No Hard Feelings

Hungover, underpaid and overwhelmed

Feelings

'Scaldingly funny and bitingly real, *No Hard Feelings* deserves a warning label: *danger, may induce binge reading*'
TORI HASCHKA, AUTHOR OF *GRACE UNDER PRESSURE*

Genevieve Novak

I exist on validation from emotionally unavailable men, biscuits, and cheap wine, and it's easier to get off with Max than a Tiny Teddy.

Penny can't help but compare herself to her friends. Annie is about to become a senior associate at her law firm, Bec has just got engaged, Leo is dating everyone this side of the Yarra, and Penny is just ... waiting. Waiting for Max, her on-again, off-again boyfriend, to allow her to spend the night, waiting for the promotion she was promised, waiting for her Valium to kick in. Waiting for her real life to start.

Out of excuses and sick of falling behind, Penny is determined to turn things around. She's going to make it work with Max, impress her tyrannical boss, quit seeing her useless therapist, remember to water her plants, and stop having panic attacks in the work toilets.

But soon she's back to doomscrolling on Instagram, necking bottles of Aldi's finest sauvignon blanc, and criticising herself with renewed vigour and loathing. As her goals seem further away than ever, she has to wonder: when bad habits feel so good, how do you trust what's right for you?

'*No Hard Feelings* is clever, funny and surprisingly sweet, and Penny captured my heart' — Toni Jordan

'Funny, biting, vulnerable and unflinching, Novak's novel is like an ocean dip: a bit salty, very refreshing' — Lauren Sams

'Gratifying, warm and funny' — *Books+Publishing*

'Wry and witty' — *Saturday Age*